from the Depths

Gerry Doyle

from the Depths

McBooks Press, Inc.

www.mcbooks.com
ITHACA, NEW YORK

Published by McBooks Press 2007
Copyright © 2007 Gerry Doyle

Dust jacket and interior designed and illustrated by Panda Musgrove. Submarine illustrations by John Kelsey copyright © 2007.

Library of Congress Cataloging-in-Publication Data
Doyle, Gerry, 1976–
   From the depths / by Gerry Doyle.
      p. cm.
   ISBN 978-1-59013-141-1 (alk. paper)
   1. Women forensic scientists–Fiction. 2. United States. Navy. SEALs–Fiction. 3. Submarines (Ships)–Fiction. 4. Sailors–Death--Fiction. I. Title.
PS3604.O9548F76 2007
813'.6--dc22

                        2007015392

Distributed to the trade by Independent Publishers Group
814 North Franklin Street, Chicago, IL 60610
(800) 888-4741
www.ipgbook.com

Additional copies of this book may be ordered from any bookstore or directly from McBooks Press, Inc., ID Booth Building, 520 North Meadow St., Ithaca, NY 14850. Please include $5.00 postage and handling with mail orders. New York State residents must add sales tax to total remittance (books & shipping). All McBooks Press publications can also be ordered by calling toll-free 1-888-BOOKS11 (1-888-266-5711). Please call to request a free catalog.

Visit the McBooks Press website at www.mcbooks.com.

Printed in the United States of America
9 8 7 6 5 4 3 2 1

This book is dedicated to my parents, who taught me the joy of fusing imagination and the written word; to Kara, whose love is an inspiration and whose red pen led me to many thoughtful ideas; to the countless teachers, mentors and friends who have supported me along the way; and to God.

Acknowledgments

I'd like to thank Dr. Kylie Vannaman and Lt. Rich Federico for their technical assistance and thoughts as I prepared my manuscript. If it weren't for their help, my characters would be limited to the technical expertise of an imaginative journalist. Thanks also to Tami Miller, Erica Meltzer, Ben Hubbard, Charlie Dickinson and Theresa Schwegel for their comments and generosity with killer ideas. Christine McClure made sure readers saw my good side. Pete Valavanis got me behind the trigger of an MP-5 (and an AR-10, and an M-4, and . . .). I owe Nhan Nguyen and Adam Brown for their expert counsel.

These people and countless others have inspired and encouraged me during the course of my career—too many to list, but without whom I would not keep putting pen to paper.

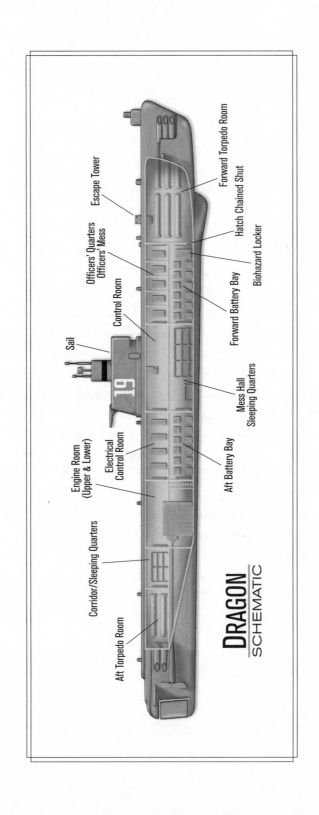

DRAGON
SCHEMATIC

Aft Torpedo Room

Corridor/Sleeping Quarters

Engine Room
(Upper & Lower)

Electrical
Control Room

Aft Battery Bay

Sail

Control Room

Mess Hall
Sleeping Quarters

Officers' Quarters
Officers' Mess

Forward Battery Bay

Escape Tower

Hatch Chained Shut

Biohazard Locker

Forward Torpedo Room

19

from the Depths

War is a contagion.

−Franklin Roosevelt

Prisoner interview

SUBJECT: Myers, Dr. Christine M.

INTERVIEWERS: Olsen, Jorge C., Rear Adm., USN
Trent, Greg L., Capt., USN

LOCATION: —**redact**—

TIME: Interview transcript is compilation of four eight-hour sessions on 03, 04, 05 and 06 June, 2007.

OLSEN: Please state your name for the record.

MYERS: No. Why am I being held here? Have I committed a crime? Do you think I'm a terrorist?

TRENT: Ma'am, we just want you to tell us—

OLSEN: We've read through your written version of what happened. It's incredibly detailed and helpful. But we'd like to go over it with you, to have you walk us through everything so we can gather as much information as possible. Get a complete picture, so to speak.

MYERS: Of course it's detailed—I'm a scientist. And it's not like I've had anything else to do. I've been here, what, four days? It's a big suite I'm in, sure, but don't think I didn't notice the door to the hallway was locked. I can't sleep. There are no windows. The television isn't connected to anything except an empty DVD player. If the orderly hadn't brought me a pen and some paper, my only entertainment would be watching the doctors examine me. That got old fast.

TRENT: Ma'am, please. We need you to answer some questions. That's all.

MYERS: Prisoners usually get lawyers. Do I?

OLSEN: You're not charged with a crime, ma'am. This is just a debriefing. You're being cared for here in this facility for your own safety.

MYERS: My safety? What about my rights? I know you haven't spoken with Gen. Patterson. There's no way he would allow me to be held in detention, with no visitors, interrogated every day—

TRENT: This isn't an interrogation.

OLSEN: Look, ma'am, it's standard. This interview is the last step in the information-gathering process. We just want to know what occurred onboard the *Dragon,* and you're the only person who can tell us. So we need to see the events that transpired through your eyes. Then we'll write a report. And then you'll get to go home, as soon as the doctors say it's OK.

MYERS: I feel fine. I AM fine. No one's bothered to show me my charts, but there's nothing wrong with my body—except for the splint on my finger—and no amount of blood work will show otherwise. I'm fairly certain that I'm suffering low- to mid-level symptoms of post-traumatic stress, though. Not that anyone's asked. And I want to leave. Now.

TRENT: It's not our decision or yours. It's the doctors'. I know how difficult all this must be to understand.

MYERS: That kind of condescending bullshit angers me. Just so you understand.

OLSEN: It's just an interview. Nothing more. We'll ask a few questions, but mostly we just want to hear what you have to say.

MYERS: Every time I close my eyes, I see the inside of that sub. It's dark, but I can tell what's waiting out there. Blood everywhere. I haven't turned the lights off in my room since I got here. Yet you want me to talk about it some more.

OLSEN: It's the only way.

MYERS: What do you want me to say?

OLSEN: Just start with your name. Then tell us the day and time when you first became involved in this, and go from there, with as many details as you can remember. Tell it . . . tell it as if you were sitting in a bar or a restaurant. Relax.

MYERS: Are you for real? Sitting in a bar? Right. Fine. My name is Dr. Christine Megan Myers. I'm a forensic scientist for the Central Intelligence Agency. My specialty is recreating violent crimes. Is this debriefing classified?

TRENT: Yes, ma'am.

MYERS: It better be.

I

I HAD WORKED with Gen. Patterson before. I don't feel comfortable discussing the details of those instances. In all of them, however, my work involved dissecting mayhem. Figuring out how someone died. When they died. How the attacker escaped.

So when I heard Patterson's voice on the phone, I knew that further sleep would be impossible.

"Dr. Myers, this is Jack Patterson," he said. His voice was like a file sawing through a lead pipe. "I apologize for the hour."

I rolled over and struggled to bring my bedside clock into focus. The glowing green display told me I was having a telephone conversation at 2:45 in the morning. It was a Sunday. The last Sunday in May.

"General Patterson. What can I do for you?"

He didn't bother asking whether my phone line was secure. A crew from Langley came once a month to make sure it was "clean," free of bugs or taps. Calls like this meant it had to be.

"We need you to examine a submarine full of dead people," Patterson said. The words, which lacked intonation or excitement, slipped through my head without registering.

"Say that again?"

He ignored me. "But we know why they're dead. It appears that the sub was flooded with chlorine gas."

"Wait, General, I'm confused. Someone launched a chemical attack on a U.S. sub?"

"No, it was an accident. That's the way it seems at this point, anyway. And it's not one of our subs. It's North Korean. Diesel-electric."

I took a breath to ask him why he was calling me, but he cut me off.

"Look, I know this is confusing. I'll sketch the situation out as briefly as I can. This submarine contained some important weapons research, and it was defecting to the United States with its crew. It was being escorted by one of our attack subs. Last night, about eleven o'clock, the escort's sonarman heard unidentifiable mechanical noises, shouting, alarms and, finally, gunfire. A few minutes later, the North Korean boat surfaced.

"The escort tried to hail it, but no one responded. They sent a boarding party over, and that's when the chlorine accident was discovered."

"How do they know it was an accident?" I asked.

"They don't know for sure," Patterson said. "But these older boats . . . you have to understand, this submarine is just barely a step up from a World War II U-boat. Chlorine gas is a pretty common danger because it forms whenever seawater comes in contact with the ship's batteries."

"So everyone on board was killed in the accident."

"Well . . . no. Everyone was dead, but not from the gas. The boarding party sent in one man wearing protective gear to search for survivors. He only looked through part of the ship and didn't find anyone alive. He did, however, find a North Korean crewmember shot to death in the conning tower."

"Shot by whom?"

He laughed, and I tilted the phone away from my ear as the unnatural, gravelly sound burst through the receiver.

"That's why I'm calling you. We're going to send a skeleton crew onto the boat to get it submerged and into port. Once it's there, I need you to tell us what happened last night. Be ready to go by six. That's about three hours from now."

"Wait, that won't work."

"Dr. Myers, it will have to work. If that's too early for you, I suggest you start making coffee now." It was tough to tell whether I had pushed him beyond his usual irritated demeanor, but it was clear he was a few seconds away from hanging up on me.

I was sitting up in bed now, the covers bunched around my waist.

"No, listen. It's not too early, it's too late. If your crew has been aboard the sub for three hours, they'll have disturbed the crime scene. I don't even know how much the man in the boarding party did, what he touched or rearranged. I can't accurately reconstruct anything if I'm working with a dirty scene."

"So what would you suggest? The ship has to be submerged when the sun comes up, and it is imperative to get it to port soon."

"Where is the ship right now?"

"About forty-five miles off the coast. It was headed here, to Norfolk."

"How will your crew be getting there?"

"We're going to insert them by helicopter. Everything's below the radar."

He already had formulated a plan, and shoehorning new ideas into it had not been his intent when he called me. I didn't need to give him any reason to dismiss my suggestions. I spoke fast, trying to convey my urgency without sounding desperate.

"Then let me go with the crew. I can get to the base in fifteen, twenty minutes. Once we're onboard the sub, I can see what they're doing and make sure they don't disturb anything vital. It's not ideal, but it's better than looking for evidence after they've contaminated the scene for hours."

For a few moments, all I could hear was Patterson's breathing.

"That's a good idea," he said. "Be here in twenty minutes. The guard at the gate will tell you where to go. I'll fax you condensed dossiers of the crew and an overview of the submarine."

I replaced the phone on the bedside table, its glossy brown surface empty of pictures or decoration. I knew better than to wait for him to say goodbye.

There was no moon, but the indistinct glow of the streetlights caused a shifting lattice of shadows to dance through my bedroom. The shapes were just gnarled tree branches undulating in the wind, but the effect was unsettling.

Without thinking about it, I reached for the light switch next to the bed. The black-and-white mysteries of the dark room gave way to a pleasant, familiar mix of colors and objects as the overhead fixture clicked on.

And the last shreds of discord were washed away by the trilling of my fax machine down the hall. Patterson was moving fast.

No time to clean up. After hopping out of bed, I threw on some jeans and a Georgetown sweatshirt over a sports bra. I winced at the mirror as my reflection tried to make its unkempt black hair look presentable. In the end, a ponytail carried the day. And as a final, habitual touch, I slipped a worn rubber band into a familiar position around my left wrist.

At the bottom of my closet was a bag I kept for nights like these, when a phone call could pull me into someone else's violent world. It contained everything I would bring from my office to a crime scene: A fluoroscope for revealing stains and fingerprints. Fingerprint-collecting materials. A portable fuming chamber for latents. Evidence bags, tweezers, magnification devices, a ruler, an angle-finder, calipers, scales, chemical ID tests. A Nikon digital and a Polaroid, a Radio Shack microcassette recorder for notes. A flashlight and a box of latex gloves.

I slung the duffel over my shoulder and jogged down the hallway into my office, the faux-Persian carpet muffling each sneaker-clad footstep. The fax machine had just finished spitting out the last page. I hadn't bothered turning on the light, but the illumination spilling through the doorway showed the printout tray was full of paper. I rolled its contents up and shoved them in the duffel bag. Although Gen. Patterson could hand me all of these documents in his office, he might have thought I had someone to drive me to the base, allowing me to read them en route. But my bag would be the only passenger on this trip.

As I turned to leave, the phone warbled again. I picked up the extension in my office, looking out into the hall. Now that I was in motion, the comforting wood-and-leather interior of my workspace seemed to be clutching at me, keeping me from more important business.

"Christine?"

"Hello, Charlie." It was my division supervisor, Dr. Charles Weber.

"I guess you've already talked to Patterson, huh?" he said. His voice was shot through with fatigue.

"Yeah. Just got off the phone. I'm on my way to the base now."

"Now? I thought . . ."

"He wanted to have a bunch of sailors on that boat for hours before I got a chance to look at it. There's no way I could have done anything useful after that. So they're going to put me on the sub with the crew, and I'm going to start working immediately."

"Christ, Christine," he said, then chuckled. "I'm glad one of us is awake enough to think clearly. OK, go get this submarine mess figured out for Patterson. He seemed pretty pissed that he had to ask for help on this one. Of course, he seems pretty pissed all the time."

"I don't think he knows how not to be angry. But we're all on the same team, right? I'll give him answers, Charlie, don't worry."

"I know you will. Be safe, Christine."

And we hung up.

Then: Down the carpeted stairs, turning off lights as I went. Past the picture of Stephen, his wife, his two kids. Then Mom. Then Stephen by himself. Then the three of us together, a happy family grinning in front of a neutral background that almost matched my walls. Through the foyer and dining room, dodging the island in the kitchen. Out the back door and into the garage, where my Jeep waited next to cabinets of power tools, two bikes and a red canoe.

I tossed the bag in the passenger seat and pulled out of the garage.

I wish I could say the night seemed evil. In hindsight, it would make sense to have left the house in the middle of a storm, with vicious bolts of lightning exploding in the sky. And maybe if nature had tried harder to persuade me, I would have changed my mind and stayed home. Pored over Patterson's reports with a cup of coffee warming one hand.

But it wasn't like that at all. It was beautiful. Maybe sixty degrees, with just a sprinkling of moisture in the air and dew on the ground. I remember rolling down the window as I backed out of the driveway and inhaling that clean, damp smell.

The house was dark. I hadn't left any lights on. The two-story Victorian farmhouse was lit only by the arc-sodium streetlights, which gave its white exterior a pale orange cast. It was too much space for me—it had been for years—but it was home. As I pulled away through the tree-lined neighborhood, yards full of coifed bushes and dormant sprinklers, the building seemed comforting and solid in the rearview mirror.

Driving through the empty streets, past blinking stoplights and slumbering storefronts, pulled me into a state of half-awake introspection. This wasn't the first time I'd been called to a crime scene in the middle of the night. And it wasn't the first time I thought of my mother on such an occasion. How had she felt, watching my dad climb into his rust and blue pickup truck to go to his job the last night she—or any of us—had seen him alive?

I never discussed with her what I did for a living. Not that she disapproved of my work, but the details would make her worry. And she already had worried far too much in her life. It would be unfair to allow her to think of me being whisked away to some far-off, bullet-pocked place, not after her husband had been summoned to a burning building and never returned. I'd been a baby, then, and my brother was too young to remember any of it, but my mother had told us.

Our city wasn't even incorporated, and its fire department was all-volunteer. My dad and six other firefighters had charged into a burning barn, a routine call in our rural surroundings. How were they to know there were two barrels of ammonium nitrate simmering inside?

Lights flickered ahead. I had been transported so far back into my past that I hadn't realized how far I'd come in the present. The gatehouse emerged, ghost-like, from the fog that had coalesced as I got closer to the naval base.

The guard checked my ID and inquired about my business with an expression of stern indifference. Another soldier stood near the gate, his M-16 held barrel-down at an angle across his broad, camouflaged chest, while two other men used illuminated mirrors to check the underside of the Cherokee.

I focused on a spot in the mist about twenty-five feet beyond the gate and tried to pretend the man in the gatehouse wasn't staring at the side of my head.

The search took a couple of minutes, and when it was over I had a laminated ID badge and a card to stick on my dashboard. Before he raised the gate, he handed me a map of the base with a route marked in red felt-tip pen. At the end of the crimson trail, he told me, was Gen. Patterson's building.

I hadn't known that Patterson had an office at the naval base, but it didn't surprise me. Branch of service didn't seem to be an issue with his work. Not that I'm certain what his work is. All the times I've encountered him, however, he has been giving orders as something unusual, dangerous and covert is unfolding.

The drive through the base was surreal. Blocky buildings came and went, just gray, ephemeral shapes in the mist. Deuce-and-a-halfs and Humvees squatted in long, perfect rows. I seemed to be the only source of motion in the entire installation.

Using the map as a reference, I knew I was nearing my destination, but the light from Gen. Patterson's office still surprised me as its diffused glow colored the mist. I never had been to the two-story, nondescript concrete structure I now was approaching. Its neighbors were hard to see but probably featured the same bland, gray color. At the top of five or six concrete steps lay the only obvious entrance, a pair of steel doors with windows inset. There was no sign telling visitors what they might expect inside.

I parked in a "guest" spot, grabbed my bag, and walked around the side of the building to the steps. The right-hand door swung open as I was on the third step, revealing another fatigues-clad soldier.

"Dr. Myers? I'm Lieutenant Weeks, General Patterson's aide. If you'll follow me, please?" He managed to smile at me, although it seemed an awkward expression for his pale face.

He held the door open as I walked through, then hurried around me and trotted down the hall. He looked at least six and a half feet tall, and it was tough for me to keep up. When he stopped in mid-stride and turned, I came within a few inches of plowing into his chest.

"Oh, I'm sorry, ma'am. I just . . . can I carry that bag for you?" he said.

I took a step backward.

"Um, sure," I said, handing the duffel to him. My first instinct had been to say "I'm fine" and continue down the hall. But he seemed earnest and almost desperate to follow decorum, and it disarmed me, just for that instant.

He hoisted the strap over his shoulder, turned, and began walking again. The slapping of his combat boots on the tile floor echoed through the empty corridor.

Patterson's office was in a corner, of course, on the second floor. Weeks opened the door for me, allowed me to walk in, saluted, then closed it behind me.

Patterson was sitting at a battered oak desk in a short-sleeved khaki uniform dotted with pins and medals. He managed to look crisp and dangerous despite the smudges of black under his eyes and stubble on his angular face. There was a dime-sized divot at his hair line, right in the middle of his head. It came, I suspected, from a glancing collision with something fast-moving and hard, possibly a bullet or a gun butt. It wasn't the first time I had seen the mark, but it always jumped out at me.

I keep track of faces that way. It's reflexive. Blame it on medical school, blame it on professional obsession, but when I meet someone, I catalogue their features. Without the skin. In the two sentences it takes to be introduced, bone structure, scars and teeth all get jotted down in a mental file. I'm fairly certain I could ID most of my friends' bodies, no matter how they died. But I don't tell them that.

The room's white walls were home to constellations of framed pictures and awards. His desk, two chairs and a U.S. flag in the corner were the only furniture. A motionless, wood-bladed fan hung from the ceiling.

"Dr. Myers, have a seat," he said, gesturing at an overstuffed brown leather chair across from him.

I complied.

"Coffee?"

"No thanks. I'm fine."

He leaned back in his chair and ran his fingers through his salt-and-pepper buzzcut. I could hear his neck pop as he clasped his hands behind his head.

"This is a tough situation, Dr. Myers, and I appreciate your assistance, as always. Your agency always has been discreet and helpful."

I nodded.

"It's fortunate that we have someone with your expertise nearby."

Without waiting for me to respond, he continued. "You'll be on the boat with sixteen men, all SEALs. Lieutenant Daniel Larsen is in command. He understands your mission and you will have great latitude in what you can do, but ultimately he is in charge. Do you understand?"

"Yes," I said, resisting the urge to add a "sir."

"The crew will submerge the sub as quickly as possible and then continue to a submarine bay here. The ship will be shadowed at all times by a Los Angeles–class attack sub, the *Hyman G. Rickover.* You know your job. Do you have any questions?"

I refused to blink as his brown eyes bored into mine. He leaned forward and rested his forearms on his desk, which was empty except for a calendar blotter, a telephone and a manila folder in front of him.

"How long had the submarine been at sea?"

"About a month."

"Did it have a history of accidents?"

"No. The sub's history is in the material I faxed you."

"Then I believe I'm ready to go," I said. That was true, but I already knew I'd think of more to ask him once I was onboard.

"Good." He pushed a button on the telephone. "Lieutenant, Dr. Myers is ready to leave."

I heard the door open behind me. "Lieutenant Weeks will drive you to the staging area," Patterson said.

He opened up the manila folder and began leafing through its contents. I was dismissed.

In the waiting area, Weeks shouldered my bag from the floor next to his feet and opened the office's outer door for me. "If you'll follow me again, ma'am, there is a Humvee waiting downstairs."

I lost track of where we were within seconds of driving away from Patterson's building. The air had thickened to a soup that was impenetrable by even the Humvee's fog lights. Weeks, however, plowed through it as if we were on an open road at noon.

He turned to look at me as he drove with one hand.

"Nervous, huh? Don't worry . . . there's no one driving on the base right now except us. We need to hurry, too. The helo was supposed to be wheels up a few minutes ago." He opened his mouth but shut it and turned back to the road without saying anything.

"Well, tell General Patterson I got here as fast as I could," I said.

I gave up trying to follow the road and watched Weeks drive instead. Although the vehicle's interior was spacious by military standards, Weeks's lanky frame seemed crammed into the driver's seat. He craned his neck toward the windshield as he drove, too, adding to the awkward impression.

"Oh, I don't think he's angry at you or anything, ma'am. He's just a pretty intense guy."

"I know," I said. "I've met him before."

"Yeah, he said you had worked together in the past."

Our conversation dissipated into the grinding growl of the Hummer's diesel engine. I could see his brow tighten as he searched for something else to say. One of his incisors was capped with silver, and his tongue fiddled with it as he thought. His All-American features were distinguished only by a somewhat prominent superorbital ridge. Genetic.

"So, you're a doctor?"

Weeks had the tiniest bit of a Boston accent, and for some reason I pictured him sitting in a pub someplace trying to make small talk with a woman who just wanted to enjoy a drink by herself.

"Mmm-hmm. I'm a physician. I also have a PhD in psychology."

"Wow! From Georgetown?" he said, gesturing at my shirt with his chin.

"That's where I got my medical degree." I pre-empted his follow-up question. "How long have you been General Patterson's aide?"

"Oh. Just a few months, now. I actually was a staff driver for some brass in D.C., but they transferred me down here."

"Ah," I said, returning my gaze to the invisible road. I could see him chewing on his thumbnail out of the corner of my eye as we rode in silence for a few moments.

"Um, ma'am? I don't want to presume or anything, but have you worked with SEALs before?"

I sighed. "I'm not really allowed to discuss my work with you, Lieutenant."

"Right, right, right," he said. "I know. What I meant was, these guys are tough. Bad news, you know? They're used to slitting throats and blowing sh–stuff up. Rough-and-tumble types."

I saw him sneak a glance at me. Maybe he was waiting for me to tremble in fear, I don't know. I managed to avoid rolling my eyes.

"I'm sure they're very professional, also."

"Yeah. Yeah, they are. You just have to be careful around those types of guys sometimes, you know? I mean, you're–"

I cut him off before he could tell me how small and defenseless I was. "I appreciate your concern, Lieutenant. However, I have no doubt that I will be able to work with them, and they with me, to get our respective jobs done."

He began to reply, but a pulsing red glow in front of us interrupted him. He downshifted, then hit the brakes as motion became apparent in the mist. He turned off the engine, and I could hear rotors thumping nearby.

I got out of the Hummer, and he ran around the back of the vehicle clutching my bag.

"Come on!" he shouted over the noise.

I could feel the edges of the rotor blast tugging at my clothes as we jogged toward the sound and light.

A helicopter squatted like a fearsome insect in the center of a typhoon of activity, its landing lights painting the scene in flashes of crimson. Black-clad soldiers were pulling themselves in the helo's side doors and helping others hoist crates into its gut. A fireplug of a man stood by the door, staring into the mist. He saw us.

"That's Lieutenant–"

"Larsen. I know," I shouted over the stutter and whine of the helicopter. "Patterson told me. Larsen's the SEAL platoon's commanding officer."

Weeks nodded, and we set a course for the lieutenant. He also was dressed in black and had a stubby assault rifle slung across his back. He wielded a clipboard like a hand-axe.

"Are you Dr. Myers?" he said as we approached. It was impossible to discern his words, but the context helped me read his lips.

"Yes. Lieutenant Larsen?" I extended my hand and saw Weeks flinch in my peripheral vision.

"You're late," the SEAL said, ignoring the gesture. "We need to move. Get in the helo." He turned and tossed the clipboard inside, then pulled himself in after it. I faced Weeks.

"Thanks for the ride. And for helping with my gear," I said as he handed the bag to me.

"You need a hand?"

"Nah." I threw my duffel at the feet of a stone-faced SEAL sitting in the helicopter, turned, hopped to a sitting position on the helicopter's deck, then swung my legs in and stood.

I was confronted with a silent wall of shadowy masculinity in the helicopter's red-lit interior. There was one seat left by the door on the other side, and I sat in it, dragging my bag to a position between my feet.

A crewman—the co-pilot, maybe—extricated himself from the front cabin. He pulled both doors shut, then grabbed a headset off the wall and handed it to me.

"We can hear each other talk this way!" he yelled. As I put it on, he gestured at my luggage. "And you need to stow that!"

I nodded and he grabbed it.

"Wait!" I said. He paused and turned to me. "Can I get something out?"

I reached in and removed the pages Patterson had faxed me. After I zipped up the bag, the crewman secured it to some webbing on the wall.

"You know how to strap in?" he asked.

I thought I did, but he didn't give me a chance to answer. A few seconds of deft manipulation left me in the grip of a six-point harness. He leaned down in front of me, flashed a thumbs-up and headed back to the cockpit.

The men around me were wearing no such restraints. As I heard the pilot and co-pilot check off switches and instrument readings, the soldiers made a show of ignoring me and each other.

Then we were in the air.

"It'll be about a half-hour ride," I heard in my headset.

"Roger," came a reply.

I looked down the line of SEALs and saw Larsen sitting at the end of the row across from me. He had the clipboard again, and his head was bowed as he examined its contents.

The man directly across from me seemed intent on using his eyes to drill a hole in the wall above my head. The cabin lights turned his face, framed by a black watch cap and matching turtleneck, a demonic crimson.

I felt like I should try to talk to him, or any of them. But the shadows in the helicopter seemed more solid and defined than the SEALs, who all looked the same. And acted the same: cold, silent.

There were no faces to scrutinize, no conversations to overhear. So I unfurled the faxes, massaging the rubber band on my wrist with two un-thinking fingers as I read.

First, the submarine's crew, an understrength complement of thirty men. The captain, Yoon Chong-Gug, had a distinguished record in the North Korean navy. He also had family in South Korea and had been working for the United States for several years. He was smiling in the picture at the top of his dossier, a mouthful of gapped teeth gleaming in contrast with his bushy black eyebrows.

When he found out he would be ferrying research from an offshore lab to a base on the mainland, he suggested the mass defection to his CIA contacts. They had arranged for the escort by a U.S. attack sub, but the details of the scheme were his.

His five officers had similar stories. All had rocketed through the ranks, their records spangled with awards and commendations. And, like their captain, they had relatives in South Korea. None were married.

The enlisted men got about a paragraph each, and few had photos. They all apparently were aware of the plan to defect. I had no idea how Yoon had managed to fill his boat with people willing to commit such a bold act of treason. Unlike the officers, many seemed to be leaving spouses behind.

There were about five pages regarding the submarine itself. Patterson had mentioned its similarity to a U-boat, and I could see what he meant.

It had the same tapered shape, flat deck and narrow beam, and its profile resembled a long rectangle with a boxy conning tower jutting from its center. It looked like it belonged in a museum someplace. Or a scrap heap.

I had never been on a submarine before, so I tried to place myself inside the schematics and walk through the boat's interior. The fore and aft torpedo rooms took up the entire depth of the sub, but the rest of the compartments had two decks. The control room was situated in the center of the boat, on the upper deck above the mess area and some sleeping quarters.

Aft of the control room were the electrical controls; below that was a battery bay. The two-level engine room fit between that compartment and a passageway to the aft torpedo room containing more controls and bunks. Forward of the control room were the officers' mess and living quarters above another battery bay. Then the torpedo room. Ten compartments in all, it seemed.

Although the Romeo-class boat was ancient by Western standards—the Russians, from whose Project 633 design it was copied, had abandoned that model by the late '50s—this particular ship was less than fifteen years old. It was the third-newest of its type in the North Korean navy, so its electronics and weapons were only half as out of date as the hull, and many of its mechanical systems had been upgraded and simplified.

The submarine's crush depth was listed as 775 feet, but the report suggested that the boat would have difficulties surfacing if it went below 650 or so.

North Korea's Romeo-class sub No. 19 was called *Yong*. The English translation of its name: "Dragon."

Its top speed when submerged was thirteen knots. I tried to imagine traveling halfway around the world at a pace a track athlete would have little trouble maintaining. They might surface every few weeks, but those moments above the waves would be seldom and furtive. And the entire time, of course, the crew's universe would consist of cold metal walls and the smell of each other's sweat.

What would it be like to suffer through such conditions for months?

According to Patterson's information, the boat's sole mission was patrolling North Korea's territorial waters. Its crew never had needed to endure an extended trip underwater. Maybe one of them had snapped.

A massive release of chlorine gas presented more questions. Patterson said it was caused when seawater interacted with the batteries. I did the chemical equation in my head. Did the cells contain sulfuric acid? That would react with the hydrogen, oxygen and salt in seawater, releasing chlorine.

Other than a hull breach, where could the water come from? The battery bays were in the center sections of the ship, but I couldn't read the schematics well enough to tell anything other than that.

I glanced up. Larsen still was engrossed in his clipboard. At some point, I would need him to walk me through the ship's systems.

And nothing in the pile of faxes told me anything useful about him or any of the other men sitting around me. A one-paragraph mission overview contained Larsen's name, and the name of his second-in-command, Lt. j.g. Jonathan Matthews. That was it.

The numbing roar and vibration of the helicopter's rotor were beginning to drown out my thoughts. And there was little for me to focus on besides the documents in my lap.

Now the SEAL across from me was checking a fastener on his assault rifle. The other soldiers also seemed enveloped in a solitary world of equipment-checking and silent contemplation.

It was impossible to move without nudging the person next to you. I felt like I should try to get to know, somehow, the soldiers I was crammed into the helicopter with. But no one spoke. Acknowledging anyone else's presence seemed forbidden.

I glanced out the basketball-sized window to my right. The shoreline fog had given way to a moonless night sky reflected in a calm, twinkling sea. The helicopter was low enough that I expected to see a wake rippling from its sides.

Sprays of stars soared above us, their glow providing the only means of discerning the horizon.

"Two minutes to target."

I would have jumped at the disembodied voice in my ear, but the straps limited me to a flinch and a gasp.

"OK, Doctor, here's what's going to happen."

Even when Larsen spoke in a conversational voice, his words had a harsh, commanding edge to them. I glanced back down the cabin and saw that his gaze matched. He unbuckled his lap belt and walked across the cabin until he was crouched in front of me, his headset umbilical stretching back to the bulkhead above his seat.

"The helo's too big and heavy to land safely on the deck. So it's going to hover above it, with the landing gear barely touching, and we're going to jump down. If the seas are too rough for that, we'll have to rappel down. Do you know how to do that?"

"No," I said. I started to explain that I had done some rock climbing, but he cut me off with a quick, savage gesture of dismissal.

"That's what I thought. If we have to rappel, we'll strap you onto Warrant Officer Grimm's rig, and he'll help you. Judging from the view up here, though, we'll be able to just hop down. Is that bag the only gear you're carrying?"

"Yes."

"Good. Grimm will take that no matter how we have to transfer to the sub. Can you jump a few feet, or do we need to lower a ladder?"

"I can do it," I said. "That's no problem."

He didn't respond this time. The red lights painted his face with unnatural shadows as he sized me up.

"Fine," he said. "I'm going to get you a life jacket—shit, you should be wearing one already—and you will leave the life jacket on until you are inside the sub, do you understand?"

I nodded.

"We'll be onboard in a minute or so. Once we're on the submarine's deck with all our equipment, we'll discuss entering the ship."

He stood and grabbed a limp, yellow life vest from the bulkhead above my seat and handed it to me. He watched as I undid my harness and cinched the vest's straps across my torso, then refastened the safety belts. He made his way back to his seat.

"I've got a visual," I heard on my headset. "Seas are calm. Looks like we'll be able to do this the easy way."

Larsen's voice replaced the pilot's.

"Miller, Henderson, you're off first," he said, gesturing to the two SEALs opposite him. "Secure the conning tower hatch, but do not enter the submarine.

"Grimm, you're carrying the doctor's gear. If she needs assistance leaving the helo, you're the man to give it."

"Yes, sir!" came the acknowledgment.

The SEAL across from me stood and disentangled my bag from the wall webbing. He slipped the shoulder strap across his chest, making sure to leave his weapon unencumbered.

"You need a hand, ma'am?" he said, making the first eye contact of our flight together. It seemed this was Grimm.

I shook my head no and moved to hit the quick-release latch on my harness. As I did so, however, the world pitched about forty-five degrees to the left. The soldiers who were standing grabbed handholds and braced themselves against the floor.

"Hold on a second," Grimm said. "We should be hovering shortly."

Indeed, the floor returned to its normal angle a few seconds later, and the engine noise swelled. Then the red dystopia of the helicopter's interior was swept away in a rush of wind and sound as a crewmember pulled himself into the cabin and yanked the door open.

"We're coming down on the stern!" the crewman shouted after plugging his helmet into the wall. "I'll signal when it's safe to egress!"

I felt a new vibration crawl up my legs from the floor. It ended with a thump a few seconds later, and I realized the landing gear had been lowered.

I reached for my harness again, but Grimm intercepted my hand and shook his head.

"No! Wait until we've stabilized! If the helo has to bounce back up, you need to be strapped in!"

"OK!"

He glanced toward the doorway, then back to me.

"I'll go first!" he said. "If you think you're going to fall or don't think you can make the jump, tell me now!"

"I'll be fine!"

Through the door I could see the top of the submarine's periscope masts. As we drifted downward, more of the boat was revealed, its hull a dull, gray interruption of the sparkling waves.

Then the helicopter crewman turned and pointed at the first SEAL by the door.

"OK, go, go!"

That soldier and the man sitting next to him stood and stepped into the night. For a moment, they disappeared. Then their heads poked up at door level, and they jogged toward the conning tower. Their motions were effortless and animal-like, a ballet of footsteps, swiveling heads and weaponry.

Both moved to the far side of the conning tower. I lost sight of them in the darkness. As I watched, however, an indistinct mass seemed to slide up the tower's ladder, then unfold itself into the silhouette of a man.

It was obscured for a moment by a structure jutting from the top of the sail but re-emerged and made three sharp gestures toward the helicopter. I couldn't make them out, but they were clear to Larsen.

"Move!" he shouted.

Grimm leaned over and whacked the release latch on my harness, then hooked a hand in my armpit and hoisted me to my feet as I tried to recover from the blow. I shuffled forward next to him, watching the SEALs in front of us slip out the door in parallel lines.

And then we were at the edge.

In my peripheral vision, I saw Grimm step out of the helicopter and without thinking, I did the same. My sneakers hit the deck before I expected them to, and I fell into a crouch, letting my knees absorb the impact. The helicopter was about four feet off the deck, I guess, but it was tough to gauge the distance in the dark.

I was at the end of a two-abreast column of crouching soldiers. Grimm pulled me toward them by my elbow. He spun to face me.

"I told you to wait for me! Pay attention!"

His teeth gleamed as he yelled, providing the only focal point amid the vague gray and black contours of his face.

"Sorry!" I said. "It wasn't far! I'm fine; I'm not hurt!"

"That's not the point! When you get instructions on this ship, you need to follow them!"

He pulled my bag off his shoulders, tossed it in front of me, then turned to watch Larsen. The SEAL leader was taking a head count. When he finished, he flashed a thumbs-up to the man in the helicopter's doorway.

The crewman returned the gesture as he began pulling the door shut. The helicopter slid sideways, then climbed and began to accelerate away from us, its dark flanks already beginning to blend in with the night sky.

The whine and chatter of its engines diminished into an irregular thumping echoing across the ocean. Soon that, too, was swallowed up by the darkness.

The SEALs had begun moving across the deck toward the conning tower, the sound of their footsteps harsh and intrusive in the sudden silence. Grimm walked after them without saying anything to me.

I stood and watched them for a moment. The sea's gentle motion tugged at the ship, making its skin seem alive, flexing with unseen muscle.

I took a deep breath, inhaling salty air tinged with diesel and oil.

And then I picked up my bag and followed the soldiers across the *Dragon*'s back.

II

GRIMM HAD TALKED to Larsen.

"I specifically told you what was going to happen and Warrant Officer Grimm told you how it was going to happen," Larsen said. "I guess you didn't listen to either of us."

He was only a few inches taller than I, but he was leaning forward, trying to throw his physical presence into each word.

"I'm sorry I jumped before Grimm told me to. It's not like there was much danger in a four-foot drop."

"We'll decide what's dangerous here, Doctor."

It wasn't a question, but he stared at me like he wanted an answer. I raised my eyebrows and stared back, listening to the slap of wavelets against the sides of the submarine. It was impossible to tell whether the SEALs huddled around us at the base of the conning tower were ignoring us or just wearing the same stoic costumes they had throughout most of the helicopter ride.

Larsen stepped back and inhaled. When he spoke again, his tone was slow and measured, as if he were addressing a child.

"OK. Now, we only have an hour or so until it starts to get light. So we need to get submerged. But the doctor needs to examine the control room before we get in there and muck it up. Isn't that right?"

I shrugged, but he wasn't paying attention.

"So what's going to happen is this. Grimm will descend the ladder into the control room and, without touching anything, will verify that it is secure. Dr. Myers will then climb down the ladder. From that point, she will have twenty minutes to collect all the observations she needs from the control area." He pointed at my head. "After twenty minutes, the rest of the platoon will enter the submarine, and we will dive. This is not negotiable. Do you think you can stick with the plan this time?"

I could feel a hard knot of fury gathering deep in my chest. But if he wanted to bully me, he wasn't going to get the satisfaction of a terse response.

"Sure," I said and shrugged again.

He wanted to scream at me to call him "sir"; I could see him biting back the words. But instead he turned and barked at Grimm.

"Go! Get in there!"

"Yes, sir," Grimm said. He braced himself on the doorframe with one hand and pulled his lanky body through the aperture on the side of the submarine's superstructure. Without waiting for instructions, I followed him in.

Mounted in the deck in front of me was a manhole-sized hatch with a ladder that stretched to the ceiling of the conning tower and down into the guts of the sub.

A few feeble traces of illumination escaped the opening as Grimm lowered himself into it, offering a suggestion of the conning tower's interior. To the right of the hatch was a waist-high, domed post as thick as a man's leg. Erupting from its sides were several sets of levers, wheels and gauges.

I glanced down and saw Grimm's watch cap bobbing down the ladder. The sub's electrical system must have survived whatever catastrophe befell the crew because he stepped into a pool of dim white light and moved out of my field of view.

Then, a few seconds later: "All clear!"

"Get down there, Myers," Larsen called from the submarine's deck.

I slung my bag over my shoulder and lowered myself into the hole until I felt my feet come to rest on the top rung. It soon was evident, however, that the duffel wasn't going to fit. I had to dangle it from my right hand while using my left on the ladder.

My slow pace drew Grimm over to the base of the ladder. I heard him say "Jesus Christ" under his breath as he looked up at me.

"Hey, Doctor, do you need a hand?"

"No, I'm fine. The bag is slowing me down, that's all." By that time it was dangling into the control room. I felt him grab it. "Thanks."

I was on the floor a few seconds later.

The first thing that struck me about the submarine was its smell, a stiff cocktail of sweat and machinery. It almost masked an odor I was more familiar with: death.

I turned to Grimm. The overhead lights made him seem more tangible, more human than he had in the helicopter's carmine interior. He looked about my age, older than I expected. Mid-30s, maybe. Dark eyes, square jaw, clean-shaven. His tanned face was punctuated by a Roman nose, which swooped down to thin lips.

A small scar—less than a centimeter—sliced through his left eyebrow, just above his pupil. His right ear was set a tiny bit higher than the other. But that nose would be what set him apart when he was lying in a morgue.

He held my bag out to me.

I took it, slung it over my shoulder, unzipped it and pulled a pair of latex gloves from a box within. "Could you stand behind me as I turn, please? Be careful to step only on empty floor."

The flash from my digital camera exploded in the cramped room as I documented its layout and contents. The ladder I had climbed down was at the aft end of the compartment. At the forward end was a bank of dials and gauges, their faces looming over a six-spoked wooden control wheel that looked like it belonged on a square-rigged galleon. To the right of the wheel was an open hatch to the next compartment forward. The opening, mounted at knee height, looked about the same diameter as a sewer cover. Moving clockwise from the hatch, I snapped pictures of a wall choked with red valve wheels and dials.

Just about all the surfaces that could be painted were the same utilitarian gray, a tone that ate up the timid light radiating from caged bulbs set above us at three-foot intervals. Running along the ceiling at the sides of the compartment were a tangle of pipes, valves and thick wires. The two periscopes were mounted in the center of the compartment, polished metal pillars that, in their "down" position, rested in a well in the floor.

In the left-hand corner of the aft bulkhead was another open hatch. A back-lighted table similar to one a photographer would use to examine negatives was positioned in a niche to the right of the door. It looked like a transparent navigation chart was clipped to its dark surface.

Continuing to my right, I photographed what looked like the sonar station—two chairs in front of the usual dials and switches, plus two rectangular displays mounted on the bulkhead and two circular ones mounted on a counter. The last two workstations were studded with bulkier valves and toggles. Crammed among them were thin, vertical glass gauges and a silhouette of the submarine punctuated with red and green lights.

But the most noticeable aspect of the final crew station was the dead man lying on the floor in front of it.

"What are those controls for?" I asked Grimm without turning to look at him.

"Diving and surfacing."

The life vest's puffy embrace was complicating every movement, so I unsnapped it and draped it on the ladder, then hung the camera around my neck and reached back for my tape recorder. Holding the cigarette box–sized black device by my mouth, I spoke.

"In control room, deceased lying prone eighteen to twenty-four inches from diving and surfacing control panel."

The man was about five and a half feet tall, his jet-black hair trimmed short on top and shaved to stubble on the sides. His blue jumpsuit was streaked with dark smudges. One arm—his right one—lay at his side, bent ninety degrees at the elbow, fingers splayed amid streaks of blood. His left arm stretched out straight toward the console. Both knees were bent a few degrees.

The floor around him was devoid of blood, although I could see a few smears near the aft periscope. I moved a few steps toward the body, scrutinizing the deck to make sure I didn't trample any evidence.

"Two entrance wounds in back, left side, superior to spine of scapula.

No powder marks visible. No blood pooling evident." I switched the recorder to my left hand and rummaged in my bag until I found a collapsible ruler. "Wounds spaced approximately . . . 12.25 centimeters apart. More medial wound located approximately . . . 1 centimeter above scapular spine and . . . 8 centimeters laterally from midline. Second wound located . . . 4 centimeters directly lateral to first wound. Wound diameter approximately 9 millimeters."

I took a picture of the ruler next to the wounds, then turned to the smears on the floor. I snapped a close-up picture of them, let the camera dangle again and stuck the ruler in my pocket. The next thing out of my bag was a bottle of Hemastix. I swabbed one of the strips near the edge of the nearest stain, waited a few moments and checked it against the results diagram on the bottle. It was blood.

"Blood stains near center of room, approximately 3.5 feet behind deceased. Smeared parallel to deceased's body."

I stood back up. The room was rife with evidence. But with Larsen counting the seconds until he and the rest of the SEAL team could storm down the ladder and take control, I had to ignore the impulse to scrutinize every surface, document every detail.

"OK," I said. "Grimm, I need your help. Without touching anything, can you tell me which controls would need to be activated for the submarine to surface, and what position those controls are in?"

Behind me, I heard the SEAL shuffle in a few feet closer.

"Well, you'd need the whole engineering crew to do a normal, controlled surface. The trim and ballast controls are on the bulkhead to starboard. Your right. But you could do an emergency blow and surface from here. Um . . . that lever there, the one with the red plastic grip, that toggles the diving tanks. Those five switches in a line underneath it control the sub's ballast tanks. They look . . . yeah, they're all in the 'emergency blow' position."

"Thanks," I said, stuffing the ruler back in my bag and digging out some static print-lift sheets. Leaning in, I could see that although some fine droplets of blood had been sprayed across the entire panel, I was going to have to check for latents on the smaller switches. But the diving tank switch . . . yep, there it was. Smears of blood on top. There would be some nice visible prints on the bottom of the grip.

I took one-handed pictures of the switches, zooming in as far as possible. Their sides were flat. Flipping them would be a two-fingered operation; the thumb would fit on one surface and the first finger on the other.

Pressing a lift sheet against the first switch, I pulled the sheet's cover off, waited for the print to take, then removed it and held it up to the light. It was pretty much what I expected—a hash of interlacing prints. Tough to determine which was most recent. The rest of the switches yielded the same result. I photographed all the sheets, framing each next to the ruler's metric scale.

The red handle, though, was going to tell us a lot more. I crouched and looked up at its underside. Even from a few feet away, I could see the contours of three pristine prints. I took separate pictures of all three. Lifting them might be a little trickier. Under different circumstances, I'd have a technician come in and remove the whole handle.

I held the tray of fingerprint powder in my left hand like an artist's palette, dipping a finger-sized brush into its contents. Trying not to breathe, I swabbed the prints with the brush until the bottom of the handle seemed coated with years' worth of gray dust.

Now I could exhale. I blew the excess powder off the prints and put the brush and powder away. A piece of clear tape pulled each of the three prints, their intricacies mapped by the powder, off the handle. I snapped images of them beside the ruler and filed them in separate evidence envelopes. The center of one print was marred by a thick vertical streak.

I ignored the voices in my head shrieking at me to slow down, hooked my hands under the dead crewman and turned him over.

He was a kid, a teenager whose cheeks were devoid of facial hair. The man's skin was the color of ash, his bluish lips providing the only contrasting hue. Thin, black brows arched over his half-closed eyes. Only a crescent of white was visible below the lids.

An exaggerated grimace distorted the sailor's mouth and exposed two rows of crooked teeth. His tongue's swollen tip poked out between the canines on the left side, pale and dry. It seemed trapped behind the yellowed enamel.

"I have rolled the deceased over to his left. He is now on his back," I said into the tape recorder after standing up. "Cyanosis evident in lips and fingers. Two exit wounds visible in left shoulder area." I leaned down and measured them. "Wounds spaced approximately . . . thirteen centimeters apart. Left-hand wound approximately ten centimeters to right of midline. Both wounds located two centimeters above clavicle."

Three more digital images captured the face, torso and full body of the dead sailor. A fourth documented the patch of deck he had occupied before I moved him.

"Deceased is cool to the touch. Moderate rigor mortis. Blood is coagulated."

There were some smears of blood on the deck where he had lain but not enough to collect in a pool. A few fibers, which appeared to be the same color as his jumpsuit, were stuck in the tacky red marks on the floor.

"Little blood evident beneath body."

The coveralls' front zipper was open halfway down his chest, revealing a T-shirt that was struggling to be white despite shadows of ground-in grease. The suit had two breast pockets, both of which were zipped, and two loose pockets sewn into the front just below the waist. Tugging the shirt's neck down a few inches, I peered down its front, trying to gather an image of the sailor's sternum.

"Dependent blood pooling visible on deceased's chest," I said after a few moments.

If I cut off all his clothes and examined him in a more clinical setting, I'd see more of the same. He hadn't been moved since he died, and the blood had settled in the parts of his body closest to the floor.

His hands were half-curled, as though he had been trying to ball them into fists but ran out of energy. On the middle finger of the right hand, I found what I was looking for: an unhealed cut traversing its tip. I photographed it.

I turned and saw Grimm, who had been staring at the seat of my jeans, now struggling to regain his austere martial expression. A guilty half-smile flashed across his face. I made it easy for him by ignoring his presence as I brushed past and walked the long way around the control room to the forward hatch.

The door, which swung into the control area, was ajar and lay against the wall, held in place by a simple latch. Its white surface and candy-red closing apparatus gleamed amid their grim neighbors.

Pulling a flashlight from my bag, I examined the edges of the opening, which was about five inches thick. The inside surfaces were scratched, and I noted similar marks around the circumference of the door. No blood anyplace.

I kneeled in front of the opening, and poked my head and flashlight hand through. The muscles in my left arm vibrated with the strain of holding me upright as I examined the floor on the other side. The flashlight's beam revealed nothing but the scuffed gray deck.

Pulling myself back through, I stayed on my knees for a moment, looking through the circular opening. There was a hallway beyond it, lighted by a series of caged bulbs set in the ceiling. It didn't look wide enough for two men to pass without bumping shoulders. A handful of closed doors were set flush with the walls.

I pivoted and looked back down the length of the control room. The hatch at the opposite end offered a circular view into the next room aft. The rubber band snicked against my skin once, twice, the sting lost amid my thoughts. The nervous routine of snapping it had begun years ago, under more stressful circumstances, and now had become a part of my normal work process.

I pulled myself to my feet, walked over and crouched next to the hatch. In my peripheral vision, I could see the tips of Grimm's combat boots reorient toward me.

The doorframe was identical to the one in the forward bulkhead, a scarred, utilitarian porthole connecting two watertight compartments. Again, no blood. But on the floor . . . yes.

I must have said it out loud.

"What?" Grimm said.

"Nothing. I mean, I found something. Hold on."

The floor on the control room side of the hatch was the same worn surface I had encountered everyplace else on the boat. But its uniformity was interrupted by a glitter in the beam of my flashlight. A cartridge casing.

I stood and took a picture of it and its surroundings, then kneeled back down for a close-up. The brass had been lying in the shadow of the hatch door. I circled it with orange chalk, then used tweezers to slip it into a plastic pouch, which I sealed and marked "CASING 1–CONTROL ROOM FLOOR."

"Hey, what is that?"

"Shell casing," I said, leaning through the hatchway. This was trickier because I had to be careful not to smear the chalk outline. I wasn't sure how I would be able to pull myself into the compartment without disturbing something vital, but as it turned out I didn't have to.

Another shell casing was standing upright against a ceiling-height cabinet or control box mounted just to the right of the hatch opening. One handed, I snapped a couple of pictures, then drew another circle, half on the deck, half on the cabinet. The casing went in a separate plastic pouch.

I extricated myself from the hatch and stood, hearing my back pop.

Grimm looked down at me, eyebrows raised. It seemed to double the length of his nose.

"You done?"

"Not even close. How much time do I have?"

He glanced at the watch fastened around his sweater's sleeve.

"Seven minutes."

"Shit." I looked around. "Did anyone leave this ship after it surfaced?"

"I wouldn't know for sure. But if they did leave, they're drowned by now or floating around in a life jacket. Our briefing said the hatches were closed when the *Rickover*'s party reached the ship. Does that help?"

I almost smiled. His government-issue monotone was edged with eagerness.

"Not really. Sorry."

Priorities and theories whirled in my head, whipped into a shapeless nebula of thought. But one idea kept floating to the surface: assuming the gun that had ejected this brass was still onboard, I needed to find it before the SEALs came onboard and kicked it into a torpedo tube or something.

"I'm going to search the ship," I said, pivoting on the balls of my feet and moving toward the control room's forward door.

"What? You're going to search . . . what are you looking for?" Grimm was following me.

"The gun that killed this man. But wait."

I stopped and turned again. Grimm's chin came within inches of bouncing off my forehead as he pulled up short.

"When you guys come onboard, do you have a plan? Are you just going to rush everyplace at once, or are there priorities?"

Grimm's confused look told me what he was going to say before his lips formed the words. I cut him off.

"What areas of the sub do you need to control first? Where are the first places Larsen will send you guys?"

"Oh. Um, we'll secure the weapons storage and control areas first. Engineering. The control room, obviously. Everything else can wait until we're submerged and underway, I guess. Why . . . hey, where are you going?"

I had walked over to the hatch and was sizing it up, plotting the best way to maneuver my way through it.

"To the forward torpedo room. I want a look at it and those other areas before the rest of you come onboard. I'll work my way back through the ship."

"You're just supposed to examine the control room. We discussed it on deck."

"Well, now I need to examine other parts of the ship. And I need to do it before the evidence I'm looking for has been disturbed or lost. I realize that wasn't part of the original plan, but Lieutenant Larsen can deal with that after he gets down here."

"We need to stick to the script. I can't let you just go off on your own."

I shrugged, but I think he missed it as I squatted down and hooked a leg through the door.

"We need to stick to the plan," he repeated, and I heard him take a step toward me. "Just follow the directions, OK?"

I envisioned myself darting through the hatch and jogging down to the torpedo room. Then that image was replaced with one of him grabbing me by the collar and hauling me back into the control room before I got my other leg through the doorway. Larsen would love to come down the ladder and see me tied to a chair or something.

Sighing, I extricated myself from the hatch and stood in front of him.

"Look, I'm sorry about the helicopter thing. I got carried away, and that was my fault. I understand that you have orders and that we have a plan. You were supposed to secure the area before I boarded the sub, right? And you did that. So now, why don't you come with me and secure the areas I need to inspect? Then, when we're sure there's no one waiting to jump out of the shadows at me, you can come back to the control room." I raised my eyebrows and smiled. Just a harmless lady doctor.

"But Lieutenant Larsen . . ."

"Grimm, we both heard what he said. But the situation has changed since we were standing on the deck, right?" I gestured around the control room. "I've gotten some important information in here, but to make it worth anything, I have to check other areas of the ship. And I have to do it before the scene is disturbed. Do you understand that?"

He shifted his weight and started to say something, but I cut him off.

"So now we just have to apply the original plan to the modified situation. It doesn't make any . . ." I halted, searching for a phrase with enough military jargon to bolster my point. " . . . any operational sense for us to wait in here when there are more important things I need to do in other parts of the boat. You can cover me, or whatever, but I need to get to the torpedo room. And . . ."

This time he waved away the rest of my sentence.

"You'll follow me. I'll enter each compartment, ensure that it is secure, and then tell you when it is safe to enter. If I tell you to go back, you go back. Clear?"

"Sure. Yes, perfectly clear." I stepped out of the way and let him get at the hatch.

I doubted it was designed for someone as tall and broad as he was, but he didn't hesitate at its mouth. He grasped the top of the frame, thrust both legs in and let their momentum carry his upper body through.

All I could see through the portal as I squatted next to it were the backs of his legs. In a half-crouch, he moved down the hallway. Each step seemed deliberate and deadly as he held his stubby assault rifle at face level.

At each doorway, he paused, brushed the area around the knob with his left hand, then shoved it open with a sudden, violent thrust of his arm. After scanning the room on the other side for a few seconds, he stepped back and closed the door. There were six of them, three on each side of the corridor.

When he got to the end, he dropped into a lower stance and peered into the next compartment through another hatch. This one seemed like it may have been designed for more comfortable use; it was oval and a third larger than those in the control room.

Without looking back, he shouted, "Clear!"

I shoved one leg through, wormed my torso after it, then pulled myself up and planted my other leg on the deck.

The thirty-foot compartment was all hallway. The floor and ceiling were the same as those in the control room, featureless metal under a canopy of pipes and wires. But the walls were fake wood panels the color of a dark wine. I guess that was what passed for luxury on a submarine.

As I passed the doors, I examined them. All but one were outfitted with brass nameplates screwed into the surface about five feet off the deck.

I arrived at the end of the corridor, and Grimm held up his left hand, clenched into a fist. I stopped.

He leaned forward, poking his head and gun through the doorway. Over his shoulder, I could see that the floor of the next compartment seemed to be about three feet lower than the passage in which we stood.

Grimm pulled himself back into the hallway, sat down and hooked his legs through the hatch opening. He scooted up and ducked his upper body into the other compartment so he was sitting on the edge of the portal.

His back filled the entire opening, and I could see it flex as he looked around the area. Then he took two steps down and away from the hatch, leaving the back of his head at eye level.

He moved away from me, sweeping the room with smooth arcs of his rifle.

This was the torpedo room. It looked more spacious than the last two compartments. I could see the fins of eight torpedoes, four on each side, mounted on racks along the walls.

Grimm continued to move away from the hatch. He stopped fifteen or twenty feet away, still facing toward the bow.

Then he straightened, letting his rifle drop to waist level. He gestured over his shoulder at me with his free hand. "Room's clear. Come check this out."

This time, I emulated Grimm's method of entry. I found myself sitting at the top of a four-step ladder overlooking the compartment. Glancing down, I saw another hatch mounted just to the right of the ladder's base. It was closed. Chained shut, actually.

My initial impression of the room had been correct. It was vast compared to the equipment-congested control room and claustrophobic hallway we had just passed through.

The center was empty except for some chains dangling from machinery on the ceiling. The space was wide enough for three men to stand shoulder-to-shoulder. Along the walls were two torpedo racks, one on each side of the room. The eight weapons they held managed to look fat and sleek at the same time, their long, shiny exteriors stretching twenty feet from snub noses to four raked fins.

The far end of the compartment—the bow—was tapered. Even the floor sloped upwards. Six tubes were packed into the space, joined by a web of controls, dials and gauges. All their doors were closed, the red levers on their exteriors set in the same horizontal position.

"Come on, Doctor, you want to see this."

The eager voice snapped my attention back to Grimm, who still was facing away from me. As I walked over, he stepped to one side.

In front of him was another dead body. This one clutched a black semi-automatic pistol in its right hand.

"Did you touch anything?" I asked.

"You saw me. I just walked in here."

The man was lying face-down. He was wearing a khaki shirt, short sleeved, with insignia sewn onto the shoulders. From the waist down, however, he was dressed in some kind of a yellowish rubber or coarse fabric suit. The top half of the suit was pulled down, its arms splayed about his midsection.

"I need to take some more pictures. Can you stand behind me again?"

"Actually, I'm going back to the control room. Do whatever you need to do here. Looks like . . . five more minutes you got."

I didn't speak SEAL, but I understood what he was trying to do. When Larsen came onboard, Grimm was going to be where he was ordered to be. I was on my own.

He walked across the compartment, pulled himself up the ladder and disappeared through the hatch.

I moved toward the approximate center of the room and started photographing. I took in the torpedoes, the tubes. A hatch was set in the ceiling toward the aft end of the room, its red and white dogging mechanism forming a three-dimensional bull's-eye. Forward of the hatch dangled equipment that seemed designed to help the crew hoist the weapons into their launch tubes. Around it all snaked the now-familiar background of exposed conduits and caged lights.

Unnatural death can seem so peaceful. If the victim doesn't have the strength or time to flop around, the life sort of ebbs from his body. I have seen beatific expressions on the blood-speckled faces of people killed by machete wounds and sniper victims slumped in their chairs as if they were napping after a big meal.

The man on the floor in front of me offered no signs of a violent end. His black hair was flecked with gray and white. Both legs lay unbent behind him, and his arms stretched over his head.

"Subject Number Two in forward torpedo room. No visible wounds on deceased's back or head," I said into the recorder.

The fingers of his right hand were curled around the pistol's grip. I kneeled and took close-up shots from several angles. I recognized the gun; it was a Chinese copy of a Russian Tokarev 9mm. The caliber markings were evident on the slide under the words MADE IN CHINA BY NORINCO. Everything was in English; the pistol was made for cheap, easy export.

I stood and pulled one of the cartridge casings from the compartment in my bag where I had stuffed them. Holding the plastic sheath up to the light, I could see the shell's headstamp: The number "71" on one side of the primer hole and "93," oriented the opposite direction, on the other. A quick measurement told me the casing was nine millimeters in diameter.

Before I examined the gun, though, I wanted to see the rest of its owner. Again ignoring the years of training and experience tugging at my muscles, I rolled him over.

The man's face was lined and leathery with a broad, flat nose. His mouth was open, but not gaping, and thin lips covered his teeth.

Brown eyes stared into nothingness from beneath bushy eyebrows. His forehead was knotted with clenched muscles.

I leaned in a bit closer and shined my flashlight into the man's mouth. His tongue was thrust forward just behind the lower incisors. Moving the light up his face, I examined the scalp. A receding hairline simplified the task.

"Deceased's lips exhibit cyanosis," I said. "No anterior cranial lacerations or contusions visible."

The floor where the man had lain seemed unmarked, but I took a picture anyway. A pair of black patent-leather oxfords were arranged side by side on the deck between the bottom torpedo tubes. I photographed them and shoved aside the urge to try to lift some fingerprints from their mirror-like surfaces.

His legs could wait, too. I saw no blood anyplace in the compartment. Not on his hands, not on the walls. Not on the spit-shined shoes. If he had a mortal wound below his waist, the suit's thick material was concealing it.

I crabbed over until I was kneeling next to the gun. It was clutched in the man's right hand, palm-up. His index finger was curled around the trigger guard. The other four digits enveloped the pistol's chipped brown plastic grips. The nail beds matched the color of his lips.

The weapon was boxy and black with just a hint of blue swimming across its worn exterior. Patches of milling marks were evident on the slide, which extended back past the grip and covered the hammer assembly.

Rigor mortis had turned the corpse's hand into a gargoyle's claw. I could feel the sinews creaking and tearing as I peeled the thumb back and wrestled the gun from the dead man's grasp. I laid the weapon on a plastic evidence bag next to me and fitted another bag over the hand.

"Connective tissue damage in right thumb of subject due to removal of physical evidence."

The gun pulled my already tangled instincts in innumerable directions. But most of the important tests would be performed in the lab, and I'd have to remove the ammunition before I turned it over to them.

So the bullets would come first.

I pulled the magazine and laid it on the bag. Inverting the gun next to it, I ejected the chambered cartridge onto the plastic, then used tweezers to pick it up. Stamped on the bottom was "71 93"—it was from the same factory as the two empties and was made the same year. It went in a separate translucent envelope, as did each of the five bullets in the clip.

Six rounds. The mag for a 9mm Tokarev could hold eight. And I doubted a submariner would keep one loaded in the chamber of a pistol notorious for its fickle safety mechanism.

Using a magnifying glass, I measured one of the bullets and took a picture of it adjacent to the ruler. Another photograph captured the head-stamp at the base of the cartridge. The casing of the live round was identical in length and diameter to the casings I had collected near the dead sailor.

I slipped a pencil through the trigger guard and rotated the gun in the air in front of me. No visible prints, no blood. My nostrils flared at the odor of cordite and oil. The acrid combination stood out even against the submarine's weighty, pungent atmosphere.

Dragging my bag, I moved a few steps aft, away from the evidential detritus arrayed on the floor around me, and dug out a handful of fingerprint-lift sheets. My first three attempts were throwaways that showed only a smeared confusion of whorls on the gun's slide. But near the back, on the left side above the grip, was a pristine, oval print the size of a quarter. Right where a shooter's thumb would rest.

After laying the gun down, I took a close-up of the print next to the ruler and sealed the sheet in an envelope.

I turned the pistol over. The serial number was stamped on the opposite side, a string of eleven letters and digits.

On the label of another evidence bag, I wrote "M21388123CE, Norinco 'Tokarev' 9mm. Mag enclosed separately. Ammo enclosed separately. Collected submarine 'Dragon,' forward torpedo room, 27 May 2007." I dropped the gun inside, then slipped the bullets and magazine into two other pouches.

Should I take a print of the man's thumb? Did I have time?

The sudden, dull echo of voices and combat-booted footsteps answered my question. I grabbed an ink pad and print paper, stuffed the envelopes into my bag and pushed it to the side under a slumbering torpedo. The shoes, too. I'd want to get the shoes. I picked them up by the laces and laid them next to the duffel.

The man's thumb, bent back at an impossible angle, was easy. I pressed the pad against it, then rolled it across the paper. The index finger was accessible, too.

The other three fingertips would be tougher to get to, though. I would have to brutalize each if I wanted a full set of prints.

A shout from the doorway interrupted me.

"Stay where you are!"

I could see the upper body of a SEAL in the hatch. He was crouching in the hallway leading to the control area, staring at me from the other side of his assault rifle.

"It's just—"

"Shut up!" He steadied the rifle with one hand and used the other for balance as he slipped his legs through and onto the steps. "Just let me check the room."

He surveyed the compartment for a moment, swiveling from left to right, then snapping his rifle down to check the deck below the ladder. I could see sweat glistening on his coffee-colored skin.

"Stay against the torpedoes there, ma'am." He lowered the rifle, keeping his right hand on the weapon and gesturing with his left.

I nodded and watched him hop down to the deck and walk to the forward bulkhead, stepping over the body. He grabbed the red bar mounted on each torpedo tube and gave it a downward tug.

After the last one, he grunted and turned to the controls that covered the bulkhead to the left of the tubes. His hands were busy among the gauges and switches. I could hear him mumbling "off . . . off . . . empty . . . off . . ." as he worked.

I laid the dead man's hand back on the floor and slipped the prints into a protective sleeve.

When the SEAL's ritual was finished, he turned to me, but his gaze caught on the corpse on the floor.

And I almost hit my head on the torpedo behind me when a disembodied voice exploded into our metallic environs.

"Doctor, get to the control room. You need to see this."

The SEAL saw my reaction. He made no effort to suppress his smile as he searched the wall for a moment and detached a handset from it. Its coiled, black cord led to a shoebox-sized speaker mounted in the midst of the controls he had been engrossed in.

"Conn, forward torpedo room. Area is secure," he said into his fist.

"Torpedo, conn. Roger. Did the doctor hear me?"

Turning to me, the SEAL raised his eyebrows. Maybe a leer, maybe just a silent inquiry.

"Ma'am? He wants to know if you heard. I'm not sure what to tell him."

Jesus.

"Yeah, I heard him. Tell him I'll be right there."

III

THERE WAS A SEAL leaning against the wall in the hallway to the control room, a hard, purposeful presence that was out of place in the corridor's false opulence.

When I had passed through it on the way to the torpedo room, it had seemed cramped for more than one person at a time to use. That first impression was correct; we both had to turn sideways to allow me to pass. But the soldier didn't seem to mind as my breasts brushed across his torso, and his eyes probed the neckline of my sweatshirt in a futile attempt to get a better view.

After I had squeezed by, I could hear him shuffling behind me as he moved back to the middle of the hallway. I had a pretty good idea which direction he—and his eyes—were facing.

Larsen was waiting for me in the control room next to the forward periscope. Four other SEALs, their weapons slung across their backs, were swarming over the equipment, flipping switches and adjusting knobs. Their voices punctuated the work with curses and an occasional gauge reading.

"Did you enjoy your trip to the torpedo room, Doctor?"

Rolling my eyes was out of the question. I settled for a shrug. Larsen blinked a couple of times. Maybe he expected more.

It was the first clear look I'd gotten at his face. It was hard and mean and dotted with hundreds of old acne scars. Nose had been broken. Chipped incisor, no cap. His right eye seemed to open a bit more than the left. The result of a wound?

"I hear you made good use of your time," Larsen continued. "Found the murder weapon, huh?"

"I found the pistol I think was used to shoot the man we found in here," I said, moving closer to Larsen as one of the soldiers shouldered his way by me. "There still are a lot of things to consider."

"Are there? Well, you're in luck: I think we've got more for you to investigate. Put it this way, we found a great place to put this guy so we can run the boat without tripping over his ass," the lieutenant said as he pointed his chin at the corpse on the other side of the room. "Come on."

Larsen turned, dodged a SEAL and walked over to the aft hatch. He swung himself through without looking back. I moved after him, tossed my bag into the next compartment and followed it.

When I stood, I almost hit my head on Larsen's equipment belt. He was standing just inside the hatch, facing me.

"Hey, watch your step, Doctor. Don't want to have an accident." He grinned, ogling me with a crooked expression that contained more condescension than happiness.

I couldn't pick up my bag without repeating the awkward movement. "Is this where we're going?"

"No," he said, taking a step back and gesturing around. "This is the control room for the electric engines. We're just passing through."

A couple of SEALs were following the same sort of routine as their counterparts in the adjacent compartment, examining and adjusting banks of switches, tapping on the faces of balky dials. Two floor-to-ceiling banks of white circuit breakers gleamed at the aft end of the compartment.

Larsen already had walked away and was hauling himself through the hatch. The illumination in the next compartment reduced him to a silhouette.

Once I stepped through, I could see why. The lighting in this compartment was dazzling compared to the dusk of the rest of the submarine. Two angular engines, each the size of a Cadillac, squatted on either side of a walkway down the center of the compartment. A SEAL was kneeling in the middle, tinkering with one of the greasy beasts.

Ducts, pipes and conduits crawled along the walls and ceiling, all leading to the engines. The compartment's floor was set a few feet lower than that of the electric control area, creating a higher ceiling and the illusion of spaciousness.

At the aft end was another hatch. To our right was a ladder leading down. Through the grated walkway I could see another black-clad figure tinkering with the machinery below us. Metallic hammering rang through the room.

"How's it looking, Martin?" Larsen said.

The SEAL in front of us turned and dragged the back of his hand across his forehead, leaving a faint trail of machine oil on the pale skin. Carolina-blue eyes bracketed a razor-thin nose.

"Everything's in pretty good shape. Couple of loose wires up here, but nothing serious. We could go right now if we had to. Miller's downstairs checking the powertrain. Hey, Miller!"

The hammering stopped.

"Yeah?"

"What's the situation down there?"

"I think we're good to go. Gimme a few more minutes."

"That's fine, Seaman. Just make sure we can get to port without throwing a rod," Larsen said.

That seemed to end their conversation. Larsen grabbed the side rails of the ladder and slid down through the hole. After slinging the bag over my shoulder, I climbed down after him.

The lower deck seemed an inverted reflection of the upper level. The bottom halves of the engines were set in the ceiling, and a strip of deck led between the wide pillars of equipment they rested on. The lighting and walkway above cast a weird grid of shadows through the area.

The SEAL we had heard from above–Miller, I guess–was whacking a domed cover on the left-hand engine. His watch cap was stuffed into a back pocket, but a head covered with a uniform thickness of wiry black hair created the same effect as a hat. He paused when Larsen stepped onto the deck and nodded, his doughy face slick with sweat.

Larsen turned to me. "We're heading back forward. Through there."

He pointed at the bulkhead behind me, and I saw another hatch. This one was as close to human-sized as any I had encountered on the boat.

A SEAL stood on the other side, his olive skin turned sallow by the anemic overhead bulbs. He was up on his tiptoes, trying to look at something to the left, outside my field of view.

"Vazquez," Larsen said as he followed me through the hatch.

The SEAL turned. He had a graceful, almost child-like face. Deep-set brown eyes, no scars, nose had been broken several times. His mouth stayed closed when he wasn't talking.

The three of us were standing between two racks of rectangular, green boxes that stretched the length of the compartment. The top shelf was mounted about chest height, and I recognized notations for voltage and resistance printed on one of the boxes. Batteries.

The open space in the middle seemed about as wide as the center of the torpedo room. Behind Vazquez, I could see two figures clad in blue uniforms splayed on the floor.

"Lieutenant, the aft battery bay seems operable, sir. I ain't seen any major damage, and we should have enough juice to turn over the diesels." He looked at me. "You here to look at the bodies? They was laying there just like that when we came through. I didn't . . . I mean, I tripped and fell on top of that one, but I ain't moved them."

"I appreciate it, Vazquez," I said. "I'll just take a quick look at these two, and then we can get them out of your way."

Vazquez blinked several times and cleared his throat before he spoke. Maybe he wasn't used to being addressed in a normal tone of voice.

"Oh, uh, sure. Thanks. I mean, you know, no big deal. I'll be through here 'fore too long."

"OK, finish up, Vazquez," Larsen interjected. "We're going to fire up the engines soon."

He swept his right arm in an exaggerated arc toward the corpses. "Have at it."

I stepped around Vazquez, who was squatting now, checking something along the bottom battery rack. The two dead crewmen on the other side were oriented in opposite directions: one faced aft, lying on his back, and one faced forward on his stomach.

The left arm of the one facing us was pulled up to his lower abdomen, and the opposite hand lay at his side, bloody, as if it had been crushed. Even in death, the man's muscles appeared taut and powerful. His knees were bent at about a right angle, making it seem as though he had expired while doing sit-ups. He was young, maybe the same age as the crewman in the control room, and his black hair was trimmed to quarter-inch bristles.

The face, though, was the most striking feature about this corpse. His eyes bulged in their sockets, the eyelids wrenched open as far as they would go, the dilated pupils staring at the ceiling.

And the rest of his face matched. His lips—like the others', they were discolored, I noticed—were pulled away from his teeth, leaving his mouth frozen in a silent scream. Flecks of blood were evident on his chin and cheeks. I kneeled down for a closer look: the red dots still glistened.

"Uh, ma'am? That's the one I fell on," Vazquez said.

I looked up at him. "How did you fall on him?"

"I was at the forward end of the compartment, and I turned around and my foot got stuck in his legs." He shrugged, and traces of crimson crept into his cheeks.

"No, I mean, how did you land?"

"Oh. Well, I was pulling my weapon around on my back, and my right hand got kind of tangled in the strap." I heard Larsen snort behind me. "So I tried to catch myself with one hand, but I was, like, falling sideways. My hand landed on the guy's chest, and I sort of rolled to the side. I swear to Jesus I ain't moved him, though."

I planted my left hand on the deck and pantomimed pushing myself to the side and turning my body.

"Like this? All your weight was on your arm, and your hand was on the corpse?"

He nodded. "Yeah, exactly."

"Did anything happen when you hit? Did you hear any bones break? Tell me what you remember."

The color spread further across his face. "I didn't feel nothing break when I landed. But he . . . the body kind of coughed, like, and there was a little blood sprayed out. I got some on my face. Wait, he ain't alive, is he?"

The SEAL's distraught expression seemed inappropriate on a person loaded down with military paraphernalia.

"He's been dead for a while. Ice cold. But inside his body, the fluids don't evaporate because they're not exposed to the outside air. They take longer to dry up. He had some blood in his lungs or throat, and when you hit him, the pressure forced air up through his mouth and took some of the blood with it. Don't worry about it."

I had a feeling I could autopsy this crewman and find out what the insides of all the other corpses onboard looked like. Vazquez's accident may have offered me an inadvertent look at what I'd read in the medical examiner's report later.

"I didn't want to mess anything up for the, you know, investigation," Vazquez said.

"Right," Larsen said. "Vazquez, go on and finish getting this battery array squared away. Doctor, do you want to look at the other one here? I'll tell you right now, though, that these two aren't the main event."

I stood up and took a picture of both corpses without bothering to tell Larsen to move out of the frame.

The second dead crewman told a now-familiar story. No visible wounds. Lips and nail beds showed signs of cyanosis, and I'm sure the toes would have too, if we had bothered to take off his lug-soled boots.

This was a young one, too, his head shaved bald. After rolling him over, I could see that his eyelids were clenched shut. The rest of his facial muscles were slack, leaving his mouth open a few degrees.

"OK, where's the main event?"

Larsen laughed. "You'll know it when you see it."

Stepping around the bodies, he moved to the forward end of the compartment. His wide frame eclipsed most of the hatch opening, but I could see figures moving in the next room.

On the other side of the portal lay a charnel house. Two SEALs walked among the bodies, stepping over or around the tangle of limbs. A quick count told me there were eighteen corpses. It was tough to tell, though, because several lay atop each other or were lost amid intertwined arms and legs.

The room was about the same size as the upper half of the engine room, making up for a lower ceiling with greater length. The left half of the room was devoted to eating and cooking.

A kitchenette with a griddle, two burners and an oven took up the aftmost corner. Forward of it were a floor-to-ceiling steel refrigerator and a pantry that was a foot or so deep but stretched the length of the compartment. Three square tables were set in front of the pantry, surrounded by stools bolted to the deck.

The opposite wall was all bunks. Three racks, most covered by curtains, were mounted at about ankle, waist and shoulder height.

And sprawled throughout were the bodies.

There seemed no pattern to their distribution at first. The corpses were oriented in myriad directions and unnatural positions. Face-up. Face-down. On their sides. Draped over the edge of a counter. One seemed to be sitting against the bulkhead, deep in thought, his forehead resting against his knees.

I took a picture, my hands moving without conscious direction.

"Pretty fucked-up, huh? Some shit went down here."

As more of the scene began to register in my brain, some of the randomness dissipated. There was a concentration of bodies around the hatch to the next compartment forward. Many of them lay parallel to the sub's long axis. The ones closer to the center of the room were arrayed in more varied alignments. And just a handful of the dead were in the aft end.

Half wore a full uniform or jumpsuit; the rest had blue pants and T-shirts. For the first time since boarding the ship, I saw signs of major violence. Blood soaked through clothing. Walls and furniture were, in places, coated with gore.

Larsen poked one of the bodies with a booted toe. But he watched me as he did it.

"It's like they decided to have a WWF match in here. Same kinda shit in the forward battery bay. Hey, you guys find any weapons here?"

The nearest SEAL turned from the galley, where he was checking the pipes around the stove and oven. He had the broad shoulders of a middle linebacker and a nose that looked as though it had gotten the business end of a stiffarm. From several yards away it was hard to see his teeth, but I guessed they might have suffered some damage in the process.

"Couple of pistols. We pulled the mags. No rounds in the chamber . . . doesn't look like they'd even been fired. And one guy had grabbed a knife from over here. That's all."

"Have you moved any of the bodies?" I asked. As twisted a mess as this was, there might be something useful concealed in the chaos.

"What?" The SEAL turned to me as though he'd just noticed my presence. "Sure we did. I cleared these guys away from the galley so I could check the wiring." He pointed his chin at a pile of three crewmembers a few feet away from where he stood.

"I pulled a guy out of the forward hatch," said the other SEAL. He was about the same height as the first but looked willowy in comparison. Long neck, slight overbite. Some kind of a tattoo on his neck.

His eyes fluttered up and down my body, settling on my face with great reluctance. "He was sort of half-in, half-out."

"Which half was in this room?" I asked.

"The upper body. His stomach was square on the lower edge of the hatch."

"So what can you tell us, Doctor?" Larsen said, following his words with an amused glance at the second SEAL.

"Bunch of dead sailors," I said. "What's in the next compartment?"

"Campbell's in there," the stockier SEAL said to Larsen. "Just more of the same."

"It's the forward battery bay. You want to see it, Doc?" the lieutenant asked.

I nodded. "Why not? I want to at least make sure the whole crew is accounted for."

"We've found thirty bodies. Doesn't hurt for you to double-check, though," Larsen said, picking his way through the carnage as he walked toward the compartment's forward hatch. "Don't want any angry Koreans jumping out of the shadows at us."

The two SEALs' attention already was refocused on their examination of the room. As I followed Larsen, I heard one of the SEALs grunt with exertion. The sound was accompanied by a meaty thud as another corpse was moved out of the way.

We emerged into a copy of the room Vazquez had been working in. The major differences, however, were the fans of blood on the batteries and the dead sailors draped across the equipment.

"Shit," I said, hearing the word before I realized I had said it. "Are you sure those weapons they found hadn't been fired?"

Larsen turned to me, his brown eyebrows raised. "Looks like your professional opinion agrees with mine. 'Shit' is right. As in 'it hit the fan.'"

There was a SEAL standing between two bodies in the middle of the compartment, applying a wrench to a tube mounted on the ceiling. He had taken off his watch cap, revealing a red buzzcut. As we began speaking, he stopped and faced us. I took note of an unblemished face, high cheekbones and a jawline that defined but didn't dominate his face. Some Native American in him, despite the red hair.

"No firearms in here, sir. Just eight stiffs and a bunch of ruined batteries."

"Ruined?" Larsen said, frowning at the soldier. The expression made his cheeks look even more ravaged.

"Yes, sir. First of all, there are a couple of bodies sort of wedged back across the lower racks on both sides. And there's a ton of water damage. We reconnect these to the electrical system, we're gonna get a big-time short, if not a fire. Gas issues for sure."

"Dammit. 'Scuse me, Doctor." Larsen shouldered his way past me to the hatch we had just passed through. "Talk to Warrant Officer Campbell, take pictures, do whatever. I have to go figure out how to get this boat to port." He disappeared through the portal.

Campbell shrugged at me. "What do you want to know?"

"Did you move anything?" I was tired of asking this question, and I wasn't expecting his answer.

"Actually, no. Well, the ones on the deck I've had to slide out of the way a couple of times. But I haven't even thought about trying to fish these guys out," he said, kneeling and pointing between the two racks to my left.

I crouched and let my eyes adjust to the dimness under the top battery rack. Lying against the bulkhead, facing away from us, was a dead crewman. He looked as if he were using the batteries as a makeshift bed. I could see some dark stains on the wall by his head.

"There are two more on the other side, plus one flopped over the top rack. Four on the deck. Do you . . . what kind of ideas do you have about what happened here?" Campbell stood and leaned against one of the racks' vertical supports and motioned around the room with his left hand.

No blood around the corpses on the floor. But one of them was lying on something. I took a picture, then tugged the object free. It was a gas mask and had been trapped under the man's midsection.

"Yeah, there's a couple more of those between the racks. Not near the bodies, though," he said.

"Hmm." I tried to allow the scene's chaos to gel into a theory. "Well, it's tough to say what happened. I understand that the initial boarding party found chlorine gas, though. And I've been told that a battery accident can cause the gas. So maybe you can help me figure this out . . . how would such an accident take place? What would have to happen?"

He smiled and gestured at the ceiling with the wrench. "Shit, that's easy, ma'am. These pipes up here? Just about all of 'em failed. I'll bet they sprayed water all over the goddamn place in here. Soak all of these cells in saltwater, and you got big problems."

"Where do the pipes go? How did they fail?"

"That I'm not completely sure about. See, this isn't, like, a standard Romeo boat. The North Koreans bought most of their fleet from China and Russia, but their last few Romeos they've built themselves. Tried to improve on the design, I guess."

"Yeah, I read that, too. This is a modified Romeo class. But . . ."

"We've actually been trained on the operation of a Romeo boat. Capturing a hostile submarine is one of our possible missions, and these things are a dime a dozen, especially with third-world navies. So I can tell you that the big stuff is laid out the same way. The battery compartments are where they should be, the control room's where it should be, the engines are, too . . . you see what I'm saying? What they changed were a bunch of details, like hatch locations, ladders, some crew quarters, stuff like that. And when you rearrange details, little changes sort of ripple through the design."

He whacked the ceiling with the wrench, the discordant sound dying in the cramped space.

"And it looks like one of those ripples was that they needed to relocate some low-pressure seawater piping. I've never heard of a submarine design since World War II that had water pipes anywhere near the batteries. I'm not sure if you noticed in the aft battery compartment, but there aren't any pipes on the ceiling . . . just a bunch of electrical conduits. But here they are: water pipes. Like I said, I don't think any of them held up. And you can see the result."

I nodded. "So . . . they just broke?"

"Nah. I told you, these are low-pressure. No way they fail all by themselves."

"But obviously they did burst," I said, squatting next to the nearest body, a khaki-clad figure with insignia boards on its shoulders. "What would cause the failure?"

"Well, ma'am, I have a theory. I'll bet you money these pipes tie into one of the ballast tank manifolds. They're supposed to carry water from the tanks only when they're not open to the ocean. So they're not designed to be exposed to pressure at depth. You following me?"

"So far, yeah."

"Well, if you set about ten valves in the wrong position, then overfilled the ballast tank or tanks that these run to, then you get high-pressure seawater running through pipes that aren't designed to handle it. Pop," he said, illustrating an explosion in air with his hands.

"Uh-huh. And then the water sprays all over the batteries. What's the first effect of that?"

"Shorts, probably. I don't see any signs of fire. And, of course, chlorine. They dodged a bullet with hydrogen. That separates out of seawater, too. You get a boat filled with hydrogen and oxygen, one spark'll turn it into a Roman candle."

I gazed at the corpses on the deck and sighed.

"Valves to the wrong position, overpressured lines, and then they burst. So where are these valves? What are the chances that they'd be set in the wrong position inadvertently?"

Campbell cocked an auburn eyebrow and chuckled.

"Inadvertently? Right. You'd have to have the world's dumbest fucking crew to leave all those valves in the wrong positions. I guess it could happen, but even if it did, the pressure gauges would tell that something had gone wrong. All of that is right there in the control room. Bunch of wheels and dials and pipes."

"And with all of these pipes bursting, all that water . . . how much chlorine is that going to create?"

"Jesus. A bunch. I've never seen a situation like this, where so many leaks were spraying so much H_2O on a battery array. In fact, I'll bet the leaks didn't stop until they blew the tanks and surfaced."

"That's what I thought," I said. "Hey, am I keeping you from work here? Larsen said we were going to move soon."

"Work? Yeah, right. I'm trying to fix some of these busted pipes, but that ain't gonna happen. This all needs to be refitted. I already called the control room and told them to isolate the low-pressure lines in the forward half of the ship and keep them empty. Shouldn't be a problem for this short of a trip. And you can see from the rest of this," he said, slapping the rack to his left with the palm of his hand, "there's nothing else to salvage. The water's already drained into the bilge bay."

I moved past him, steadying myself on a support as I stepped over a body. I stopped at the forward end of the compartment. The hatch, which was designed to open into the next room, was shut.

"Where does this go?" I asked.

"Forward torpedo room. It's jammed, though." He watched me as I looked over the room. "So come on, spill it: what do you think happened to these people?"

The battery rack on the left side of the compartment ended about two feet short of the forward wall. The resulting space was occupied by what looked like a gray refrigerator about as tall as a man, and wide enough that even Campbell's broad shoulders could probably fit inside.

"Hold on," I said. "Is this thing standard?"

"Uh, no. No, I have no idea what that is."

"Did you look at it at all?"

"Not really. Shit, I've only been in here a few minutes, it seems. Just trying to check out all the equipment."

"Well, come here for a second. Can you tell me what that says?"

Two-inch-high lines of Korean characters were stenciled across the door of the locker . . . refrigerator . . . whatever it was. A shiny handle was set on the left-hand side next to a numeric keypad.

He smirked at me. "You know I'm the only person on this sub who can? I spent a little time at the Presidio language school. Let's see. *We-uhm. Duh ruh oh jee mah say yo.* That means something like 'Danger. No open.' No, 'Do not open.'"

But I didn't need his translation to figure that out. The spiky biohazard symbol stamped on the door above it told the same story.

"And you said you didn't examine this when you came in here?"

"No, not really. I told you, I was checking out all the batteries and the busted pipes."

"You don't know what's in there?"

"Maybe it's medical supplies or some shit. I didn't open it."

I slipped a finger under the handle and applied the tiniest bit of pressure. There was no give.

"Jesus! What the hell are you doing?" Campbell stepped on one of the dead crewmen as he lunged toward me.

"Whoa, whoa, relax," I said, turning to face him and holding my hands up, palms-out, in front of my chest. "I was just trying to figure out whether the lock mechanism was functioning."

"Well, I hope it fucking was! Didn't you hear what that writing on the door said?"

"Yeah, but it could be anything. Medical supplies, maybe, like you suggested." I watched his eyes as they tracked my body language. "Anyway, the handle didn't move at all. Seems locked up tight."

"Good thing, too. Let the technicians at the dock put on some bio suits and open it. Our job's just to get this boat back to port in one piece." He paused and closed his eyes. His barrel chest expanded under the black turtleneck, then deflated as he released the breath in a deep sigh. "We've all had biowar training, you know? And honestly, that stuff really puckers my ass. So if we can just let that storage bin be for now, I think we'll all be better off. You know?"

"I do know. I understand. And you're right, there's no reason to actually open it. So how about I just take a few pictures, look over these bodies and then get out of your hair?" I smiled. If nothing else, Campbell deserved that much for offering me the longest conversation since I had joined up with the SEAL team.

He flashed a half-grin that extended to his green eyes.

"Ah, don't worry about my hair, ma'am. I'm about done here, anyway . . . none of this shit is fixable. I'm going to head up to the control room in a sec."

"And I think I'll follow you before too long. Thanks for your help, Campbell."

"Not a problem," the SEAL said, then reached back toward the ceiling with the wrench, fighting with a pipe fitting.

I kneeled near the forward hatch, looking aft, then stood back up. I took a wide-angle picture of the compartment, kneeled again and photographed the bodies wedged between the battery racks.

Interesting. Two of the four bodies on the floor wore khaki uniforms decorated with various insignia. I rolled them over and took face shots.

Both of them were older men. The taller of the two, who was lying closest to me, had thick eyebrows and gray hair interlaced with the occasional black strand. His features poked at the back of my head, digging for a memory. I set my bag down on a clear patch of deck and opened up the dossier Patterson had given me.

Yes. It was Yoon, the captain. His tongue lolled from his mouth like that of a hanged man, and the other officer wore a similar expression.

Rolling over the other two crewmen on the floor, I saw that their countenances were twisted into the same grotesque, bug-eyed visage.

"I'm done here," Campbell said, bracing himself against the battery rack frame as he stepped among the splayed limbs and moved toward the hatch.

"Thanks again for your help. Oh, hey, before you go, I have a question for you: are the bodies stuck between the racks electrified? I mean, can I touch them without getting shocked?"

He nodded, then frowned. "Usually, I'd say you're pretty safe touching them. But with all the water that was in here, I wouldn't do it, personally."

"Right," I said. "I'll stay on the safe side, then."

"All right. See you, then. Uh, good luck." He started to wave goodbye, then stopped in mid-gesture as he realized he was still holding the wrench. He shrugged, smiled again and ducked through the hatch, the stock of his rifle clanging against the edge.

I turned back to the sailor atop the lower battery rack to my right. My imagination provided me with an image of Larsen rolling his eyes as he saw my unconscious body lying on the deck, smoke rising from my fingers.

Nope. A closer examination of the four crewmen arrayed amid the batteries would come later, when I had more assurance that I wouldn't be barbecued for my efforts.

I zoomed the camera in on the sailor's head, capturing the spray of reddish brown on the bulkhead next to it. The rest of his body seemed free of injury.

The two lying between the racks on the other half of the compartment weren't facing the wall. The one closest to me had a continuous necklace of bruises encircling his throat. Even from a few feet away, I could see the exophthalmos of his eyes. They bulged, staring through the shadows at the bottom of the rack above him. I snapped a picture.

The other crewman was lying on his side. The area just under the center of his forehead seemed obliterated by a blossom of red. My flash showed a massive injury where his nose would be. The bridge of it had been flattened, and I could see a few teeth poking through the ruined remains of his upper lip. It was like someone had dropped a cinder block on his face.

"In forward battery bay. Subject Number Three lying atop lower battery rack, supine, facing center of compartment. No visible damage to trunk or limbs. Face distorted by major blunt trauma centered on nasal cavity." I took a breath and turned to the other body. "Subject Number Four lying forward of Number Three. No visible damage to trunk or limbs. Tongue is protruding from mouth . . . no measurement possible, but about four centimeters appear to be visible."

"Ecchymoses evident on, uh, right side of subject's neck, continuing to other side," I said, noting the bruises. "Manipulation of body impossible."

I faced the other side of the room.

"Subject Number Five lying supine on opposite side . . . port side of submarine. Trunk, limbs appear undamaged. Dark stain evident on bulkhead. Deceased is facing stain." The corpses on the deck deserved a few observations as well. "Four subjects on floor of compartment. Bodies had been moved before photographs or observations recorded. No wounds visible on any of deceased. Extreme cyanosis visible in lips, nail beds. Tongues protruding from mouths several centimeters. Eyes exhibit extreme exophthalmos."

Standing, I held the camera over my head and used it to scan the top rack to my left. The other body Campbell had mentioned was wedged way back there, facing the wall. I photographed it.

"Subject Number Ten inaccessible at this time. No wounds visible."

"Hey, are you talking to us?" A male voice snapped my attention to the aft hatch. The head of the SEAL who had been examining the oven in the other compartment was thrust through the opening.

"Oh. No, I'm just recording some observations. Taking notes."

He glanced around the room and whistled. "Wow, looks like the party wasn't just in the galley." Refocusing on me, he continued. "Well, we're done in here. Feel free to do whatever."

"Thanks," I said. But he already had pulled himself back into the next compartment.

The evidence I most wanted to inspect was just a few feet away: bodies mutilated in a way I hadn't seen elsewhere on the submarine lying undisturbed where they had fallen.

But the threat of electrocution may as well have been a steel wall between me and the corpses.

I thought about the dead crewmen in the galley. Leaning over, I could see through the hatch into the other compartment. The SEALs had cleared out, leaving most of the bodies piled like refuse near the center of the room. The haphazard patterns of blood on the walls reminded me that some of the sailors in the galley had obvious wounds. There also were two officers still unaccounted for.

OK. I'd sift through the human debris in there, then make my way to the control room. I needed to sit down and evaluate everything I had collected so far.

I stepped toward the hatch, but stopped as a thought tugged at me. Turning, I saw again that the forward door was closed. I couldn't recall seeing another sealed hatch as I had made my way through the ship.

The latch mechanism seemed simple: a red wheel set in the middle. Two arrows the same color were painted above it, accompanied by some Korean characters. Well, it was righty-tighty, lefty-loosey, right?

I grabbed the wheel with both hands and twisted counterclockwise. It moved perhaps a quarter-inch, then stopped. Bracing my feet against the rack on one side and the biohazard locker on the other, I tried harder, throwing my back muscles into the effort. Nothing. Attempts to turn it clockwise met with the same result.

I'd have to get one of the SEALs to give it a shot later.

I picked up my bag and ducked back into the galley area. Glancing around the compartment, I didn't see any khaki, the color I had begun to associate with the submarine's officers. But then . . . there. Near the bottom of a stack of bodies to my right, next to one of the tables.

To get to this man, I'd have to pull four or five corpses off him. I didn't want to risk dropping one and causing postmortem damage that could hamstring a later examination. So a photograph of his face would have to do. I crouched next to the lifeless mass and tried to frame a shot.

It was surreal. The SEALs had laid the corpses so they were all oriented in the same direction, head upon head, feet upon feet. The result was a precarious pillar of contorted, tortured expressions six deep.

The officer was the second from the bottom. Zooming in with the camera, I captured his countenance. One eye was screwed shut as though he had just tasted something foul; the other was open, its brown pupil rolled up several degrees. His mouth was sealed by bluish lips.

His face was round and fleshy. The expression frozen on it seemed even more horrific in such a soft, baby-like countenance.

I stood. One more officer should be in here someplace. It took me a few moments to pick him out of the remaining corpses. His attire had thrown me off.

He was lying by himself near the room's aft hatch. The man wore the same uniform pants as the other officers, but a T-shirt replaced the matching top. Its white fabric was polluted by reddish-brown splashes around the neck.

Even from across the room, I could see where the blood had come from. The left side of the man's face was savaged, crumpled inward right where the bone structure was strongest. Another pool of dried blood had spread from beneath the officer's head.

Beneath his head? That meant the SEALs hadn't moved this one.

"Subject Number Eleven found to starboard side of aft hatch, galley area. Severe blunt trauma evident." I tucked the tape recorder between my elbow and body, snapping a picture of the scene. "Impact occurred just below deceased's right orbital socket. Zygomatic process collapsed. Some dentition visible."

Crouching down next to the man, I studied the back of his head and continued talking.

"Slight deformation of posterior cranial vault evident. Blood pooling evident on deck around deceased's head."

I measured the area covered with blood on the deck and the wound on the man's face, then stood and zoomed in for a shot of his features.

His hair was black and cut a tiny bit longer than that of the other bodies I had examined. A bushy unibrow stretched across his forehead, and his undamaged eye was closed. Extrapolating from the left side of his face, I could imagine high, angular cheekbones framing a beak-like nose.

Standing, I looked around the room. They said they had found two pistols and a knife. The butt of a pistol could do damage like this if someone swung it like a roundhouse, barroom punch. A quick check of the compartment showed no other weapons. The bunks also were empty. I'd have to ask the SEALs what they did with the guns.

I hoisted my bag onto my shoulder and turned my back on the room, slipping through the hatch into the aft battery bay. It was empty except for the two crewmen on the floor, who had been stacked on top of each other on the starboard side of the aisle that ran through the middle of the compartment.

Martin and Miller both were on the top level of the engine room now; I could hear them swearing as they worked. Miller noticed me climb up the ladder and gestured at me with his chin, keeping his hands inside the guts of the port-side engine. Several streaks of grease now sliced across his face, camouflaging his soft features.

"Hey, uh, we're about to start 'em up. You probably want to head forward to the control room or whatever. It's gonna get real fucking loud."

"Thanks," I said, pulling myself to a sitting position on the catwalk, then standing. "That's where I'm heading now."

Miller grunted and turned away.

The two SEALs in the electrical control room had been joined by the ones I had seen tidying up the galley. None of them glanced at me as I slipped through the compartment, their heads bowed to panels of blinking lights and quivering indicator needles.

I squatted and wiggled into the control room. It was a maelstrom of activity, with SEALs flipping switches and calling out gauge readings to one another. There was no sign of the dead crewman.

Larsen stood unaffected in the center of the action, his arms crossed, watching his men work. He did nothing to indicate he had seen me emerge into the scene.

"Time?" he asked, keeping his eyes focused on the SEAL settling into the steering station.

"Ah . . . 0450 hours, sir," came a voice from the left side of the control room.

"We need to get down," Larsen said, again speaking to the air in front of him. "Find out what the status on the engines is."

"Aye-aye, sir." The SEAL who responded was standing at the station to the left of the helm. His posture seemed hunched and predatory, and I realized he had to duck just to stand in the compartment. He reached up to a metal box mounted on the wall next to his head and depressed a switch. I recognized it as part of the intercom system I had encountered in the forward torpedo room.

"Engineering, conn. How're the engines coming along?" he said.

A tinny voice responded from the speaker. "Conn, engineering. We're ready to go on both shafts."

The lanky SEAL turned to Larsen. "Sir, engineering reports that the engines are ready."

"Very well. Start the diesels."

"Engineering, conn. Fire 'em up," he said into the speaker.

"Aye-aye, sir," it replied.

I heard a clang from the compartment I had just left. Crouching, I could see that the SEALs had sealed the hatch at the aft end of the room.

Then a vibration tickled the soles of my feet. It stopped, started, then erupted into a rumbling crescendo. The deck hummed with unseen energy, making it seem as if we were in the belly of some slumbering monster that had coughed and awakened.

"All ahead one-third," Larsen said.

"All ahead one-third, aye," the SEAL next to the helm replied. The man standing at the control station advanced two chrome levers mounted on a waist-high panel to his right.

Without any reference point, I was caught off-guard by the sudden shift in my personal inertia. We were moving.

"Prepare to dive and snort," the SEAL commander said.

"Prepare to dive, aye," came the reply. The hands of the SEALs on my side of the room flitted amid the snarls of pipes and valves there.

"Uh, excuse me. Could you move a little bit?" a voice said behind me.

It was Campbell, looking almost apologetic. "I need to get in here."

Larsen turned, bracing himself on the forward periscope, and acknowledged my presence.

"Doctor, we don't have room for you in here. Go to the officers' mess in the next compartment. Young will show you where it is." He pointed to the forward hatch, then swung himself back to his original position.

"Sure, no problem," I said, though my words seemed drowned out by a room full of indifference. I dodged my way to the hatch and into the hallway on the other side. The SEAL I had seen in my first trip through still filled the cramped space, leaning against the bulkhead. That must be Young.

He looked like a perfect California surfer dude, with an effortless tan and features that would make cheerleaders melt. His face had no flaws that I could see, besides the lechery in his gray eyes.

Young raised his eyebrows. "Coming through again?"

"Which one of these doors is the officers' mess room?" I said. His eyes now seemed fascinated by the GEORGETOWN written in blue across my sweatshirt.

"Yeah, it's this one," he said, peeling his gaze from my chest long enough to point at the forward-most door on the left. "You probably want to go in there and have a seat. Now that we're underway, we're gonna dive pretty soon. It could get . . . rough."

"Right, thanks," I said, trying to compress myself as much as possible while I shuffled past him.

"You need a hand? Diving in a submarine ain't like riding a subway."

"No, I'm fine."

The door looked like a man's shoulders would brush the edges of the frame when he passed through. The room on the other side was compact as well. It was about as long as a picnic table and arranged the same way, with uncushioned benches fixed on the walls around it. There was enough space inside the door for two people to stand side-by-side, but everyone else in the room would have to sit.

The room's walls matched the hallway, their brown surfaces gleaming with artificial wood grain. A hutch for making coffee or tea was set in the wall to the right of the door, and the walls were bare except for four black-and-white photos of a submarine, one on each wall. It was the *Dragon*, I assumed.

I tossed my bag on the table's white laminate surface and slithered in, leaving the door open. As I sat, my stomach and inner ear told me that my world was reorienting.

The change was subtle at first. The engine vibration seemed to take on a deeper, more muted timbre. I could hear water rushing into ballast tanks, metal creaking under new stresses.

And then my bag began to slide across the table. I held onto it, feeling gravity tug me toward the bow of the sub, and glanced up as I saw a figure move into the doorway. It was Young, his eyes glittering in the hallway's gloom. His smile revealed a single flaw: a mouth full of aimless, crooked teeth.

"Going down?" he said.

IV

THE WORLD LEVELED ITSELF OUT before too long. Young watched me the whole time, chatting at the side of my head through the doorway.

"Yeah, this feels like about fifteen degrees. Not too steep, you know, or we'd just keep going down. Couldn't stop. These old boats are weird that way." He paused and listened for a moment. "Almost there. We're not going very deep because we're using the diesels. There's this big snorkel thing that sticks up above the water and gets air so we can use the engines. So we're only, like, sixty feet down."

I turned to him and flashed a tight-lipped smile, then began sifting through the items in my bag.

"Only sixty feet down," he continued. "But it's still dangerous. We get a hull leak, we might not come back up. Or if the snorkel fails, the engines'll suck up all the air in the boat. Zzzzzzwhup! Hey, what's that?" I had pulled the Tokarev out as the dive ended and the floor once again represented where "down" was.

"Norinco M 213." I laid it on the table, then set the bags of shells and casings down next to it.

"Shit, lady, you can't just bring a gun with you when—"

"It's evidence," I said, speaking to the pistol as I held its bag up to the light. "Would you mind giving me a few minutes to myself? I need to look through all of this stuff. Thanks."

"Sure, whatever," he said, and after a moment I heard him step back down the hallway.

By the time I had emptied the duffel, the tabletop was all but covered by evidence bags. The light was better in here: four bulbs' illumination was diffused by square, white covers.

I had a gun, which looked as though it had been fired twice. I had a dead crewman, who looked as though he had been shot twice. Fine. Who shot him?

Flipping through the index of pictures on my camera, I found the one I was looking for and held it next to the sub's dossier. The man was wearing an officer's uniform, and . . . he was indeed an officer. Lee Tae-Uk, the ship's executive, had been the one holding the gun in the forward torpedo room. Although he wasn't smiling in my picture, his broad nose and thick eyebrows were unmistakable.

So Lee shot . . . who? I fidgeted with the rubber band, spinning and tugging it.

I was fortunate on that count. Of the twenty-four enlisted men on the ship, seven had photos attached to their profiles. The dead man in the control room was one of them.

His blue coveralls made more sense now; he was the top non-officer in the engine room. A mechanic, in essence. His name was Ahn Do-Ri.

An officer shot a mechanic twice in the back, then went to the forward torpedo room. Was he going to launch a torpedo? Fire on the U.S. escort?

I let the photos of that compartment take me back to the moment when I first saw the room. The torpedo racks all were full. And, seeing the massive cylinders again, I doubted one man could manage the loading operation. Were there torpedoes already in the tubes, maybe?

The weapons dominated the room's features. Torpedoes, tubes, launch controls.

But another detail separated itself: the suit covering the corpse's lower body. The yellow fabric seemed florescent in comparison to the somber background. What was this suit? Why was he half-wearing it?

Even assuming I had identified both the attacker and the victim, those facts still seemed minor and overshadowed by the things that remained unknown. And perhaps unknowable.

"How's it going, Doctor?" Larsen's voice pulled me back into the dining area's bleakness. He had appeared in person this time, leaning against the doorframe.

"Things are a little confusing," I said, gesturing to the bench to his left. "Maybe you can help me out."

He sat, laying his rifle next to him.

"Help you? How can I do that? I'm just a sailor, a simple submarine driver."

Men and their macho idiosyncrasies didn't bother me. I had even been engaged once, when I was in my late 20s, although, as Mom would say, it just hadn't worked out. With my odd schedule, it was tough to meet men, and most of the guys I hung out with were co-workers. Stephen too, of course, whenever I was in Washington. None of them ever had been able to dent my patience with testosterone-inspired behavior.

But now I reached over and closed the door, a sudden rush of black emotion clouding my thoughts.

"What is your deal? Really, can you tell me that? As far as I'm concerned, we're on the same team here, trying to accomplish the same thing. But since I climbed on your helicopter, you've treated me like some kind of an obstacle to your mission." I tried to keep my tone conversational, but each word seem to detonate in the tight quarters, filled with anger I couldn't hide.

His expression didn't change. I don't think he even blinked. He pulled his watch cap off and tossed it on top of his rifle, then ran his fingers through the blonde buzzcut the hat had concealed. Taking a deep breath, he screwed his features into a caricature of clenched muscle, then relaxed and exhaled. His off-kilter eyes bored into me.

"Yeah, we're on the same team, Doctor. General Patterson called us both, right? Called us and told us there was some fucked-up situation on a submarine, and we needed to fix it. Except he told me that my men and I had to take control of the submarine—without knowing who was on-board, really—by helicopter insertion and then navigate it safely to port." He placed both of his hands palm-down on the table, as if he wanted to prevent them from doing something more drastic. "That's a pretty tall order for most people, but we're fucking SEALs. Our job is to put a boot in someone's ass before they even hear footsteps. This kind of operation is what we do, and no one does it better.

"Then I'm told, just before we're scheduled to take off from the base, that there's someone else being included at the last second. A civilian. A civilian who is going to be examining the boat while we're trying to operate it. 'Yes, sir,' I said. 'No problem, sir.' You know why I said that? Because I've never met a civilian who could keep a SEAL platoon from fulfilling its mission."

He leaned toward me. I could see the edges of his nostrils twitch.

"And our mission is to get this sub back to port in one piece, without any complications. Nothing you do onboard will be worth a damn thing if we don't make it to shore."

"I know that. I've tried to stay out of—"

"No, Doctor, you haven't. You've ignored at least two orders I've given you, and if your presence on this boat weren't so damn important to the general, I'd just stick you in one of the officers' quarters and have Young lean on the door until we were in Norfolk."

I sighed and nodded. "I'm sorry. The first time, that wasn't deliberate; I just jumped off the helicopter without thinking. And I'm sure that's the kind of thing that worries you about involving civilians in your missions. But all this," I said, gesturing at the collection of plastic bags and envelopes on the table, "is absolutely vital. I needed to find the gun that shot the man in the control room, and it wasn't in the control room. I knew we had limited time. So rather than risk it being moved or tampered with once you and your men came onboard, I left the control room to find it."

"Understandable. In your situation, I might have done the same thing," Larsen said. He crossed his arms, the limbs sturdy and powerful under the turtleneck's ribbed sleeves. "And that's why you're not locked up. I'm not asking much from here on out, Doctor."

I was sick of the way he spat out the title like it was a pejorative.

"You don't have to keep calling me 'doctor.' Christine is fine."

"OK, then, Christine. As I said, I don't require a whole lot from you in the next few hours before we make port. You can examine what you need to examine, take pictures, dust for fingerprints, whatever it is you do. Just understand that this is my boat. If you're in the way, no matter how important you might think your work is, you have to move. If you're interfering with my men as they operate this thing, then you're in the wrong place. Do you read me?" He raised his eyebrows, an expression that showed his question wasn't rhetorical.

"I understand, Lieutenant. And believe me, I don't intend to get in the way of you or your crew. OK?"

"OK. I'm glad we're on the same page."

"In fact, I don't think there's much more for me to collect. Autopsies, that kind of detailed analysis, that will all be done on shore. I've sketched together a rough scenario that, hopefully, the lab technicians can solidify."

"Oh yeah? Let's hear it. I'm interested in what went down on this relic. In fact, I've got some more evidence for you," Larsen said, drawing two black automatic pistols from his waistband and laying them, butt-first, on the table.

"What are these?" I asked.

"The firearms we found in the mess hall. This one's cockeyed–the barrel's bent. The other one seems fine. Both mags are full, eight rounds each."

I leaned in to look more closely, knowing as I did so that any value as evidence had been lost when the SEALs picked up the pistols and inspected them.

"Nine millimeter. The bent one's got some blood and hair caught on the front sight. Probably used as a club," I said. "Norinco, same as the one I found in the forward torpedo room."

"What else?" Larsen said as I sealed the weapons inside separate plastic bags and put them away.

I pulled up the wide-angle image of the crewman in the control room and slid the camera over to Larsen.

"That's the guy in the control room as I found him. I checked his picture against the dossier General Patterson gave me. Have you seen it?"

Larsen nodded.

"Good. Well, this guy's an enlisted man, Ahn Do-Ri, a mechanic. He worked in the engine room. As you can see, he's still wearing some sort of coverall. Those streaks on it are grease, I'm guessing. He was shot twice in the back. Those are the wounds in his left shoulder area," I said, reaching over and advancing to the close-up of the bloody holes in his back. "He was lying next to what Grimm told me were the controls to surface the sub in an emergency. Is that right?"

"Yeah," Larsen said, snicking a fingernail against the viewscreen. "Right there . . . ballast tanks, emergency blow switches."

"That's where he was. I took fingerprints from the switches. The only usable ones are from the big handle. And I know they belong to this man."

"You can do that without a lab?" Larsen looked up from the camera display.

"Not accurately, no. But the body had a cut on its right middle fingertip that hadn't healed. Here are the fingerprints from the handle," I said, holding the pouch up between us, "and you can clearly see the mark duplicated in this print, which was positioned where the middle finger would be. You're right that the others can't be positively identified without a fingerprint technician, but based on this, I think I can confidently say that this man left those prints on the emergency blow handle.

"So here's the first thing you can help me with: would a mechanic, in the normal operation of the sub, be working those controls?"

"That was easy," Larsen said, laughing. "Nope. Not ever. This guy's a grease monkey. When he's awake, he spends his time running or maintaining the diesels. I'd be surprised if he often passed through the control room, let alone worked in it."

I had popped a blank tape in my recorder and turned it on. I wanted to make sure all our thoughts and conclusions didn't escape the moment.

I put it on the table between us. "OK. Finding his fingerprints on the handle was unusual—"

"But not impossible," Larsen interrupted. "How do you know those prints are recent and not from, say, a month ago when he took someone else's shift for them?"

"We know it because the prints were preserved in blood. What's more, I think lab tests will show the blood is his."

"Got it. So he pulled the emergency blow handle. And then someone killed him."

"You'd think that," I said, taking the camera from him and cuing up a different picture. "But you're wrong about two things: He was shot before he pulled the handle. And the gunshots didn't kill him."

"What are you talking about? You said he was shot twice in the back . . . how is he going to pull the handle after he's dead?"

"That's just it. As I said, the gunshots didn't kill him. Look at this." I gave the camera back to Larsen. "See the wound position? Right there near the top of the shoulder. And the exit wounds are slightly higher. Those bullets didn't hit anything vital."

"He could have bled to death."

"Not much chance of hitting a major vein or artery in that area. And even more telling is the lack of blood on the floor beneath the body. He bled, all right, but not nearly enough to kill him."

"Shot twice, but not mortally wounded. I guess I can buy that. But it doesn't mean he wasn't shot *after* he pulled the lever."

"Evidence in the control room suggests otherwise. Remember the wide shot of the compartment? Blood stains near the middle of the room. Smeared in a direction parallel to Ahn's body. Combine that with the way his body was oriented, and I see this: He was shot before he got to the panel and fell there in the middle of the room. It took him a few moments, but he dragged himself back to his feet and moved over to the emergency blow switches. Then he collapsed for good. Died a bit later."

"Use small words," Larsen said. "What killed him, then?"

"Chlorine. He was in bad shape before he was shot. We'll have to wait for an autopsy to tell for sure, but I think my theory is pretty much on target. You can see it on the close-up of his face."

Larsen examined the image after I brought it up on the camera. "Damn. He was in some pain."

"It's more than that. Look at his lips."

"They're . . . blue."

"Exactly. His fingernails are in the same condition. It's called cyanosis, and it's caused when the blood isn't carrying the oxygen it should. Now, in the absence of any other evidence, we wouldn't have much idea what caused him to be so oxygen-deficient. But there was a massive release of chlorine on the sub. That's what the initial boarding party found, right?"

Larsen nodded.

"So," I continued, "we look into the symptoms of chlorine. And we see that, in high concentrations, it causes pulmonary edema. Fluid in the lungs. It's a nasty gas, chlorine—besides that effect, it also reacts with your tissue, and one of the byproducts is hydrochloric acid. Which, of course, breaks down the tissue further. Basically, your lungs drown in blood even as they're being destroyed. You cough and cough, but all that comes up is blood, and eventually, your lungs can't introduce enough oxygen into your bloodstream, no matter how deeply you breathe.

"Vazquez inadvertently helped us out on this one. When he fell on the corpse, a mist of blood sprayed out. This corpse, remember, showed no obvious mortal wounds. So we can surmise that there was internal bleeding in its pulmonary system. I think that we would see the same thing if we cut open Ahn."

"He was gassed."

"Right. He already had inhaled quite a bit of chlorine by the time he got to the control room. He wouldn't have survived even if he hadn't been shot."

Larsen rubbed his face, igniting a more noticeable glow in his already ruddy cheeks. "So who shot him?" he said, gnawing on his thumbnail.

"Someone aiming into the compartment, probably from aft to forward."

"Oh, come on. How the hell would you know that?"

"Well, I can guess at what direction he was facing when he was shot based on the bloodstains. His back was facing aft and, uh, starboard. And based on the angle the shots hit him—traveling upward—we can surmise that he was shot from a position lower than shoulder height."

"The aft hatch."

"The aft hatch. So I looked around that doorway and found two shell casings. Both 9mm." I rattled the baggies in front of him, then set them back on the table.

"You find the gun those came from, and you find the gun that shot Ahn. And that was luck on my part. It happened to be in the first compartment I checked. The forward torpedo room. Here, can I see that again?" I shuffled through the digital images. "This guy was lying right there, with the pistol in his hand."

"Uh-huh. Who is he?"

"Lee Tae-Uk. The dossier says he's the sub's executive."

"Executive? Lemme see that." Larsen scrutinized the folder. "Executive officer, is what it means."

"So how does he fit into the officer hierarchy?"

"He's essentially the second-in-command. Executive, as in, he executes the commands the captain gives."

"So here he is, lying in the torpedo room, holding a gun that matches the shell casings I found."

"Nine millimeter?"

"Yup. It's a Chinese-made gun, a copy of the old Soviet-bloc military sidearm."

"Oh, right. The Tokarev."

"Exactly. Chambered for 9mm. Two rounds were missing from the magazine, and the headstamps on the bullets in the mag matched the ones on the shell casings from the control room."

"Looks like he's the shooter, then."

I sighed. "I know you're getting tired of hearing this, but only a lab test will tell us for sure. They'll check his hand for residue that matches the gun. But based on everything else I've found, yeah, he pulled the trigger."

"Let me guess, he's got the cyanosis, too?"

"In spades. He asphyxiated right there on the floor. Which leads me to another question you can help me answer, Lieutenant. I have no idea what this outfit he's wearing is. He's got the normal officer attire on his upper body, but what's the suit he's got on his legs?"

Larsen squinted at the screen on the back of the camera, again exaggerating the fleshy moonscape on his cheeks. "That's weird. It's a pressure suit."

"For diving? Like a wet suit?"

"No, it's semi-pressurized. It allows you to float up from, I dunno, two hundred feet or so without as much danger of getting the bends. Basically, you use it to escape from a crippled sub."

We sat in silence for a moment. I stared at the shell casings, each one a glimmering, golden reflection of the lights overhead, and somehow fought off the itch to snap the rubber band. In Larsen's flinty eyes, the neurosis, however minor, would be a weakness.

"He was trying to escape," I said, hearing Larsen take a breath. But I plowed ahead. "How? What, does he just open up the conning tower and start swimming?"

"Not the conning tower. The escape tower is in the torpedo room. On the ceiling just aft of where he's lying. You open the inner door, pull yourself into this tiny compartment, close the hatch, flood the space, then open the outer hatch."

"And float away."

"You got it. Looks like he didn't make it that far, though."

"He wouldn't have survived even if he had made it out of the submarine. But wait: If he were trying to get out, why was he still holding the pistol? Wouldn't he have to put it down to put on that suit?"

"Maybe he hadn't gotten around to putting the gun down."

"He took the time to remove his shoes and pull on the legs of the suit. Can't do that while holding a gun."

"Yeah. I guess he picked the gun back up, then."

"There was no one else around! Why would he pick it back up? He wanted to get out of the submarine. There's no reason to hang around."

"Something scared him."

"Scared him? What?" The pages of the dossier fluttered as I pulled it off the table in front of him. "Everyone in here is accounted for. And except for Ahn, they're all on the lower deck. Some of them may have died from other injuries, but most are clear chlorine victims."

Larsen crossed his arms again and leaned back. "Fine, then. You tell me: what makes a man pick up his weapon when he's in the middle of trying to escape?"

"I'm saying this is a situation where we have to examine the circumstances. And the circumstances dictate that there was no one alive to pose a threat to him. Or if there were, they were in as bad shape as he was, if not worse. Something obviously made him grab the gun again, but it wasn't . . . hold on."

"What?"

I closed my eyes, trying to allow my subconscious to piece together the scene. It was like watching an old newsreel, the details jumping in and out of focus.

"Keep in mind that he crouched and shot through the hatch. He didn't climb into the control room before he fired. He couldn't wait that long to shoot. There was time pressure."

"I'm not sure—"

"Let me finish. Ahn was facing away from him when Lee pulled the trigger. So why rush? Because he had to shoot before Ahn reached the diving controls . . . he was moving toward that panel when he was hit, remember. Lee shot him, saw him fall and stop moving, then continued through the compartment and went to the torpedo room."

Larsen shifted in his seat.

"Once he got there," I continued, "he was ready to escape the sub, but something happened. Something that made him strip off the top half of the suit and grab the gun again."

"Ahn wasn't dead."

"Yes. Ahn had gotten back up and hit the emergency surface switches. Lee heard the tanks blow, felt the submarine begin to rise. He says 'Oh, shit,' picks up the gun and tries to get back to the control room. But he doesn't make it."

"And that was all she wrote," Larsen finished.

I opened my eyes. Larsen had a half-smile on his face, like a man who had just finished a steak at a five-star restaurant.

"Goddamn, Christine," he said. "I understand why General Patterson wanted you onboard. You might as well have been here videotaping everything while it happened."

"But look at all this," I said, sweeping my arm in the air over the table full of evidence. "We might have a good idea of what went down in the actual shooting, but we don't know why Ahn was trying to surface the ship, we don't know why Lee wanted to stop him, and we sure as hell don't know what happened to the other 90 percent of the crew."

"It's true. That stuff on the lower deck is a clusterfuck. It looks like the world's deadliest bar brawl. I know you've probably never seen that kind of violence, but in my . . . what?"

He had caught me rolling my eyes this time.

"Please. I study violence for a living. And I'm guessing that you've never seen thirty dead people on a submarine before, either."

"OK, then, what's your opinion? What happened?"

"Specifically? I'm not sure yet. Generally, though, there was a big fight. I realize you could have told me that." Larsen had targeted me with an exaggerated shrug, his eyes wide and mocking. "But I can tell you this much: violence always has a motive. I don't know if we'll be able to pin down who was on what side at this point, since all the bodies have been moved around, but I think we can figure out what they were fighting over. And I'll bet it has something to do with that biohazard locker thing in the forward battery bay. Did you see that?"

"Uh, yeah, I guess. Why do you think it's important?"

"It just seems to be at the epicenter of the worst violence, it's in the compartment where the chlorine was generated, the captain was lying a few feet away, *and* it's not a standard fitting on a submarine. Didn't you say the sub was carrying weapons research?"

"I didn't say that."

"Now that I think about it, it was General Patterson."

"Well, I have no idea what the research was, or what the locker was for. But I do know that as long as I'm in control of this boat, we're not opening anything that is marked a biohazard. Period."

"Don't worry. No way I'm poking my head in there. My investigation from this point is pretty much going to be sifting through the evidence I've already collected. But I think that refrigerator, or whatever it is, is too out-of-place to just ignore."

"Fine. Sift all you want. But you're going to have to ignore it until we get back to shore and get a biohazard team on the boat."

"I said I wouldn't open it. It's locked with a keypad, anyway."

"Just so we understand. Now, if you'll excuse me for a few minutes, I need to go make sure the boat's not sinking or anything."

Larsen used the beverage hutch to pull himself to his feet, then opened the door and stepped out without shutting it behind him. I heard his footsteps disappear down the corridor.

Young still was standing across the hall, picking at something under his index fingernail. He laughed.

"You got the case solved yet?"

"No, but you're the prime suspect," I said, staring at the ceiling.

There was something else nagging at me, an out-of-place thread in the scenario I had woven. The locker . . . the bodies . . . injuries, chlorine . . . and . . . the torpedo room. Something was out of place. The door to the battery bay wouldn't open but not because it was jammed.

"Shit. They locked it."

I browsed through the digital images until I found my documentation of the torpedo room. Yeah, there it was: the closed hatch.

Standing up, I grabbed my bag, pushed past Young and headed forward.

The SEAL in the torpedo compartment was sitting on the edge of one of the torpedo racks. Dark-brown skin, perfect white teeth. Long face, matching thin nose that flattened toward the tip. Superorbital ridge marked by at least two small irregularities—waves, almost—over each eye.

He looked up as I swung myself into the room, then stood as he saw my expression.

"Is there a problem?" he said.

"No, no," I said, waving him off. "I just need to check something in here."

Looking at the hatch in person, I saw what had caught my attention in the photo: A chain, each link the size of a child's fist, was wrapped five or six times around the dogging wheel's lower edge and a nearby pipe, secured with a fist-sized padlock. The pipe had bent a degree or so.

"Hey, could you come here for a minute?" I asked.

"Sure," he said as he moved in behind me.

"What's your name?"

"Seaman Richard Jakes. Why do—"

"OK, Richard. Is this setup, with the chain and the closed hatch, is this normal?"

The odor of gun oil and perspiration washed over me as he leaned over my shoulder.

"Nope. These things . . . you're not supposed to be able to lock them? I don't know why you'd chain it up like this."

"Huh." That was all I could manage to say as my mind churned through the information.

"On the other hand, ma'am, it's not like this is a state-of-the-art boat or nothing. Maybe it kept swinging open, or wouldn't stay open, or something, and they just secured it like that to keep it out of the way. You never know. I've seen North Korean equipment before, and they can find a way to cut corners with just about everything." He straightened. "Is that what you needed?"

"Yeah, Richard, thanks," I said, snapping a picture of the chained door and bent pipe. "I think I'm done here. I'll get out of your way."

He stepped back a few paces as I moved over to the ladder. "I don't see anything else unusual in here, if that's any help. Besides the dead guy."

"Thanks," I said again, already halfway through the hatch.

Young was at the aft end of the hallway now, squatting and talking to someone in the control room. He didn't seem to notice as I returned to the officers' mess area.

I sat back down and closed the door.

The mental filmstrip I had for the three body-strewn compartments was shapeless and filled with gaps. So much fighting . . . but over what? And why had the forward battery bay hatch been sealed?

I tried to picture the sailors grappling with each other, punching, rolling on the floor. Green death billowing from the forward battery compartment. Some had brought gas masks, but they had been lost in the fray.

Why had the crewmen stayed? Why, their lungs burning, stomach muscles tearing as they tried to cough away the searing pain in their chests, hadn't they run? The chlorine had no doubt infiltrated the rest of the submarine, but not in the concentrations that must have been present around its source.

But two men *had* run. One went to the control room in a bid to surface the ship. The other shot him. My impressions of those events were much clearer, but their motivations still were lost in the haze of the battle on the lower deck.

Start from the beginning. Pipes burst over the forward battery bay. Chlorine begins roiling from the spoiled batteries.

Oh, Christ, this wasn't going to get me anywhere. I didn't know whether that was the beginning or not. My imagination was supplying most of the details.

Facts. Just plant the facts in a blank script, and see whether they connect to one another and form a plot.

I rubbed my temples, trying to massage away the sudden spears of frustration and stress.

There had been some kind of conflict in three compartments on the lower deck. How did we know that? Because there were dead people tossed about the rooms, some of whom featured visible injuries.

All the officers except one lay among the devastation there. Lee had made it to the forward torpedo room. But the lower door from the battery bay was locked. Did he chain it shut behind him? No, it was locked when he fled the fight because he entered the control room at its aft end and continued to the torpedo compartment. There was one sliver of storyline.

Maybe Lee wasn't involved in the fight, though. Maybe he came from another part of the ship, farther aft. Except he died as a result of chlorine inhalation. There wouldn't have been enough of the gas in the rest of the sub to have caused that kind of massive pulmonary damage so fast. So he must have been in the thick of the violence at some point.

Same thing went for Ahn. Everyone onboard had been part of the struggle in three chlorine-saturated rooms.

And I knew the burst pipes were a deliberate act, or an act of gross incompetence. Who would instigate a chlorine accident on a submerged submarine? It was a desperate move that seemed to guarantee the demise of whoever arranged it. The thirty corpses proved the truth of that.

Lee had left the fight to shoot Ahn. Why had Ahn left the fight? To surface the submarine. Why would he do that? Or, more important, why was he the sole crewman who sought to do so?

I pushed those questions to the side as I felt my imagination begin to dump speculation into the blanks.

All the other hatches I had seen had been open during the fight. So an escape route was open. But, again, no one tried to flee. There was a motive there. The pain and fear chlorine inflicted was too much for a person to just shrug off. The sailors stayed in the area for a reason.

Now my thoughts were beginning to chase each other around in my head. Anchored in the center of the whirlpool, however, was one image I couldn't let go of: the biohazard symbol on that refrigerator in the forward battery compartment. An electronic lock, its technological complexity decades ahead of any of the sub's other equipment.

That told me something important was inside. And the stated reason for this sub's importance was the weapons research it carried. I shook my head and allowed myself to fall over the edge into a supposition. It was a small one, I told myself, and could be changed later as evidence warranted.

The locker held whatever intelligence information the United States was so keen on getting. Nothing else on the boat presented any value to a nation that hadn't fielded a diesel-electric sub in fifty years.

If that were true, it might explain the motivation for a free-for-all on a submarine. It might also offer a reason why someone triggered a gas accident that submariners would consider the stuff of black nightmares.

Not a concrete reason, for sure, but it provided a small glint of rationality in what otherwise appeared to be a scene of wanton violence.

The door swung open, and Larsen walked into my forensic daydream.

He sighed as he sat, pushing himself down the bench and hoisting his legs onto it. I could hear his neck crackle as he swiveled his head.

"Tough day at the office, Cap'n Nemo?" I said.

He looked up at me. If I had been standing, his expression would have made me take a step back. Then it melted away and he laughed.

"Nemo. Right." He let his head loll back and closed his eyes. "You know, this submarine capture business is one of our most peripheral missions. I mean, I imagine that someone who studies violence for a living knows that SEALs spend most of their time conducting covert operations in places where conventional forces would fail. Rescues, high-value target elimination, demolition, intelligence gathering, you know. Not taking over antique submarines."

I winced and nodded at the "violence for a living" comment. I deserved it this time.

"I mean, hell, this is only our fourth time aboard a boat like this," Larsen continued, opening his eyes and focusing them on me. "I'm not sure where they found a spare Romeo lying around, but they did, and we worked on its operations. We had general training on the operation of a sub, and knew the layouts of several more advanced models . . . Russian nuke boats, mainly. But then these North Koreans decide they want to give Uncle Sam an early birthday present and head over here in their submarine to deliver it. So, of course, we learn how to take control of such a boat, just in case they lose their nerve at the last second or something."

"Looks like you guys have done a fine job so far," I said.

"Nothing's blown up. We're not taking on water. We're on course. And hey, when we get a little closer to the coast, we'll be in waters that are shallower than this tub's crush depth, so that's a comfort."

He glanced at his wrist, checking the time.

"Are we on schedule, Lieutenant?"

"Yeah, we should get there in plenty of time." He leaned forward and pointed at my chest. "So, I've come up with a theory about what caused that zoo of death downstairs. Want to hear it?"

"Shoot."

He pulled an imaginary trigger with his pointing finger, then chuckled.

"Pow! OK, here's the deal. I'm not sure why this wasn't obvious to me before, but it sure as hell is now. There was a mutiny."

"Tell me why," I said.

"It's not too hard to figure out, actually. This boat was defecting, committing treason against its home country. Everyone onboard was part of the conspiracy. But do you know how hard it is to get thirty people to go through with an act like that, let alone keep it a secret?"

"I was wondering about that myself earlier."

"See? It makes sense. But stay with me. When they got close to the coast here, the dissenters decided to make their move. They probably arranged to do it while most of the crew was sleeping. You saw all those bunks down there. But someone woke up. The alarm spread. Pretty soon everyone's fucking pounding on each other down there."

"But the chlorine . . ."

"I'm getting there. It's not going well for the mutineers. So one of them, in a last-ditch move, starts the water leak in the battery bay, which just happens to be adjacent to the room where most of the fighting was taking place, and tries to gas the crew into submission.

"There were a couple people with gas masks in the forward battery bay, right? They were trying to fix the leak, but they couldn't really separate themselves from the fight and ended up losing their masks and dying anyway. Meanwhile, one of the good crewmen—the ones who wanted to defect—is like, 'fuck this,' and runs up to the control room to surface the ship and ventilate it."

"Hold on a sec," I said, tapping the table with my fingertips. "I was going to ask you about that . . . is surfacing the ship pretty standard if there's an accident like this?"

"You're catching my drift. That's right—if the atmosphere is contaminated, you surface and ventilate the whole thing. Otherwise, you can't recirculate the air and you're screwed. So that's what the mechanic, whatever his name was . . ."

"Ahn."

" . . . Ahn, that's what he was trying to do. But one of the mutineers, the leader, I'll bet, sees him go. He chases him. Pops a couple caps in him."

"Sure, but why did he then try to escape the sub?"

"Because if you don't surface the sub, the whole thing's going to be filled with chlorine and you're fucked. And remember, he doesn't want us to get hold of the boat. So he's just going to abandon ship, maybe leave the hatch open so it starts flooding, and float to the surface."

"Float to the surface? If he floats to the surface, he'd still have big problems. So he's just bobbing in the ocean, miles from the coast?"

"But he's not dead. And all the other witnesses are!" Larsen punctuated the sentence by pounding his fist on the table, making the evidence on it jump. "This close to shore? He'd get picked up before he died of exposure or thirst. Then he can tell whatever story he wants. Maybe he becomes the good guy, tried to thwart a mutiny, ended up being the only survivor. It doesn't matter. All that *does* matter is that he's prevented us from getting the intelligence we wanted, and he keeps us from ever knowing what happened on the boat."

He leaned back again and raised his eyebrows. "See? It all fits."

"It makes a certain amount of sense," I said. "But there still are lots of things we don't know. That *don't* fit."

"Yeah? Like what?"

"If you're going to stage a mutiny, why wait until you're just hours away from the end of a journey that took months? Why not try to take over the ship when you're still near the coast of your homeland, where the sub can be recovered?"

"Maybe they just had to work up their courage. They probably didn't start to worry about the defection succeeding until they realized how close they were to the United States." Larsen waved his right hand in the air between us, dismissing my questions. "It's not really important."

"Not important? Well, how about this: If they wanted to take out the crew while they slept, why not just trigger the chlorine spill and seal off the galley and sleeping area? That would kill everyone in there without risking any of the mutineers' lives."

"Poor planning. It happens."

"Well, someone took the time to seal off the front hatch in the forward battery bay. Why?"

"What are you talking about?"

"Go check it out. Someone wrapped heavy-gauge chain around the locking wheel in the torpedo room and secured it to a pipe so the hatch couldn't open."

"Could just be busted. That happens, too. Or maybe the mutineers didn't want to give the crew more than one way out when they started their attack. Look, when I left this room, you were all upset because you couldn't figure out why all those people were dead down there. And you're an expert." Larsen had raised his voice a few decibels. "So please, Doctor, I'd like to know if you have a theory now. Do you?"

I didn't blink as he stared at me.

"I'll bet I can put something together," I said.

V

"YOU'RE ON THE RIGHT TRACK in trying to come up with a motive for the fight," I said. "There has to be a motive, you see . . . you're not going to get thirty people brawling, thirty people who have military training and are used to submarine life, over something small like an insult or stolen magazine. Something major went down here."

Larsen shifted in his seat. But he was listening.

I brandished the camera at him. "And these pictures show us where the epicenter of the violence was: on the lower deck, in three compartments that likely were flooded with chlorine. And we both can agree that the gas was not an accident, right?" I paused and he nodded. "Further, we know that both Lee and Ahn were involved in the melee, or at least were in that area, because both expired due to chlorine exposure.

"So everyone on the sub was down in those three compartments when they were flooded with a noxious, painful, deadly gas. There was a way out, but only two left. I promise you, if you're involved in close combat in the middle of a chlorine cloud, you're going to break it off and try to get away. But none of these people did. Why not?"

"It's your world," he replied.

"Something kept them there. Chlorine gas is brutal. I told you what it does to the body when it's inhaled. Whatever their motivation for staying, it was powerful. And important."

"Oh, Jesus. No—" Larsen said, but I didn't let him finish.

"Yes. Come on, are you going to tell me that the biohazard container isn't utterly out of place on this sub? That it probably has nothing to do with the intelligence that we're after? Think about it. It provides a motive."

"OK, let's say you're right. Let's say it provides a motive: mutiny. Someone didn't want it to fall into our hands. What the hell is your point?"

"Not mutiny. If you were fighting for control of the sub, why would you focus your efforts on an area that had nothing to do with it? Secure the sub, turn around, head back to Korea."

"No!" Larsen said, his voice resonating through the room. "You're not listening. I told you, they were trying to kill the crew sleeping down there."

"Lieutenant, *you're* not listening. If it was just a fight, they would have been falling all over each other—all of them, not just the mutineers—to get away from the gas. But they stayed."

"I take back what I said about knowing why the general wanted you on this boat. Where the hell is this theory going? I'd like to hear how it tells us any damn thing."

I held up my hands. "Whoa, whoa. You're right. It's not a complete theory, and it doesn't tell us exactly what happened. But I think the more we find out about that locker, the more we can piece it together. It's at the heart of the motive. That's all I'm saying."

Larsen pulled himself to the end of the bench and glared at me, his face knotted with irritation.

"And here's all I'm saying: You try to open that fucking thing, and I'll make sure you don't move more than three feet the rest of this trip. That's if I don't throw your narrow ass out the emergency hatch. Do you understand me?"

"Don't worry," I said, trying to keep a neutral tone. "I'm not going to open it. I don't want to, and I don't need to. That's for the technicians on the shore. But—"

The vibrations in the floor, which had long since faded into a familiar background sensation, had stopped. I could feel the deceleration as the water's drag began to bite into the sub's sides.

"What the fuck?" Larsen said, standing. He wrenched the door open, but stopped when a speaker on the wall, which I hadn't noticed before, addressed him.

"Sir, the diesels have stopped."

"I'm aware of that," Larsen said after mashing the "talk" button. "I'm on my way. Sit tight."

I expected him to turn around and growl at me to stay where I was. But he threw himself out the door and down the claustrophobic hallway without addressing me. After a few breaths, I followed.

"What's going on?" Young asked. He had been standing in the middle of the corridor, watching Larsen disappear through the hatch to the control room, but turned to face me when he heard my footsteps.

I saw his confused expression and felt his breath, sour and hot, on my cheek as I pushed by. I ignored him and crouched next to the hatch. Larsen was a few feet into the control room, facing to my right.

He must've seen me move at the edge of his vision.

"We don't have room for you in here, Doctor," he said, pointing at me. Without waiting for an answer, he addressed someone outside my view. "What happened, Lieutenant Matthews?"

"We're not sure, sir. We were making revolutions for eleven knots. Then the engines cut out."

"What did Miller say?"

"Nothing, sir. No word from the engine room."

"What do you mean, 'no word'? Didn't you call down there?"

"Yes, sir. But there was no answer."

"Is the intercom working?"

"It was when we ordered the engine start-up. But I can—"

"Who's in the aft torpedo room? Vazquez? Call him. Tell him to go find out what the fuck happened to the engines. Tell him to get Martin up here."

"Aye-aye, sir. Torpedo room, conn. Go to the engine room and report back on the engines' status. Send Martin to the control room."

"Conn, torpedo room," a distorted voice replied after a few seconds. "Aye-aye. I'm on my way."

"Sir, couldn't we just send someone from the electrical control room to check?" asked the unseen man to Larsen's right.

"No. Find out how much the batteries have charged. Can we make headway with the power we have?"

"Aye-aye, sir. Electrical, conn. How are the batteries?"

They seemed insistent on using the awkward introductory decorum at the beginning of each intercom exchange. I suspected it was born more of training than any practical use in this situation.

A different voice replied from the speaker, its boyish timbre and Southern twang evident despite the electronic background noise.

"Conn, electric. We've only got one battery array online, 'cuz the forward bay is trashed. So right now we're at about 10 percent of our total capacity."

"Electric, conn. What kind of speed can you give us, and for what duration?"

"Well, that's . . . I mean, conn, electric, we're not in too good shape there. We can run the creep motors for a couple hours, maybe, and give you twenty-five, thirty-five minutes at two-thirds throttle with the main electrics. You want us to switch them on?"

"Electric, conn. Stand by. Sir?"

"Diving, are we stable?" Larsen said, taking a step to my right. All I could see were the backs of his legs now.

"Hovering at sixty feet, sir," said another crewman I couldn't see. "We're not going anyplace."

"Right. Tell electric to continue to stand by. I want us to get back underway with the diesels and charge the batteries up a little more."

"Aye-aye," the first SEAL he had addressed replied before relaying the instructions to the electrical compartment.

Then the speaker's crackling flooded the control room again. Larsen's legs jerked.

"Ah, conn, engineering. I dunno what's wrong with the engines, but . . . um . . . but Miller and Martin aren't here."

"We already knew that, Vazquez," Larsen said.

"They're just not here," Vazquez repeated. "I looked on both decks."

"Young, get in here!" Larsen yelled, half-turning toward the hatch. I stood back and let the SEAL climb through.

"Lieutenant Matthews, take Young, Wilkes and Henderson down to engineering. Find out what the hell is going on with the engines." He seemed more annoyed than worried. "Get Young working to see whether we can start them back up. And find Miller and Martin. Go!"

A chorus of "aye-aye, sirs" erupted in the room as the four SEALs headed through the aft hatch. When they had gone, Larsen strode back over to my side of the room and took a knee in front of me. I knew what was coming.

"Doctor, you stay in the next compartment while we figure out what is going on. Once things are secure, you'll have free rein on the boat again. Campbell!" he said, standing back up. "You're with the doctor."

The SEAL snapped to attention at his post near the ballast tank controls, trying to erase the surprised look from his face. "Aye-aye, sir."

Larsen dismissed us by turning his back and starting a hushed conversation with whomever was sitting at the steering station. Campbell walked over to the hatch and climbed through as I moved out of the way.

"Weird stuff, huh?" he asked, pulling his rifle around to the front and fiddling with its folding stock. "Did you hear all that?"

"Sure did. I'm trying to figure out where two SEALs could disappear to on a submarine."

"It's not a big deal, I'll bet. Nothing in this sub works right all the time. They probably went to go do something else, but the intercom was busted when they called up here. Maybe they're trying to get the forward battery bay online."

"What about the engines?" I said, raising my eyebrows.

"Like I said, nothing here works. They step away for a couple of minutes, and the engines slip a little out of whack. There are a million things that could have happened. They might have gone to the head or something."

"Walked off to take a leak and shut off the engines before they went?"

The sickly lighting made it difficult to tell, but Campbell's face seemed to flush to the same color as his hair.

"Well, uh . . . the lieutenant will get it figured out." He scratched his head, focusing on some invisible attraction on the floor. "Something minor happened, you know? That's all. Lieutenant Larsen's not going to be happy about it, though, no matter what excuse he gets."

I laughed. "I'm sorry, I didn't mean to embarrass you."

Campbell shrugged, but reddened further. "Look, I'm not worried. Are you worried? Don't you need to get back to your evidence and stuff?"

"Relax," I said. "Sure, I need to get back to my evidence and stuff. Although I don't think it's going to take us anyplace new."

"What do you mean?"

"I know what happened with the shooting. But the piles of bodies downstairs are a little harder to figure out. There's some information that we don't have, and it may have died with the boat's captain. Sometimes that's just the way it goes."

I turned to walk back to the mess room but stopped. Campbell bumped into me, gripping my shoulder as I stumbled.

"What?" he said.

"The officers' quarters are off this hallway, right?"

"Should be," he said, taking a step back and looking at the doors around us.

"Well, then, you can help me right now. Which of these rooms is the captain's?"

His mouth dropped open, then formed a smile as a visible wave of understanding washed over his face.

"Oh, I see." He looked at all the placards and pointed to the doorway to my right. "You're right on top of it."

I turned the handle set flush in the door and pushed. The panel, just as narrow as the one in the entrance to the officers' mess, swung inward.

Standing in the hallway, I considered what was revealed.

A bunk along the far wall, cabinets mounted three feet above its surface. A man-sized locker was set in the wall next to the pillow. To the right of the door, a writing hutch was framed by more cabinets. The desk's surface was clear except for a brown blotter and a stack of manila folders in one corner, and a straight-backed metal chair was pushed under it.

To the left of where the captain's legs would have fit sat a safe. Its bottom and back were welded to the floor and wall.

The bunk was made, a coarse gray blanket pulled up to a pillow-width strip of crisp, white sheets. Except for the safe, all the surfaces in the room had been milled from the same fake-wood tree as the paneling in the hallway.

There were a couple of pictures hanging on the shadowy wall over the bunk. I could see the light glinting on the glass, but couldn't make out the frames' contents. A few more pictures were scattered on the walls—submarines, uniformed men, a North Korean flag.

"You gonna go in?"

"Give me a second, Campbell."

Was this a crime scene? Could I traipse about in Yoon's bedroom, trying to gather a scrap of evidence that . . . oh, hell, let's face it: I didn't even know what I was looking for. I wanted to talk to a dead man, and the items he left behind might let me do that.

I could do it on shore.

But I had the time to do it now. And the curiosity. That was what pushed me into the spartan living area.

I took a picture through the doorway before I stepped inside. And once I stood in Yoon's quarters—the dimensions were about the same as a king-sized mattress—I documented its contents as well.

"Do you need me to—"

"Could you just stand outside for now? There's not much room to maneuver in here." I sighed, turning to him as I heard the harshness in my voice. "Sorry. I don't think there's space enough for both of us to stand without tripping over each other."

"No problem. I'll just hang out here." He took a step back into the hallway and draped his forearms across the top of his rifle.

The safe was begging for my attention. But there were other, less obvious things to examine first.

I pulled prints from all the cabinet handles in the room. The lift sheets showed concentrations of prints; whoever opened these doors grasped the same part of the handle each time. Holding the sheets up to the light,

I could see that the few discernible prints in the muddle were similar, if not identical. Another one for the lab to verify.

Snapping on a fresh pair of latex gloves, I pulled at the cabinets over the bunk. Nothing. There was a polished metal lock on each set of doors. I didn't feel like forcing one open, not when there was more to explore in the room.

I just about fell over, however, when the cabinet over the desk swung open, the force of my unresisted tug causing me to take a few unsteady steps backward. I heard Campbell shuffle toward me.

"You OK?"

"Just lost my balance for a second." I already was leaning forward, shining my flashlight into the cabinet's interior.

A squat bottle of brownish liquid sat on the far left-hand side. The label was just a confusion of Korean characters to me, but there was a faint odor wafting from it that made the packaging irrelevant: whiskey.

Stacked next to the bottle, filling up that half of the cabinet, were a collection of hardbound books. A few had English titles, too—the captain was a Stephen King fan. I took a picture of the open cabinet.

The other half held file folders separated by black metal slats. Each folder had a colored label on its outer edge marked by a few characters. I looked down at the desk. The folders it held were identified the same way.

I reached for the desktop files but stopped myself and took a picture first. Using tweezers, I opened the cover of the top file. It was some kind of an official report—or maybe it wasn't; it could have been a collection of Korean nursery rhymes and I wouldn't have been able to tell. But it was laid out with several headers above the body text and a series of numbers across the top of the page. If there were no other leads to be found, I could give these papers to Campbell and ask him what the subjects of each were.

Turning 180 degrees, I walked a few steps to the opposite wall and the locker set in it.

"What about the safe? Aren't you going to . . . ?"

"Just wait," I said, scrutinizing the locker's latch mechanism. It looked like it had a hole for a padlock but featured no other means of security. "It's not going anyplace."

I took a picture of the locker closed, slipped a pen under the door handle, opened it and took another picture. The interior was about eighteen inches wide and divided into three sections. The top and middle sections were open, but the bottom portion contained two closed drawers.

The highest shelf was about the size of a shoebox. An array of hygiene implements was scattered on it, including a shaver, toothpaste, brushes, a mirror and soap. The middle area was maybe three feet deep. A dress uniform top and pants hung there, as did three pairs of khaki pants and shirts. A pair of spit-polished shoes sat beneath them.

Using the pen again, I pulled the top drawer open. It held shirts and underwear, each white item folded with razor creases. The clothes were stacked to the top of the drawer, smelling of soap and starch spray.

I pushed it closed and opened the bottom drawer. Socks and some folded civilian clothes—jeans and T-shirts—filled its interior.

Well, why not? The underwear drawer had always, for some reason, been a popular place to stash valuables.

Using a ruler, I lifted each item of clothing up and looked beneath it. Nothing was stacked between the socks, jeans or shirts, and the bottom of the drawer was bare. I measured its depth and compared it to the exterior . . . nope. No false bottom. The top drawer also held clothes but no clues.

So. The safe.

It had a lock mechanism about the same diameter as a can of soda. A vertical handle was mounted beneath it, and I could see from scrape marks on the weathered gray metal to its left that it swung in an arc in that direction.

I glanced up. Campbell was standing in the door, looking down at me and the safe.

"Think it'll open?" His voice was tinged with an enthusiasm that he tried to hide behind a blank expression.

I shrugged, grasped the handle and pulled. Nothing.

"Evidently not. But the captain wouldn't be much of an officer if he just left the boat's safe unlocked, would he?" I stood. "Ten bucks says the key is in his pocket. I'll go down and search him after they get this engine room business straightened out."

He took a step back as I moved into the hallway again. I chewed on my lower lip, then spoke.

"Larsen said the dead guy in the torpedo room was the executive officer. Would his room be around here anyplace?"

"What was his name?" Campbell asked, looking at the closed doors again.

"Lee." I dug in my bag for the dossiers. "Lee something. Tae-Uk. Lee Tae-Uk."

"Yeah, I think the XO's quarters should be off this passageway. Lee . . . Lee . . ." He walked down the hall, then stopped at the door just aft of the mess room. "This is it."

As I swung the door open, I was struck by how similar this room was to the captain's. It might have been tighter by a few square feet, but the layout was the same. A locker against the aft wall, a bunk, cabinets above it, and more cabinets hanging over a desk. No safe, though.

The wall over the bunk had twice as many pictures mounted on it. More framed photos of landscapes and ships were visible on other surfaces. A snapshot of a smiling man in uniform, his arm around a petite, striking woman, was taped to the bulkhead over the desk's writing surface. I paused, trying to take it all in.

"Hey, what are you doing to your hand?" Campbell said.

"Nothing. Just thinking. It's a rubber band I wear on my wrist." I had decided what I wanted to look at first.

Walking over to the bunk, I could see that the pictures next to it were of the same woman, with or without the man, who I now recognized as Lee. The photos told silent, one-frame stories of happy times. I moved back a few feet and captured the whole scene in a digital image. Using lift sheets, I took prints from all the room's handles. As had been the case in Yoon's quarters, there were clusters of similar—if not identical—prints on all the surfaces.

And like the captain's locker, Lee's was not secured. I opened it the same way. The top shelf held shaving and cleaning items. Uniforms, both dress and daily, hung in the middle area. The top drawer held olive socks and white underwear; the bottom one contained assorted non-military garb and a stack of white undershirts.

I closed both, then sighed and crouched again.

It was a waste of time to poke through this stuff. The underwear drawer held nothing but undergarments. The other drawer held only . . . wait. As I lifted up the pair of slacks at the bottom of the pile, I could see the spine of a thin, leather-bound book.

Using the ruler, I kept the book visible without touching it and with my other hand took a picture of where I had found it. Then I reached in and pulled it free.

"What? Did you find something?" Campbell moved into the room behind me.

"Maybe. It was hidden, so it probably has stuff in it that he didn't want other people to find. That could be something that answers some of my questions about what happened on the boat . . . or it could be gossip about the enlisted men. Hey, could you step into the doorway?"

"Oh, sorry," Campbell said, shuffling back out of my way.

I stood up and opened it to the first page.

The book was about the size of a postcard and maybe a finger-width thick. The pages inside were white and unlined. The first was filled with spidery Korean handwriting, as were the next few.

"It's a log or a diary. Not official, I'm guessing."

I closed it again and checked the back cover. It also was unmarked, brown leather. But about two-thirds of the way through the book there seemed to be a gap, from which protruded the edge of another sheet.

When I opened it to that page, a folded piece of paper fell out and fluttered to the floor.

"Shit," I said.

I made sure to mark the place in the book where it had fallen from with my finger. Leaning over, I could see that the white paper was blank on the sides facing us. But the faint impressions of Korean characters were visible through the thin, pale material.

"Is it a letter or something?"

"I don't know. We're going to leave it folded up for the time being." I picked the white square up with tweezers and placed it back in the book.

"You're just ignoring that book? What if it's—"

"Calm down. The locker was the first thing I examined. Should we just forget about all the cabinets and other stuff in the room now?" My voice was loud, louder than I intended. The crime scene was my domain, and his inexpert advice grated on my professional nerves.

"Whatever," he said, raising his palms in mock surrender. "You stay in here, I'll stay out there."

"Sorry . . . Campbell? I didn't mean to snap at you. I'm just trying to concentrate here, and you have to trust me when I say it would be a mistake to get too fixated on this book. It could cause us to overlook something more important. OK?"

"Sure. You're the expert," he said. "Don't want to get in the way."

Annoyance still permeated his words, but he was just going to have to get over it.

Putting the book on the lower shelf of the locker, I focused on the desk area. The desk had only one ornament: another framed picture of the woman I had seen in the photos by the bunk. This was a black-and-white head shot with a soft filter that turned the woman's porcelain skin cloudy.

Her eyes looked out over a desktop calendar blotter, each of its days crossed off in red ink. It looked like it belonged on the desk of a CEO, not a submariner. Notes and numbers were crammed into each date box and in the margins.

But my gaze kept coming back to the woman. I didn't remember seeing spouses listed for any of the officers. A girlfriend? I checked the dossier again and found that I was correct: Lee was unmarried. It said he had two brothers living in South Korea, but they were his sole relatives, according to the dossier.

I walked back over to his bunk and re-examined the pictures there. The backgrounds were nondescript in most, just a jumble of urban scenery or pastoral countryside. But several included recognizable North Korean landmarks.

Lee had some pretty strong feelings for someone he was leaving behind forever in a hostile country.

Campbell's curiosity had overcome his bruised ego.

"Is there some clue in the pictures?" he asked.

I turned and smiled at him, hearing the change in his tone. He was standing in the doorway again. "Most of the guys on the *Dragon* have few if any ties to the PRK. But Lee seems to have quite a fascination with a North Korean lass."

"He's a traitor! I knew it. Lieutenant Larsen said the same thing, that Lee was found with a gun in his hand."

"We don't know he's a traitor. Come on, we have to be careful not to jump to conclusions here," I said. "At this point, it's interesting–but that's it. She could be, I don't know, a prostitute. There are lots of possibilities."

Campbell wanted to say something but kept silent as I continued to explain my work to him. He didn't look annoyed anymore. He looked interested, an expression that didn't seem to be in the rest of the SEALs' repertoire.

"What's your first name?" I asked.

He blinked. "Uh . . . what?"

"Your first name. I'm not a SEAL. I'm allowed to act like you're a person."

"Oh. It's Brandon. Brandon Campbell. Everyone calls me Campbell, though."

"OK, Brandon, it's like a puzzle," I said, but he was right. "Campbell" just seemed more natural. "If we try to make the pieces fit some preconceived image, we could force them to be something they're not. See what I'm saying?"

Campbell nodded. "Near my parents' house, there was this overpass that had a big water stain on one of the pillars. One day someone noticed it looked kind of like the Virgin Mary. The next day there was a three-foot mound of flowers and candles around it. You see what you want to see. Me, I just saw wet concrete."

"I don't think we're going to find anything that dramatic," I said, my smile widening as I turned back to the officer's quarters. Campbell smiled back. Alongside the aura of black-clad killer he shared with the rest of the SEALs, it was unexpected and gentle.

The storage space over Lee's bed had a lock mechanism but swung open. Revealed was the executive officer's book collection: two shelves crammed with Korean titles. Nothing I recognized. And I wasn't surprised to see another photo of the woman taped to the inside of the left-hand door.

Files filled vertical wire racks inside the cabinets mounted above the desk. They were color-coded, labeled and incomprehensible to me. As was much of the Korean officer's life.

"Just curious—you know anything about Korean culture? From your training?" I asked Campbell.

He shook his head. "Not really. It's an intensive course, but it's still basic. At least it was when I quit."

"Well, we're coming back here," I told Campbell. "I'll need you to translate the file names in the captain's room and in here so I can catalogue them."

"Sure," he said. "That shouldn't be too tough."

As I sealed the leather-bound book in plastic and slipped it in my bag, a shadow fluttered in the hallway's meager lighting. It was followed by the appearance of another SEAL behind Campbell. I hadn't met this one yet.

"Lieutenant Larsen wants you two in the control room," he said, addressing Campbell but speaking to both of us. He still wore his stocking cap, which seemed to blend in with his swarthy face. "Situation update."

Campbell nodded, and the other soldier turned and headed aft. I already was moving toward the doorway.

"What do you think is up?" I asked Campbell as he moved to the side.

He shrugged. His body language conveyed unconcern, and he said nothing as we walked toward the control room.

I swung myself through the hatch and into a crowd. Most, if not all, of the SEAL contingent was in the room. I could see a couple more crouched on the other side of the aft hatch, listening and watching.

"Myers, just stand out of the way," Larsen said. "Myers," huh? Guess I was one of the guys now.

As I stepped back, Campbell entered the room. The SEAL from the forward torpedo room squatted in the hallway.

"People, here's the situation," Larsen said. "Seaman Young says the engines were not shut off, they were sabotaged. Is that correct, Seaman?"

Young was standing next to the aft door, leaning against the wall with his hands at the small of his back.

"Yeah. An oil line was cut. Oil pressure dropped, the temperature rose, and eventually it tripped an automatic cut-off switch."

"Did you all hear that? The line was *cut*. A sabotaged engine." Larsen looked like he wanted to pace, but the SEALs and control equipment left him no room. "What's more, Miller and Martin are missing. Really missing. They're not at their posts in the engine room, and they're not anyplace else on the sub. Do you read me?"

I expected consternation to ripple through the assembled soldiers, but they just waited for Larsen to continue.

"That means one thing: there is someone besides us on this boat. Now, our job is to get to shore. Our adversary obviously wants to keep us from doing that. So two additional objectives have been added that we must accomplish. First, we must ensure that the boat is not sabotaged further. Second, we must find the saboteur and neutralize him."

He looked at Young. "The engines. Can we get them running again?"

So, the surfer dude also was a mechanic. The question seemed to deflate him a bit. He pulled his right hand from behind his back and scratched at his tanned neck.

"Well, kind of. I can fix the oil line, and because the engines cut off before the temperature got too high, there's no permanent damage. But we lost enough oil that we can't safely run them now. So . . ."

"What, we're stuck out here?"

"No, sir. I can consolidate the oil supply to one engine. I would recommend running that one diesel until the bats are charged up, then switching to electric power for the rest of the run. I'd estimate we can make about six, seven knots on one screw."

"Fuck me running," Larsen said. "Chief, is that going to hurt steering?"

The SEAL who had fetched us from Lee's quarters was leaning on a panel near the control wheel. In the somewhat dimmer room, his features were even tougher to make out. Dark skin, dark eyes and facial hair, ears covered by his watch cap.

"It shouldn't affect us too much," he said. "We'll have to compensate a little with the rudder, and that'll make us lose a little headway. It will work, though. We'll get where we're going."

Larsen banged on the gleaming attack periscope next to him.

"Damn right we will. Listen up! Young, you and Wilkes are the engineering department. Henderson, you're security. Get down there, get that engine serviceable and tell us as soon as it is," Larsen said, holding his hand up above the milling SEALs. "Everyone: We are in a combat situation now. There is at least one hostile onboard. No relaxing, no taking anything for granted. Treat everyplace you go on this boat as new, potentially dangerous territory. Clear?"

The room reverberated with a chorus of "Yes, sir!"

"Good. Engineering department, get down there. And bring me Miller and Martin *now*. I'm goddamn serious—the plan has changed. Everyone else, return to your stations."

The SEALs acknowledged the order and scattered. As the room emptied, I noticed Larsen looking at me. When he caught my eye, he strode over to my corner.

"You're staying in the officers' area. We just don't know what's out there, and right now, the boat's operation—and your safety—are the overriding concern, not your investigation."

"I understand," I said. "But . . . how could there be someone onboard? All the Korean crewmen are accounted for."

"I don't know. Frankly, I don't care," he said, his expression stony and focused. "We're getting the submarine to port no matter who's trying to stop us or what their motivations are."

"Don't you—"

"I'm only going to say this one more time: The enemy's name and his motives are not my concerns. Overcoming that enemy is. And that's what we're going to do. Maybe after we make it to shore and pick this tub apart, we'll find out who we're up against, and you can help us figure out what makes him tick. But right now, I could give a flying rat's ass. Campbell?" he said, turning away from both the SEAL and me. "You're security for the doctor. Ensure her safety. And make sure she stays put. Now get out of the control room, Dr. Myers."

"Uh, c'mon, ma'am," Campbell said as Larsen walked over to the SEAL by the steering console. "We need to get back to the officers' quarters."

He stood aside as I climbed through the hatch, then followed me. As soon as I was back in the mess room, I motioned him inside and spoke.

"Look, what's the deal here? Did Miller and Martin just decide to take a break, or are they missing? Larsen didn't even seem worried until just now, even though two of his men apparently went AWOL on a boat where it's impossible to be more than fifty yards from your commanding officer. What is going on? You can't tell me this is just some contingency that you guys train for."

"We train for everything," Campbell replied. "No, seriously, that's not just a line," he said, hearing me sigh. "To you, Lieutenant Larsen seems like an unreasonable hardass, or whatever, because you're not a SEAL. You don't know how we operate or what we do. What he said about our objectives . . . that's totally correct. We have a mission, and we're going to carry it out. Getting distracted by some weird event isn't going to help us accomplish that. Unless this person attacks again, we're not going to focus on anything except getting the submarine to shore. Because that's the best way to fulfill our objectives."

"Campbell, I'm getting a little tired of being treated like I'm an idiot. Larsen's not being focused. He's being bizarre. It doesn't add up."

"What? What do you mean?" He was blushing again, trying hard to establish eye contact with the wall behind me.

"I mean I understand the importance of concentrating on the task at hand. I understand that, above all else, the *Dragon* needs to be in a dock in U.S. waters. OK? I get all that. But it's fucking ridiculous to pretend that the disappearance of two of your men is just another bump in the road.

Larsen's keeping something from me. So are you."

I was leaning on the table now, trying to force him to hear the truth of what I was saying.

"I don't know what you mean," he replied, his voice neutral, eyes still avoiding my face. "But it's not going to help us, at this point, to worry about what's going on with Miller and Martin. So just let it go. Shouldn't you focus on the evidence here, anyway? Try to put together another theory?"

Slumping back in the bench seat, I shook my head.

"Let it go? Fine. Whatever."

I made a show of grabbing some of the evidence off the table and holding it up to the light. But my mind was infected with anger. Not really at Campbell. At Larsen, who I was sure had ordered his men to keep quiet about whatever had happened. There always was a bigger picture, always—and the missing SEALs were part of it. In this closed system, the mistake of ignoring any event would be magnified.

Folding my hands in my lap, I closed my eyes and counted to ten. When I opened them, Campbell was staring at me, his freckled brow wrinkled in consternation.

He cleared his throat. "So . . ."

"Do I come here often? No. And yes, I'm single; I don't even have any pets. There, now we've gotten that out of the way. How about doing a little work?"

I pushed the evidence between us to one side. "Here," I said, thumping Lee's book into the clear space on the table. "Read me what's on the pages where we found the folded-up piece of paper."

He kept his eyes on me as he reached out and grabbed its leather spine.

"Make sure not to lose the place," I added. I put a fresh tape in my recorder, set it in front of Campbell and started it. Grabbing a pen and notepad, I sat, eyebrows raised, and watched him open the book.

"Are you sure you're—"

"Dammit, Campbell," I said, interrupting him. "I'm over the missing SEALs. I'm happy and smiling. See? Not worried at all. Now, this book, this is evidence. It's in Korean. You can read Korean. So read the evidence and help us all out."

About four expressions flashed across his face. I could tell he was wrestling with whether to be angry, hurt, embarrassed or agreeable. In the end, a combination of all emerged.

"OK, I'll read it. Noooooo problem." He cleared his throat. "By the way, there are page numbers along the top here. I'm looking at page seventy-nine now, just for future reference. Let's see . . . The page starts in midsentence."

"Can you look for the beginning of the passage, please?" I said, jotting down "Pg. 79" in the notebook.

He flipped back, ran his finger down the page, and started speaking again, each word separated by a pause as his mind re-formed the characters into English.

"Uh . . . '27 April, 2007. We . . . have been submerged for . . . for longer than any of . . . ' uh . . . 'the officers can remember. Even with the . . . smaller crew, the *Dragon*'s walls seem . . . ' um, 'seem . . . to press against our minds and bodies. Is there a world outside our ship's'—sorry, I don't know this word—'world of sunshine and . . . stars? Such a . . . reality seems far . . . taken,' no, that's not right . . . 'far . . . removed from ours.'" Campbell halted. "This guy's quite the philosopher, huh? The Korean Socrates."

I said nothing, just nodded as I scribbled notes.

"Anyway. 'Removed from ours. And the worries of my . . . duty, my mission . . . press down on me as well.'" Campbell stopped again. "This might be kind of rough, OK? I just wanted you to know that. I'm better at understanding Korean than speaking it, so if he gets really complicated or fancy, it's going to sound odd."

"Don't worry about it," I said, looking up and smiling. The expression was genuine, and had the effect I wanted: he smiled back, and I could see his posture relax. "We're lucky you went to language school."

"We'd be luckier if I had stuck with it," he said. "I got bored after six months, and it was only a sixty-three-week program. Same thing that happened with college—it just stopped being interesting."

"So you found something harder to do?"

"You got it. BUD/S training, SEAL qualification."

"And you're not bored yet?" I could tell he got the joke.

"Look at all the exotic places I get to go. Seriously, I don't have any regrets. I grew up in Oklahoma City—ever been there? It's no place special. If I weren't here, I'd be there. I mean, I *like* what I do because it takes serious effort and thought to prepare for a job like this and even more to do it. With something like languages, which were always kind of easy for me, I just quit trying, I guess. Now if I quit trying, I let down seventeen other guys whose lives are depending on me. It's a purpose." Campbell took a deep breath, then shrugged as he ran out of words.

"I can tell you for a fact that if you weren't here we'd probably all be out of luck. You're doing great."

"Good," he said, then continued translating. "'It is a great . . . duty that I have been given. An important one. A . . . vital one. But if it comes time to . . . carry it out, will I do my . . . commanders justice? Has . . . their trust been out of place?' Wait, I think that's 'misplaced' instead of 'out of place.' OK, 'has their trust been misplaced? I would like to . . . ' ah, 'imagine that I am strong enough to . . . prevail and overcome the great . . . obstacle that may come. But to my comrades it will seem like the most . . . low, shameful sort of . . . betrayal.'"

He stopped reading and waited until I had finished writing.

"Sounds like he's planning something," Campbell said.

"Maybe. He could just be referring to the defection. Keep going."

"'I try to . . . imagine the . . . serpent being loose in the world—even in a place as . . . powerful as America—and it makes me . . . shudder. That, and only that, will give me the strength . . . to condemn the *Dragon* and her men to the sea's . . . depths.

"'Still, the . . . knowledge of what I . . . must do if that happens appalls me. The nearer we get to America, the more . . . certain my,' uh, 'heart becomes that it will . . . come to pass. And I cannot allow that.'" Campbell tapped the page with his finger. "OK, now, that sounds pretty clear. He can't allow the sub to arrive in Norfolk." He didn't wait for a response before continuing. "'So the mission's . . . importance can overcome my . . .'

damn, this is tough . . . 'personal . . . shortcomings. I think it will force me to be strong and . . . dutiful.

"'My burden also is . . . lowered by knowing someone else shares it. Captain Yoon, too, knows what I–what we–must do. He has told me that he will make sure the serpent does not leave this . . . submarine. That his . . . soul, like mine, is . . . heavy with this . . . responsibility gives me strength.

"'Yesterday in his . . . quarters, we discussed our . . . nearness to the American coast and what we . . . might have to do. Hours later, when I was . . . sleeping, he . . . slipped a . . . letter under my door. The fact that he understands how I feel–and . . . feels the same way–makes me less alone. And feeling alone in this . . . tiny world is the worst . . . ' something. 'Worst . . . emotion I have ever experienced.'"

Campbell closed the book on his finger.

"Is that the whole entry?" I asked.

"Yeah. About two, two and a half pages. So what do you think?"

I could tell he had drawn his own conclusions. They might not be far off from where my mind was taking me.

"Well, it brings two questions to the forefront: First, what is the serpent? And second, was the captain involved in precipitating whatever happened here?"

"Face it, Doc, there was a mutiny. All Lee's talk about having a terrible burden, feeling like he was betraying his friends . . . what the hell else could he have meant? I admit, though, it surprises me that the captain was in on it too. Could be a double-agent kind of deal, you know: he tells our CIA guys one thing, then turns around and ruins the whole operation."

"It's certainly possible. But what about the serpent? I'd like to know what he's referring to."

"Serpent . . . well, isn't the submarine called the *Dragon?* He might just be saying that they don't want the boat to fall into U.S. hands."

"That makes sense. But what's so special about the boat?"

"Dunno. Just national pride, maybe. They don't want the filthy Americans to take her over."

"It might fit with the mutiny scenario. But there's one other thing I'm curious about: I think the piece of paper stuck between the pages is the letter he mentions in the book. Could you read it?"

"Sure," Campbell said, unfolding the sheet and laying it on the table. "There's no date on it.

"'My . . . shipmate, my honored . . . colleague, my friend: I understand your fears and concerns. They . . . weigh on my heart as well. But I know that you, like me, are . . . aware of what will happen if the . . . serpent leaves this ship.

"'And the nearer . . . we get to America, the more I, too, fear that we will have to take such a . . . horrible action. In some part of your mind–the . . . ' ah, 'emotional part, the human part–what I have asked you to do appears wrong. To . . . sacrifice so many men, to . . . condemn them to death for something they don't completely understand seems . . . wicked.

"'But the . . . rational part, Tae-Uk, that is what we both must focus on. Because in my imagination, I can picture the serpent reaching shore. I can picture the great . . . suffering that would . . . come. This is what we are . . . preventing.

"'So we continue on, knowing that we . . . hold great . . . responsibility. I am confident in you. I know you have the strength and courage to do . . . what is necessary. And I will stand by you, fight beside you, to make sure we . . . prevail.

"'Capt. Yoon Chong-Gug.'"

"They're frightened. Both of them," I said.

"Terrified."

"But the serpent isn't the submarine," I continued as Campbell refolded the paper. "It can't be. Otherwise 'if the serpent leaves this ship' makes no sense at all. And the captain . . ."

"Is the leader of the conspiracy," Campbell finished. "Those two were working together, obviously."

"Right, but to what end? What is this serpent thing?"

"I'll bet it's in here." Campbell pointed his chin at Lee's book. "I'll read through the whole thing."

"No, I don't think the answer's there. Look at the general terms he used when writing. It's pretty standard for a diary . . . it's written as if to a confidant, but all the details are left out in case someone finds it."

"So we're stuck, then. Why not just read the diary? We might get lucky."

"Because the captain is at the heart of this. He gave Lee his orders," I said, standing up. "And if there's any documentation on something so super-secret and important, it'd be locked up. Human nature. Military protocol. There are only two locks on this boat: on the biohazard container and on the captain's safe. I'm not about to open that locker, but the safe . . ."

"It's locked."

"Where would the keys be? The captain would have them. It's not like he's going to leave them lying around for someone to find."

"But you can't leave this compartment. It's too dangerous, like Lieutenant Larsen said."

"Yeah, I know. If the bogeyman didn't get me, Larsen would. That's why we're going to go ask him if you can go collect some evidence."

Campbell stood, too, bringing our faces about a foot apart.

"Oh, sure. He'll go for that."

"Is it hurting anything to ask him? If he says no, I'll stay here and you can check the diary for anything else useful. And he's already pissed at me, so it's not like I have anything to lose."

"I'm not—"

"Fine, I'll do it," I said, stepping into the hallway and striding toward the hatch to the control room.

"Hey!" I heard from behind me. He jogged after me and, in a tiny, paranoid corner of my brain, I expected to be tackled. But I reached the door unmolested.

"Your funeral," he muttered as I crouched and rapped on the hatch's edge.

"Lieutenant Larsen?"

The SEAL leader was standing next to the navigation table at the aft end of the room, reading something on its surface. He looked up and skewered me with an expression of disgust and annoyance.

"What? Do you need a bathroom break or something?" he said.

One of the four or five other soldiers in the compartment snickered.

"No, thanks. I actually have a favor to ask."

"A favor? You need something from me? Why, I'm honored." His mocking tone made my knuckles whiten on the lip of the door, but I stayed silent as he walked over to me, stopping a few feet away. "What, Dr. Myers?"

"I left out a step in my examination of the captain's body. It's crucial to the investigation."

"Too bad. You stay in the officers' quarters until we reach shore or catch the saboteur."

"And I will," I said as he started to walk away. "I'm not going anyplace. Just let Campbell go down there, look at the body and come back."

Larsen turned back toward me. I prepared myself for a sneer. But after a few breaths, he spoke, looking at me but addressing Campbell.

"You understand that the situation has changed," he said, then continued without waiting for Campbell to reply. "Henderson says the forward battery bay is clear, but he hasn't searched any compartment other than that and the engine room. I was going to send Vazquez to help him, but I suppose I can send you, too. Grab whatever evidence the doctor is looking for if you see it. Then get your ass back up here and report."

"Aye-aye, sir," Campbell said.

Larsen pushed the intercom button. "Vazquez, meet Campbell in the engine room and back him up as he goes to the forward battery bay."

"Uh, conn, aft torpedo room, I copy. Aye-aye, sir," came the reply.

"There you go, Doctor," he said, going back to the nav station. "Move, Campbell."

I let Campbell pass, speaking to him as he climbed through the hatch. "Check his pockets."

Larsen didn't turn to face me, but I heard him laugh.

"Check his pockets? You forgot to check his pockets? That's rich. You're quite the sleuth."

I ignored him and locked eyes with Campbell, who nodded and headed aft.

VI

AS I WALKED BACK to the officers' mess, I marveled at how little resistance Larsen had presented. I had expected a speech about how I was asking him to risk the lives of his men for some puny piece of information I had been too stupid to deal with myself. And he hadn't even asked what the missing evidence was.

I couldn't figure him out, and it made me uneasy. It was impossible to count on him being either helpful or hostile. Was that deliberate? Or was he an unpredictable jerk to everyone? I didn't like being kept off-balance. When you try to figure out the motivations of the dead, they don't change while you're working. Living people are harder to analyze.

I sat down on the bench, which was still warm.

The submarine's jarring combination of human and mechanical stenches had faded from the foreground of my senses, I noticed. And my world had shrunk to one thirty-foot hallway. It was easy to forget that there was another reality beyond the metal and wan lighting.

It might have been subconscious. My mind, knowing how terrifying and inhospitable the environment I was submerged in was, focused on other things. The conduits on the ceiling were solid, tangible, arranged by human hands. The deck's grayness added to its solidity. When you stood on it, you weren't underwater. You were in control, on unyielding steel.

As I let my thoughts drift, I felt the floor once again flutter with vibrations. So they had gotten one of the diesels running.

The fact settled in my brain, accompanied by an abrupt feeling of disjointedness. The engine had started. Oh, good. In my house, the start-up of my air conditioner registered in the same way. But that house, that life . . . they seemed separated from me by more than a few dozen miles of ocean.

I didn't feel far from home. I felt like home was a dream, and the sub's confining, protecting walls were my real here and now. Claustrophobia and fears of drowning weren't a part of this world. And it wasn't as though I were ducking them, trying to keep my mental energies focused on other things. Those worries were, like the sea, shut out by the submarine's pressure hull. There was no other way to deal with them.

In a more academic setting, the phenomenon I was witnessing in myself would have made a fine research paper.

Amid these abstractions swam a table full of evidence. Fingerprints. Blood. A gun, shell casings, bullets. Photographs. And it all meant . . . what? They were artifacts of actual events, immutable actions that had already occurred. But the events, however concrete they may have been to their participants, were growing more and more ephemeral to us here in the present.

I could tell Patterson who shot whom on the *Dragon*. The obvious murder had an obvious answer.

"Lee kills Ahn, tries to escape," I muttered to myself.

I imagined an invisible audience in the room, the ship's officers gathered there listening to me try to surmise how they died.

Chlorine. Most of them had died in an invisible, inescapable torture chamber. Their throats burning, their lungs screaming for oxygen as they filled with blood and acid.

A few had died faster, their heads staved in by massive blows. One had been strangled, right? I thought back . . . yes. In the forward battery bay. Those were easier to deal with. Common violence. Humans had a facility for dispatching one another, and their work was simple to discern and examine.

But aside from the most brutal psychoses, our species didn't off one another without reason. Territory. Property. Anger. What did all the men in the *Dragon*'s belly die for? What was the rationale behind their demise?

Larsen's voice cackled in my head. "Mutiny, you dumb bitch," I heard, my mind supplying the pejorative and the smirk with which it would be delivered.

On a gut level, mutiny worked. The *Dragon*'s mission had been one of treachery to its crew's home country. That implicit treason was bound to chafe, to create second thoughts.

Had the captain ordered them to turn around? Had half the crew, so close to a new life in the United States, rebelled and fought him?

But the scalpel edges of reason eviscerated this scenario. If there had been a battle for control of the ship, why had none of it centered around the control room?

As the possibilities whirred through my mind, a word kept slithering to the top: serpent.

It was dark, its enigmatic nuances shrouded in shadows and secrecy. Lee's diary and the note from Yoon indicated that it was at the heart of whatever conspiracy they had launched. The answer, the serpent's nature and identity, was someplace on this boat, and that fact taunted me.

The sound of the footsteps in the hallway outside must have been buried in the strata of my thoughts. I didn't notice that a SEAL was standing in the doorway until he spoke.

"Doctor, Lieutenant Larsen needs you in the control room, ASAP."

I glanced up, the shards of my theorizing scattered by his words. "What?"

"Something's come up."

"Right," I said. I tried to collect myself, to focus on his clean-shaven face, its surface gleaming with a sheen of perspiration. He held his rifle across his chest, one finger resting on the trigger guard. No, it was *inside* the guard. "What happened?"

"The lieutenant will tell you," he said as I stood up.

The urgency in this voice set something off inside my chest. It was the feeling of a patient who sees a terrified expression on her doctor's face.

"Let's go," I said.

Inside the control room, Larsen and Matthews were discussing something over the nav table. Both men seemed intense but not angry.

Larsen looked up as the SEAL and I entered.

"Doctor, you and I are going down to the forward battery bay." He straightened and nodded at his junior officer. "Matthews, you have the conn. You know what to do if Miller is found."

"Yessir," the other man said. He stood, and I realized he likely was the tallest person on the sub. Angular features and a hooked nose like a beak. He had tiny eyes wedged into deep sockets in his narrow face. The bone structure wouldn't look much different without skin.

"Christ in a whorehouse," Larsen mumbled as he gestured me closer. "You remember the procedure when Grimm was securing the first few compartments?"

"Yeah," I said, frowning.

"That's how it's going to work now. I'm going first into every room. When the room is safe to enter, I will hold up my hand like this," he said, making an "O" with his thumb and first finger. "Keep behind me at all times. If I start shooting, don't run. Stay down. If you're near the hatch, duck back through it. OK?"

"Got it. But—"

"Not now. Just follow me."

He made eye contact with Matthews again, and the act made me shudder. Larsen's glance had contained just a whisper of something I hadn't yet seen on this submarine: fear.

We moved through the electrical control room. Its occupants stood at their stations, acting focused and industrious. But I could feel everyone staring at us as we passed through. Larsen interrupted the silence as he got to the aft hatch.

"Word of warning—it's going to be really loud in the engine room. Impossible to talk. So just watch me carefully, all right?"

"OK," I said. He had waited for me to reply, and his sudden show of concern raked across my already jangled nerves.

I was aware that the vibration in the deck had become joined by an identical noise, a sort of rumbling hum that permeated the air. As he opened the hatch, it exploded in a tooth-rattling flood.

Stepping through the hatch after him, I plugged my ears and watched him close the door. In front of us stood Young, his rifle in hand. His face was smudged with grease, the grime standing out like fresh bruises.

He nodded at Larsen, who crouched and looked through the grated floor. Below us were two more SEALs, one of whom was covering the aft door with his rifle while the other bent over a piece of machinery a few feet away. The one watching the door glanced up, saw Larsen, and made three quick gestures.

Larsen moved to the ladder and climbed down as I watched. When he reached the bottom, he looked up and gave me the "clear" signal.

I followed him, coherent thought obliterated by the torrent of noise from the engine. The sound and the room's brilliant lighting made me want to duck, to run, to get away from the interruption of the submarine's dull interior.

On the bottom deck, Larsen already had opened the hatch and was aiming his rifle through it. He stepped into the battery bay: after crouching and waiting for his OK, I joined him.

The door clanged shut behind me, and I felt my body relax as the engine's fury was diminished by the steel bulkhead.

We were standing in a room I had been in before, and in which function, not comfort, was king. But compared with the officers' quarters—and occasional trips to the control room—the slight change in surroundings felt like a trip to an open meadow.

Larsen was at the opposite hatch, scanning the galley.

"Vazquez! What the fuck are you doing?" he yelled.

I tensed and scrabbled for the door latch behind me.

There was a response from the other room, but it was made incomprehensible by the two rooms' acoustics.

"I don't care if you're hungry—this boat isn't secure! What the fuck could . . . no, don't talk anymore." Larsen had straightened up now and stepped through the doorway.

I moved forward, around the two bodies I had examined earlier. Larsen continued to scream in the galley, his vitriol directed to my left, out of my field of vision.

"Put the goddamn bread down and get back on station, sailor! I want you by the forward hatch covering CAMPBELL'S MOTHER-FUCKING ASS!"

Vazquez jogged across the galley and stopped near the door at the end of the room opposite me. His swarthy complexion was flushed, and he was sweating.

Larsen waved at me to follow him. He didn't look at Vazquez as he stepped into the forward battery bay.

The SEAL tried to smile at me as I passed, but the expression died on his face and never made it to his brown eyes.

In the next compartment, Campbell stood facing us, flanked by the two-tiered racks that stored half of the sub's batteries.

"Sir, what was going on out—"

"Fucking Vazquez was over by the food locker gnawing on a hunk of bread. Unbelievable." Larsen held up a hand to stop the question forming in Campbell's mouth. "Tell us what you found."

Campbell had been trying to maintain a poker face, but he was too pale to pull it off. His voice matched his pallor as he pointed into the space between the racks on the port side.

"It's . . . well, I came in here and started going through the captain's pockets. I finished without any problems. But as I stood up, I saw Martin."

Larsen had taken a step toward the rack before Campbell finished.

"Goddamit," I heard him say under his breath. Then, louder, "God *damn* it!"

Over his shoulder, I could see what Campbell was referring to. It was Martin, the SEAL who had been working in the engine room.

There were bruises on his neck, but he hadn't been strangled. He was lying on his right side, chest toward the bulkhead, on the lower battery shelf. His head, however, faced the opposite direction, toward us.

"What the fuck, Doctor, was his neck broken?" Larsen said.

"Could be postmortem," I said. "But I doubt it. The bruising's not going to occur like that if it happened after he was dead. So yeah, looks like someone snapped his neck."

"Like a pretzel," Larsen said. "Like a—" He stopped, grasping the bridge of his nose. When he spoke again, his voice was level, empty of emotion.

"I need you to learn everything you can about what happened to him, Christine," he said. "Campbell will cover you. When you're finished, call up to the control room, and I'll send down cover for you two to return to the top deck."

He swung himself into the galley area and gestured for Vazquez to follow him.

I turned to Campbell. "What happened here?"

"It's just like I described. I was standing up, and I saw the body. Then I called the control room."

"You haven't moved it?"

"Moved what . . . oh. No, I haven't moved the body." He looked at the floor, then back at me. "What happened to him?"

"You got a flashlight?" I asked. He unclipped the light from the barrel of his rifle and handed it to me. I turned it on, shining the sterile white beam on the body. "I don't have any of my stuff down here. So this is going to be pretty inexact.

"Legs appear intact. No visible wounds there. Same with the torso. Look, I can't get to the body at all to examine it. There isn't any indication he died of anything except a broken neck."

"That's all you can tell?"

"That's all I can tell about the cause of death," I said, trying not to hear the desperation in his voice. "But tell me this: how do you carry your weapons when you're not planning to use them?"

"Like this," he said, slipping his rifle under his left arm and onto his back. Its strap now lay across his chest.

"That's the position Martin's weapon is in," I said. "See?"

The SEAL's rifle was lying with him on top of the batteries, about a foot and a half away from his contorted face, its strap still looped across his chest.

"He was surprised. Thoroughly surprised," I said.

Campbell's gaze was fixed on the weapon. "He didn't even get a chance to fight back."

"No. But it was quick," I lied. It may have been instantaneous, or he may have suffocated to death, his frantic attempts to breathe stymied by a severed spinal cord.

"Why is he in there?" Campbell asked.

"Impossible to tell. But we have to surmise that he was thrown, not shoved in, because of the possibility of electrocution. You couldn't touch him once he was touching the batteries." I paused, drumming my fingers on the flashlight's barrel. "Could be that whoever did this threw him between the battery racks, hoping he'd blend in with the rest of the corpses. But his head lolled back and gave it away. That's just a guess, though."

"His head . . . how could someone do that?"

I couldn't tell whether Campbell wanted a motive or a physical mechanism. A clinical answer seemed best. I felt a sudden compulsion to do anything I could to eradicate the mixture of wonder and fear I heard in his words.

"It would take a lot of strength. But remember that Martin was surprised. He didn't have a chance to resist. If you suddenly apply a bunch of torque to someone's head—well, the attacker would have to be very strong, but not superhuman." I didn't add that Martin's injury would have been fatal long before his head was facing the wrong way. If murder was his assailant's only intent, the injury was far more brutal than necessary.

"And we have to just leave him there. Dammit!" Campbell was angry now. It comforted me. "He deserved better than that. But we're gonna find who did this. Right, Doctor?"

"The attacker is on the submarine, obviously," I said. "They're not getting off until we surface."

"Yeah, and we're not gonna surface until we find that asshole," Campbell said, pushing past me to the aft door.

"Hey, Campbell?" I asked. "I don't get it. Why were you guys so cavalier before, when Miller and Martin were just missing, but now you're all out for blood? What's changed?"

He remained facing away from me. I could see droplets of sweat suspended in the red bristles of his hair. "You don't understand. *Everything's* changed now."

No other explanation seemed forthcoming. I watched Campbell's shoulders rise and fall as he took several deep breaths.

"Did you find the keys?"

"What?" he said, turning around, the words "the fuck are you talking about?" hanging unsaid in the air between us. Then his impatience melted into understanding and relief that I had changed the subject. "Oh, yeah. Yeah, I found 'em."

He dug in one of his front pockets for a moment, then tossed me a silver ring with four keys on it.

"Good work," I said, taking a step toward him. "I think this is going to help us figure out a lot of what happened and what's going on now."

"You want to go back upstairs?"

"Yeah. I'll see what I can find in the captain's safe." I reached out and touched his shoulder, resting my fingertips on the coarse material of his sweater. "We're going to figure this out. OK? And whoever killed Martin . . . they're not going to get away. Once we have some more answers, we won't just have to sit here anymore. We can act, be the aggressor."

I was in a bizarre world where a trained killer twice my size needed to be comforted. But Campbell seemed heartened. His face had regained some of its color.

"Let's go. Stay behind me," he said, stepping into the galley.

He first scrutinized the right side of the room, the eating area, then turned his attention to the opposite wall. The bunks, some of which still were shrouded by thick curtains, seemed to worry him. The barrel of his rifle moved with his head, ready to spray bullets into anything that threatened us.

I followed a few steps behind. I swept my gaze over the bodies still piled among the tables and cooking area. The neat stacks fit with the ambiance of the rest of the submarine: everything was in its place, and no space was wasted. Even populated with dead people, the room seemed neat and ready for inspection.

The refrigerator and pantry doors glittered, reflecting the bulbs spaced across the ceiling. The stove range was crumb-free, all the pots and pans stowed in some cabinet. The sink was devoid of even a stray droplet of water. The oven was . . . full?

"Campbell, hold on."

He crouched and brought his rifle to bear on the opposite side of the room, and instead of diving for cover, I channeled the burst of terror into a single blink. My muscles quivered with the effort.

"What?" he said.

"I think . . . there's something in the oven."

"In the oven? Hiding?" He gestured for me to stay where I was and moved sideways, staying in a crouch, keeping his weapon's front sight on the oven door. When he was about ten feet away, he spoke again. "It's a person. I can see hair."

I could make out that detail too, now. The back of someone's head was pressed against the rectangular glass window in the oven door.

Campbell crept closer. I stopped breathing. Each beat of my heart seemed to betray the SEAL's stealth. When he was an arm's length away from the oven, he reached for the door handle, keeping his right hand on the trigger.

Hooking one finger on the handle, he yanked it and hopped back. "Don't move! Don't move!"

An arm flopped out, and I thought I could hear the gun firing, could see the bullets' impacts on the person crammed inside the oven. But Campbell didn't shoot. I saw why: There was no volition behind the arm. It was limp.

"Oh, shit. Ohshitohshitohshit. Christine, come over here."

Campbell stood up, his rifle falling a degree at a time until it dangled by its strap, pointed at the floor. His shoulders slumped, and I'm sure he didn't realize his mouth was hanging open. The expression made him look like the teenager he probably was.

The racks had been removed from the oven. In the resulting space— about the same size as two side-by-side milk crates, but deeper—was a person. All we could see was his back, which was clad in black. The head was facing away from us, and one arm was tucked out of sight. The other still lolled out the oven door. I could tell from the bizarre angle at which it hung that the shoulder had been separated or dislocated.

I could see no movement in the figure's torso.

"Campbell. Campbell. Brandon, are you there? You with me?" I watched the SEAL straighten, his green eyes focusing on my face. "I need you to help me get this guy out."

"Out?"

"He's wedged in pretty good. If we can get his upper body out, we can pull him the rest of the way."

Campbell stepped forward and hooked his hands into the armpits of the body—it was a body, there was no way this guy was alive—and tugged. As I had predicted, the torso came free, and once it did, Campbell's momentum caused him to pull it the rest of the way out.

"Miller," he said.

I recognized the SEAL, too. His face was peaceful, eyes closed, unmarred by injury.

It was a remarkable contrast to the rest of his body, which had been folded and contorted like a cherry stem. His shins were snapped, the lower legs telescoped toward the knee. His right arm was shattered by more fractures than I could count. The man's back seemed to be in about the same shape.

Miller's neck was discolored, a purple half-circle betraying the method of his death.

"Strangled. From the front. He was dead before they did this to him. Campbell? He was already dead."

The SEAL stood next to me, blinking, his fists clenching and unclenching.

"We need to tell Larsen," I said. "Hey! Brandon!"

I had seen mutilated bodies before. Political prisoners and drug informers tortured until they could only be identified by dental records. What we had found in the oven was, to me, shocking in its circumstances, not its appearance. Campbell, however, seemed paralyzed by the crumpled heap on the floor.

"Larsen?" he said, still not looking at me.

I stepped between him and the body.

"Yes, Larsen. Look at me!" I said. "You need to pull it together. Your commanding officer should be apprised of the situation so you and your platoon can react and respond."

I had hoped the commanding tone and military jargon would slap him back into awareness, or at least allow him to let his training take over. He stopped blinking, and I could see his pupils contract as he focused on me.

"Shit. Where's the . . . ?" He glanced around the room, looking for something. His gaze landed on the speaker box next to the aft hatch, and he walked over to it. "Control room, galley. We've found Miller. He's dead. Lieutenant Larsen, I think you should come down here."

"Roger," came the reply.

The crisp, businesslike exchange made the world seem a little more normal.

"What the hell is going on?" he said, remaining by the door.

"I don't know. I think Larsen's going to want an answer, too, and at this point there's nothing I can tell either of you. Miller was overpowered, strangled. It might have been a sneak attack, but . . . hey . . . where is his gun?"

"What do you mean?"

"His rifle. It's not strapped to him." I crouched down, ignoring the corpse as I stared into the oven's black interior. "Toss me your flashlight again."

Its beam answered my question. The gun was lying against the oven's back wall.

"Never mind. The rifle's in here. But . . . odd."

Campbell joined me as I trailed off. "What's odd?"

"Whoever did this took the time to remove Miller's weapon from his body, then stash it in the back of the oven. But why didn't they just take it? Wouldn't having a gun be an asset if you were trying to sabotage a submarine or kill its crew?"

"Goddamn, it doesn't look like they need a fucking gun."

"No, Campbell, think from a military point of view. You're a soldier.

You're outnumbered. Will you be better off if you're armed or unarmed?"

"I'd take the rifle over my bare hands any day. But you have to remember, he's outnumbered. So far, he's tried to be sneaky, to avoid a frontal attack. Shooting people would give away his position, maybe trap him someplace."

Campbell was a SEAL again, confident and matter-of-fact.

"So he doesn't have to use it," I said. "But he'd at least want it around in case he *did* get cornered. He could do a lot more damage that way."

From the aft battery bay came a crescendo of engine noise cut short by the clang of a hatch. Campbell spun into a crouch, bringing his rifle up in a fluid arc. Then he relaxed.

"Where's Miller?" Larsen said, stepping into the compartment.

"Over here," I said as Campbell pointed toward the oven. When Larsen saw the body, an unreadable expression flashed across his features.

"How did he die, Myers?"

"Strangled, it looks like. I'd need an autopsy to confirm."

"So all these broken bones and shit . . ."

"Occurred after he was dead. Probably inflicted in an effort to fit him into the oven." The alternative, that the wounds were the result of violence for violence's sake, chilled me.

"Who could have done this?"

"A strong man. It takes less to create these types of wounds than it does to twist someone's neck 180 degrees."

"You have a theory about what happened?"

"It's all speculation. There's no useful time frame, no evidence other than what we see here on the body. You want some guesses?"

"I want whatever you can give me," he said, his voice as calm and pleasant as it had ever been since I'd met him.

"Well, let's see," I said, kneeling next to the corpse. "Look at his fingernails here. They're clean. No blood or bits of flesh . . . that probably means he didn't fight back. Which is odd, considering the marks on his neck. He was strangled from the front, like this," I said, choking an invisible target. "These are some serious bruises, too, so we're talking about a bunch of force applied. Miller likely was unconscious within seconds.

"Now, what else do we know? Nothing conclusive. But there is one more interesting fact to note: Miller's rifle was removed from his body and stashed in the oven with him. As I told Campbell, if you were trying to sabotage a submarine's mission, why wouldn't you take any firearm you could get your hands on? Especially when you know you're facing armed opposition?"

"Put it together for me."

"There's nothing to put together. I'm sorry. He probably was surprised but was attacked from the front. Don't those sound mutually exclusive? He was killed and disarmed, but his rifle wasn't taken. Counterintuitive again. And wait," I said as Larsen began to give an order to Campbell. "One other important thing. Both of these bodies were concealed. Whoever is doing this wanted to keep their deaths a secret. Why? There is no chance the disappearance of two of your men would go unnoticed, whether the bodies were found or not."

"I appreciate your help, Dr. Myers. But what you've given me is one big question. It's time we start searching for an answer. Campbell, are these two rooms secure?"

"As far as I can tell, sir."

"Good. I've got point. Campbell, cover our flanks. Myers, you stay between us. We're going to the control room."

At the hatch between the battery bay and the engine room, however, we stopped. Larsen opened the door, wincing at the pounding machinery, and waved the SEAL guarding the door into our compartment. After closing the door, he spoke.

"Shut all the hatches to the engine room. They are to remain closed at all times. You stay on the lower level and keep your weapon on this door," Larsen said, pointing to the portal between the battery bay and engine room. "If it opens, you shoot whoever comes through."

"Aye-aye, sir," the SEAL said. "No one gets through."

"That's what I want to hear. Now let's go."

As we moved through the engine room, I watched the SEAL Larsen had spoken to spread his instructions to Young and the other soldier using signals and pantomimes. All three moved with a gravity and assurance that suggested anyone who tried to capture their compartment would see blood spilled.

The electrical compartment was filled with more unasked questions. The SEALs worked without speaking, but their postures and glances still gave away their mood. Larsen ignored them as, one by one, we maneuvered through the hatch to the control room.

He walked to the center of the room, resting one hand on the attack periscope. The soldiers made no attempt to act disinterested. I wasn't sure anyone was breathing.

"Sir, we don't—"

"There is no uncertainty: we have an enemy combatant onboard," Larsen said, cutting off Matthews. He glanced around the room, craggy features now adding to his air of authority. "He is stealthy. He is strong. He has killed two of us, and he's going to pay for that.

"Our primary mission is to deliver the *Dragon* into American hands. And we will. But we no longer can afford to be reactive. Lieutenant Matthews?"

"Yes, sir."

"Order all the compartment hatches sealed. No one is going to enter or leave their area without notifying the control room first."

"Aye-aye, sir." Matthews slouched over to the intercom, dodging low-hanging pipes. "Attention, all compartments: secure and seal. Remain in place and call the conn if you have to leave station." He turned back to Larsen.

"Yes. Wait, leave that one open," Larsen said as one of the SEALs near the forward hatch moved to close it. "We'll be dealing with the doctor a lot from here on out. Campbell, you're attached to her permanently.

"Gentlemen, as soon as we switch to electric power, this guy isn't going to have any noise to hide behind. And that's when we're going to go get him. For now, sit tight. And Dr. Myers, head back to the officers' mess, please. I'll need to speak with you in a moment."

I made eye contact with Campbell. He seemed to have recovered a little more of his military demeanor, giving me a slight nod when I gestured toward the open hatch.

In the hallway on the other side, I ducked into the captain's room.

Campbell followed me without speaking.

The keys sparkled as I held them up to the light, rippling reflections across the walls. I felt gleams of hope flutter through my chest in response and realized that my outlook had shifted. This was no longer an abstract investigation. It was a search for safety in the face of a brutal enemy.

The third key I tried turned in the lock, and the door swung open, revealing two shelves stacked with papers and folders. I grabbed them all and tucked them under my arm.

"Don't you want to take pictures or anything?" Campbell said as I stood up. His monotone suggested he already knew the answer.

"No time. If Larsen's going to go after the saboteur, we need to give him as much information as we can. This 'serpent' thing clearly is the motive for everything that has happened on this boat. Finding out what it is now, for our own sake, is a bigger deal than wondering later whether we documented everything perfectly when we found it."

"What if it's not in there?"

"Then we hold out until we hit the shore, then tear apart the sub rivet by rivet until our questions are answered." I walked out of the room and down the hall to the officers' mess. Pushing the evidence on the table to the side, I spread out the documents from the safe.

Campbell took a seat across from me.

"Lot of reading material," he said.

"What I need you to do is glance at all the labels, all the headers, and look for key words: 'serpent,' obviously. But also things marked 'top secret,' 'confidential,' and so on. Words that tell us there's something important inside. If there's a ship's log in here, we'll want to read that, too."

The room's bright lighting seemed harsh and antiseptic now, illuminating our desperation. Were we desperate? I realized my grip on the table's edge was hurting my fingertips. Sitting back, I watched Campbell thumb through pages, his lips moving as he read.

"Are you worried?" I said, my thoughts blurting into the silence. My wrist hurt. The source of the pain was a red welt where I had been popping the grimy rubber band against my flesh.

He looked up and spoke without hesitation. "Our training makes us the best soldiers on any battlefield. But I've never seen anything like this. That's all I know." The rest of his thoughts were hidden behind his eyes, and after a few unblinking moments, he returned to his work.

His answer disquieted me more than anything I had witnessed so far. Bodies didn't upset me. Death's nuances, quirks and unpleasantries were academic, just pieces of a crime scene. But the totality of the events on the *Dragon* added up to something more than death. Something that was outside my experience, too.

"Here's something," Campbell said, piercing my mental fugue. "'Most secret.' It's the only reference of that kind so far. You want me to read it?"

"No, let's gather everything that looks important first, then read through it all at once."

He grunted and began poring over the documents again. I picked up the file he had pointed out.

Its contents were impenetrable. But I noticed several tables of numbers near the back of the folder. The column headings were in Korean, though, so I could have been looking at the medical records of the ship's cat or a recipe for buckwheat pancakes.

Or secret weapons files. I kept myself from telling Campbell to forget the rest of this stuff, to just read these papers. An answer, any clue, seemed more necessary than breathing.

But I was silent, tearing at a hangnail with my teeth as he went through all the files and documents, pushing most to the side and stacking the rest in a pile in front of me. By the time he was finished, I was surprised I could speak without screaming.

"Well?"

"Got no more files, but seven individual pages. None say 'serpent,' but they're all stamped with warnings and secret designations and shit."

"But nothing about the serpent?"

"Not in the labels. Where do you want me to start reading?"

"Doesn't matter. That one," I said, pointing to the top of his pile.

He began to translate, each sentence again riddled with pauses. "'To: Capt. Yoon Chong-Gug, Commander, No. 19, *Dragon*. From: High Command, Special Projects . . . Division. Orders are . . . as follows: Meet with . . . research vessel No. 2 between 2000 and 0400 hours 28 January. Research personnel will load . . . codename *Serpent*'—hey, I think this might be it—'codename Serpent into . . . containment . . . structure. Delivery of research to . . . Facility No. 99 expected 31 January. Crew should not be . . . informed on mission. Officers on . . . need-to-know . . . basis only.'" He stopped. "It gives a routing number and stuff, but that's the end of the text. There's no date."

"It's kind of fuzzy on the details," I said. "Not particularly concise. Where's the research ship? Where is Facility No. 99? What is Serpent?"

"Yeah, exactly. It should spell all that shit out."

Campbell was becoming more profane. There were worse ways to deal with stress.

"It assumes he knows where he's going and what he's going to carry," I said. "He's been briefed. This order is a formality."

"It's too secret to write down?"

"Maybe. If that's the case, we're wasting our time here."

"Fuck it," he said, dropping the page he had just read onto the bench next to him and grabbing the next one. "This has the same header . . . wait, no, the 'From' section reads: 'Fleet Command West.' Not familiar with that one. But the North Korean submarine fleet is pretty secretive."

"Uh-huh. So what is it?"

"Um . . . 'U.S. surface and . . . submerged units may be . . . patrolling area.' And then it lists a bunch of ships. Looks like the *Kitty Hawk* battle group."

"Terrific," I said. "What's next?"

"Another one from Fleet Command West. 'Orders are as follows: *Dragon* will accept reassignment of officers, as requested. New . . . command staff members include: Lee Tae-Uk, commander; Choi Ji-Sung, lieutenant; Hyun Yung-Pyo, lieutenant . . . ' These are the orders that pared down the crew to the size it is now."

"Interesting. Yoon brought Lee onboard. How long were they planning this thing?"

"The orders are marked January 2," Campbell said. "It's got a locator tag on it, too. Looks like they were in port. So this essentially is the complement for the 'Special Projects Division' mission. They let him hand-pick the crew."

"I don't know anything about North Korean military culture. Is that typical?"

"It's not typical anyplace, let alone there."

"Nothing about this fucking sub is typical," I said. "Keep—shit!"

The epithet had been triggered by Matthews, who had appeared in the doorway, his angular body wraithlike against the dreary background.

"You two: The situation has escalated. Lieutenant Larsen and I will need a briefing on whatever you have that may pertain to who we're dealing with."

"Whoa," I said, my words stopping him as he began to return to the control room. "What do you mean, 'escalated'?"

He looked at me, dark eyes peering from a face that looked more birdlike every time I saw it.

"Young, Wilkes and Henderson are dead."

Now Campbell jumped in. "Dead? Who . . . when did this happen?"

"We're not sure. We gave the order to shut down the diesel and switch to electric power, but the engine kept running. MacDonald, Ridder and Reyes were sent to see what happened."

"And the engine room crew was gone?" I asked.

"No. Young's body was on the top deck, Wilkes's and Henderson's on the bottom deck."

"I'd like to see the bodies," I said.

"That's not possible. We're locking the ship down. All our personnel are going to be in the electrical compartment, the control room, this compartment and the forward torpedo room."

"Did their bodies have any visible wounds?"

"Young's neck was broken and so was Henderson's. Wilkes's head is bashed in. It looks like he was slammed face-first into the port diesel."

"Oh, Christ," Campbell said.

"No one heard anything?"

"If there was anything to hear, it was drowned out by the engine noise. Look, we don't have time for this. Lieutenant Larsen and I will be back in a few minutes." He turned and stalked down the hallway.

I stared at Campbell, who looked ready to shoot his own shadow if it made a threatening gesture.

"Did you hear that?" he said, leaning across the table. "Did you hear that shit? All three of them dead, man! Fuck this. I'm going out there, and I'm going to ventilate this motherfucker."

"He's not getting away," I said. It was going to be impossible to calm him down if his fear gelled with bloodlust.

"Yeah, no shit," he said, standing.

"Wait! I need you to read some more of these. There's something vital in here. Something that can help us, that can tell us who's . . . who's . . ." My words disappeared, smothered by a new, disquieting idea.

Campbell's anger melted into confusion, then concern. He put his hand on my shoulder and squatted next to me.

"You OK?"

"Sit down, Campbell. I know who did it."

VII

"WHAT?" HE SAID, pushing himself up and back into his seat as though my words had flung him there.

"It's a matter of access. Who could have killed both engine room crews? The killer would have had to be able to move without anyone seeing him, attack with total surprise and get away before the bodies were discovered," I said, then waited for the information to sink in. "You following?"

He nodded.

"There is one person we *know* had the access and the opportunity. Vazquez."

"No. He didn't do it."

I hadn't even finished saying the SEAL's name before Campbell delivered the denial.

"I know it's hard to think of being betrayed by one of your friends, but it happened. Look at what the North Korean crew did."

Now Campbell was shaking his head.

"You don't understand. It's not possible. Vazquez didn't kill them, I promise you."

"Ignore your loyalty for a second. You guys stormed onto this boat and checked every compartment. Every single one. There was no one else onboard to commit these crimes. That's the first point. The second one is that no one was killed until the engine room was sealed off from the rest of the boat. Secrecy for the killer. And the killer obviously didn't come from the forward part of the ship—the upper deck, anyway.

"And then there's the fact that all of the people killed didn't put up a fight. Even Miller, who was attacked from the front. Why? Because they knew their killer. He walked right up and murdered them.

"Finally, Miller's rifle. Vazquez left it for one reason: he already had one. It all fits."

Campbell hadn't stopped shaking his head.

"You tell this to Larsen and Matthews, and they'll say the same thing. Vazquez didn't do it. He's on our side."

"What is your problem?" His esprit de corps touched off a flare of irritation. "I list 8 million reasons why Vazquez is the biggest suspect, and you brush it all aside by telling me no, it's just not possible. And I just thought of another reason: he was supposed to search for the bodies, but, conveniently, he didn't find them."

"You just have to trust me," he said. "I know for a fact that Vazquez didn't do anything to Miller and Martin. And if he didn't kill them, why would he have killed Hendy, Wilkes and Young? You don't have a motive, either."

This I could handle. It made it easier to dilute the frustration in my voice.

"That's correct. I don't have a motive. In some cases, though, you don't need one to find out who did a crime." I softened my tone further and ticked off each point on my fingertips. "He's the only person who could have gotten into the engine room unseen. His familiarity to the victims accounts for the lack of struggle. He left the rifle because he didn't need one. And he didn't 'discover' the bodies of the first two men he killed."

"Well . . . yeah," Campbell said, shifting in his seat. I could see a drop of sweat trickle down the left side of his face, pausing for a moment on the high cheekbone. "I guess he fits in with all the evidence."

"Not only does he fit in, but no one else on this ship even comes close."

"But here's the thing." Campbell was straightening the stacks of paper now. "He didn't find the bodies because he wasn't supposed to. At first."

"It might be easier for you to stop lying to me, or at least tell a lie that makes sense. Just a suggestion."

"Lying? No, Vazquez was . . . look. I shouldn't tell you this."

"Jesus Christ! Decide now: fuck me over again, like you did the first time I asked you, or tell me what happened to Miller and Martin."

"They didn't just disappear, OK? You were wondering why no one was upset—well, it was because Larsen told them to leave the engine room, to pretend to vanish."

"He ordered them to vanish."

"Yeah."

"Why the hell would he do that?"

Campbell still was focused on the papers, but I could see his cheeks flood with abrupt color.

"To, uh, scare you. Keep you confined in one place. It gave him a reason."

I laughed, making him look up, his features pinched and confused.

"No, no, I can figure it out from here. He didn't want me snooping around that locker downstairs. And, you know, I'm just a little girl, a woman among men, probably checking her makeup every five minutes and trembling in fear when left alone."

"It's not—"

"So, because it wasn't enough to just fucking *order* me to stay put for the rest of the trip, he creates some ghost story to keep me out of his hair."

"He didn't say that, he just—"

"Didn't say that? What did he say, then? How many times did he use the word 'bitch'? Just curious."

"It was only . . ." Campbell said, trailing off.

I stayed silent, realizing that he was waiting for me to interrupt him. He cleared his throat and continued.

". . . only supposed to spook you. To keep you . . . OK, fine. He actually said that, 'to keep her out of my hair.' He said just ordering you around would get you riled up, make you start talking back and causing trouble. But if you wanted to stay put, if you felt endangered . . ."

" . . . then I'd stay in the mess room and cry myself to sleep. Yeah, I got that. Sweet Jesus. No wonder you people were so freaked out when you found Martin's body. Either Miller had taken his 'mess with the bitch's mind' orders a little too seriously or somebody else onboard took him out. I can see how that would be hard to comprehend."

"You're not a bitch," Campbell said.

"Nice of you to say. I *am* pissed off, though. I hope you realize, too, that none of this clears Vazquez."

"What? I just told you—"

"You told me the disappearances were staged. But you saw those bodies. They were real. He still is the only one with access. He still was familiar to the dead guys. But mainly, he's remaining my top suspect because I'm not going to take a damn thing you say from now on seriously."

"Oh, come on. That's not fair. I've helped you."

"You also lied to me. If there weren't a murderer still running around loose on this ship, I'd just finish my investigation without saying another word to Larsen or any of you other jock stuffers."

"I'm sorry, OK? It didn't seem like a big deal."

I threw the manila folder from the safe at his chest.

"Shut up, read through this and let me cool down."

He spread its contents on the surface in front of him, careful to avoid looking at my face.

Larsen. That ass. All that discussion about scenarios and motives was just shooting the breeze, killing time until Operation: Keep the Woman in Check kicked into action.

I started writing a mental report to Patterson. I doubted he'd do much besides stand shoulder-to-shoulder with his fellow pistol-waver. But I could make sure my boss, Charlie, got a copy of the report, too. He would be as upset as I was now. I could hear his voice, a cultured East Coast baritone iced over with anger: "Hmmm. If they're going to work that hard to keep us from helping, maybe we shouldn't help at all next time."

And as often as Patterson and his units asked us for help, that might be a deadlier public-relations poison.

"Hey, um . . . this is serious. This entire first page is all security warnings. 'Secrets of the Republic . . . punishment is death . . . unauthorized access . . . ' blah, blah, blah, lots of shit like that."

I said nothing.

"Well, it seems like a big deal to me," Campbell said. "Let's see. Next page . . . this is all super-technical. Probably over my head in English, too, ha ha."

The self-deprecating humor died in the air between us. But my stomach fluttered with sudden, unexpected anticipation. I was getting the sense that we were on the cusp of uncovering something vital.

"Well, find some words you understand and go from there. Larsen and Matthews are going to walk through that door any second."

He flipped through the pages, then stopped. He stared at the document, motionless except for the slow, steady downward movement of his jaw. Looking at me, he tried to speak, but the words disappeared into a squeaky rasp.

"Holy shit," he said after swallowing and massaging his throat.

"What? Holy shit, what?" I said.

"It's a man. The Serpent is a man." He turned the folder around to face me. There was an outline of a man, longhand notes jotted in boxes next to red marks on the figure.

"What does the title say?" I said, pointing at the text running across the top of the page.

He reoriented the folder again. "It says . . . 'Serpent. Healing.' Healing something. 'Healing ability,' uh, 'skeleton, muscle, organs.' There are some other words in there I don't know. Medical stuff, maybe."

Blood pulsed through my temples. The information set my imagination spinning, but I tried to ground myself by asking more questions.

"The text, the handwriting . . . what does that say?"

"I can do that. I can read this." Even across the table, I could hear that Campbell's breathing had accelerated, too. "This one here on the guy's left forearm—wait, no, it's his right forearm, he's facing us—says 'break, much blood inside.' No, not inside, 'internal.'"

"A fractured bone, massive internal bleeding. Is that all it says?"

"No, there's a time written next to it. 1100, 09/19/05. And then underneath it . . . I'm not an expert, but it looks like a different person's handwriting . . . it says . . . dammit, I don't know that word. Something 'complete.' It's referring to the bone."

"Probably a notation about the fracture healing. Keep going."

"'Scans show . . . density 110 percent normal. No . . . evidence of harm in tissue. Scar tissue small . . . ' er, no. Not 'small,' but something like that."

"'Minimal,' I'm guessing. The bone has repaired itself to a strength beyond its original condition, that's what the density is telling me. And the massive bleeding seems to have been controlled rather quickly if there's no evidence of tissue damage." A thought plowed into my consciousness, knocking aside my medical evaluation. "Wait, that's not all it says, is it? There's a time and date by the second entry, isn't there?"

It was tough to tell in the artificial, shadowless light of the mess room, but it looked like some of the color had drained from his face.

"Yeah. Yeah, there's a time. It says, '0234, 09/20/05.' But that can't . . . maybe I'm misreading it."

"I thought they used Arabic numbers."

"I know. It can't be right, though. Can it?"

The dimness of the hallway to my left seemed to take on sinister qualities, providing a breeding ground for my fears. What could hide in the uncertain light? And could these walls and corridors offer us a place to hide if it came after us?

"Doctor? You with me? Look, this can't be correct. It's saying that a broken arm healed in something like fifteen hours. I've had a fucking broken arm, OK, and it took weeks to get back to normal."

I blinked, still focusing on what we couldn't see. "Read another entry," I said. My voice sounded flat, disinterested. It was an instinctive facade hung over feelings I hadn't even begun to sort out.

"But what about—"

"Just do it."

"Uh . . . here's one for the upper body. Looks like his stomach area. 'Bullet wound. Thirty-caliber handgun . . . ' It just talks about the gun for a bit. 'Bullet perforated lower . . . ' I don't know what the hell word that is. Uh, 'liver damaged.' More massive internal bleeding. This one's

138

1300, 10/31/05. On Halloween. Motherfucker."

"Hold up the chart where I can see it," I said. He did so, and I noted where the red mark was. "It probably says perforated intestine or bowel. I can see why the liver was damaged. Now read the rest. There's more."

"'No . . . ' something—wait, I think that's wrong. 'No . . . no . . . no transfusion. No transfusion needed. Bleeding half-normal after two minutes; stopped after five.' What?" He saw me lean forward on the table and cradle my head.

"Nothing. Keep going," I said without looking up.

"'MRI'—hey, they just use the English letters for that—'shows . . . ' dammit, there's that word again. Let's say it's intestines. 'MRI shows intestines undamaged. Liver functions test normal.'"

"And?"

"And . . . '2350, 10/31/05.'"

I looked up and saw the concern on Campbell's face. "I'm sure you're picking up on a trend here. A broken bone healed in less than a day; tissue and organ damage healed even faster. They're deliberately injuring the subject—the Serpent—and keeping track of how his body reacts."

"But this is impossible," he said. "Fucking impossible . . . he's gutshot, but totally fine hours later?"

"Scan a few more of those. Tell me if they don't fit the pattern."

He was silent for a moment, his eyes flitting across the page. "'Stab wound . . . shoulder' . . . shit," he said under his breath. "It's just a bunch of injuries. Just looking at the dates, none of them took more than 24 hours to heal. What the fuck is this? Some kind of a super soldier?"

"You knew something important was on this sub. So important that they sent you guys out to capture and control it. So important that its entire crew is dead." I was dismayed to find that I still couldn't put any emotion into my words, not even fear. "Weapons research. That's what my dossier said was onboard, weapons research. Well, this right here, if we're reading it correctly, is one hell of a weapon."

"Wait, what are you telling me?"

"I don't know," I said, trying to summon reserves of discipline to bolster my professional detachment. "Just keep reading. See if you can find a page header for 'physical abilities' or 'changes' or 'growth' or 'transformation' . . . shit, I don't know. Something like that."

He gave me a confused glance, but dived back into the folder.

"I don't have any clue what you're looking for. There's a ton of information in here. If there's some kind of specific data that you're trying . . . wait, how about this? 'Physical timeline.'"

"Timeline? Maybe. Tell me what it looks like."

"Bunch of dates and times down the side with typed entries next to them. *Really* fine print."

"Let's hear 'em."

"The first entry is for 1200, 07/07/05. 'Gene sequence modified.' That's all it says."

"Next?"

"Same day, an hour later. 'IQ test. Subject's intelligence shows 45-point increase.'"

"Smarter. Next?"

"Same day, thirty minutes later. 'Strength test. Subject's upper- and lower-body abilities show 165 percent increase.'"

"Stronger. Keep going."

"Same day, another half-hour later. 'Subject shows signs of paranoia.'"

"Too much of a good thing can be bad for you, Campbell."

"What the hell are you talking about?" he said. He looked worried, as if my words held malice toward him.

"Read me the last entry on the page, and I'll spell it out for you."

"Fine, the last entry; '1800, 07/16/06. Serpent frozen for transportation.'"

I leaned back, trying to brace myself against the solidity of the wall behind me. "You getting it yet?"

"Getting *what?* You said you'd spell it out, now spell it the fuck out!"

Footsteps in the hall ended as Larsen spoke from the doorway: "Spell what out?"

Matthews was standing in the hall, still stooped a bit despite the higher ceilings. He was chewing on a toothpick or matchstick.

"Come in and I'll tell you," I said, sliding down the bench to make room.

"We really don't have time for this, sir," Matthews said, but Larsen waved him off.

"Is this something we need to hear, Myers?"

I nodded, and when Larsen saw Campbell's troubled expression, he sat and motioned for Matthews to do the same. It took the taller officer several seconds to wedge himself into a place at the table.

"Talk to us," Larsen said. For the first time I noticed a tiny scar by his left eye, the one that didn't seem to open all the way.

I stacked the materials we had found in Lee's and Yoon's quarters in front of me. Pulling the folder from Campbell's hands, I placed it, closed, on top of the stack of documents, then took a deep breath.

"I've found some things," I said, looking into Larsen's face, then Matthews's. "First of all, Yoon and Lee were working together. If there was a mutiny, it wasn't started by either of them. They had plans, but I don't think they involved sabotage or betrayal. I'll get to that in a moment.

"A more pressing matter is the deaths of your men. First Miller and Martin, and now the latest engine-room crew. Larsen, I'm trained to solve crimes. I analyze the situation and come up with an explanation that fits the evidence. And all the evidence pointed to Vazquez as the killer. No, I know what you're going to say," I said as Larsen held up his hand and opened his mouth. "Vazquez couldn't have done it. Blah, blah, blah. Save your half-assed bullshit. I know you lied to me."

The searing anger about the way I had been treated bubbled to the surface again. It was clear and certain, and I let it carry me.

"Don't bother yelling at Campbell. I would have made you tell me if he hadn't. But now, of course, Miller and Martin aren't just missing— they're dead. And so are Young and . . . wait, I can remember these names . . . Wilkes and Henderson. Right? Five of your men dead. The engines sabotaged. Seems like there's *someone* trying to stop us, doesn't it?

"Except that doesn't fit with the fact that all of the sub's original crew are accounted for and also deceased."

I paused, took a breath. Campbell's expression hadn't changed, and

I expected one of the officers to interject something. But they waited for me to continue. Larsen's poker face was perfect; Matthews's was marred by a twitch under his left eye.

"I believe that the deaths of the *Dragon*'s crew and the deaths of your men are connected. First, the Koreans. There was a massive battle and, essentially, a chemical attack on the lower deck. Two men made it out; one tried to surface the sub. One tried to kill the other to keep him from doing that.

"There's more. See, Yoon gave Lee orders of some kind. Orders in respect to something called 'the Serpent,' and how it couldn't be allowed to reach the shore. About how he had to do something unthinkable if its escape seemed imminent. Sounds like something that might precipitate the deliberate release of chlorine gas on a submarine, right?

"So they were fighting over the Serpent. But what is the Serpent? Well, we can guess that it has something to do with the weapons research this boat is carrying. The information that caused our government to send a SEAL team—minimally trained for such a mission—to take over a sub, and me to figure out what had gone down."

Larsen lost it then.

"Myers, you better not have—"

"Larsen, shut up," I said.

He looked like he was about to swing at me. I saw death in his eyes. But instead, he stood up and grabbed Matthews's arm, halfway to hauling the taller man to his feet.

"Come on, Lieutenant, this cunt is wasting our time. Campbell, get out in the passageway. Keep the door closed. She is not to leave."

"I can tell you exactly what you're up against, Lieutenant Larsen. Is that a waste of your time?" I said as he walked out. Larsen spun around.

"Then tell me. But if you opened that locker, I'll shoot you." Although his voice was soft, there was no compassion or humor in it.

"I didn't open anything. I told you I wouldn't. I *promised* I wouldn't. And you went and launched some dumb fool-the-bitch operation instead of taking me at my word."

He sat back down and folded his hands on the table.

"Talk."

"A file in the captain's safe discusses the Serpent. It details a soldier in whom mortal wounds heal in hours. It talks about strength increases. Intelligence increases. And insanity. You know what the last entry in the report's timeline says about the Serpent? It says 'Serpent frozen for transportation.'"

I watched understanding flicker across Matthews's face. The matchstick fell into his lap. Larsen still was fighting to defuse his emotions.

"The Serpent was in that biohazard freezer. It got loose. The crew fought back. Everyone died. And now we're its next targets."

For a few heartbeats, all was still, the scene a portrait depicted in stale air and severe lighting. I felt calm, again in control of the crime scene. The evidence had added up, as it always did.

"So we're fighting the Serpent?" Campbell said.

"It appears so. It all fits," I said, sliding further into my professional persona. "A massive amount of strength was required to inflict some of the wounds, both on the crew and on our people. The enemy is strong. Probably brilliant as well, which explains how he's been able to avoid you so far. And if he were wounded or incapacitated in the fight against Yoon and his men, he's fine now."

"This . . . person . . . was frozen and then came back to life?" Larsen said. "Sounds like bullshit."

"It *should* sound like bullshit," I said. "Ice crystals form in human blood when it's frozen, and they puncture the red blood cells. Not to mention the serious complications of depriving tissue of oxygen for long periods of time. But if you asked me yesterday, I'd tell you it was impossible to genetically modify a person like this, too."

"Tell us more about this soldier," Matthews said. He tried to lean his elbows on the table, but the proportions were all wrong, and he settled for crossing his arms across his chest.

"No, wait," Larsen said. "Why do you think this Serpent was in the freezer, why do you think it killed all those Koreans, and why do you think it's what we're fighting now?"

I met his gaze. "Why am I suggesting it was in the freezer? Because we have several sets of orders here that discuss this sub picking up the Serpent from a floating laboratory. And then we have these specs that say it was frozen for shipment. Connect the dots." I didn't wait for him to get angry again. "Why do I think it was responsible for the crew's death? Well, honestly, I don't think it killed all of them. Many of those guys died of chlorine inhalation and complications from it. But there are a lot of really brutal wounds in the three compartments below us, and I didn't see any bloody weapon lying around.

"Plus, the chlorine leak was in the compartment with the locker. One of the compartment's doors was chained shut, which I have been told is not normal procedure. And finally, we have personal correspondence that discusses just such a horrific scenario if the Serpent were to get loose.

"Now, as for why I think it's responsible for the deaths of your men . . . well, the only other suspect is exonerated by your idiotic prank. Yet something clearly has killed, by brute force, five SEALs. Does that cover everything?"

Larsen looked at Campbell. "What did you read about the Serpent?"

"Exactly what she just said, sir," the SEAL said, snapping his head toward the officer. "This thing, whatever it is, can apparently heal like a motherfucker and is smarter and stronger than he was before. He's definitely called 'the Serpent,' and this sub was definitely sent to pick him up."

"Now answer Lieutenant Matthews's question, Myers," Larsen said. "What can you tell us about this thing? How do we fight it?"

I pointed at the stack of documents. "The only thing we know for sure is that freezing it made it harmless. But apparently not dead."

"So we just need to zap it with some ice cubes? Fantastic. What a load," Larsen said. But he stayed in his chair.

"No, I didn't say that. You aren't planning to ship it; you're planning to kill it. And according to these healing tests, it's susceptible to normal attacks. Bullets, knives, clubs, whatever. You just need to keep shooting it and make sure it's dead, because, as Campbell put it, it can indeed heal like a motherfucker."

"How is it hiding from us?" Matthews spoke again, his eyebrow twitching with increasing frequency.

"It's smart," I said. "Its IQ probably is at genius level. What you have to do is systematically eliminate all possible hiding places. Make a sweep, from point A to point B, and make sure there is no place, absolutely no place, it could be lurking."

"Bilge bays, lockers," Larsen muttered.

"Exactly," I said. "If you eliminate everyplace it could be but one, then it will be in that last place. Being systematic is the key. No matter how smart this thing is, it can't escape that."

Larsen and Matthews looked at each other. Then Larsen stood again.

"Thank you for your help," he said to me, but he had already turned to face Campbell before the sentence was finished. "Dr. Myers and these documents are key. You are responsible for keeping all of it safe." Then, to both of us: "We're going to hunt this thing. Your compartment will remain unsealed, but if there is gunfire, serious fighting, lock it down."

There was resolve and violence in his voice. But I wasn't comforted.

"We should also contact the escort sub," I said. "Even if there's nothing it can do immediately, it should know what's going on."

"Out of the question," Larsen said. Matthews was shaking his head as his superior spoke. "We don't contact them because it would give away our position. They don't contact us for the same reason. Unless we start sinking, the *Rickover*'s orders are to monitor us, protect us from other vessels, and report to shore anything that happens. We'll win this fight on our own."

He walked out the door, and Matthews extricated himself from his seat and followed. Before he could disappear around the corner, I spoke again.

"Wait."

Matthews turned and raised his brows, making his eyes appear even more deeply embedded in his head.

"The other thing is . . . based on what we've read, the Serpent is probably insane. Don't expect him to behave rationally all the time. Insanity isn't predictable."

"Oh. Right," he said, frowning in my direction. Then he nodded and walked out of sight.

Campbell looked like he'd be a lot more comfortable if he had something to shoot at. He was blinking too fast, as though dust had contaminated both his eyes.

"Eleven versus one. There's no way he can escape," the SEAL said. He wanted me to agree.

"If they do it right, there's no possible place for someone to hide. I was serious when I said they had to be—what is that?" I paused, feeling a new sensation creeping through my feet and up my legs. This was much less obvious than the diesel engines—just a tiny, constant shiver in the deck that would have been imperceptible in any other setting.

Campbell saw the look on my face. "It's the electric engines. We're moving again."

As he spoke, I could feel my inertia pull me aft as the sub picked up speed. I smiled.

"It's nice to be getting closer to home, isn't it? How fast can we go with the electrics?"

"Well, we've only got one operable battery bay. So even though we can max out at thirteen knots, we only can travel about seven nautical miles at that speed. But we're still at least twenty nautical miles from shore."

The diesels should have been rumbling underfoot. They would have been a comfort, a sign of mechanical well-being and progress. But my thoughts flashed down the hallway, through the control room and electrical compartment and visited the space where five men, now, had been brutalized.

"I don't think Larsen wants to risk having a crew in the engine room anymore," I interjected.

"Yeah, exactly. So we'll go at five knots or so on the electrics and only switch to the diesels if it looks like we can't stretch it into port."

"That means we're still four hours from shore. Jesus."

Campbell reached across the table but stopped short of taking my hand.

"I know. I don't like it either. Shit," he said, pulling his hand back and resting it on his rifle. "How do you stay so calm? It's not like I've never seen a dead body before, but when I saw Miller, I . . . I kind of locked up. I couldn't react. That should never happen to a SEAL. You were fucking icy down there, though."

"It's nothing to be proud of," I said. "I've seen a lot, that's all. You learn to look at it clinically, or you can't do your work. You were thinking like a person, like a human being."

"I don't like just sitting in here. I'd rather be with the other guys hunting down the Serpent."

"I'm curious to see what they find."

"What?"

"You know, just from an intellectual point of view." I was serious. I had discovered that my fear had once again retreated into the background, leaving my scientific mind to wonder how such a being functioned. "Don't misunderstand: I want it dead, too. Or at least captured. My first priority is getting back to shore with a pulse. It won't bother me if preserving our lives means ending the Serpent's."

He seemed satisfied with my answer. Then he tilted his head and stared into space.

"What would it be like to go against a whole platoon of these things?"

"That's the question, isn't it? It seems like this is the prototype. But I'd be scared to see a whole bunch of these unleashed on a battlefield. He's been unarmed, too, remember."

"You don't have to sound so admiring," the SEAL said.

"I don't admire it any more than you do. Goddamn, Campbell, give me some credit. You just said as much yourself: the Serpent, solo, is a serious threat. Imagine what a squad of Serpents carrying automatic weapons would be capable of."

"They can die. And we would kill them."

"Uh-huh. So here's a question for you: Say the U.S. uses this research and makes its own Serpent. What would that be like?"

He laughed. "It's just a weapon. Right? Like a gun. We make it, we aim it, we shoot it."

"You seemed a little more concerned about bioweapons when we first noticed the freezer in the battery bay. I believe you said something about letting guys in rubber suits handle it. As opposed to heavily armed SEALs."

"I trust my commanders," he said. "I don't trust some foreign army with a bunch of Petri dishes. Doesn't bother me if our brass decides to deploy this thing."

"It doesn't bother you? Are you serious? A person isn't a gun. And this particular person is barely a person—it's like a Human Being, Version 2.0. What if they wanted to upgrade *you?*"

"You don't get it. We *are* weapons, a sword in the hands of our commander and country."

I snorted. "Oh, please. What kind of poetic, bullshit patriotism is that?"

"Like I said, you don't get it. If they wanted to upgrade me, if they thought it was safe—and if that's even possible—then, yeah, I'd do my duty."

"Just like the soldiers they tested atomic bombs on? They were doing their duty, too."

"What's your point? I have a job to do, and I'm not afraid to do it," his voice had grown louder. "Right now, my job is keeping you safe. Later it might be taking an inventory of our ammunition or something. And if my duty eventually included being 'upgraded,' then I'd follow through."

I thrust my hands over my head.

"I surrender. Forget I mentioned it. Really, I have no idea how they made the Serpent. Surgery? Gene splicing, maybe? Perhaps they gave the test subject a spiked drink. I can't wait to autopsy this one and find out." Campbell nodded when I said "autopsy."

"It was only a matter of time," I continued. "You can build bigger guns, better armor . . . but in the end, you still have the same soldier wearing it. If you can manipulate a person's genes to improve them, why not give yourself an unequaled edge?"

He shrugged. "I told you, it doesn't bother me."

"It bothers you that we have to fight this thing."

"Yeah. But we'll kill it."

"The idea of creating beings like the Serpent, though, that isn't disturbing to you. Right?"

"I'm sorry, I'm not a doctor. I'm just a SEAL," he said, each word leaden with sarcasm. "If you want some kind of debate over this, you'll have to find someone else to have it with."

"I'm not trying to start a fight," I said. "I guess I'm just thinking out loud. It's one of those things that's too big to just keep inside your head."

I paused, my eyes unfocusing. The evidence, the SEAL, the room's spare furnishings all wavered and became indistinct. I tried to allow my thoughts to crystallize in the blurriness.

"It's like this." I returned my gaze to Campbell's face. The paleness I had seen before had been replaced with a flush of annoyance. His eyes flicked to the rubber band, and I stopped playing with it. "You've heard the phrase 'the genie's out of the bottle,' right? It sort of ties in to the nature of science and knowledge. Knowledge in itself isn't bad—it's the application that can be unethical and dangerous.

"But the thing about knowledge is, once you discover something, you can't undiscover it. And what we have here is the apparent discovery of how to improve the human body and mind. A concept that, in the abstract, is a good thing. After all, people constantly strive to better themselves. If they didn't, health clubs and diet plans would be out of business."

I hadn't lectured students since grad school, but it felt like I was doing it now. If this had been a class, I would have waited for laughter at my last line. But Campbell remained silent, brows raised, eyes curious.

"However, in reality," I said, answering his tacit question, "knowledge can't exist in the abstract. As we have seen in the Serpent. Now that we can make soldiers who are faster, stronger and smarter than normal people, what happens to the normal people?"

"We kick its ass," he said without hesitating.

I sighed, reaching for the folder.

"I've been to college," he said.

"What?"

"I told you. I went for a year to Oklahoma State. I took a couple of philosophy classes. I speak some Navajo, too. That's one of the hardest languages in the world, did you know that?"

"I don't understand," I said. But I did. I could see where he was going, and I felt guilty.

"My point is that I think you're wrong, and it's not because your vocabulary is too complex. You know?"

"I'm sorry," I said.

"Look at the history of war. Someone invented the sharp rock. And then the spear. Then the bow and arrow, and the gun, and eventually the nuke. But we're all still here. The way I see it, if we're smart enough to invent something, we're smart enough to figure out how to deal with the consequences."

"I'm not that confident," I said.

"I guess I am."

We looked at each other for a couple of heartbeats, and then he smiled and shook his head. "But we're definitely both on the same team."

"In that case," I said, "let's see if there's anything in that folder about how the Serpent was created. Just so we have something to do while we're waiting for its ass to be kicked."

He pulled the file back and started flipping through it again.

"It probably would be toward the front, right?" he asked, continuing to pore over the pages.

"Yeah, probably." I pulled my legs up onto the bench and rested my chin in my hand.

A few minutes ticked by. I tried to be as silent as possible, straining to listen for any indication of how the search-and-destroy operation was going. All I heard was my own heartbeat and intermittent, muffled voices from the direction of the control room.

"How about this? It's a section titled 'Transformation effects.'"

"Haven't we already read about that?"

"No, we looked at the timeline. It had a different heading. The only reason I brought this one up is because the first subhead is 'Treatment beginning.'"

That sounded promising. I didn't expect to find anything of immediate use to us, but the scientist in me was clamoring to know more.

"Well, just skimming through here, it says the subject was 'infected.' That's the word it uses. Um, I'm having a hard time with some of this stuff. This might be 'genetic material' or 'gene material.' Whatever it is, the treatment is changing it, according to this."

"Pretty much what I thought," I said. "Alterations that drastic have to be rooted in the DNA. I wonder how they started the changes. What else does it say?"

But he never got a chance to answer my question. Matthews's head poked around the edge of the doorframe.

"Campbell, front and center. You're coming with us. We need the manpower."

Campbell looked at Matthews, then me, then back to his superior. "But what about her?"

"If we're successful, she'll be fine. If we're not, it wouldn't matter if you were sitting up here, would it? Now get to the control room."

He didn't wait for an answer, but Campbell stammered out a weak "aye-aye, sir" to the empty doorway.

He stared at the space where the officer had been for a moment. Then his resolve caught up with him.

"Time to go," he said, patting his rifle as he pulled himself to his feet.

I was being left unprotected while an insane superman prowled the ship's corridors. But I managed to smile and squeeze a joke out of the tension. "Just try to leave it in one piece, OK?"

"No promises. This thing fucked with the wrong platoon." He paused in the doorway. "You'll be safe."

I nodded, and he slipped away.

As his footsteps faded in the hall, I probed my psyche, trying to pin down the feelings stirring within it.

There was fear there, sure. The room now seemed more like a trap than a haven; there was one way out, and the unbroken walls offered no place for a hunted doctor to cower.

Cower? Did I want to cower? The Serpent was like nothing I had encountered before. I made my living bringing secrets into view and un-raveling the stories revealed by the physical evidence. But this thing was obscured from view. The only tools I could bring to bear on it were imagi-nation and speculation.

Still, death was something I understood, had touched and studied. The prospect of experiencing it firsthand did not, I discovered, chill me.

So, fear. Fear of the unknown. I labeled it and placed it in its own men-tal compartment. But I knew it wouldn't stay caged there.

What was this other emotion poking at me? Pulling it into the light of conscious thought, I saw it was curiosity. That made sense. If I didn't know what we were facing, wouldn't I want to find the answer to that question?

It was more than that, though. The doctor in me—the person who made up most of who I was, I realized—wanted to take the Serpent apart and see its physical machinery. Healing a broken bone in less than a day . . . damn! That kind of process could lend itself to study for years. And how did the Korean researchers discover how to augment a person's in-telligence? I knew most of that information was in the file Campbell had been reading to me. But I wanted to roll up my sleeves and dig it out of the Serpent's cells myself.

OK, then, add curiosity to the mix.

Tagging behind it was its distant relative, competitive spirit. That was the best way I could label it. This situation on the *Dragon* was a mystery, and my job was to solve it. And I wanted to know—*had* to know—what had happened onboard the submarine before we got here. The faded, grainy movie was playing on a loop in my head, the blank spots mocking me.

My guesswork sketched in scenes, however, providing a storyboard for the mayhem that had taken place.

Start with a close-up of the biohazard symbol on the refrigerator door. Pull back until we can see the whole thing. Then, with a reptilian hiss, the door cracks open, releasing trickles of water vapor into the sub's dull atmosphere. A hand reaches through the crack. Still shots show a crew-man cowering in fear. An officer barking orders. Sailors rushing to con-front the beast, which tosses them aside like wadded-up pieces of paper. A different officer—Lee—watches his hands tremble as he twists the valves that will send water streaming into the battery compartment. He hopes the desperate move will lay the Serpent low.

But he failed. We knew that, now, beyond a doubt.

Blinking, I hauled myself out of my imagination. Yes, a desire to solve the mystery, to figure out whodunit and why it was done, was pushing me as well.

The last emotion I could sort out from the background of my thoughts was anger. It still tugged at me, cultivating resentment and doubt wherever it could.

I was angry that Larsen had lied to me. He had treated me like a teenager who couldn't see what was good for her. With such a flimsy plan! That was insulting, as well: the idea that he thought he could fool me with his moronic fabrication.

Of course, when he needed something examined, wanted clues gleaned from the crumpled bodies of his men, he had no qualms about bringing me out of my cell. He had reduced my surroundings to one room, had limited my investigation to one long conversation. He was a prick. My resolve to torpedo him in my reports to Patterson and Charlie solidified.

I realized, too, that I was angry about being here at all. There wasn't any rationality behind this fury; I was just upset that I was stuck in an underwater prison surrounded by death, endless questions and a killer. I had a beautiful home and a safe bed, and that was where I belonged now.

The minutiae of everyday life called out from a place deep inside me. I wanted to see early morning sunlight kissing the cherry blossoms in my backyard as I made breakfast. I wanted to lie on my sofa and read a worn paperback with a glass of wine on the brass-trimmed coffee table next to me. I wanted to worry about meeting someone new, about keeping a doctor's appointment, about remembering to call my brother or my mom. Even the lingering ache of a failed relationship was a familiar friend whose company I missed.

I had spent ten years at the CIA, applying as a freshly minted psychiatrist. Two years doing profiling. The rest reconstructing death scenes. In the middle, for about three years–two years, eleven months, eighteen days, I knew the dates and had not been able to forget them–I had dated, lived with and agreed to marry Tom Jenkins, a field agent I met on assignment. Two years ago, on June 11–another date I had failed to erase from my memory–Tom had told me over dinner that we had grown apart. And he left. There was no pretense of trying to remain friends. The few men I dated after that, I was sure, could feel the sliver of distrust wedged inside me.

Fucking hell, why had I become so introspective? I couldn't remember ever immersing myself in my thoughts like this before, trying to find answers within them.

But I knew why. Glancing around the room I was sitting in provided ample explanation. There was no exterior world to focus on, no windows to look out of, no yard to pace in. My universe had been compressed from a place with a sky and a horizon to the interior of a steel tube.

The longer I stayed in it, the greater that compression became. From the entire sub, to the upper deck, to one compartment, to one room, and now to myself. I had reduced the totality of my existence to my own consciousness.

The epistemology of it all was fascinating. I wanted to let myself be swept away by the rumination. But the documents and evidence strewn across the table's glossy surface wouldn't allow me.

I had to focus on the stark, tangible situation that confronted us. A Serpent on the loose needed to be stopped, maybe killed, then studied. A scenario needed to be constructed to explain why twenty-eight Koreans lay dead in the *Dragon*'s belly, with two more sprawled on its upper deck. And the keys to all of it lay here, in front of me, dependent on my ability to fit them together.

I considered closing the door, then decided against it. The contrast between the hallway's uneven, shadowy ambiance and the mess room's brilliance offered the only reminder that there was more to life than just four gray walls.

Pulling all the evidence within arm's reach, I leaned over the table, trying to see the pattern that would make everything clear.

VIII

THE SHOTS MADE me jump.

There were three of them, pop-pop-pop, the sound made muffled and distant by the boat's steel walls. As I sat there, immobile, my senses quivering at attention, they were followed by a long burst of automatic fire.

Then silence.

The shooting didn't just die away—it vanished, leaving no echoes behind. I wanted to hear shouting, yells of victory, but there were none. Was that the hammering of combat boots running along the metal deck?

I waited for someone to walk through the doorway and tell me what had happened. I tried not to let my brain invent horrible, deadly explanations.

But it became too much. Standing, I thrust my head into the hall, first looking forward—nothing—and then aft. Through the hatch to the control room, I could make out feet scuffing about, and I crouched to see more.

The room's aft door still was closed. There was one . . . no, there were two SEALs in the compartment. Both had their rifles unlimbered and were facing the sealed hatch, but they didn't seem panicked. I felt the alarm begin to subside in my chest.

One of the men was Grimm, his nose jutting from his face like a sail. The other was a stockier SEAL with a Mediterranean complexion whom I'd heard referred to as "Chief." He wore braces, and the bridge of his nose was irregular, almost jagged—I couldn't tell whether it was genetic or the result of a fist.

Neither was doing anything different from what SEALs, at least those I had observed, did when they were waiting for something to happen. Or maybe they had been ordered to watch the door and blast whatever came through it.

They didn't even look at each other, just kept staring at the hatch. It didn't seem as if either had seen me.

"Do you think we should . . ." the chief said, but Grimm crushed the rest of his question with one curt word.

"No."

I also had wanted to shush the man. My ears were the only way I could tell whether we were the victors or just the remaining victims.

A hatch clanged. Both SEALs flinched, but neither repositioned himself or lowered his weapon. I could see Grimm adjusting his grip on his rifle.

The sound hadn't come from the hatch to the control room, however. Its locking mechanism remained stationary.

More noise was audible now. Men's voices, yelling, their words indistinct. The shouts were tumultuous, full of urgency and growing louder.

Then the wheel on the hatch began to turn, and the two soldiers took a step back. As they moved, they brought their rifles up to their faces, the short barrels pointing like deadly appendages toward the doorway.

The wheel stopped. So did the commotion on the other side.

"Stand down. It's Larsen," a voice shouted through the door's thick steel.

"You're covered," Grimm yelled back.

He and the chief lowered their weapons, but even from my vantage point, I could see that their knuckles were white. If something threatening thrust itself through the doorway, they wouldn't waste much time bringing the rifles to bear on it.

As the hatch swung open, Larsen came into view, and my heart accelerated again. His face was flushed, sweaty and freckled with blood. He stepped into the control room, then turned toward the door.

"OK, pass him through."

"No, I'm fine!" came a voice from the other side. Vazquez hooked his left arm through, shrugging off a hand on his opposite shoulder. "I can fucking walk. I got all the way up here, didn't I?" He ducked and worked his way through, only allowing Larsen to offer an occasional steadying hand.

When Vazquez stood, my breath caught in my throat. His right arm was soaked in crimson from elbow to wrist. He let it dangle, keeping pressure on the forearm with his other hand. His childlike appearance was gone.

I left the doorway to the officers' mess and moved down the hallway, listening to more SEALs pile into the compartment. But when I crouched at the doorway it all stopped.

They turned toward me, guns raised, except for Vazquez, who stood behind them, panting. I froze, unable even to beg for mercy. The barrels of their rifles seemed to be the unblinking eyes of Death himself, and I couldn't look away.

Larsen broke the spell.

"Hold your fire. It's the doctor."

As a unit, they relaxed. A couple slung their weapons on their backs and tended to Vazquez. The rest began to talk all at once. The SEAL leader caught my eye and beckoned me into the compartment.

"Two more dead," he said after I had worked my way through his men.

"Did you get the Serpent?"

"No. Dammit. Vazquez got off a few rounds at him, but there's no body. Nothing."

I glanced at Vazquez. The men who were aiding him were trying to persuade him to sit down on the nav table.

"Let me look at him," I said, taking a step toward them. "We need to get that bleeding under control."

But Vazquez straightened up and half-turned away from me.

"No! I don't need a doctor. This . . . this is nothing. It's not deep, didn't hit any arteries."

The vehemence in his tone stopped me. Jakes, the SEAL who had been manning the forward torpedo room, gestured at me with a half-open medical kit. His watch cap was askew, revealing a close-cut afro.

"It looked a lot worse when we found him, but he's right, it's not deep. Just long. I'll slap a bandage on it, and he'll be in good shape." Jakes pulled a gauze pad from the kit and unfolded it.

I was doubtful. Spatters of blood dotted the floor where it had dripped from Vazquez's fingers. But his face wasn't ashen, and he didn't seem to be in shock.

Larsen tapped me on the shoulder. "The Serpent got him."

And you want me to tell you how he did it, I thought as I turned back to him. Great. Once again, I was welcome in Larsen's operation.

"We sent one team of three men forward of the engine room on the lower deck and another team aft. Campbell was stationed in the engine room, covering the flanks of both teams.

"Campbell, get over here," he said, then continued talking to me. "When Vazquez shouted, he was the first to respond, so he saw . . . well, he can tell you."

Campbell now stood next to us. He also was flushed, and although his rifle was held in an at-ease posture across his chest, I could see his index finger flexing on the trigger guard.

"Tell her what you saw, Warrant Officer Campbell. And start from the beginning, because I don't know the whole story, either."

The SEAL had been staring at nothing, but Larsen's voice got his attention, and Campbell addressed the platoon leader in a crisp, official manner.

"Sir, I was holding position on the upper deck of the engine room. I could see Fire Team Bravo through the aft hatch, five-by-five. The area below me was clear after Fire Team Alpha headed forward on the lower deck. Then I heard a clatter and . . . and a yell. It was Tracy, I knew it was him, you know, because he's got that hick accent, and he yelled something like, 'What the hell?'" His demeanor was becoming more conversational. "So I yelled for Bravo to back me up, climbed down and ran into the aft battery bay. Well, there was no one there. That was where Vazquez was supposed to be. So I knew something was wrong. Then I hear, like, a struggle further forward. And a couple of seconds later, three shots."

He paused, his eyes unfocusing again.

"You're doing fine, Campbell," Larsen said. It took all my willpower to hide my surprise at the grandfatherly note in his voice. But his face was still and cold.

"Right. Thank you, sir." The SEAL pulled himself back into the story. "So I've got my rifle up, and I say, 'Vazquez! Tracy!' And right when I say that, Vazquez goes flying by the hatch to the galley. I mean, flying. He was horizontal, like he had been shot out of a fucking howitzer. I hear him hit something and land. And then he starts shooting.

"So I advance toward the doorway. I'm ready to shoot. If this thing so much as sticks a toenail into my view, it's getting blown off. But right before I get to the doorway, the shooting stops. And I hear Vazquez yell, 'Get him! Fucking get him!'

"I crouch and look into the galley. Nothing in there. I mean, nothing moving. Mac's body was lying to my right. I could see his feet, and I knew he was dead. I can't explain it. Just the way they were lying, it wasn't natural."

I was lost in Campbell's recollections. The slain SEAL was clear in my mind, the sound of gunfire reverberating in my ears.

"I couldn't see Tracy yet. But I moved sideways a little, and I could see Vazquez lying there. He had impacted the stove area. There was a dent. But he was sitting up, fucking with his rifle, trying to get another magazine in there one handed. His right arm looked like a mess. All I could see was blood.

"'Where'd he go? Where's the Serpent?' I'm yelling at him. He looks up, and he's like, 'It's gone.' Behind me I hear Bravo. It's Chacho talking to me, I know it's him, because he's asking, 'What's going on, who started shooting?' So I felt it was safe to advance."

He looked at Larsen, questioning, unsure.

"You had backup. You had a platoon member in danger. You did the right thing," Larsen said. I couldn't tell whether he meant it. But I sensed that, sincere or not, such a reassurance was the only way to get Campbell to continue.

"That's what I thought, sir," the warrant officer replied. "I entered the room. Vazquez was facing me, so I immediately scanned the area behind him from where I was standing. It was clear of threats. Then I turned around, and that's when I saw Tracy.

"Paul . . . Jesus, man, Paul," he said, his voice wavering. But he kept going. "I saw his eyes blink. He was still there. He was still with me for a second. But there was too much blood. There was nothing I could do. The gash was huge! All the way across his throat! It was like someone had tried to saw his fucking head off . . . there's no way anyone could have survived that."

The last sentence was directed at me. As Larsen had, I nodded, trying to encourage him. If Campbell's assessment of the wound were right, it was true: there wasn't much chance of repairing such damage here on the sub, let alone replacing the lost blood.

"MacDonald was lying next to him, a little more toward the doorway. That's how I saw his feet. He was face-down . . . I mean, he was on his stomach. I could see his face because his head had been twisted around. Not as bad as Martin," he said, looking at me again, "but it was pretty obviously broken. His eyes were open, and they were pointing in two different directions."

"What about the Serpent?" Larsen said after a moment.

"No sign of it. Nothing moving. I didn't hear anything running away, anything like that. The bunk area—you know where I'm talking about? Across from the crew's mess? It was all shot up at the aft end."

"That's where he was standing."

I jumped. Vazquez had come up behind me as we listened to Campbell.

"How's your arm, Seaman?" Larsen asked him.

"It'll be fine, sir. Just a scratch. Look," he said, waving his injured limb around and wiggling his fingers. I winced, but he seemed unbothered by the movements. "Put me on point when we go out again to kill that bastard."

"We'll see about that," Larsen said. "Now, Campbell's told us what he saw. What about you? What happened down there?"

"I was covering Petty Officers MacDonald and Tracy as they passed through the aft battery bay. After they were clear of that compartment, I maintained station, both to provide security and to ensure that the target did not exit the galley area, if it was in there." Vazquez didn't seem as consumed by his memories as Campbell had been. He had adopted the tone of an official report, signed and in triplicate. "Approximately ten seconds after entering the galley compartment, MacDonald looks to his right—starboard—and says, 'What's that?'

"He did not appear nervous or afraid. Just curious. Both he and Tracy walked to starboard, outside of the area I could view through the open hatch. A few seconds later, Tracy yells, 'Hey! What the hell?' roughly simultaneous to a clattering sound, as Campbell mentioned.

"At this point, I was moving forward cautiously, trying to provide backup without giving away my position."

He stopped and looked at Larsen. But he wasn't after kind words. Vazquez had the air of a man who knew he had made the right moves and wanted his boss to know it. Without waiting for an audible response, he resumed speaking.

"Sounds of a struggle continued, and then I heard a sort of gurgling noise and a thud. At that point, I charged through the doorway.

"Tracy was on the ground." He looked at Campbell, reached out and squeezed his shoulder. "You're absolutely right, man. There's nothing anyone could have done for him. The asshole had slit Tracy's throat open with his own combat knife. Tracy was trying to hold his throat with his hands, but it was clear he was losing strength quickly. His chest and the floor around him were covered in blood.

"In front of him, facing toward me, was the Serpent. He . . . it . . . was engaged hand-to-hand with MacDonald. There was no way I could get a shot, so I moved in to use my knife."

"Wait, hold on a second," Larsen said, gesturing for Vazquez to stop. "You saw the Serpent? It was right there in front of you?"

"Yes, sir. It was about six and a half feet tall. Clearly Asian. It had those slanty eyes and darkish skin. The thing was freakishly big, sir, musclewise. Its shirt had ripped, like the Incredible Hulk. We're talking immense knots of muscle on its arms and chest."

"So it was wearing clothes?" I asked. "Was it the remains of a Korean naval uniform?"

"I don't know about that, ma'am. It could have been. Looked like dark pants, maybe, and a similar-colored shirt. But as I said, it was all in tatters."

"That's really a pretty secondary point for us to discuss, don't you think?" Larsen said. "Vazquez, let's hear the rest of it."

"Aye-aye, sir. As I said, it was fighting with MacDonald. But the action was pretty one-sided. MacDonald had brought his weapon to bear on the Serpent, but it had, one handed, reached out and wrenched the barrel to the side."

"Bent it?" Campbell said. "Holy fuck."

"No, just changed his aim. Pushed it away. At that point, MacDonald fired three times. Not a burst, but singly triggered rounds. Its other hand was on his face, you see, and it was slowly twisting his head to the left. MacDonald's left. And right after he fired, it just put a little more effort into the twisting and MacDonald's head snapped all the way around, it seemed like.

"MacDonald dropped, and the thing's eyes focused on me. The pupils were huge . . . I couldn't see any whites. It was like staring into the bottom of an oil well. I lunged at it, planning to strike it with my knife.

"But it just moved so incredibly fast. You have no idea. I got my hand to the hilt, but that's it. Its hand had almost beaten mine there. And with its left, it swung at me with Tracy's knife."

"I thought it had grabbed Mac's rifle," Campbell interjected.

"It had . . . with three fingers. It was still holding onto the knife when it did that, and when it killed Mac, it let go of the rifle barrel. So it attacked me, so fast I didn't even know it was happening, really, but I guess I had anticipated it, because I had brought my arm up to shield my face. So it cut me, but it's better than opening my jugular.

"And then—this was probably dumb, but it was instinct—I moved in closer, to try to avoid giving it another chance to swing with the knife. It didn't fight me, just dropped the knife, grabbed my shoulders and threw me across the room."

"I saw that," Campbell said. "Jesus Christ, you were moving fast."

"No one knows that better than I do," Vazquez said. "I slammed into the galley's stove, not head-first, thank God. Saw a few stars. But I could see the Serpent stand there for a second, then take a step toward me."

"And you opened up," Larsen said.

"I unloaded on that cocksucker. But . . . but . . . you just don't understand how it moves. It's so fluid. Fast, like a water snake. I was shooting at it, tracking it with my weapon, but it just accelerated across the room, bounding, ducking, sliding. And then I had burned the whole clip.

"I tried to watch it; it seemed wary for a moment, and I thought that would give me time to reload. But I couldn't–dammit, sir, I couldn't get the magazine in without looking. It was because of my fucking arm. All that blood. So I take my eyes off this thing and try to load a new clip. I knew Campbell had to be coming soon, so I yell, 'Get it! Fucking get it!' or something to that effect.

"I didn't even see Campbell come to the doorway . . . I just looked up and there he was. He starts screaming at me, wanting to know where the Serpent was, but it was gone. It was fucking gone. I *had* it sir. I *had* it, and I let it get away." Vazquez balled his left hand into a fist and whacked himself on the side of the head with it. He no longer seemed childlike. His dark complexion was flushed, veins popping out on his neck.

"Whoa, easy," Larsen said, grabbing his arm. Vazquez twisted away, staring at the floor. "You did everything you could do. You played it right; this thing is just superhuman."

"Yeah, I guess," the SEAL replied. "But I should have nailed it. Less than twenty feet away . . . full auto . . . and I didn't hit anything."

"But you survived, and your actions probably saved some more lives. Now we know what this thing looks like, what it can do. And that'll help us kill it."

"And I want in on that mission, sir. This thing owes us some blood," Vazquez said, looking up at Larsen, then me, his brown eyes glittering. I felt my insides recoil at the intensity behind them, as if his gaze had groped at some deep, personal part of me.

"We'll make it pay, Seaman, don't worry." Larsen turned his attention to me, and his next words were not surprising in the least. "So what do you think of all this, Doctor?"

"Well, you were with Fire Team Bravo, right?" I said. Campbell wandered over to an empty workstation and sat down. Vazquez returned to the nav table, picking at the bandage on his arm.

"Yeah. I was on point." Larsen tugged at his ear as he spoke. I could see dense musculature rippling under his close-fitting black sweater. Even when he was trying to calm down he looked deadly.

"So what did you see when you arrived in the galley?"

"Exactly what both of them described. To the right of the hatch, two bodies: MacDonald and Tracy. To the left, Vazquez, sitting against the back of the stove. Campbell was down on the floor next to him, trying to make sure he was OK. Reyes had walked a little farther into the room and was covering the forward part."

"Wait, Reyes? Who's Reyes?"

"Seaman Dom Reyes. They call him 'Muchacho,' or 'Chacho' for short."

I remembered the name now. "Go on."

"He was covering the forward area. Ridder, the other man in Bravo, was standing behind him and to his right, covering the starboard bulkhead where the bunks were."

"And there was no sign of the Serpent."

"Besides the two dead men and a third covered in blood? No, no sign at all."

"Come on, Larsen."

"We didn't see it, OK? It might as well have turned into a bat and flown away."

"Everyone was in the galley compartment?"

"That's affirmative."

"Did anyone shut the aft hatch after you came in?"

"What are you getting at?"

I held my hands up in a warding-off gesture, preparing for the anger I expected. "Well, if you didn't close the door, the Serpent could have gotten past you and your men and into a different part of the sub."

"Shit." There was no anger in his voice, just disgust. "You're right. We could have trapped it in there. But even with the doors open, there's no way it could have slipped through. Not with four people looking for it."

"It would seem that way," I said. "But from everything Vazquez has told us—and he's the only one who's seen this thing and survived—it's not subject to normal rules of movement and visibility. I can't think of a logical way it could have run by you. Our situation seems to be getting less and less logical with each passing minute, though, doesn't it?"

"You got that right," Larsen spat.

"How about afterward? Did you guys close the hatches behind you when you came back up here?"

"Pigfucker!" His yell made a couple of the men in the compartment turn around, but he ignored them. "We were too busy trying to stay tactical, and Vazquez was hit. It seemed a lot worse then. So, basically, no. Except for the aft hatch of the electrical control room, all the doors still are wide open."

"More ground to cover."

"Yeah, no shit. We'll get it next time, though. The tactics were sound; if Tracy and Mac had been more careful or if Vazquez had gotten a lucky shot, we wouldn't be having this conversation." I sensed a little revisionist history in his comments. It was almost as though he were figuring out how to word a report about what had gone wrong.

"May I offer a suggestion?" I asked.

"Can't hurt."

"Don't go after it again. Sit tight in the control compartments. Wait until we get to shore, and then you can send in a wave of shock troops. Or shore personnel can just flood the whole thing with nerve gas. There's no reason to risk any more of your men."

He was shaking his head, sighing.

"That's not an option. Believe me, if I thought we could take care of this thing without putting my men in harm's way—especially given what we know now about what this thing is capable of—I'd do whatever it took. Unfortunately," he said, jerking a thumb aft, "if the Serpent wants to kill us all, it can do so. Just start a fire in the fuel area. Or if it's not feeling suicidal, it can get into the electric motors and pour water on them or something. And then we'll be back to square one, because we'll have to get back into the engine room to start up the diesels."

"So you can't let it go."

"No. It's got to be stopped, killed, or at least contained in a compartment where it can't threaten us or our mission."

I looked around the control room. The SEALs seemed restless. Vengeance was in every eye, every clenched jaw. Vazquez's face remained fixed in a predatory stare that radiated across the room at me.

"What about the *Rickover*? All this gunfire, they've got to be thinking about sending–"

"They aren't. They're not going to interfere unless someone tries to sink us, and there's no way for them to board this piece of shit without us surfacing anyway."

"Well . . . how far are we from shore?" I asked, turning to Larsen.

"Not as close as either of us would like. Chief!" Larsen called across the compartment. The SEAL directing the helmsman strode over to us, stuffing his cap into his back pocket. His head was shaved and shimmered with perspiration.

"Yes, sir?" the man said. His brown eyes regarded me for the barest instant before coming to rest on his superior.

"How much progress have we made? When can we expect to put in?"

He half-laughed. It was the sound of utter cynicism. "We're making six knots, and that's being generous. When we were running the diesels, we were making about eleven. Seven on just the one. Add it all up, and–the last time we checked the chart, anyway–we were seventeen nautical miles from port."

His scenario was a little better than the one Campbell had outlined.

"Three hours," Larsen said to neither of us.

"That's right, sir. About that long. We crank up the amps, we can cut that in half. But we'll run out of juice before we get there."

"No more estimations, Chief. Sit down with Reyes and figure out the top speed we can make to reach port as quickly as possible. No margin of error. No safety net. I want to exhaust the batteries when we pull into our slip. Clear?"

"Yes, sir. Reyes! Come over here," the chief said, scooting around me and gesturing Vazquez off the nav table.

Larsen's intense gaze seemed lost someplace outside the control room.

"Lieutenant Larsen?" I said. He faced me, but he still was looking through me, searching, I guessed, for some plan to preserve us. Then he blinked.

"Yes, what?"

"Is there any way we can send for help?"

The idea was now attractive to him at some level. I could see the novelty of it register in his face. But then he shook his head.

"No. Not a chance. I told you before, it would compromise our secrecy."

"But if—"

"But if secrecy weren't our goal, Myers, we'd just tow this scow back to port, and we wouldn't be onboard and, let's see," he said as he counted the names on his hand, "Young, Henderson, Wilkes, Miller, Martin, Tracy and MacDonald wouldn't be dead."

"That's a big sacrifice," I said, not looking away.

"No shit." But there was no regret in his voice. "Sometimes, though, we don't get to do things the easy way. Obviously there's something important on this sub, and I think you'll agree with me when I say that the rest of the world does not—repeat, does not—need to know about it."

"Are there any circumstances in which you'd compromise the element of secrecy?"

He didn't say anything, waiting for an explanation for my question before he answered it.

"Because what if it's just me, I'm the only one left?" I continued. "Or what if we're in danger of losing the sub, not to our enemies' spy satellites, but to the Serpent itself? If it kills us all, we're dead and Patterson doesn't get his intel."

"If the *Dragon* is in danger of falling out of our control, I'll think about using the UQC," he said. "But it's not going to happen. Now, I hate to cut this conversation short, but I have to go lead my men."

And I was an outsider again. At least he hadn't told me to get out of the control room.

As I looked around, however, I saw how unreasonable such an order would be—not that he would hesitate to give it anyway. There were six men in the room now. That left three elsewhere; I assumed they were in the electrical compartment, to which the hatch now was closed.

Seven people in here, including one unarmed civilian. Larsen and Matthews were conferring near the steering controls. The chief was seated at the nav table with the smaller of the two men I first had encountered amid the corpses in the galley. He chewed on his lip as he scribbled on a piece of paper. Hispanic features, tattoo of a fist on the right side of his neck. That would be Reyes, then. Another man was operating the helm. Campbell was still at an unused workstation, staring at nothing.

The moment when I met Larsen and the other SEALs now seemed distant, as much a part of an alternate reality as my home back on land.

What about the Serpent? We had seen it face-to-face now and had some kind of a report on its capabilities.

My question about its clothes, however, hadn't been as meaningless as Larsen had thought. I couldn't figure out why its shirt was ripped and tattered, as Vazquez had described it. First of all, why would it be wearing any clothes at all? Did the technicians who packed it into the refrigerator have an overreaching sense of modesty?

Second, even if it had been wearing clothes, why were they ripped? It had already undergone its physical transformation, so wouldn't it be dressed in items that fit it?

One explanation kept hammering at me, demanding to be let to the forefront. I told myself I didn't want to give it precedence because there still were other avenues to consider. But there was a much stronger, much more human reason for trying to avoid it. Fear.

Because if this "improved human" were indeed still improving to the point where it was growing out of its clothes, we all had a lot to be afraid of. Every moment we waited, it was getting stronger and, I had to assume, smarter. So maybe Larsen was right in wanting to launch another search-and-destroy mission as soon as possible. He just didn't realize the depths of his wisdom.

I crossed to the other side of the compartment. No one I passed looked at me. Neither did Campbell, who was at the workstation next to the one

I sat down in, running his fingertips over the blued finish of his rifle.

All the SEALs were focused. And that was good. I just doubted they were thinking about the situation from every possible angle. It was a skill I had learned not in the classrooms of Georgetown, but at the countless crime scenes I had stepped into since then.

If you succumb to tunnel vision, you lose. Period.

In a fetid Guatemalan hallway overlooking a village square, I had seen mortal evidence of that mistake. I remembered the sun scalding my eyes as I walked from my jeep, accompanied by three Army Rangers and a local officer. Four American-trained counter-insurgency troopers—sent to the village for some noble purpose, their commander had assured me through a flinty-eyed interpreter—lay dead, head to toe. Their assault rifles had full magazines. None had struggled with his attacker. Blood soaked into the floorboards from four slit throats, the air thick and wet with its coppery smell. A single set of red footprints led away from the corpses.

It had seemed an impossible crime; four men with automatic weapons overcome by one with a boot knife. But as I waited in the tiny, patchwork airport for my flight back to civilization, puzzling through what I had seen in the village, I remembered a flier posted on an adobe wall near the square. "Desfile el sabado." Parade Saturday. The day the soldiers' bodies had been found. I could feel a connection.

A few phone calls filled in the rest. The parade's purpose was to celebrate the opening of the district's new, communal deep well. Its champion was the village's mayor, noted for his socialist leanings. The parade would culminate with a speech in the square.

My job was to explain it all, and I did. I had felt satisfaction and disgust as I delivered my report to Charlie, who would pass it on to some Special Forces commander in South America, who would use it to help future assassins avoid the same fate. The case, more than most of the others I had worked on, had almost overwhelmed my love for my work and its challenges. I typed up a resignation letter and for nearly a month debated handing it to Charlie. But I didn't.

What I told him: The four soldiers had been moving into position to either shoot the mayor or just ignite panic by firing into the crowd. As they moved through the hallway, intent on murder, someone had slipped in behind them. He killed the man at the rear of the column, and the three in front had been too confident, too fixated on their task and target—"hunter's hard-on," fighter pilots call it—to notice as the body was lowered to the floor in silence. And they had died the same way, one by one, oblivious, their life spraying out into the afternoon as cheers outside concealed the sound of their last gurgling breaths.

What were the SEALs fixating on? Victory. That was clear in their posture, their attitude toward ass-kicking. Larsen also wasn't allowing himself to get too distracted by the specifics of each fatality. In his view, that was my job, to pore over the reports he let me hear and tell him what had gone wrong. But even that was starting to fade. He wanted to know what the Serpent was and where it was, not how it had done what it did.

That was a mistake. Know your enemy—who had said that? It was applicable here. No other parameter was changing. Not the battlefield, not the conditions, not the combatants, unless you counted our dwindling numbers as a change. So to ensure victory, we needed to know more about the one unknown: the Serpent itself.

The thing that was most troubling about it was its brain. If the person the Korean scientists had used as a subject was at least of average intelligence, we were up against a genius now, a murderous Stephen Hawking. If it wanted us dead, the Serpent could find a way to make it happen.

So it was acting according to some plan. Was there a pattern? It had killed two engine-room crews. So it wanted the sub to stop, to lose power. Or maybe it was just working its way toward the control room. It wanted to take over the sub—that much made sense.

No one on the outside was expecting communications from us. If the *Dragon* changed course, maybe got within a mile or so of shore and then stopped, no one would investigate until it was too late. The Serpent would have made it to land by the time another boarding party arrived. I had no illusions that it was incapable of swimming that far.

Stop it, Christine, I told myself. I was making a trap of assumptions, creating walls that could keep the truth from being seen. This thing was insane, right? Hadn't the report said that? Basing my model of the Serpent on rational motives was like trying to build a skyscraper out of gelatin.

Even serial killers, however, had motives, reasons for their behavior. The rationality in those reasons lay in the heads of those who were driven by them. We on the outside could only look for patterns—that all-important word again—and try to divine what twisted mechanism was at work.

The control room was filled with the ebb and flow of low-voiced conversation. Campbell still sat next to me, offering no sign that he realized anyone but himself was in the compartment.

"Hey," I said.

Nothing.

"Hey, Campbell," I repeated.

He turned his head toward me, his fingers still scurrying around the surface of his rifle, stopping here and there to tighten a fixture or check a switch position. The dullness that enveloped his face took my breath away.

"What?" The word matched his expression.

"What's the UQC?" I said, trying to ignore the vacuum of emotion in front of me.

"It's the underwater telephone." He jerked his head up and to his right, to the aft of the compartment. "You can use it to talk to other subs." Then his head dipped again, concentrating on his weapon.

I looked in the direction he had indicated. Maybe that was it: what looked like a telephone handset buried in the readouts and pipes over the sonar station. At least I thought it was the sonar station.

Well, that was good to know. Assuming I was able to figure out how to operate it, I could use the device to call for help if the Serpent ate the rest of the SEALs. For some reason, the image made me giggle. I waited for one of them to turn around and glare at me, but it didn't happen.

What I most needed, I thought, was to get Campbell poring over the Serpent's documentation. As if it were an appliance or something that we just had to read the instructions for to figure out. But I was certain there was more useful information in those documents. The bulk of it would be academic, no doubt, of interest to scientists and our own country's weapons researchers, but there had to be more on the thing's capabilities. Its tendencies, perhaps. A weakness.

Reyes and the chief were standing, reading a piece of paper Reyes held between them. Reyes looked at the other SEAL and nodded, scratching the back of his buzzcut. They both moved to where Larsen and Matthews still were submerged in planning.

When the chief spoke, it broke through the hushed mood. This wasn't a scheming, hypothetical murmur. It was clear, loud and factual.

"Sir."

Larsen and Matthews both stopped talking and turned. Matthews remained leaning against the wall, hunched as always.

"We've finished looking over the nav and battery data. And there's some good news."

"Finally," Reyes interjected, but none of them paid attention.

"If we allow no margin for error, we can increase our speed to 7.5 knots. More good news: the tide will be working with us, so we'll make even more headway. Call it 8 knots—but that's just an estimation."

"Good thinking on the tide, Chief," Matthews said.

"Reyes's idea," the chief said, cocking a thumb at the other SEAL, who shrugged and smiled. "We're 16.6 nautical miles from port."

"Two hours." Larsen was the one jumping in this time.

"Two hours, four minutes and thirty seconds, actually," the chief said, looking at the calculations on the sheet he was holding. "Assuming we won't be doing any evading, accelerating or major course changes, that's how long it'll take us. If we're not there yet, we'll have to fire up the diesels again. Or the one that works, anyway."

Larsen was nodding to himself, digesting the numbers. Then he spoke in his command voice, each syllable crisp and important.

"Chief, give the order. Adjust throttle for seven and a half knots. Ridder, steady as she goes."

The SEAL at the steering workstation replied without looking away from his gauges. "Aye-aye, sir."

"Aye-aye, sir," the chief said, then hit the intercom button. "Electrical, conn. Make turns for seven and a half knots."

After a moment: "Conn, electrical. Say again, seven and a half?"

"That's right. Don't go over that speed."

"Aye-aye, sir," came the crackling reply. And a few seconds later, we felt the infinitesimal surge of acceleration.

"The clock's running out on this motherfucker," Larsen said. I couldn't tell whether he was referring to the Serpent or our situation in general. Campbell stood up next to me.

"Are we gonna go get this thing? I want a shot at it." The resolve in his words was such a contrast to the expression I had seen on his face moments before. Even his posture seemed more aggressive.

"Don't worry, Campbell," Larsen said. "It'll be sucking your rifle before this day is over. We have a plan, by God, and our enemy is not going to get away from this platoon."

"What's the plan?" I asked. I knew my question was unwelcome, but, as ten percent of the surviving force, I had a right to know.

"Well, Dr. Myers, I thought I'd wait and tell my men first. Is that OK with you? Or do you have some new, vital piece of evidence that can help us?" He wanted the second question to be as sarcastic as the first. But I could hear the need buried in it.

"It's your ship," I said.

"You're goddamn right it is. Lieutenant, go brief the electrical department." As Matthews walked away, Larsen continued to the four SEALs gathered around him: "We are going to contain this thing like a trapped animal. We don't know how it thinks. But it doesn't know how we think, either. It knows less about us than we do about it. And that's our advantage."

He was right, I thought. But I was surprised about where he took that conclusion.

"There will be two three-man teams—Charlie and Delta. One will be assigned to the two compartments aft of the engine room and the other to the three lower deck compartments. Another man will be stationed in the engine room once it is secured. The hatches to the engine room will be closed behind each team, and of course the hatch between the forward battery bay and the torpedo room is chained shut.

"The key here is containment. No matter which section the Serpent is in, it cannot leave. The only people that will be able to pass through those hatches without being killed are SEALs. We will utilize code phrases to make sure this is what happens.

"When the fire teams wish to re-enter the engine room or either of the control rooms, which they will do only after either eliminating the Serpent or establishing that their sector is clear, they will shout a phrase through the door. For this operation, the phrase is . . ." He paused, looking at a scrap of paper in his hand. "The phrase is: 'Who's in the Super Bowl?' The correct response—the *only* correct response—is 'The Bengals.' And the only correct response to that is 'They're going all the way.'"

I had a hard time believing any of the soldiers could say that without laughing, but they all nodded, solemn.

"What if the Serpent is in the engine room?" I asked, again drawing a poisonous look from Larsen.

"It won't be in the engine room because that's the first place we'll examine, and we'll be doing it with both teams, so I don't think it's going to slip through. Do you approve?"

He didn't care what I said, and I didn't answer. But I understood why he was so confident of the plan's success.

At the worst, three men would die. But if that happened, it would give away the location of the Serpent, telling us which section it was in. The hatches would be closed behind each team of SEALs, so if their quarry tried to get out without knowing the code phrase, it would be shot up when it was vulnerable, climbing through the hatchway.

At best, of course, one of the teams would locate and kill the Serpent. No matter what happened, the Serpent would be discovered and contained. Larsen wasn't going to make the same mistake twice.

The tactics involved were sound and logical, at least to my inexpert mind. But in my gut, I felt only that we would see more blood spilled in the *Dragon*. Whose blood it was became clear soon enough.

IX

THEY LEFT ME ALONE in the control compartment with the helmsman. His name was Ridder, Seaman Charles Ridder. "Call me Chuck," he said.

Chuck seemed undisturbed by the events we had witnessed so far, and those that were unfolding now weren't his job. His job was to steer the sub and keep it on course. With his eyes always locked on the indicators in front of him, he at least gave the appearance of working hard to do so.

I addressed the back of his head, which still was clad in a stocking cap.

"How long do you think they'll be gone?" I felt tiny and vulnerable just sitting there waiting for something to happen.

"Who knows?" He rotated his head a few degrees toward me as he spoke, revealing dark, sleepy eyes set in a pale face. One front tooth capped, old burn scars evident on neck. He was short, about my height, and his hands seemed delicate and graceful on the ship's wheel, like a pianist's. "I guess the faster they get back here, the better their trip went. Right?"

It was rhetorical. He already had returned his mental energies to the task of keeping us on an even keel.

I wanted to ask him another question. I *needed* to ask him another question. There was no more work to do now, nothing to occupy me while I waited for some resolution to this bizarre conflict I had descended into.

"So, you're not worried, Chuck?"

This time he spoke to the control panel.

"Worried? About what? There's no place to go. Nothing to do but wait to see if I get a chance to shoot anything."

It might have been stoicism, but it sounded more like boredom. Before I could come up with another half-assed comment, he continued.

"Lieutenant Larsen knows what he's doing. Doesn't really matter whether they get the Serpent or not. If they don't get it and it tries to get in here, I blast it. Ain't but one way for it to get into this compartment. And right here is the only place you can run the boat from. We're in control. Safest place in the world."

Except anyplace else, I thought. Anyplace but a second-hand submarine filled with bloodthirsty soldiers and their predatory prey.

"Larsen said the boat could be sabotaged from outside the control room. That's why they're out there hunting it."

"Yeah, it could stop us from moving. But all the diving controls are right here. We want to surface, we can surface. Not a damn thing it can do 'bout that."

"What about the fuel tanks? It could start a fire."

He shook his head. "Why would it do that? The sub sinks, the Serpent dies."

More silence. I imagined I could hear—or feel—footsteps reverberating from other parts of the sub. But nothing concrete, nothing to tell me whether I had more or less to be afraid of.

My professional attitude had all but eroded. Shreds of it still lay draped across my consciousness. But the small part of me that could view the situation as a detached observer said I was less a doctor and investigator than an unwilling participant in a nightmare. That was eating at me. I could do nothing to influence my plight, not even make intelligent conversation with Chuck the sub driver.

"Do you know how to operate everything in here?"

"Well enough to do my job. I keep the boat straight and level, check the chart to make sure we're not drifting."

"Yeah, but what about the other stuff? The diving controls, for instance— if it came down to it, would you know what you were doing?"

"Why does that matter? I could get us surfaced or submerged, probably. The sonar might be a little hard. I could work the periscope. We all basically know how to work every station on the sub. Why—do you wanna launch a few torpedoes at some cargo ships?" He followed the witticism with a bray of laughter.

"You and I might wind up being the only ones left on this boat," I said. Just trying to be rational. Just trying to evaluate all the options and possibilities. "Say we are. Could you get us to the surface safely? Call for help? Do you know how to operate the . . ." What was it called? " . . . the UQC?"

"I told you I could surface the boat. And the Gertrude is simple, like working a telephone. Just relax, OK?" Now his voice had a little emotion—annoyance. He chortled as another idea hit him. "Besides, if you and I are the last ones left, I'm sure we can find something more fun to do."

Stepping away, I pretended to examine something on the deck. Not that he was watching me. But I had felt a shiver of apprehension at a clumsy come-on I should have ignored or ridiculed. You're too wound up, I told myself.

I had to be more clear-headed and calculating. You're not trying to solve a crime, I thought, you're trying to prevent one: your own murder.

Because that's what it was about now, right? Survival. Of the SEALs, sure, but it was becoming a lot easier to consider ways to get only myself out of the sub in one functioning piece. The SEALs could take care of themselves—they thought so, anyway, and had the military hardware to give themselves a better chance. All I had was a rubber band.

What I needed was a gun.

Chuck's rifle was on the floor next to him. I doubted he'd let me borrow it while he drove. Maybe his knife? Would he give that up?

Wait, no: I didn't have to beg for cutlery. There was another firearm, one that no one would mind if I borrowed. The Tokarev.

Chuck saw me move toward the forward door.

"Hey, where you going?" No surprise or alarm. What trouble could I get into, anyway, petite little girl that I was?

I contemplated lying. But why? Was there some reason I'd had this surge of distrust?

"I'm going to get a gun," I said, watching his reaction. For a moment, he didn't have one. Then a nod.

"Yeah, good idea. The more firepower the better." Again without pulling his eyes from his work.

But before I could duck through the hatch, a sound interrupted the control room's tranquility. I might have imagined it; the noise was fleeting and hushed. A glance at Ridder, however, told me my instincts were correct. It was a faraway gunshot.

Then another noise jumped into the still air around us. It was a soft whirring, like the breeze blowing across my ears.

After a moment, I figured out what it was. The intercom had switched on.

No one was speaking. But I could hear something in the background. Heavy, labored breathing, like a draft animal. And some scuffling, indistinct activity.

There was a moan, again in the background, but clear, identifiable and human. A hatch clanged open.

"What . . . Hello? Sir?" It was Vazquez. Despite the electronic distortion, he sounded drugged, or as if he had just awakened from a deep dream. "Where are you? Where are y–"

The word was cut off. And then he screamed.

The sound pierced my guts like an ice pick. I had never heard so much pain. There was fear, too, but the pain rose to the top like an oil slick, obscuring everything beneath. Somehow every raw vibration of Vazquez's throat was evident to us there in the control room.

There was no modulation, no change in pitch. Just a long, hoarse cry that continued, continued, continued until it disappeared over a cliff. I heard a deep, ragged intake of breath and expected to be assaulted with another wave of anguish. But instead, Vazquez spoke. Pleaded.

"No. No, you don't have–AGH!" He yelled, a high yelp that again was laden with undeniable agony. It was accompanied by a sharp crack. "Oh, God. Oh, God. Campbell, help me! Someone. Someone–AGH!" Another crack.

I sensed Ridder leaving his post and walking toward the speaker box, mesmerized.

"No. No! Please! No! Just kill me. Please. Just kill me. Justkillmejustkill mejustkillmeno! NO! NO! NOOOOOOO!" And Vazquez's voice disappeared, cut off by another clang.

A new noise swept over us, a slight mechanical vibration followed by a whoosh, like a snippet from a tiny, gurgling stream. I realized it wasn't all coming from the speaker.

"Door's open. He flooded the tube," Ridder said next to me, his voice unsteady.

I looked over at him. He was now staring at a workstation a few feet aft of the speaker. There were eight sets of lights, three lights each, one red, one yellow and one green. The second set from the right now was green. All the rest were red.

I grabbed Ridder's left forearm.

"You have to stop it. You have to do something." I wasn't even sure what I wanted him to stop. All I knew is that there was horror welling up inside me, a visceral intuition that something unthinkable was about to take place. But he paid no attention.

We were standing like that, him staring at the array of lights, me digging my fingers into his arm, when a different, louder noise echoed through the sub.

It was like a burst of air rushing out into the sea. And then I knew.

"Oh, shit. He . . . oh, shit," I said.

Ridder had become aware, on some thoughtless level, of my hand and pried it loose. He spoke in a monotone. Maybe answering me, or maybe just giving voice to his own thoughts.

"Torpedo tube just fired. No fish in the water." We both saw the green light change back to amber.

My stomach was curled up into itself in fear and nausea. Ridder's words seemed to be coming from another room.

"He shot him out. Vazquez. Oh, fuck, Vazquez."

The intercom clicked off.

The silence in the control room was crushing me. Vazquez's screams still were bouncing around inside my head, and I needed something to make them go away. Something to replace what I had heard in his voice.

"The Serpent's in the aft torpedo room," Ridder said. There was resolve in his voice, and I clung to it, trying to keep from drowning in my own hopelessness.

"He's not getting out. Get in there, guys. Shoot him up. Come on, come on," he continued, still staring at the torpedo tube indicator lights, if that's what they were, and sounding like a man rooting for a football team on TV.

There were no echoes of activity from other parts of the sub. But I didn't trust my ears anymore. I knew what I wanted to hear, and I had no doubt that my brain would supply the correct sounds to comfort me.

Still, those might be running feet. That might be the clatter of armed men climbing a ladder. Shouting voices? Perhaps.

A metallic thud. That wasn't imagined, was it? A hatch closing, slamming shut. If Ridder heard it, he wasn't showing any sign. He stood next to me, his arms at his sides.

"I can't believe this shit," Ridder said, more dismayed than fearful. "How'd it get him? Why'd it shoot Vazquez out the fucking torpedo tube?"

I had no answers.

"What should we do?" I asked.

"We wait. Goddamn, I hope they're on their way to killing that thing."

"Did you . . . do you hear anything? Like the lower-deck team?"

"No," he said, his certainty further pummeling my spirits. "A hatch closed, but that's all."

I tried to collect myself, to grab the remains of my tattered composure. Our actions now would be our salvation or our doom.

Wait, "salvation or doom"? No, that wasn't a path I wanted to go down. Come on, Myers, you're a medical doctor! A pro! What's more, the SEALs expect you to wilt. You're supposed to collapse under pressure, be frightened by all the unexpected death. Right? Isn't that why Larsen arranged the disappearing act earlier?

Was I going to give him that satisfaction now?

So it was my ego, not my training or resolve, that pulled me back into functionality. I didn't care. I just felt exhilarating relief that I was able to shove my dismay and panic into the background. But a tiny, chattering voice deep in my psyche was telling me that I wouldn't be able to do this again, no matter how much I needed to.

Ridder still seemed a little lost. His face's funerary pallor was a white beacon in the compartment's uncertain lights. Expressionless. Motionless. It was tough to tell whether he still was breathing.

"We got Campbell!" The words, shouted from an unknown distance, still were clear. There was more yelling, an impossible puzzle of simultaneous orders, this time accompanied by bumping and heavy footsteps.

It all was coming from the next compartment aft.

"Get him in! Get him in! Cover!" Closer this time. Was that a moan?

Ridder remained a statue. He jerked, though, when there was a pounding on the forward hatch.

"Who's in the Super Bowl?" a voice shouted at us.

Ridder turned and stared at the door. Did nothing.

"The Bengals," I whispered. He directed his stare at me, blinked, then yelled a reply.

"The Bengals!"

A pause. Then, "They're going all the way!"

The hatch's wheel began to turn. It struck me that Ridder hadn't even picked up his rifle.

But the door swung open before either of us could have reached it. Larsen climbed through without looking at us, then turned and reached back into the electrical compartment.

"Here, give me . . . hey!" He interrupted himself with a yell. "Close that fucking hatch! OK. Now, just lift him up . . . yeah. Pass him to me. Ridder, get over here."

As Ridder stumbled into motion, I saw Campbell's head push through the doorway, his eyes half-open. Larsen cradled his shoulders. With Ridder's help, they got his upper body through, then his legs. They laid him on the floor.

"Myers!" Larsen said, but I already was on my way to the prone SEAL. His right thigh was soaked with blood. I knelt next to him.

"Dock-er?" Campbell slurred.

"You're gonna be fine. Ridder, lift up your hands for a sec." He had been applying pressure to the wound, which, I saw, had been caused by a bullet. "Larsen, get me that first-aid kit."

The lieutenant gestured through the doorway, and a hand extended through with the olive-green box. I set it on the floor and yanked out a wad of gauze.

The black fabric of his pants had torn a little around the wound, and I tugged the rip wider.

Yeah. A bullet hole. Distended flesh around a perfect, round puncture, the whole site coated in crimson. No powder burns.

Not too much blood on the floor, either, and I didn't see any bubbling out of the wound. The femoral artery seemed to have survived. I felt around on the back of his leg . . . yeah. Exit wound.

I rummaged in the kit and found some white antiseptic powder, which I sprinkled into and around the hole. Grabbing more gauze, I packed it against both injuries. Campbell winced, but I noticed his eyes showed a little more presence now.

"Campbell, buddy, you're going to be OK," Ridder said.

"Hold this gauze here. Don't let up the pressure," I told him, switching my attention to Campbell's neck.

I took his pulse. Strong, steady, somewhat elevated. So he wasn't too far into shock. His skin didn't feel clammy.

His eyes, though, told me something different. And I soon saw why.

The back of his head was a bloody mess. I probed the wound and was relieved to find that it wasn't mushy. The skull might be fractured, but it had held its shape. His pupils were dilated, though. Worrisome.

"Gimme a flashlight. Someone . . . thanks," I said as Larsen handed me the one from his rifle. I waved its beam across Campbell's eyes. The pupils irised a little bit at the bright light but not as much as they should have.

"He's concussed. The gunshot wound isn't bad; nothing life-threatening right now, although he's a little low on blood. We need to get him lying down after I bandage this. That's all we can do right now."

Larsen nodded. There were several SEALs crouching on the other side of the hatch, watching as I worked.

"He'll be fine," I told them. I wrapped the wound, then observed the dressings for a moment. No blood was soaking through yet. Good. I cleaned and dressed the back of his head.

"Doctor? Christine? Is it bad?" This was Campbell again, sounding clearer and more composed. I suspected he still had been reeling from the knock on the head when they brought him in.

"You're going to be all right, I promise. We're just going to take you into the captain's quarters and get you in bed."

"Yeah. Yeah, I'm . . . tired."

"Get someone else in here," I said to Larsen. "He needs as much support as possible when we move him, and that leg shouldn't move at all."

He didn't seem to mind being ordered around. And although I was more used to dealing with corpses than the blood and screams of the living, it felt good to me, too. This was something I could handle, could fix. Just a bullet wound and head trauma, real-world situations that presented no surprises.

Another SEAL climbed through and, under my direction, he, Larsen and Ridder hoisted Campbell up and carried him to the captain's quarters. Campbell now had the presence of mind to protest and tell anyone who could listen that he could walk just fine.

"No," I said to him after we had him in bed. "No walking, no moving. Just lie there. I'm being honest when I say you'll be fine, but you're going to make things worse if you try to get up. Doctor's orders."

That drew a wan smile. But it was sincere and peaceful.

"Yes, ma'am," he said.

We left Ridder to finish attending to him and moved back to the control compartment. Larsen pulled me over to the nav station after telling Reyes to take over the helm.

"Listen, I want the truth. Is he going to make it?" he asked me, his eyes serious.

"I'm certain the bullet wound isn't mortal. It's all flesh, maybe nicked the bone—there's no way to tell at this point. But the major artery in that area didn't get hit. He's not going to bleed out." I stopped, considering my next words. "The concussion is minor, too, as far as I can tell. If he were in a hospital, I would bet my life and yours that he would survive with few difficulties. But if his brain starts swelling here, there's nothing we can do about it."

"What are you saying?"

"I'm saying that as long as there are no complications, Campbell's in no immediate danger. But if there are, his chances are a lot worse. He needs a hospital." I wasn't too concerned about my bedside manner. I doubted Larsen was, either.

He considered what I had told him for a moment.

"Shut the hatch," he said to one of the SEALs in the electrical control room, and the door slammed shut.

Then he regarded me again. "Dr. Myers. Two more men are dead."

"I heard it."

"We all did. The intercom channel was open to every compartment in the ship. We all got to listen as the Serpent did Vazquez, flushed him like a fucking goldfish," he said, his entire body radiating anger. "Why would he do that? Why would he broadcast that to the rest of the boat?"

Ah. He wanted my opinion. I was the expert again, but I was tired of my oscillating status. It was just too much.

"You're acting as if you respect my views. Why is that?" My professional voice resurfaced, even and neutral.

His pocked face reddened. A vein snaking across his forehead pulsed like a buried parasite.

"Don't fuck with me. Not now, Doctor. This is serious, and I don't need static from you."

I let him stand there for a moment as I reached back, shook my hair loose, then refixed it with the elastic band. To me, we weren't surrounded by exposed wiring and gray steel. We weren't floating hundreds of feet underwater. Or if we were, it didn't matter. This was my ground now, and I wasn't giving it up.

"All you've done so far is mess with me, Larsen." Still a neutral voice. "Lied to me. Tried to trick me. Probably called me mean names behind my back, too, but I don't really give a fuck about that."

Now I ratcheted up the volume, taking a half-step toward him.

"Lucky me, though, you actually need me around sometimes. So you send for me, give me some problem to solve and then stick me back in my cage when I'm done. If my conclusion agrees with yours, then you're a genius. But if it doesn't, I'm an idiot. Funny how that works, huh, tough guy? No, shut up," I said.

Larsen had taken a breath, but I didn't give him a chance to turn it into a reply.

"People start dying, and you want answers from me. But if I do anything that seems remotely inconvenient to you, you act like it's my problem, not yours.

"And now you want me to psychoanalyze the Serpent? Tell you why he did what he did? And, let me guess, tell you what he's going to do next?" This felt good. I let myself ride with the deep current of fury. "You're such an asshole."

He wanted to hit me. I could see the fantasy playing out behind his eyes, him lunging forward, me crying out and falling to the deck. Stupid bitch, his look said.

"Shut up," his mouth said. "Shut up right now."

"Shut up? Or give you advice?" I dialed it back down to a conversational level. "That's the problem. You want me to do both. And as of right now, I will not. If you treat me like a person, like a professional, like an *equal*, we can work together."

The change in tone caught him like I had wanted it to, a flurry of jabs followed by an uppercut. He was off-balance. Was I angry? Was I reasonable?

The important question to me was, would he be reasonable?

"What do you want?" He had stepped back as far as I had moved forward. Point: me. I let us slip back into the submarine, the semi-audible vibrations of the engines, the naked lights, the coils of wires and pipes overhead.

"I want respect. I want to survive as much as you and your men do. I'll use everything at my disposal to help the good guys win this one."

His face was still red, but it contained no violence anymore.

"I respect you."

"And I believe you." A lie, but a necessary concession. "I just want you to show it. I'm not a soldier, but I'm an expert that you need on your team."

"I'll respect your judgment and opinions, Doctor. But I need you to respect my authority."

There we go. This one was almost over.

"I respect your authority. You're the commander, the mission leader. It all comes down to you. I trust you to use my skills in the best way possible."

"Fine. We'll need them." No way was I getting an apology. This was what I wanted, though.

"And there's one other thing," I said, continuing before he could rile himself up again. "I want a gun."

"A gun?"

I gestured at our surroundings.

"We're fighting a war. I'm the only one here who can't shoot back. I'm not saying I want to go out on any raiding parties or anything like that. But if it comes down to it, I might need to defend myself."

"You know how to use a firearm?"

"It's required for the places the CIA sends me."

"Assault rifle, too?"

"Sure. But I'll settle for a pistol."

And then he did something that told me I had accomplished far more than I had hoped. He unsnapped a flap on his utility belt and handed me his sidearm.

"Model 1911?" I said, feeling the heft of the .45 in my hand.

"Yeah. Some people don't like the small mag, but in my book, being able to stop someone with one shot is more important than being able to shoot them three times."

"Thanks, Lieutenant." I held his gaze, creating a solemn moment between us. Then I jerked my head toward the aft bulkhead. "Now, let's figure out how to tackle the Serpent."

Larsen walked over to the nav table and sat down, motioning me into the seat of the adjacent sonar station. Ridder had returned to the helm. If he had found anything unusual or interesting in our exchange, he had shown it by keeping his eyes forward and his body stationary.

"So what advice can you give me about this thing?" Larsen said after I was seated.

"I'm not sure yet. What happened back there? I mean, obviously, I heard the intercom, all the screaming and stuff." I struggled to fight off another wave of trepidation. "Who was with Vazquez? Campbell. Who else?"

"Matthews. He's dead. We . . . we had to leave the body back there. Like the others."

"Matthews, Campbell, Vazquez. Do you know who was on point? How the group was organized?"

Larsen shook his head, picking at the surface of the table as he looked at me. "I don't know for sure. I'd guess Matthews was in front. His body was in the torpedo room—we could see it through the hatch."

"You didn't go into that compartment?"

"No. Campbell was in the area between the engine room and the torpedo room, lying face-down, feet pointing aft."

Larsen had been paying attention to me as I investigated earlier. He knew what I wanted to know before I asked it.

"Facing forward. OK. What's in the compartment he was found in?"

"Nothing important. Storage lockers. A short bulkhead of bunks. A bilge-pump station. Why?"

"Just trying to set the scene a little. So Campbell was in there. Matthews was in the torpedo room . . . did you get a good look at him? Could you tell what had happened?"

"He was kind of curled up on his side, facing us. Blood all over the place. His face was sort of smashed in. But we knew he was dead because his neck had been ripped open, almost all the way around," Larsen said, emotion slowing his speech. "Like I said, though, I just got a short glimpse of the compartment. We grabbed Campbell and retreated."

"No sign of Vazquez?"

"You heard what happened to him."

"But did you see any indication of a struggle? Anything like that?"

"There was a cap, a stocking cap like this," he said, pointing to his own head, "lying on the deck near the tubes." He closed his eyes for a moment. I saw the orbs jittering behind their lids, trying to reconstruct an unpleasant memory. "And the port side tube door was smeared with blood. The starboard door was open."

"Did you see the Serpent?" It couldn't have gotten past them, and such a massive presence would have been hard to miss.

"That's the thing," he said, looking at the tabletop. It was the first time I could remember him being unwilling to make eye contact. "We didn't . . . I mean, we were just recovering Campbell. That was our first priority, you know? We were focused on him. I didn't want to risk sending any of us into the torpedo room with Campbell lying right there."

He was embarrassed. And judging by the twitches along his jawline, he was angry that he was embarrassed. The SEALs had rushed in to try to rescue their comrades and abandoned the idea of containing the Serpent on one part of the sub at any cost.

"But nothing was visible through the hatch?" I cut him a little slack. No point in continuing to prod him in a tender spot.

"No. Nothing moving, nothing in our field of view. We got Campbell, we pulled back, and nothing got past us."

"What about Campbell's rifle?"

"Huh?" His eyes returned to mine.

"Campbell's rifle. He didn't have it when you guys brought him back. Was it on the floor by him?"

"Shit. No, it wasn't. The Serpent must have it now."

"No need for stealth anymore. It knows we know it's there."

The million-dollar question was forming on his lips, but I beat him to it.

"This is all speculation, all right? I don't think we really need to know exactly what went down back there at this point, but here's my guess: The

Serpent was in the torpedo room. Matthews entered first, and the Serpent attacked him, probably using Matthews's own knife to kill him before he could react. Vazquez tried to engage, but the Serpent incapacitated him. Threw him against the wall, maybe, or just hit him. I think he survived initially because the Serpent still was dealing with Matthews's struggles.

"Campbell, meanwhile, is bringing up the rear and sees all this." I knew I was presenting a much more concrete-sounding story than the evidence warranted. But the movie theater in my head had opened again and was showing yet another horror flick. "I doubt he tried to climb into the torpedo room. Whether he did or not, the Serpent shot him, maybe with Matthews's rifle. It drops Matthews and moves over to Campbell— remember how ungodly quick it is—and bashes him with the butt of the rifle. But it doesn't finish him off.

"Why? Because Vazquez is regaining his senses. The Serpent knows Campbell isn't an immediate threat, so he returns to Vazquez and . . . and . . ."

Larsen was engrossed in my narrative, his mouth open.

"And what?" he asked.

The movie faded. I was back in the control room, looking at a black-clad SEAL's confused expression over the nav table.

"To a certain extent, we know what happens next. I think he broke some of Vazquez's bones to make him fit in the tube . . . his collarbones, maybe? And then stuffed him in the torpedo tube and shot him out."

"Dear God. Every time I think about that it seems worse."

"Yeah. I know." I was trying not to let my imagination place me inside Vazquez's body. I didn't want to know how he felt as he was mutilated, what was going through his mind as the tube door slammed shut, cutting him off from light, air and life. "But that's not why I stopped. I'm thinking. Trying to understand why the Serpent broadcast the whole thing to the rest of the boat."

"To scare us?"

"That seems the most obvious answer, doesn't it? A little psychological warfare, trying to tell the rest of us what it's going to do when we finally meet it face-to-face."

"You think there's something else?" No sarcasm this time. It seemed an honest question.

"We keep ignoring the fact that it's insane. We can't always ascribe rational motivations to its actions. I think, more than any tactical advantage, it just wanted us to know it was there, let us into its world. Serial killers do this all the time—subconsciously leave reminders, clues about where they're coming from. Keep in mind that 'where they're coming from' is an extraordinarily bizarre place. You and I can't go there, nor would we want to. But the more they tell us about it, the more we learn about them. And the more we learn about them, the easier it is to catch them."

"Or kill them."

"That too. I think that's the best plan for the Serpent, don't you?" Graveyard humor. Neither of us laughed.

"OK, Myers. It's trying to give us a glimpse at its 'world,' whatever that is. Can we use that against it?"

I nodded. "I think we can."

"Goddamn, there has not been enough good news today. Tell me what you're thinking."

"It wants us off the sub."

"Off the sub? I don't get it."

"Why would it go through the trouble of shooting Vazquez out the tube? Why not just snap his neck and be done with it?"

"I wish it had."

"Me too. But instead of just killing him, it went through a fairly elaborate procedure. And based on what you told me you saw, I think it was in the process of doing the same thing with Matthews when your team opened the hatch from the engine room and went in after the other men."

"It wanted to shoot them both out?"

"Yes. It hadn't had access to the torpedo tubes before, or any other way of physically removing its victims from the boat. But this time it did."

"So why didn't it shoot any of the others off? Miller, Martin, any of those guys?"

"Two reasons. First, it would have had to fight through more people to get to the tubes at that point. And second, it's not dumb: It knew operating the tubes would give away its presence and location. It still was trying to be covert at that point. But in this case it had the opportunity and no reason not to take it."

"It was sort of sending a message, then? 'Get off my ship'?"

Larsen's determination and enthusiasm were palpable.

"Not consciously. But that's what it's feeling, I think. For whatever reason, sole ownership of the *Dragon* is important to it. We could speculate for hours about that. Maybe it feels like a conqueror and the sub is its spoils after killing the crew. Or maybe it sees this as its own private world, and we have intruded into it. Honestly, I think the least-likely explanation is that it has some definite plan for the boat and we're preventing it from carrying out that plan."

"It wants us off," Larsen said, still wondrous. "And how can we use that against it?"

"We could–"

"A classic trap," he interrupted. "We know what you want. We'll offer it to you. We'll kill you when you try to get it."

"Be careful. The Serpent is not stupid. You don't want to underestimate this thing just because its head isn't screwed on straight."

"Yeah, yeah, I know." Larsen wasn't listening to me, though, I could tell. His mind was whirling with plans for the Serpent's demise.

"Hey." The voice from the other end of the room was weak and marbled with pain. Campbell was in an awkward, sideways crouch on the other side of the open hatch, his injured leg stuck straight out down the hallway.

"Jesus, Campbell, what the hell are you doing?"

"Get back in bed!"

Larsen and I had both yelled at him at the same time, our words tangling.

"I will." He sounded like he was about to keel over. "But . . . but I found something."

"Found something? What the fuck are you . . . Reyes! Get him back in the captain's quarters."

As the SEAL moved to comply, Campbell kept speaking, somehow injecting some urgency into his deflated voice.

"OK. I'll go back. But come . . . come with me. You need to see this." He disappeared behind Reyes as the other man pulled himself through the hatch and into the next compartment.

"You know what he's talking about?" Larsen asked me, standing.

"Not a clue. He might just be hallucinating, in shock. Or . . ."

"What?"

"Or he might be having some brain issues. Swelling, as I mentioned before."

"Fuck." Larsen stood there, staring at the doorway.

"That would be a big problem," I said. "But he also might have something to tell us. I'm going to go talk to him, at least to see whether there's anything else wrong."

But Larsen began walking before I did, arriving at the door in four or five purposeful strides.

"Let's go," he said as he went.

Campbell was resituating himself in the captain's bunk when we walked into the room. It was crowded. Larsen, Reyes and I couldn't do much more than stand there without bumping into one another. Reyes rubbed at the tattoo on his neck as he regarded Campbell.

"Reyes, get back to the control room," Larsen said, and sat down at the captain's desk as the SEAL left.

Campbell had found a notebook, one that I recognized.

"Hey, where did you get that?" I asked. He had a bullet hole in his leg, but that didn't mean I'd excuse him for rummaging around in my stuff.

"Your bag. It was blank. I just needed something to write on." He coughed. "Actually, I didn't go get it. Ridder did, when he brought me these."

He waved a sheaf of papers, which I also recognized. It was the report on the Serpent.

"You shouldn't be reading, Brandon," I said, moving to take both away from him. "You've got a concussion, and the best thing your eyes can look at is the ceiling."

Campbell pulled the report and notebook to his body and warded me off with his other hand. "No, this is important. I'm not going to just fucking lie here while my friends are getting killed." His voice swelled, incongruent with his pale face and blood-soaked bandages.

I felt a hand on my arm. "I'll take responsibility for this," Larsen said as he gestured me back from the bed. "I want to hear what he has to say."

"So do I. But I don't want him to worsen his injuries, either," I said, remaining where I was. "You tell us what you found, and then you give those papers to me. Larsen may be your commander, but I'm your doctor, and you'll be in a lot worse shape if you don't follow my orders."

Larsen removed his hand. "I agree. Tell us what's on your mind. But I don't want to see you out of this bed again until we're in port."

Campbell lay back on the pillow, staring at the ceiling for a moment. He seemed drained by the discussion. But after taking a deep breath, he opened the notebook.

"It's like this. I wanted to read more about the Serpent, see if there was anything else in there that would help us fight it." I remembered thinking the same thing, casting about for some advantage we could cling to. "So I just started translating as best I could, writing down everything. It's easier that way, helps put together the context a little better."

"You translated the whole thing?" Larsen asked.

"No way I could do that. It would take hours. Days, maybe. But I started in the places where we already found useful information. And I saw we made a big mistake."

Even though I had no idea what he was going to say next, I felt cold. Giving any edge to the Serpent, no matter how small our miscalculation had been, was suicidal.

Campbell must have seen something in my face. "I know. It makes you feel like . . . like something horrible is waiting. Something we should have seen, but didn't."

I found myself unable to say anything. I just wanted to hear the bad news, whatever it was, so I could face it instead of just fearing it.

The SEAL propped himself up a little higher, wincing.

"But it's not as bad as it could be. As far as I can tell, we know what the

Serpent's true capabilities are. We weren't wrong about those. The problem is, the Serpent isn't what we think it is."

Another inadvertent shiver fluttered through my body.

"Then what is it?" Larsen asked. "Animal? Vegetable? Mineral?"

"Uh-uh. None of the above. We assumed it was a person who had been modified and improved. Well, that's not right. The Serpent is a virus."

"A virus." This new piece of information wasn't quite registering in my brain.

"Yeah," he continued. "It's a disease, a man-made bug that alters the genes of its host. That's what the *Dragon* was sent to pick up, and that's what was stored in the locker on the lower deck."

"And it got loose," Larsen asked, all the sureness of command drained from his voice.

The three of us were silent for a few moments, lost in our thoughts.

My voice punched through the tranquility, surprising me. "It infected someone on the *Dragon*. The crew tried to fight it off. Everyone died, but one crewman tried to surface the ship. That's how desperate he was to survive. But Lee knew—because the captain had told him—what would happen if the virus got loose. He couldn't take that chance."

"It's still here on the boat. Oh, shit. Motherfuck. We're all infected," Larsen said. I couldn't tell whether he was angry or overcome by anxiety.

"Not necessarily." This was again in my professional sphere, a monster I had slain before. "Depends on the vectors by which it spreads. And I'll bet that's in the report. See anything in there, Campbell?"

The warrant officer, despite his injuries, seemed more composed than Larsen or I. But the paleness of his freckled skin gave away the severity of his wounds.

"Yeah. We got lucky: it says the virus only can be contracted through bodily fluids. Something about membranes."

"Mucous membranes. Yeah, that makes sense. Many viruses aren't very hardy. A little light, a little air, and they're dead. Besides, if you're developing a virus as a combat system, you want as much control over it as possible."

"Here's what it says: 'Subject initially infected by injection.'"

"That's about what I thought. It's designed to create a super soldier, not an uncontrollable outbreak."

Larsen jumped in now. "Then how did the crewman get infected to begin with?"

"We'll probably never know," I replied. "There are lots of ways. If there were a spill of whatever was stored in the locker, he might have gotten some on his hands, then touched his eye or nose or mouth. All it takes is carelessness."

"And look what happened," Larsen said, amazed.

Loose lips sink ships, I thought. The inappropriateness of the joke made me laugh in spite of myself.

"The other thing is, you're only half-right about the purpose of the virus," Campbell said after a few awkward seconds. "In the summary here, it says it first was developed to be a defensive weapon, for use on friendly troops."

"Right. Making them stronger, faster, et cetera."

"Except there were some serious problems, the biggest being insanity. The more time passes after infection, the more nutso the subjects become. I mean, not just slightly crazy, but psychopathic."

"Not someone you'd want in a foxhole with you," Larsen said.

"These guys just start killing indiscriminately, it says. And worse, their hormones get all out of whack—go through the roof, really—so they're looking to screw, too. Killing and fucking machines."

Campbell's chest was heaving now. Whether it was from the effort of speaking or his reaction to what he was saying was impossible to tell. I knelt by him and rested a hand on his shoulder.

"Relax. You're doing great."

Larsen crouched and patted his arm. After managing a thin smile at both of us, Campbell continued.

"So instead, they decided that the best use of the virus as a weapon would be to send someone into enemy territory—even a civilian city—and have them infect themselves with an injection. Then they get loose. Start killing. And raping. So they spread the virus. And there's more killing."

"Fuck," Larsen spat. It was as if even hearing the idea of such warfare had contaminated his mouth.

"So that's two things we were wrong about," I said, "but nothing catastrophic. And it explains some things, like why the Serpent . . . that is, the infected host, would be wearing the remains of a Korean navy uniform."

"But I thought we had accounted for all the crew," Larsen said. "I had Grimm double-check after Miller and Martin disappeared, and there were thirty bodies, same as before."

"Maybe there was someone on the boat who wasn't listed in the manifest."

"Go on, son," Larsen said. It was as if he had been listening to my thoughts. "Is there anything else we should know?"

"Uh, well, the insanity is connected to the brain enhancements. As the neural—is that the right word?" I nodded and he continued. "As new neural connections form, they get fucked up. So although the result is a higher IQ, like eighty to one hundred points higher, they're all out of whack."

"What about its other capabilities?" I asked. "There's got to be others."

It's not that my concern for Campbell's health wasn't still there. Seeing him squeezed into the bunk, pale and fragile, was painful. There was a sense of trust, a gossamer bridge between us that I had managed so far not to wreck. But there was a scientist in me who no longer cared about that. I wanted to hear more. I wanted to hear everything.

"You know it's stronger. That happens almost right away. Its senses all are much better than normal. But the biggest change, and the one that takes the longest to happen, is the skin."

"The skin?" Larsen said. I'm not sure how my intuition arrived at the place it did, but I knew what Campbell was going to say.

"Yeah. It changes, too. It can slowly adjust to its surroundings, like a chameleon. The, uh, pigmentation chemicals change. They become sensitive to electricity and can be controlled by the body."

"What you're telling me," Larsen said, "is that this thing, besides being stronger than a normal person, smarter than a fucking rocket scientist and totally insane, is also *invisible?*"

"I don't think so. Not invisible. It seems to be more like camouflage, like fatigues you don't have to wear."

This was disturbing. It also explained how the virus' host had sneaked up on all its victims and stayed out of sight when it decided not to fight.

"So you think it has all those capabilities now?" I asked. "Does it say how long it takes for everything to set in?"

"Yeah, that was one of the first pages I looked at." He paused and flipped back a few pages in the notebook. "Uh . . . strength increases first, accompanied by a drastic rise in caloric intake, within fifteen to twenty minutes of infection. The mental changes come next, within thirty minutes to an hour. That's when the insanity starts to appear, too."

I stood up, backed away and leaned against the cool, metal wall. Larsen and Campbell both stared at me.

"I think I see it all."

"See it all?" Larsen had stood up now, too. He looked ready to shake an answer out of me.

"It's a Korean sailor. He wants us off the submarine because it's his submarine. We're invaders, the enemy. He also wants to get to shore, you know? Because he knows there are women there. But . . . oh."

"But what?" Larsen said.

"There might also be another reason why he's trying to kill off all of you. Not just because he wants you off the submarine. But because you're competition."

"Competition?" This time it was Campbell speaking, bewildered and frail.

"Yeah. Competition. For me. I'm the only woman on this boat, and he wants me."

X

WE WERE BACK in the control room, except for Campbell, who was napping in the captain's quarters. I had reneged on my threat to take away the documents and notebook, but I didn't think he had the energy to do more research. And despite our concerns for his health, neither I nor Larsen would have been upset if he finished translating all the reports.

Larsen now was trying to come up with a plan. He and Grimm were sitting at the nav table, I was standing nearby, and Ridder continued to steer the boat without comment or complaint.

"We know what it wants," Larsen said.

"How? The Serpent's insane. Didn't you just tell me that?" Grimm replied, sitting back and crossing his arms, his nose pointed at Larsen like a fleshy spear.

They had been going in circles for at least fifteen minutes.

"Myers is an expert, OK? She knows insanity; she can give us a better idea of its motivations than anyone else on this ship."

"My theory is just a sketch. I don't want either of you to get carried away thinking I can read this guy's mind," I interjected. The discussion had started with a report from me but degenerated into an argument between the lieutenant and Grimm, who now seemed to be the next-highest-ranking SEAL.

Grimm pointed to me, but kept his eyes on Larsen. "See? *She* even says she's not sure. We shouldn't risk everything on a hunch."

"There's nothing else we can do! Haven't you figured that out?" Larsen said.

"He's right," I said. "It's only going to get stronger and smarter, and if we let it take the initiative, we don't have much of a chance."

"Oh, really?" It was Grimm's turn to be irritated and condescending now. Maybe he'd learned it from Larsen. "How would you know whether we have a chance or not? There are seven of us and only one of it."

"Eight, actually, including me. But one of those eight can barely lift a pen, let alone an assault rifle," I said. "You let the Serpent decide the rules, and we're playing a losing game. Simple as that. But if we make it react instead of attack, we have a built-in advantage."

"And we know what it wants," Larsen said. Back to step one.

"Sure, fine. We know it wants us off the boat, and we know it wants her. Correction, we *think* it wants us off the boat and wants her. Even if those guesses are right, how do we use them to our advantage?"

Grimm had conceded, even if he didn't realize it. Maybe now we could decide on a course of action instead of chasing our tails around the control compartment. I beat Larsen to the answer.

"We take advantage of its insanity. Set up a situation that seems too good to be true but is too enticing for it to pass up."

"Right, yeah, got that. Any specific ideas about how to pull it off?" Grimm again responded to me by speaking to Larsen.

The lieutenant was gone, lost in some tactical wonderland in his head. We watched him in silence.

"OK," he said. "Myers, you're going to be bait."

Bait. I didn't like to think of myself as a worm on a hook, but it was our best chance of luring it into a trap. I knew that. And most worms weren't armed, I thought, feeling the barrel of the .45 dig into my back where I had tucked it into my jeans.

"The trap," he continued, "is going to be the forward torpedo room."

"Wait, hold on." Grimm hadn't objected to using me as a lure, but this wrinkled his face with consternation. "The forward torpedo room? There's only one way in there."

"Exactly. And only one way out."

"The problem, sir, is that the 'one way' happens to go through the fucking control room. Are we really going to let the enemy walk through the most important area on the ship? What if it decides to just close the hatches to the compartment?"

"Then we storm that room, have a big shootout, game over."

Grimm wasn't convinced. "Look, I don't care how sex-crazed this thing is, if it gets the chance to control the boat, why wouldn't it take it? The Serpent is the smartest thing on the sub, isn't it? Isn't that what you said?"

Now he was addressing me. It was uncanny how much he resembled Larsen's old persona.

"Sure, its IQ is probably twice as high as any of ours. But—"

"Shut it, Grimm," Larsen interrupted. "Even if it stays in the control room, and I don't think it will, we can attack from two sides. Myers is in the forward torpedo room, holding a .45 behind her back." Damn straight I would be. "Campbell is where he is right now, in the captain's quarters."

Grimm wanted to protest again. But Larsen's verbal pre-emptive strike left him squirming in his chair, swallowing his words. His dark eyes were mutinous.

"Campbell's in there. Ridder's in the officers' mess. The rest of us, we head aft, to the engine room. Then we descend to the lower deck and go forward. Except for one man, who crams himself all the way aft in the engine room, between the powertrains. Beneath that little overhang? You know where I'm talking about? He stays there and watches."

Grimm seemed a little less upset. But he couldn't stop himself this time.

"We're leaving the guy to go one-on-one with the Serpent?" he blurted.

"First, it's not the Serpent. It's just a guy who's been infected with the Serpent."

Who cares? I thought. Call him Ishmael, it doesn't matter even a tiny bit for our purposes. Larsen had arrived at the same conclusion.

"Oh, hell, I don't care. Let's keep calling it 'the Serpent.' That's not important. The guy in the engine room isn't going one-on-one. See, the hatch to the electrical compartment is open. And so is the one to the battery bay, the one right in front of our guy on the lower deck of the engine room. So he can see the men covering him, look them right in the eye.

"But what he's really watching is the upper deck of the control room. Because he's waiting for the Serpent to run through into the next compartment."

"But how is it going to know Myers is up there?" Grimm said. "Are we going to announce it on the PA or something?"

"No need." I could handle this one. "It knows I'm here already, trust me. Its senses are way jacked up, and if it hasn't heard my voice, which is doubtful, it certainly can smell my pheromones."

My comment transformed Grimm into a skeptic again.

"*Smell* you? Are you serious? It's going to smell the bait like an animal in the woods and just walk into the trap? I can't believe I'm hearing this."

"If we had told you yesterday about what was going to happen after we boarded this boat, would you have believed us?" Larsen said. "Of course you wouldn't have. This virus thing goes beyond our training and experience. But it's real, because we have nine dead SEALs to prove it."

"It'll know I'm there. It will also be drawn to the forward torpedo room because it offers more opportunities to jettison his competition."

I tried not to think too hard about the second point, but Vazquez's screams still lingered in my ears.

"The Serpent's a fucking fruitloop," Grimm said. The SEAL had to believe what we were saying, but, by God, no one was going to stop him from belittling our quarry.

"No doubt about that," I said.

Larsen picked up his narrative again. "So it's going toward Myers. As soon as whoever's in the engine room sees the Serpent pass through, he signals the other four guys. They form up in the engine room."

"And attack from behind?" I asked.

"Not yet."

His answer made me uncomfortable. If the monster is rushing toward me, I want the good guys right on its ass. The .45 was reassuring, but I'd feel better if my assailant were distracted by, say, automatic gunfire from its exposed flanks.

"But relax, Myers, you're not alone." He put a comforting hand on my forearm. I couldn't believe it. "The two guys covering the passageway are the signal, and they're also what we're counting on to make sure the Serpent never gets to you. When Campbell sees it, he opens up."

"From his bed?" Grimm said.

"Yeah. He shoots through the doorway. And that signals two things. One, it tells Ridder to swing into the passageway and open fire. Two, it tells the guys in the engine room to charge forward. The Serpent's not going to make it to the torpedo room. I think it most likely will run from Ridder's fire—no way to dodge bullets in a confined space like that—and the other guys'll catch it coming through the hatch into the control room. Boom."

What he didn't say, but what I knew his military mind was thinking, was that if it somehow made it to the torpedo room, the game would also be over. There was only one functioning door in that compartment, and the SEALs could just crouch there and blast the Serpent from a protected position. The bait might get eaten, but they'd trap their animal.

Grimm had warmed to the plan. He hadn't said anything, but his face was clear and unworried as he considered the details.

"You're right: if it decides to stay in the control room, we can attack it from two sides. So . . . basically, we're clearing out, giving it a shot at something it really wants, then attacking its flanks. No place to go."

"Nowhere to run, baby," Larsen agreed. "Classic snare ambush."

"The key thing, though," Grimm said, addressing me again, "is whether it's going to go for the bait." I was starting to hate that word. "Is it going to just charge after Myers? Are the temptations going to cancel out its smarts?"

"They will," the bait replied. "We're basically going to offer it the exact things that motivate its actions, and we're going to present the illusion that it can obtain them without any resistance. It's driven—that's the thing that cancels out its intelligence. When we present it with the chance to get exactly what it wants, it's not going to be able to pass it up."

I wasn't doing a good job explaining it, but both Larsen and Grimm seemed to get the idea. I had more to say, though.

"What we have to be careful about—and what you have to make sure everyone is perfectly clear on—is that this is not a person we're dealing with. It's beyond normal. Superhuman. So it's going to move faster and react faster than we expect."

"You saying we can't do it?" Grimm asked.

"No, I'm just saying we have to be careful. Remember what Vazquez said about the Serpent? How it moved so fast he couldn't hit it with fully automatic fire? Well, I think Ridder will have a much better chance at getting it because, as the lieutenant says, it won't have anyplace to dodge. But other things, like how fast it moves from place to place, will seem impossible. For instance, I think Campbell will start shooting a lot sooner than the guys in the engine room expect. This whole thing is going to be over in a flash."

"It's about time," Grimm said, picking at the top of the nav table.

"Don't worry, Myers. We've seen what this thing can do. No one's going to underestimate it. This is our best chance to take it down."

I looked at Larsen. "I know it is. Just don't . . . you can't give it any slack. If one person doesn't take it seriously enough, we're all fucked."

And maybe we already were. Maybe this was just whistling in the dark, imagining we could conquer an immortal foe. But the one thing I was sure about—and that I was convinced Larsen believed, too—was that this was our only real choice. If it worked, we survived, mission accomplished. If it didn't, we died. But inaction would result in death that was just as certain.

"What about this skin camouflage stuff?" Grimm asked.

"Shouldn't be a factor. As long as it's moving and isn't stopped in front of a background, its skin can't possibly adapt fast enough. And if it's wearing clothes, you'll be able to see those no matter what."

"Jesus, this is fucked-up," Grimm said to no one.

"OK, couple more questions," I said. "First, what if it's not in the aft torpedo room anymore? What would have stopped it from going elsewhere?"

"Nothing, I guess," Larsen replied. "But if it's in the galley area or anyplace on the lower deck, the five-man team will be positioned to ambush it."

"But it won't go after the bai . . . it won't try to get to me. And then we lose our tactical advantage."

"So we adapt. Even if we don't have all the cards, we'll still win the game. Five on one. I'll take those odds, even if it's not the optimal situation."

"Well, OK," I said. I wasn't reassured by his cockiness, but I also didn't have any suggestions for making the plan airtight. "The other question is, who's going to be steering the ship while we're doing all this?"

"Yeah, thought of that one, too," Larsen said. "I checked our course, and there's no turn charted for another hour or so. If we maintain speed, the drift won't be too bad. Plus, after we kill this thing, there's no reason to rush back to port, and we can slow down and conserve batteries."

It made sense. Drifting off course was at the bottom of our pile of priorities. I had only one more question now.

"When are we going to do this thing?"

I was sure that the more we sat around and talked about it, the less at ease I'd feel about being dangled in front of a psychopath.

"We'll do the briefing in the electrical control room. Might as well get started now."

No. That was a problem.

"Hold on. We can't do it in there."

Grimm and Larsen, who both already had stood up, stopped and regarded me without excitement.

"Why, Myers?" Larsen asked.

"The Serpent's hearing. We don't want it to even get a chance to pick up a word of the plan, and for all we know, it could be sitting with its ear pressed up against the hatch from the engine room."

"She's right," Grimm said. He sounded surprised at his own observation.

"Yeah, good point." Larsen turned aft, then forward. "OK, we'll do it in shifts. Brief half the team in the forward torpedo room, then move them back to their posts and brief the other half. Then we'll get this show on the goddamn road."

I was pretty eager to shove off, too. It was amazing. I couldn't even remember how it felt to be paralyzed, in mind and body, by fear. But I knew I had been in that exact state, what, less than an hour ago? Time seemed irrelevant.

Now that we had a plan, I had a lifeboat of rationality, and I was motoring for shore as fast as I could. So was the *Dragon* itself, I hoped.

I sat in on both the briefings. If nothing else, it was just convenient: I already was where I needed to be for my part in the operation.

The first group comprised me and Larsen—of course—as well as Ridder and the guy they called Chief. He got there first and introduced himself as Master Chief Petty Officer Carl Moretti.

"This is our shot to catch the Serpent off-guard," Larsen said. He had given up on calling the infected crewman anything else, even after we explained the true nature of the Serpent to the rest of the SEALs. "The doctor will be in here. Ridder, you will be in the officers' mess. Campbell will be in the captain's room. The rest of us are going to clear out and act as though we are searching the ship."

"But we're not?" Chief asked.

"No. We're trying to . . . I know you like football. The Giants are your team, right?"

Chief nodded.

"Well, it's like we're the safety. And we're acting like we're not covering the receiver, trying to lure the quarterback into throwing it to him. But after he lets go of the ball, we turn on the jets, close in and intercept that motherfucker."

"Myers is the receiver. And the Serpent's the quarterback. The ball, too, I guess."

"You got it, Chief. So we back off, head down into the lower deck, leaving one guy to covertly watch the hatch to the electrical control room. When he sees the Serpent rush through there, we're almost ready to go for the ball.

"Ridder, that's where you and Campbell come in. Campbell's going to be watching the passageway through his door. When he sees something—anything—come through there, he's going to start shooting. That's when you swing into the passageway and open up, too."

"You need to move fast," I interjected. "Don't expect it to move like a human. In fact, I wouldn't even bother to look for a target. Just start firing."

"We'll leave that to Seaman Ridder. I don't like the idea of just shooting blindly at whatever happens to be there." It was the first time I had heard Larsen contradict me without any disparaging comment. We had indeed turned a corner.

"Got it, boss," Ridder said. Then he continued to me in his characteristic monotone. "I got a quick trigger finger. If there's anything in the passageway besides air, it's gonna have about a millionth of a second to start dodging. But I won't miss."

"Damn right, you won't. Ventilate that thing. And even if you don't, it's going to retreat toward the control room. That's when the cavalry arrives," Larsen said, warming to the story. "It's running full-tilt at us, a bunch of hot lead chasing it, and what does it see? A bunch of pissed-off SEALs with MP-5s. You're the rock, we're the hard place, and it's a bug caught in the middle."

"I like it," the chief said. "Is she going to be OK, though?"

"I'm fine," I answered for Larsen. "I've got a weapon, I know how to use it, and if it makes it to the doorway here, I'm going to pop it as it climbs through."

"Well, then. You want me to get the rest of the guys in here?" The chief stood up, got a nod from Larsen and climbed up the ladder and out of the room.

"You cool, Ridder?" the lieutenant asked.

"Sure. I'm always cool." I had no argument on that one. But then he turned to me. "And don't shoot me in the back."

"Jesus, that's the least of your problems. Get in the officer's mess and figure out the ideal position to hide," Larsen said. After the seaman had left, he continued. "You stay cool, too, all right? I know you're not going to panic and shoot one of us. But I don't want you to worry that we're not on our way. We're covering you."

"I know. I don't have any desire to be the one shooting at this thing. And I trust you."

Grimm and two other SEALs interrupted our moment by clambering down the stepladder into the compartment. One was the black man who had been stationed up here right after they boarded the sub. Jakes. The other's name was . . . something Hispanic. Rodriguez?

"Reyes, we're going hunting," Larsen said.

Yeah, that was it. Reyes. I couldn't remember the last time I'd forgotten a name so quickly.

"That's good news, boss, 'cuz I got a fine, government-issued rifle I've been itching to use," Reyes replied in an accent that was part street, part Spanish.

Larsen gave his spiel, again using the football analogy. I was a casual sports fan, but I knew what he was talking about, and it was a perfect parallel to our plan. There were no questions after he finished describing how dead and bullet-riddled the Serpent was going to be when this was over.

"So when do we go?" Jakes asked.

"No point in waiting, Seaman," Grimm said. "I don't have anything better to do."

"Assemble in the electrical control room, and *no talking*," Larsen said. "We don't want it to have the slightest idea that we're about to kick its ass. I'll be in there in a minute after I brief Campbell."

He watched the others leave, then turned back to me.

"You sure you don't have any problems with this?"

"Problems? What problems would I have? I'm just sitting here waiting for a homicidal super-soldier to come after me, and I can't think of a single reason why that would bother me." The expression on Larsen's face told me he didn't realize my sarcasm was good-natured. "No, relax. It's not anything I'd normally sign up to do, but I know—just like you do— that this plan is our best shot. I'm ready, no reservations. Let's do it."

He smiled. "Fuckin' A, Doctor." He held the expression for a moment, then turned to leave. But as he was about to climb through the door, he called over his shoulder: "Next time I see you, I'm going to shake your hand over this thing's steaming corpse. You're all right." Then he left without waiting for a reply.

Glancing around, I tried to find the best place to position myself. As far forward as I could get, for sure. No way was I going to be near the hatch. I settled for standing between the torpedo tubes' loading doors, trying to ignore the pressure-suited body Jakes had shoved under the portside torpedo racks.

All these torpedoes . . . damn, that was irony. Each could rip apart a warship and send it plummeting to the ocean floor. Yet they were useless against our foe, unless we wanted to blow ourselves up in the process. The torpedoes still radiated danger, but it seemed small in comparison to the more immediate threat roaming the ship.

I had become accustomed to this environment, I realized as I peered inward. Here I was in a submarine. So what? No one was at the wheel. What did I care? We were on the sub, and that wasn't negotiable. Meanwhile, we had a job to do.

It was as if Larsen were in my head giving me a pep talk.

I was listening for a hatch to slam, some indication that the game was afoot. But I realized after fifteen minutes or so that they were leaving the hatches open. So the next thing I heard would be gunfire, if the plan unfolded as we hoped.

Crouching down, I could see the entire doorway to the officers' mess. But no sign of Ridder. I guessed that was the way it should be.

And Campbell. Boy, was that a tough assignment. I still was amazed he could think straight, let alone read, let alone stand guard with an assault rifle. But, I reflected, he didn't have to hit anything. He was just a human tripwire.

What was he thinking while sitting there—lying there?—on the coarse, gray blanket, staring at the doorway? The same things I was, I imagined. Trying to focus on the task at hand without letting the details freak him out. That was my strategy. And it was easier to do than worry about what might happen to me. Or to him.

I pondered hiding the pistol behind my back. But why bother? I doubted the Serpent would be deterred by the sight of a gun in my hand.

It would take actual bullets to dissuade it, and I was ready to deliver them. Let's see . . . yep, there was one in the chamber, I saw as I worked the slide and ejected an unfired cartridge into my palm. I loaded it back in the magazine.

Ready to go. Ready to fight.

Nothing to do but wait.

I remembered playing hide-and-seek with my brother when we were growing up. The woods behind our house were overgrown, choked with bushes and vines. Perfect, in other words, for two kids to frolic in and be fretted over by their mother when they came home covered in poison ivy.

I had been . . . eight? Something like that. I felt swept away by the waiting and anticipation that I had felt then, as I felt them now. Hiding in leafy, green undergrowth down in a gully. Knowing that if I just waited long enough, Stephen would come by, maybe humming to himself like he always did when he was thinking.

I was never afraid in the woods. My brother and I spent countless summer hours wandering in them, alone and together, charting the topography of our childhood playground. In the woods, I discovered a refuge from my mom's sadness, which never seemed to fade. It was also where I first realized that I could predict, without understanding why, exactly what tactics Stephen would use when I hid from him.

When I was a kid, while all my friends were having sleepovers and beating on piñatas at each other's birthday parties, I was begging Mom to let me camp out in the woods. The trees and greenery were safe. Serene. Distant. I could pick my way through them and discover new truths, always confident that I could return to where I started. And it was the only place where Mom felt comfortable with me and Stephen being out of her sight. Whenever I went on a date in high school, and when Stephen left to go to college, her face—and I'm sure she didn't realize this—sagged into a caricature of despair, just for a moment. We both understood why, but it was wrenching to see. I've never looked in the mirror and witnessed that expression on my own face. That was another reason I enjoyed hiding in the woods.

An odd, metallic report echoed through my reverie. I raised the .45. The .45?

Oh, shit. My heart began hammering against my ribs as the verdant forest was replaced by steel. Leaves became rivets, branches became wires and pipes, and I no longer was a little girl enjoying the thrill of an innocent game.

I still was standing up, my nostrils flared at the scents of growth and rot that now were stale sweat and grease. Blinking, I looked around, listened. How long had I disappeared into that daydream?

Had anything happened? There was no way I could have dreamed my way through automatic gunfire. The trap had not yet been sprung.

Then I heard it again. A hatch being not just closed, but slammed shut. The noise was funneled down the hallway and blasted into my compartment. The Serpent? Or the SEALs returning empty-handed?

The burst of machine-gun fire answered my question. I resisted the urge to throw my hands over my ears, instead steadying the .45 in a two-handed grip.

Beyond its blue-black barrel, a fight unfolded, its violence slowed by the adrenaline screaming through my veins.

Before the initial shooting had even faded into memory, I saw Ridder—his legs—step out from the officers' mess into the hallway. Even in the weird slow-motion, he moved much faster than I expected from such a sedate person. As I became aware of that thought, I saw him silhouetted by the muzzle blasts from his rifle.

It was as if there were a strobe light at the aft end of the corridor. The shell casings weren't quite falling. The flashes just caught them, a frame at a time, in various stages of their descent. I suppose I could see them between shots, but the hall's dim light, compared with the brilliant staccato explosions of Ridder's assault rifle, might as well have been total darkness. And I somehow could hear the empties tinkling onto the deck.

He stood there, his legs braced maybe shoulder-width apart, and fired. I couldn't see his upper body at all, but I could imagine his face. Emotionless. Sleepy, even, but not blinking as he held down the trigger and sprayed whatever was in front of him.

Was there anything in the hallway? There was a shadow—not his—dancing on the wall, evident but indistinct. Ridder still wasn't moving. If the Serpent were charging down the hallway, the SEAL wasn't giving up an inch.

Then he did move. Not back, but forward, and he stopped shooting. As his legs disappeared from my view, an oblong black object clanked to the floor where he had stood. A magazine. He had burned an entire clip and was giving chase.

I, however, felt as though my back had been welded to the torpedo-launching mechanism I was leaning against. What if it turned around now and hit him when he was reloading? It could break him, shove him out of the way and be at my throat. If I stayed here and covered the doorway, the distance and my pistol would protect me.

Ridder started shooting again. The world had speeded up a little, and now the gunfire was slurred together into a continuous ripping sound. And on the other side of it, I heard voices. Yelling.

"Hold your fire! Hold your fire!" The shooting stopped.

Had they gotten him? I heard no panic. But none of the ebullient screams of success I'd expect if they were standing over the Serpent's "steaming corpse," either.

That detached me from my position. I ran over to the doorway and peered through. All I could see, once again, were the backs of Ridder's legs. But they were in the control room. And through the tiny doorway, in the spaces around and between his limbs, I could see SEALs piling through the compartment's opposite hatch.

I climbed up the stepladder and into the hallway. My feet almost skidded out from under me as I planted them in a pond of cartridge casings. The bulkhead at the far end of the hall was gouged with bullet impacts, and intermittent sparks dripped from the ceiling where ricochets had torn through exposed wiring. Everything was shrouded by a thin, gauzy haze of gunsmoke.

The pistol remained in front of me in both hands, held at a slight down angle as I walked forward. When I got to the captain's quarters, I glanced in and saw Campbell sitting on the edge of the bed, his rifle in his lap and a pile of spare clips on the floor.

"Did we get him?" The fighting had given his voice new purpose and energy.

I shrugged and gestured with my head toward the control compartment. "I'm trying to find out. He didn't get to the torpedo room."

"I know. I saw him go by, then come back. You were right—he was so fast. Just a blur."

I left him loading a new clip into his rifle and continued to the end of the hallway. Ridder had moved from the hatchway, and I climbed through.

Four SEALs were at the aft end of the compartment in a loose semicircle, alert, weapons ready. Ridder was standing to my right, facing Larsen. They seemed to be arguing, Ridder's dainty hands buttressing his points with angry gestures.

"He did *not* pass us, Seaman," Larsen said.

"I'm not saying he did, sir. But I saw him—just for a split-second—and he turned and ran back in here."

"And after that?"

"I dunno. He was through the hatch, and I couldn't see him anymore."

"Well, he's not in here, obviously." Larsen gestured at the posse of SEALs without looking. "Did you hit him?"

"Fuck if I know, sir. I ripped off an entire mag, reloaded and tried to hit him through the doorway, even though I couldn't really see him. That's when you guys came through the other door."

"No shit. You were shooting blind. We're lucky you didn't gun me down."

"I was *trying* to hit it, OK? It moved so fast," Ridder said. He was annoyed again. It seemed to be his personality's only setting besides "tranquilized."

Larsen shifted his gaze to me.

"Did you see it?"

"No. I heard Campbell shoot . . . wait, no. First I heard two hatches shut, I think. Then I heard Campbell start firing, and then I saw Ridder step out and join in."

"There's no way it could have gotten past us."

"Well, it did, obviously, because we're here and it isn't." That was from Grimm on the other side of the room. Larsen must have been thinking the same thing, because he didn't argue or react.

Some of the smoke from the hallway had drifted into our compartment, making it seem as if we were having a conversation in a fog bank. The SEALs' expressions were ebbing from focused excitement to disgust to worry.

"I heard you talking to Campbell, Myers. What'd he say?"

"Not much. Just that he saw it pass twice, once going forward and once aft. He wanted to know if we had gotten it."

"Well, who the hell knows the answer to that?" Larsen wasn't looking for one from any of us, as he addressed the question to the ceiling. "OK, men, we're going to resecure our stations for now. We need to rethink the situation."

And as he spoke, I saw movement. From the right side of the compartment, in the light-starved corner between the nav table and the sonar station, a human shape manifested and flung itself toward the aft hatch. It was so fast, though, that I think my brain was just filling in details where I couldn't see any.

"Look!" was all I had time to say.

Before that one-syllable exclamation had made its way out of my mouth, the apparition was at the doorway. Its movements didn't seem to have any beginning or end; it was just a seamless blur.

It slipped through the hatch, and as it did so, it grabbed Seaman Jakes. This was evident only because he jerked backward and started screaming.

His back thudded against the doorway, and his screaming was drowned out by a roar of gunshots. An assault rifle—the same type the SEALs used—was poked through the opening between his left side and the hatch frame.

Next to me, Ridder fell back, a mist of blood hanging in the air where he had stood. He bounced off the wall next to the steering station and landed face-down. The back of the SEAL's black sweater was cratered with exit wounds.

I knew my adrenaline was pumping again, but nothing was slowing down. Jakes thrashed around, his eyes wide, all of his teeth visible as his vocal cords vibrated with pain and fear. The blood was draining from his face, turning his ebony skin an ugly ashen color.

The hand clutching him had latched onto his right side, just below the ribcage. Its fingers were swarthy, tips digging into his flesh. Jakes dropped his rifle and clawed at the grip with one arm while trying to keep himself from being pulled through the door with the other. Both were losing efforts.

"Jakes!" Grimm rushed forward and grabbed the man's shoulders, paying no attention to the gun barrel protruding from the next compartment.

But the rifle disappeared. The Serpent needed its hand for something else.

"The door! It's trying to shut the door!" I yelled. The SEALs didn't move. All had raised their weapons, but except for Grimm, none showed any capacity for action or speech.

Jakes's wails hit another register, then disappeared into a high-pitched whisper as his throat gave out. The hand's grip had intensified, judging by the paleness of its knuckles, and the fingers now seemed to disappear into the SEAL's sweater. But despite the strength displayed there, Jakes wasn't moving through the doorway.

Was Grimm winning this fight? No. There was no way. The Serpent was using Jakes as a shield.

"I got him! I got him!" Grimm yelled, trying to keep his hands from being pinned between his comrade and the hatch's edge. But he *didn't* have him. He had to know that. "Come on, somebody help me!"

"No! Shoot through him! Shoot through him!" My voice again, and I couldn't believe the conviction I heard there, didn't know where it was coming from. Someplace deep inside me, I was certain what was going to happen next. "It's going to close the hatch! Shoot now!"

I heard a wet, muffled pop as one of Jakes's ribs failed. He wasn't going to survive this encounter. If his liver hadn't exploded from the pressure being applied there, his innards were mangled beyond repair. But I knew the man—the thing—behind him had no intention of leaving it at that.

"Goddamnit, Grimm, get out of the way!" I had brought the pistol up to a shooting position, and my finger tightened on the trigger.

"Belay that! Belay that!" It was Larsen this time. "Hold your fire, all of you. Myers, don't you shoot!"

He moved toward the door, directing as he went. Above all the confusion floated Jakes's continual, wispy scream.

"Moretti, Reyes, grab his arm! Shoot when he's clear of the door!"

"Larsen, no! It's going to get away! Open fire! Someone fucking . . . shoot through Jakes!"

If the SEAL in question heard our debate over his fate, he didn't show it. His eyes were staring at something far in the distance, unfocused by the white-hot anguish anchored in his lower torso.

Then the brown orbs crossed, a comical expression that seemed horrific and nauseating now. His body jerked once, twice. I heard thumps accompanying the movement, a hollow sound like someone being punched in the sternum.

Grimm fell backward, pulling Jakes on top of him as the Serpent released its grip. The hatch swung shut at the same time.

A combat knife was buried in Jakes's back between the ribs on the left side. Right into the heart, I knew without examining him.

"Oh, fuck! Jakes! Jakes, man, are you OK?" That was Grimm. Either he hadn't seen the weapon protruding from the SEAL's back or he didn't realize what it meant.

"He's dead," I said, dropping the pistol to my side.

Grimm looked up at me, an innocent, hurt expression more appropriate of a child than a soldier.

"I tried to save him," he said.

I didn't reply. I knew what he had been trying to do, but I also knew he'd had no chance of success. I felt my energy fall away, leaving me too drained to scold or praise. All the resolve that had guided me—steadied my aim and detached me from my emotions—deserted me.

Reyes stepped forward, reaching for the hatch's wheel. His rifle was balanced on his hip with his other hand. Open the door, then shoot; that was his plan.

"Wait! Don't do that! Don't open the door," Moretti said, beating me to it. At best, Reyes's weapon would be ripped out of his hand. At worst, his arm would be ripped from its socket. No matter how he positioned himself, he would be in close quarters with the Serpent, and that had proved fatal to everyone who had found themselves in the same situation.

The SEAL stopped, then stepped back. But he kept his rifle pointed at the hatch. That decision I agreed with.

"You did the right thing," Larsen said, kneeling next to his de facto second-in-command, who still was trapped under Jakes's body.

No, he hadn't. Moretti and Reyes were looking back and forth between Larsen and me, their faces unreadable.

"And you . . . how dare you give the order to shoot one of my men!" Larsen said to me, standing up and pushing his way through Reyes. His feet straddled Ridder's head, but he didn't look down.

"The Serpent was killing him with its hand," I said. "And it was using its other hand to close the hatch door. Jakes wasn't going to survive. Now we may not, either."

He knew I was right. I could see the hopelessness in his eyes, the look of a leader whose affection for his men had pushed him into the wrong side of an impossible decision.

"I'm sorry Jakes died," I continued. "He didn't deserve that, and he didn't deserve to be shot by his friends, either."

No anger now. Now Larsen stared down at the puddle of cooling blood around his boots. He didn't blink, his mouth twitching with half-said words, as the two other SEALs helped Grimm to his feet.

"It keeps getting worse," he said, speaking at me but not to me. "Unreal. Fucked-up. Shit in a blender."

I had no quarrel with that assessment.

"Sir?" It was the chief.

Larsen shuffled his feet, turning to face Moretti.

"Sir, what do we do now?"

It was as plaintive a question as a professional killer could ask. The honesty in it was obvious, and so was the importance of a direct, decisive answer. I doubted Larsen was up to it.

But as he had so many times already, he surprised me.

"We figure out some other way to kill it. It wants to make sure it's the only thing getting off this boat. I want to make sure it's unloaded in a casket." His body language had changed with each syllable. He had begun speaking as a beaten man, but now his spine was straight, unafraid. "Surrender isn't a choice. It never was, never has been and isn't now. We fight until we win. That's the only outcome."

Then the lights flickered and expired, thrusting the world into invisibility and our fears into full view.

XI

THE SEALS' REACTIONS WERE QUICK and, I'm sure, instinctual. They may have saved us.

"Lights! Lights!" Larsen yelled.

All their rifles had flashlights mounted under the barrels, and before his command disappeared into the darkness, the SEALs had switched them on. There was a swirl of beams, each isolating a fragment of the scene as they swung through the compartment.

Grimm's face, no longer stunned or melancholy. Jakes's body, seeming like a prop, a piece of scenery caught in a spotlight. The empty crew stations. Tendrils of gunsmoke suspended in the dead air. The never-ending contours of the walls and ceiling, which now appeared more organic, like the veins and arteries of a monster. Flashes of hands, belts, guns, boots.

Then, without further orders, all the beams were focused on one spot: the door. It still was closed. The locking mechanism was motionless.

"It's dogged, sir," Reyes said. It sounded like his clipped Latino accent, anyway. All the SEALs' features were just another part of the darkness.

"Keep 'em on the door. Nothing's getting through," Larsen said.

"What the hell just happened?" The shouted words floated out of the darkness behind me.

I spun, trying to find the source, but slipped on Ridder's blood and sat down hard.

I was facing the steering station, and my gun was pointing at nothing. An empty hatch, pulled out of the black by a flashlight beam from behind me.

"Campbell, relax. Stay where you are," Larsen yelled. Shit. Of course the voice was Campbell's, emanating from the captain's cabin.

"What's going on? My flashlight is . . . I can't get it to turn on."

"We'll take care of that in a second. Sit tight. There's been some kind of failure in the electrical system."

A failure? As if it had just occurred by itself.

"Grimm, tell me what just happened," Larsen said, returning his attention to the control room.

"Power's gone." Grimm was back together. One trauma had shattered him, the next had given him resolve. "Probably a fuse or two."

"Just local?"

"I doubt it. I can't feel the engines anymore. Can you? The air's stopped circulating, too."

I found that if I didn't let my eyes be drawn to any of the lights, I could make out the shapes of all the SEALs. Grimm was standing just to the left of the aft doorway, his height giving away his identity. Larsen had moved to that end of the compartment and was crouched to the right of the other three men.

"He pulled the plug," Chief said.

"Yeah. No lights, no engines . . . nothing. Chief, go check our depth," Larsen said.

Moretti had been standing next to Larsen. He detached himself from the group and walked over to the helm.

"Will any of the instruments be working?" I pulled myself upright using the seat next to me.

"Damn near everything in here is analog," Moretti said as he moved past me. "Outside of taking a hammer to them, these gauges don't stop ticking. They don't need power." He paused, examining the readings.

"Hovering, sir. Rock-solid at one-eight-zero feet. We're coasting, at two knots and slowing."

"So the situation—"

"Is all fucked up," Reyes interrupted Larsen, who just laughed.

"It is, isn't it?" the lieutenant said. "Stuck in a submarine with no engines, no air conditioning, not even enough light to read a *Penthouse.* Fortunately, we brought our own nightlights. This ventilation business, though . . . Grimm, you know how much air we got to breathe?"

"Half a sub? Five . . . six of us? We can live for hours."

"It can outlast us, though," I said. "If we just sit here and do nothing, we can last for hours. It's a matter of conserving oxygen. But if we try to do anything, the air gets burned a lot faster. And just like the Serpent survived the chlorine gas, it can survive a little carbon dioxide."

"It's started the clock on us, huh, Doctor?" Reyes again.

"I'd say so. It's trying to force our hand."

"Smart," Larsen said. "It's got better senses than us, so it takes away the light. It's got better lungs than us, so it takes away the air."

"Hey, sir? If it's still in the electrical control room, it can hear what we're saying."

"So the fuck what? Can it even understand English? It's not like we're discussing national secrets here. I'm sure it didn't expect us to *not* notice we were in the dark and running out of oxygen." But as he spoke, Larsen moved over to Grimm and flashed several hand signals in the beam from his gun barrel. He ended by pointing aft.

Reyes and Moretti seemed to understand what had taken place. The chief again took up station near the door, while Grimm and Larsen strode toward—and past—me. I grabbed Larsen's arm, but he put his finger to his lips before I could speak. He pointed to his eyes. OK. I was looking at him.

He pointed at himself, then Grimm. Used two fingers to imitate legs walking. Pointed forward. Grimm's light caused shadows to flutter across the walls from the eerie pantomime.

Larsen and Grimm were going to the forward end of the ship. Got it. Then he held out his hand, palm up, in front of him and started drawing shapes on it with the index finger of his other hand. What?

I shook my head and shrugged.

He tried again. Tapped the side of his head, then did the hand-drawing thing again. There was something familiar about the action. And then I had it: he was tracing football plays on his palm, like a sandlot quarterback.

Now I nodded. He put his finger to his lips again. They were trying to be covert. It made sense; if the Serpent were indeed in the next compartment, it could hear us plot in the control room. So they were going as far away as they could and working out our next move.

Grimm stepped through the hatch, and Larsen was about to follow. Then he turned, pointed at all of us and made talky-talky motions with his hand. Act normal. Don't let the Serpent know anything's up.

And he, like Grimm, ducked into the hallway, and their lights and footsteps receded. Even though I knew—or at least assumed—that they'd be coming back, dividing our already paltry forces made me uneasy.

I fantasized about writing a report on all this, each word barricading the *Dragon* into the past. I wanted to walk into Charlie's office, through the door reading DIV. SUPERVISOR that was always open, and toss a report on his desk. We had a routine. I'd stand there, and Charlie would put on some reading glasses, run a hand through his curly gray hair and thumb through the report's first few pages. Then he'd look up, invite me to sit as if he'd forgotten I was there and ask me, "What did you see *between* the lines?" I'd fill him in on the "outside the assignment" observations I'd taken in, providing a larger context for what I'd done and the people I'd worked with. For both of us, this was the most interesting part of the endgame, where I could speak in unofficial terms about subjects that weren't officially supposed to exist.

I knew there would be a certain tangible comfort—one I yearned for—in our conversation, and in obscuring the most jagged details of this assignment with several pages of technical jargon and filing the whole experience away. But I had to survive it first.

Moretti and Reyes weren't paying any attention to me. Both still waited by the aft hatch, their lights and concentration focused on it.

Reyes crouched in front of it; the chief was off to one side. They didn't want to give the Serpent a clean shot at both of them at once, I guess. I sat down between them, my back against the nav periscope's cool, polished surface.

Moretti looked at me, his face turned into a caricature by the light beneath it.

"Making yourself comfortable?"

"Why not?" I replied, laying the .45 in my lap. "I can shoot just as well from down here. Maybe even get a better angle through the hatch."

Reyes sat down too, without comment.

"What are you doing, Seaman?"

"She's right. I can see through the doorway better this way. And here," he said to me, pulling something from beneath Jakes's legs, "if you're going to cover the door, cover the damn door."

He handed me Jakes's rifle.

"It's an MP-5, 9mm, 30 shots in the mag," he continued. "The selector on the side there'll tell you whether it's set for single, burst or full auto fire." I knew all of that, of course, but if it kept him talking and not focusing on the dead man lying nearby, he was welcome to run through its entire design history.

I saw motion to my right and realized Moretti had sat, also.

"I've never killed anyone sitting down," he said. "But I don't like the idea of being killed myself when I'm not on my feet."

"I know this thing is fast—we all saw that," I said. "But I don't see any way it can open the door and attack us before we get a shot at it. We've got a big defensive advantage." The bigger gun hadn't boosted my courage, but it felt comfortable in my hands. And I believed what I said: we'd see the hatch wheel turn and have plenty of time to react before the Serpent could do anything more than be a target.

"Yeah, well, we've had a big advantage this whole time, haven't we? I mean, sixteen of us? One of it? And it's pitching a shutout. The scoreboard says Serpent: 11, SEALs: 0."

"If we had known it was here when we came onboard—"

"We would have just nuked this tub," Moretti finished my sentence. It wasn't what I had been planning to say, but his solution was appealing. "Shit, maybe we still should. We've all got some C-4, little door-busting charges. If the Serpent's gonna track us all down anyway, we could just blow this thing, crack the pressure hull and make sure it doesn't get away."

Neither would we, of course.

"I don't think we're quite there yet. I'm not ready to give up," I said.

"Who's giving up? Our mission now is to kill this thing, and if it looks like we're not going to survive that mission, we better make damn sure it doesn't get away."

"Mortally wounded, the heroic soldier hides a live grenade under his belly until the enemy troops stumble onto his position."

Moretti ignored my sarcasm. "You're missing the point. We want to survive. Obviously. But if it looks like we can't do that—and it's getting to that point, wouldn't you agree?—we should make sure it doesn't either."

"Hey, can we talk about something else?" Reyes said. "I mean, seriously. We're sitting here in the dark with a couple of fresh corpses, and until someone tells me how to get out of this fucked-up mess, I'd like to pretend it ain't here."

What else could we pretend we were doing? Holding an armed slumber party?

"Some cards would be nice," Moretti said.

"Yeah. You ain't never won a hand against me, Chief. Be good to get back to shore with a little extra cash."

It was unbelievable. But it was right.

"Maybe we could make some s'mores," I said, and Reyes giggled. An honest giggle, like a Cub Scout on a campout who'd just heard a dirty joke. A Cub Scout with a fist tattooed on his neck.

"Or talk about girls," Moretti said. "Just no ghost stories."

No, we didn't need any of those.

The air was still. I hadn't noticed it moving much before the power went out, but its utter tranquility was tangible now. It was a wool blanket of close, unpleasant smells. If the darkness had been complete, I might have guessed we were in some bizarre combination of machine-parts factory and nineteenth-century hospital.

"You know what this shit is like?" Reyes said. "It's like sitting in my parents' garage. My brother, my homeboy Mike and I would go out there in the summer, after curfew, and sit there in the dark and pass around a jay. It was so much like this, with the smoke and the flashlights. We'd be burning up, but we couldn't open a window to cool off because of the smell. And we wanted to talk, but we had to whisper because my parents' room was right over the garage."

"You got any smoke?"

"Sorry, Chief, I left it in my footlocker. Maybe the doctor's got some. What do they call it . . . medicinal?"

"All I have is some aspirin. Sorry, guys. But hey, if we can get the underwater telephone working, I can call someone. He'll charge extra, though."

We had gotten all the mileage we could out of the pot jokes. It seemed as though we should be sitting in a circle, but the hatch demanded our attention. Looking away from it felt like death.

I didn't want to listen to my thoughts in silence.

"Well, you know what it feels like to me?" I said. "I wasn't kidding about the s'mores thing. It reminds me of being on a campout, you know? Like inside your tent, with flashlights, staying up after the adults have gone to bed."

"Break out the porn mags and dirty jokes," Moretti said, his braces flashing as he smiled.

"Naw, man, she totally was a Girl Scout. Right?"

"Nope. Never did anything like that. But I grew up in West Virginia. So I had mountains and trees in my backyard. Camping was what we did on the weekends, for fun. When we were kids, we'd make Mom go with us, sort of like a family social event. Then once we got older—and knew our way around the woods—we could go out there by ourselves."

"West Virginia. Yeah, you have the accent. I couldn't place it right away," the chief said.

"Oh, come on, I'm a city girl now. College educated, even."

"But you still got some country in you. That's cool, Doc, that's cool." Reyes, by contrast, sounded as if he'd been born in a land of concrete and steel and never had left. "So did your dad take you hunting and shit? You look like you know what you're doing with that MP-5."

This wasn't a conversation I'd ever expected to have.

"My dad. No, he didn't take me hunting. He, uh . . . I didn't know him very well."

"More of a mama's little girl? You probably had a brother, didn't you? I'll bet Pops hung out with him all the time."

I could see Moretti shifting in my peripheral vision, trying to make eye contact with the other man. "Reyes, shut up."

"What? I'm just—"

"Quit giving her shit, all right? Why do you want to hear about her personal life? Are you gonna tell her about how *your* pops had to kiss some gangbanger's shoes back in the 'hood?"

"Damn, man, I was just making conversation. Forget about it."

"You know what? It's all right," I said, throwing myself into the middle of their exchange. It *was* all right. I didn't care. Discussing my childhood—or anything else—didn't seem painful or dangerous right now. "Go ahead. Ask me anything you want."

And we were in the tent again, playing truth or dare, probing each other's secrets.

Reyes looked at me, then Moretti, then back to me.

"Anything?"

"Go for it."

"Why do you keep fussing with that rubber band on your wrist?"

It wasn't the first time I'd heard that one. I tried not to just fall into a rehearsed answer.

"It's a story of love, death and carcinogens," I said.

"Sounds like a good one," Reyes said.

"A bad one, actually. A very bad one. I took up smoking a couple of months after I took my second job at the CIA. The one I have now." I paused, thinking back to the first butt, handed to me as I stood over a dismembered field agent in Serbia. "It's something a lot of us do. It calms you down, gives your fingers something to do and kills your taste buds a little bit. You can't smell as much.

"And there's something about the act of smoking that separates you from your surroundings a little bit, I think. The smoke is kind of like a wall. It detaches you from the rest of the world if you want it to. That's helpful.

"The day I first put a rubber band on my wrist was . . . there's only one other point in my life that even comes close to being so horrible. And I was really too young to remember that one. This was about two years ago. In September. I had been sent to New Orleans the night before, to a crime scene in an Upper 9th Ward housing project. The local cops had found a decomposing body in an abandoned apartment there and escalated the case to the feds when they found a Koran and a couple of folders with Arabic documents in them. Nothing conclusive, of course, but the body appeared to have been tortured, and of course they assumed it was terrorism. That's what I read in the case summary on my red-eye flight.

"So I go into this apartment: God, more water stains than wallpaper, creaky floors, a decrepit moldy smell that would have been overwhelming if it weren't for the even more powerful reek of rotting flesh. There's the body. Male, slumped over, tied to a chair in the middle of the room. Right off the bat, I'm guessing this person's been dead about a week—long enough to smell, but not long enough to totally disintegrate. I can also tell that the locals were right about torture: the body was naked, and you could see elongated burn marks on the legs and groin region."

"Fuck," Reyes interrupted. "You see that all the time? I mean, that was normal for you?"

"People find all kinds of interesting ways to kill each other," I said.

"I seen bodies before. But they were shot, like, just lying there," he continued.

"Let her finish," Moretti said.

I took a deep breath. I couldn't remember telling anyone this story in so much depth, not even Stephen.

"I put on a surgical mask. There's a trick where if the stench is really bad, you smear a little menthol jelly on the inside of the mask. I did that. I walked over and kneeled down by the chair, looking up and trying to get a good look at the body's face. And . . . and it all fell apart."

"What, the body?" Moretti said. I could hear the image in his incredulous voice.

"No. Me. I recognized the face. A guy I started at the Agency with. He was just out of school then, like me, and had the psychology background. But he was leaning toward field work, clandestine intelligence collection."

"You knew him. Shit, man," Reyes said.

"I got it together, barely. I finished my work and headed back to Norfolk. Wrote a draft of my report on the airplane. In other circumstances, it would have been, you know, intellectually interesting. The documents were a red herring, the body was left where it would be found . . . but none of that was really important. I just kept seeing his face. Whenever I closed my eyes."

"What was his name? The guy in New Orleans, I mean," Reyes said.

Moretti shifted a little bit. Even though he still wasn't looking at me, I could sense his discomfort.

"John Smith. No, I'm totally serious. He had the perfect name for his job. I didn't even know him all that well, but it was enough, you know? It was enough to make it matter in a way that other cases didn't. And I must have gone through two packs by the time I got back to my house, where my fiancé was waiting.

"He had made dinner. All I wanted to do was try to get some footing and pull myself back together. But you know what he did? Before I could even really figure out what to say to him, he told me that we weren't right for each other and that he was leaving me. I started crying. Then he walked out.

"I stood on the back patio, dinner cooling on the table, smoking the last couple of cigarettes I had. But he was a smoker, too. It struck me that I wanted to be done with this day, with this feeling, forever. So I quit, cold turkey. Started wearing a rubber band, and whenever I had a craving for a nic fix, I'd snap myself. I guess I got kind of used to having it on because now I wear one all the time, and I play with it when I'm thinking or when I'm nervous. It's like my version of biting my fingernails. And that's it. Boring story, right?"

"How the fuck did you *get* this job?" Reyes blurted.

"I was looking for work after college. Government jobs have good benefits. I started in profiling—I don't know, it seemed really interesting and challenging. And it is." I stopped myself. It was too glib, too easy for this conversation. "Look. I feel like . . . for basically my entire life, I've been dealing with my mom's psychological damage. Exit wounds, really. I'm used to trauma, and I know I'm no good at helping people get over it. But I'm great at figuring out *why* it happened. If you want a deeper explanation, you need to hire someone to psychoanalyze me. Now come on, ask me something I *really* have to think about."

Moretti dived back into the conversation. "A treehouse. You have a treehouse when you were a kid?"

The abrupt change in direction was refreshing. I could remember the vibrant green leaves of the tree outside my bedroom window. An oak, I think. It was like being in a treehouse, sometimes, sitting there in my room, reading a book, watching the sun make dancing patterns on the floor.

"No. There were plenty of trees around the house, but most of them were either too close to it or too small to build in. We climbed them all the time, though."

"Tomboy?" Moretti said. "I kinda figured that, too."

"Not really. It was just me and my brother playing, most of the time, because my school friends lived too far away to walk to. So I guess I was a little more rough-and-tumble, maybe, just because I hung out with him so much. Mom made sure I knew all the social graces."

"It was just you and your brother, huh? Kinda like me," Reyes said. "You know, he wanted to join the Navy, too. All those recruiters came to the high school all the time."

I could hear something in his voice, a seed of wistfulness that he tried to cover with bravado.

"But he didn't join?"

"He got killed." If Reyes had been looking at me to begin with, he would have glanced away, fastened his attention on something else. "After that, Mom and Dad was like, 'You're getting out of here.' So as soon as I was eighteen, I joined up. Worked my ass off. Now here I am."

"Where'd you grow up?" I asked.

"L.A. We lived in Silver Lake, but my pops had a, like, a convenience store in Carson. José–that's my brother–and I, we would go help him out. You know, put shit on the shelves, mop the floors."

"Cheap labor," Moretti said.

"I know, right? But we was there the first two times the place got robbed, man. I saw a guy stick a Magnum in Dad's face. And after that Mom was like, 'they ain't working there anymore.' Pops hires a couple of dudes, they turn out to be gangbangers. But he didn't know that at first. They started shaking him down, like making him give them cash out of the drawer or they'd all come back at night and burn the place down. He was scared to fire them. Shit, I would've been too. He ended up closing the store 'cause of those fuckers."

Reyes snapped back to the present. "Anyway, they're still there, in the same house. Mom's got her Navy flag hanging out front, every day. I don't worry about them anymore. Mom, though, she worries about me. All the time."

"I know what that's like," I said. "Where you from, Chief?"

"I'm from New Jersey. I'm twenty-eight and have a middle-management position with a world-class troubleshooting and demolitions firm. I'm a Pisces, I like soft music and loud romps on the beach, and I'm disease-free." Moretti was getting into the spirit of this. "Can I buy you a drink?"

I laughed at his remark, but the joy dried up inside me as an image sprung into my mind. That kid–Patterson's aide–trying to make small talk in the Humvee. The scene pulled at my heart with its normalcy. And its distance.

"Sure. Make it a double," I said, trying to mask the sudden ache with more frivolity. "What's a nice guy like you doing in a place like this?"

"Ah, you know." Moretti showed no indication of having noticed my mood. "Couple years of community college, I was bored, broke and completely directionless. So I did what any sane person would do in that situation: I joined up."

"You really from New Jersey?"

"Yep. Hoboken. Nice place, if you don't mind all the concrete and garbage. You played in the woods? We played in the alleys."

"I bet the chief would rather have grown up in your 'hood," Reyes said. "He's into all that outdoorsy shit."

"Can you blame a guy for wanting to enjoy nature every once in a while? I'm daydreaming about a nice trout stream right now."

"Nothing more relaxing than fly-fishing," I said. "Beer cooling in the stream, fish tugging at your line."

"Hear that, Chief? You're in. I'm out of the picture."

"No way, Reyes. She's out of both of our leagues. A doctor, remember? Not spear-carriers like us. We don't even know her first name."

"It's Christine."

"What's up, Christine?" Reyes said. "I'm Dom." It was an odd set of introductions, done with words but no eye contact.

"And your first name isn't Chief, is it?" I said to Moretti.

"Just Carl."

"We call him 'Chief' because that's what he is—master chief petty officer—and he thinks he's a badass," Reyes said.

"Quite a title."

"Well, I'm quite a guy," Moretti replied. "I keep everyone in line when the officers aren't looking."

As he finished his sentence, we no longer were sitting in total darkness. It was only for an instant—subliminal, almost—but there had been an increase in the room's ambient light. The moment was accompanied by a bang from the other side of the closed hatch, and a hiss that was audible even through the tempered steel.

"What the fuck?" Reyes had snapped from a sitting position into a crouch, his rifle never leaving the door.

"It's a fuse. Sounds like one blew. Everything in here turned on for a split-second," Moretti said. He delivered this news with the same

230

inflection he had told me his name and rank. "The Serpent is tinkering with the works over there."

He was right, I realized. The indicators and screens must have switched on just long enough to add a few watts of illumination to the compartment. The overhead lights hadn't come to life.

"What's it doing?" Reyes hadn't changed positions, his legs coiled beneath him.

"Who knows? Who cares? Can't do anything about it except sit here and wait for our air to run out."

"Yeah," I said, picking up Moretti's angle. "Just relax. It'll have to come through that door sooner or later, and then you'll get your chance to shoot it."

Reyes caught on now, too. The less the Serpent thought we were worrying about it, the lower its guard would be when we made our move. And it didn't hurt our mental well-being to whistle in the dark, either.

"OK. I'm cool. So what were we talking about? The chief?"

"Why would we do that? I'm boring. Just another ex-English major with an assault rifle. Now, the doctor here, I'll bet she could tell us some stories."

"Seriously, call me Christine. I'm not operating on you or anything."

"What kind of doctor are you?" Reyes asked.

"Two kinds. I'm a physician; that is, I have a medical degree. But I also have a doctorate in psychology. That just makes me a psychiatrist, one of millions."

"Jesus! How long do you have to be in school for that?"

Moretti chuckled at Reyes's amazement.

"Eight years. But I started a year early. Then when I was done, the CIA hired me."

"Uh-oh. She's going to have to kill us now, Reyes."

"Calm down," I said. We were back in camp again, our man-made surroundings as insignificant as they were invisible. "It's all aboveboard. I'm a federal employee, just like you two."

"So what do you do?"

Ah. That was crossing the line, wasn't it? But hell, the three of us had seen enough already to fill ten classified reports.

"That, I'm really not supposed to talk about. But I started as a profiler. A couple of years in, some people higher up the food chain decided I had an aptitude for forensics and nudged me in that direction. So I've been doing that for the last eight years. Basically, it's the same thing I've done here. Go over a crime scene, check out all the physical evidence, examine the corpses. Then figure out who did the killing, and why."

"For the CIA?" Reyes wasn't going to let it go.

"Reyes, you dumbass. Her job is cleaning up after people like us, I think, and I'm pretty sure we should leave it at that if we want this conversation to go anyplace." Moretti winked at me.

"Fuck! I hate this shit! I hate this pretending!" Reyes's yell was unexpected and shrill. "I fucking want to grab the Serpent and just squeeze. Choke it. Then shoot it. Then jump on its head until it splats like a fucking watermelon. But we're sitting here, talking like we ain't on the wrong end of a—"

"Reyes! Shut up! Belay that talk right now, or I'll come over there and flog your ass."

The seaman was looking over at Moretti now, his face unsure whether it wanted to be angry, afraid or dejected. But he was quiet. The tension hung in the air between the two men like invisible electric lines.

The graphic violence in Reyes's words shocked me. Where had it come from? Did all the SEALs have this same savagery packed away inside them?

"Reyes." Now I was a therapist. I tried to soften my voice, use it to create safety and certainty in our dark prison. "You're OK. Listen, I want you to tell me something. When you think back to when you were growing up, what is a golden moment that jumps out at you? When you were having fun, just being yourself and not worrying about anything? When everything was right?"

He blinked. "What?"

"I know you've had those times. We all have. See, you're never stuck someplace unpleasant, not as long as you've got your brain with you. You always have access to the things that make you happy."

He was listening now, wanting to believe. "Well, uh. José and I, we'd go down to the park. If you go around dinnertime, it ain't so crowded. So the sun's going down . . . "

"The smog makes the sun orange that time of day," Moretti interrupted.

"Yeah, exactly. Everything's kind of glowing. But we'd play 21—that's a basketball game—until it was too dark. Then we'd go home and have dinner after Dad closed up the store for the night. It was perfect."

"I told you about the trout stream," Moretti said. "There is a place in upstate New York, near Ithaca, that as far as I know, the rest of the world never discovered. A buddy of mine showed it to me. You can't even drive there. You have to park by the side of the highway, then hike for maybe a half-hour, and then all of a sudden you're on top of this beautiful gorge with a crystal stream at the bottom. Talk about happy places. If I could somehow retire there, I'd get myself discharged right now. Maybe slap an admiral or something."

"Then what would you do?" I said.

"Fish. Drink. No plans beyond that. It's kind of the way I live my life. The Navy is the longest commitment I've ever made to anything. And I can tell you, honestly, that qualifying for SEAL school changed my life. Other than doing nothing and trout fishing, there's no job I'd rather have."

"Why?"

"There are, what, six billion people in the world? One thousand of those are smart enough, strong enough, to be a SEAL. Do the math. And look at the operations we're trusted with," he said, glancing around the darkened control room. I couldn't tell whether he was being sarcastic. "I've never been part of something so important before."

"I hope you get back to that stream sooner rather than later," I said.

Reyes was nodding. I had calmed myself, too. Our recollections had touched a part of me that had been overrun by the *Dragon's* horrors. But before I had finished that bit of introspection, there was motion behind us.

We turned and saw Grimm, squinting into the beam from the light on my gun, step through the forward hatch. He pointed at me and Moretti, then jerked his thumb back the way he had come. Grimm stood to one side as we passed. He was going to stay in the control room, which was good, because I didn't think Reyes could handle being alone with his thoughts, let alone repelling an attack by the Serpent.

Campbell still was sitting in the bed, I saw as we walked down the hallway, and he managed a wave with his free hand. At the end of the corridor was an oval of faint, unsteady light. It was the hatch, its shape defined by the light from Larsen's gun.

Climbing through after Moretti, I saw the lieutenant standing at the opposite end of the compartment, where I had waited for the Serpent to fall into our baited trap. The dark shapes of the torpedoes seemed to point to him, as though he were standing at an altar or in front of a throne.

Larsen waved us over, and when we stood a few feet away, he began speaking in a voice just above a whisper.

"We're running out of options." That wasn't the encouraging message I had been looking for. "The Serpent can keep the engines off-line, can keep the air scrubbers off-line and can prevent us from fixing any of it."

"What about the diving controls? We've got those in the control room," Moretti said.

"Yeah. But without electrical power, we can't do anything except an emergency blow. So all of a sudden a foreign sub surfaces off the coast of Virginia—so long, 'top secret.' Don't bother, Doctor." He had seen me take a breath. "I know secrecy isn't our biggest priority anymore. But the other problem is that the Serpent could be off the boat the second we broke the surface. There's an escape tower like the one in here," he said, pointing to the hatch over our heads, "in the aft torpedo room. I think we all can agree that allowing this thing to reach shore would be a disaster."

"Can we call for help? What about that underwater telephone thing?" I asked.

"Without electricity, it's just a useless chunk of metal."

"So . . . what? What do we do?" Moretti asked.

"We consider the tactical advantages. Grimm and I have been over all this, forward and backward. We have the numbers. We can get the initiative. But no matter what, it will be the defender. All we can do is hope that our hand trumps the Serpent's."

"Wait a second. So we're just going to charge in there after it?" I said.

"We don't expect you to participate. You can stay in the control room, just to make sure it can't get in there, no matter what. And we're not 'charging in.' We have a plan, and we'll execute it."

"Tell us the plan, then." Moretti couldn't quite cover up the disappointment in his voice.

"As I said, we're not going to rush into a bad situation. We've got its location pinned down for the first time: the Serpent is in the electrical control room."

"Whoa," I said. "That's a huge assumption. The hatch is shut. It could be anyplace on this boat aft of the control room."

"Well, we heard it banging around," Moretti said. "It's working on the electrical systems. Or messing them up more. Whatever. The point is, it's making a lot of noise. It's in there."

"But what's stopping it from leaving before we launch our attack? Or from slipping out the aft door the second it sees us turning the wheel on the forward hatch?"

"Calm down. We know it's still there. And we made sure it wasn't going to get out of that compartment without us knowing. I can't even take credit for that one.

"When we were preparing to storm into the control room, Grimm grabbed a belt off of one of the Koreans and tied a wrench to one end. Then he tied the other end to the dogging wheel on the engine-room side of the aft hatch. As we ran through there—he was the last man through—he closed the door and sealed it."

I was getting the picture. "The wrench lies on the floor. But the wheel has to spin for the door to open, and if that happens, the wrench gets picked up and dropped back onto the deck repeatedly by the belt."

"Making a loud noise that, without the engines running or anything, we could hear all the way up here," Larsen finished.

That *was* clever. And in all the time we had been sharing campfire stories in the control room, we'd never heard the wrench banging on the floor.

"So like I said, we know where it is." The lieutenant wanted his confidence to be contagious, to infect us with its fervor. But I seemed immune. "That puts us on an even footing with the Serpent, whereas before, it knew where we were, but not vice versa."

"What we need are some stun grenades," the chief mumbled.

"You're not bullshitting. Open the hatch, lob a few through, wait for the bang and follow it with some bullets. Unfortunately, that's not one of the cards in our deck."

"What about a door-busting charge? We could toss one in there and—"

"Nope. We thought about that, Chief, and the problem is, it might wreck something in that room that we need in working order. After we kill the Serpent, we have to be able to bring this boat back online. If the Serpent's out of the picture, secrecy becomes our number one goal."

So we were back to just charging through the hatch.

"The way we make this work is by creating the same effect as a stun grenade, though. This thing's senses are all pumped up to superhuman levels. If we start shooting and pin it down with the lights, the sudden noise and flashes will fuck with it enough to get us all in the room before it can fight back. From there, we can engage it on our terms."

That was a gamble. Larsen was hoping the Serpent's abilities would work against it. But so far they had proved most effective against us.

"That's the plan?" I couldn't stay quiet. "Open the door and pull the trigger? Hope you hit something this time?"

Larsen and Grimm had already explored this territory, I could tell. The lieutenant was patient, nodding.

"It's not ideal. But we have certain advantages, and this allows us to use them. Since we don't have the luxury of waiting it out or regaining control without a fight, we have to act."

Larsen's face, drained of color by the indirect lighting, was emotionless. The effect was that of a scarred, disembodied head floating in the darkness, granting us wisdom from the spirit world.

Moretti turned his light on me, destroying the illusion.

"I know you don't think this makes any sense," he said. "But we're SEALs. We do impossible jobs. And as weird as it sounds, we've trained on how to enter and secure a one-door room. That's the situation we're facing now. So we're not just relying on blind luck."

"You have to think logically about it. We'd like to get on its flanks—but we can't. We'd like to attack from several angles—but we can't. We'd like more of an element of surprise—but . . . do you follow?" Larsen said, poking his palm with a finger as he made each point. "We do have a few aces, though, and now's the time to lay them on the table."

He was making the same argument over and over. And I was incapable of thinking about it anymore.

"Fine. We charge the Serpent and overwhelm it," I said.

Larsen was waiting for more from me. I had nothing left.

"Remember, it doesn't know we're coming, and we have superior numbers. That means—"

"Enough, Chief. I know what it means, and I believe you guys. So go do it. Let's get it over with."

The SEALs glanced at each other, unsure how to handle the abrupt lack of resistance. Larsen recovered first.

"That's exactly right, Myers. No reason to hesitate. Chief, go fill Campbell in. He's going to stay where he is for this operation. Except . . . don't tell him out loud. Write it down on the notepad he's got in there."

Moretti turned to leave, then paused. "I can't wait to kill this bastard." The words floated across to us as Moretti continued out of the compartment. And I could tell then that they were more sincere than anything else he had said to me.

After Moretti was gone, Larsen addressed me again.

"I can tell you're not thrilled with this plan. But it's the best one we can execute under the circumstances."

Execute. Maybe not the greatest choice of words.

"I believe you. Are you trying to convince me or yourself?"

After a long silence, he replied, resting one hand on a torpedo's flank.

"I'm confident in my men. And I never doubt we'll win any fight, even when we're outgunned."

"I want to ask you something before we go up there," I said.

He nodded. "Go on."

"I'm confident in you and your men. But if things . . . if the fight doesn't go the way we want it, if Campbell and I are the only ones left, what then?"

He had thought about this, too, because his lips pursed as he bit back a quick answer.

"What?" I asked. "Tell me what you were going to say."

Larsen sighed and looked at the floor, further destroying his supernatural aura. He was just a man, the gesture told me. A man whose first words a few minutes ago had been, "We're running out of options."

"I will tell Campbell this personally. I'm going to collect C-4 from everyone and give it to him," he said. "I know this sounds shocking, all right?

"If we get wiped out, Campbell is going to detonate the plastic explosives. That much bang is going to breach the hull, and . . . well . . ."

Sometimes suicide was rational, I thought.

He needed me to say something. "It's OK," was all I could manage.

I wasn't choked up by shock, as he had expected, but by a feeling of utter hopelessness that had swept over me. I pictured Campbell packing a wad of C-4 onto the bulkhead over the bed. Setting a timer, hands steady. Sitting there, watching it count down, the numerals from the device reflecting in his green eyes.

"If we can't kill the Serpent, there's no way you two can survive. Even if it doesn't come after you, it's in control of the boat, and that's unacceptable. It can't be allowed to escape."

"It can't be allowed to escape," I repeated.

"Don't try to stop Campbell. Even with his injuries, he still can–"

"I won't try to do anything. I'll sit there next to him."

I would, too. I could see myself added to the scene, and my despair deepened.

"But it won't come to that," Larsen said. I could tell he meant it, but again, the words were insubstantial to me.

He waited for me to speak. Then, after squeezing my shoulder, he walked by, leaving me staring at the *Dragon*'s dormant torpedo tubes. The executive officer's body lay a few feet away. Is this how he had felt after the captain warned him of the consequences of the Serpent's escape?

What had he thought as he turned the valves? As he listened to the hand-to-hand fighting below him? As he chained the . . .

"Wait!" My yell ruined our secrecy, but I was too excited to notice Larsen's anger as he paused on the stepladder.

"What? Keep it down, Myers."

"Come here," I said, walking toward him. He stepped back down to the deck but didn't move.

"Look," I continued, pointing.

"Yeah, it's a closed door. Explain what you're thinking, Myers, because we can't afford to—"

"No, it's not just closed. It's chained!" This time I contained my exuberance in a stage whisper. "Locked and chained! If we go through there, you guys can get behind him. Attack from two sides."

"Come on. Unless we blow the lock up, which would obviously be dangerous in a room full of torpedoes, we're not getting it off. This door is worthless to us."

"But there's a key to the lock. And I think we can find it."

"I'm listening."

"Either the captain or Lee chained this door up because they were the only ones who knew the plan for trying to prevent the Serpent's escape. So one of them has a key to this thing. We already have the captain's key ring."

Larsen moved back up the ladder. Even though he had expressed confidence before, there was more urgency and less resignation in his movements now.

"You search the XO. Where are the captain's keys?"

"In his room. Campbell might still have them."

He disappeared through the door, and I walked over to Lee's body. It had stiffened up since I first examined it, but the suit was loose-fitting. I was able to pull it down past his waist without too much trouble.

I had never searched a corpse in the dark. It might have been macabre in different circumstances, but now nothing—not the body, not the torpedoes, not the eerie, dead stillness of the immobilized sub—spooked me. All that mattered was finding new hope for survival.

But his pockets held nothing. Shit. We'd have to toss his cabin, and without direct lighting, that would be a long, frustrating exercise.

It turned out to be unnecessary. Larsen's light bobbed back into the torpedo room, and he knelt next to the lower hatch, trying the keys on the captain's ring. It didn't take long.

"Got it." The words were whispered, not yelled, but they conveyed a sureness that, this time, resonated through me. We had drawn an ace.

Grimm entered the compartment as Larsen and I disentangled the chain from the door's locking mechanism.

"Did you find it?" He saw what we were doing and didn't wait for a reply. "We divide up. Two teams, two men each."

Larsen finished with the chain, handed it to me and stood. "Yeah. The lower-deck group has three compartments to get through, but they've got to be as stealthy as possible. Even breathing too hard could fuck this up. We need to make it think we're only coming from one direction."

"The attacks need to be simultaneous."

"Of course." The men weren't addressing one another, just thinking aloud. Between them, the plan continued to take shape. "When the flanking team is in position, they'll signal and attack. The other team will hear the signal and enter the room."

"What if the Serpent makes the same noise as the signal?"

"Team B—that's the flankers—they'll bash the hatch cover with the wrench there. Three times."

"Then they'll go."

"Yes. Both doors open at the same time, both point men enter. It can't cover two hatches at once."

But it could attack one man. Whoever was closest, perhaps. This wasn't going to be a casualty-free operation unless the Serpent was paralyzed with surprise.

"Gotta be careful of friendly fire, though," Larsen said. "We can saw

240

this cocksucker in two, but the first men through the hatches are going to be looking right at each other."

"It might use one as a human shield," I said, Jakes's tortured face flashing through my thoughts. "You have to—"

"We will," Larsen said. "This is it. This is when we win, no matter what the cost. If it means shooting through me, I want my men to do it. Whoever's first through the door might get killed right off the bat. There's no guarantee it's going to be indecisive. It might just pick a door and attack."

"But it's our best shot," I said.

"No," Grimm replied. "I'd say it's our only shot."

XII

REYES AND GRIMM WERE CROUCHED by the hatch next to Jakes's corpse. No giggling in the tent now. Neither seemed aware of my presence at the other end of the room. The light from their guns was trained on the door a few feet away, turning them into silhouettes against a gray background.

They were waiting for the signal. So was I.

I had a job in this operation. After they went into the electrical compartment, I was to shoot anything that tried to move from there into the control room. Not "anything not wearing black" or "anything that doesn't give the correct signal." Anything. If the SEALs won and survived, they'd return through the lower deck. Larsen wanted to make sure that at least one escape route was inaccessible to the Serpent.

If the two SEALs in front of me were worried about getting shot in the back, they didn't show it. I wondered if I looked as unruffled. I wasn't uncomfortable with my role, with the automatic rifle I was cradling or with Larsen's .45 tucked into my waistband. And the other possible task Larsen had given me was lurking in the dark places of my brain. I kept it sequestered there.

Larsen had put his hand on my shoulder after Grimm went aft to get Moretti and Reyes.

"You know there's a chance of failure. None of us believe we're going to fail, but sometimes it's not . . ." The right words had seemed just out of his reach. Or maybe he just didn't want to say them. Instead of finishing his sentence, he had raised his eyebrows, looking for acknowledgment.

It's not in the cards, is what you want to say, I had thought as I nodded.

"If none of us come out of that room, and if the Serpent's not dead, you need to make sure it doesn't get away. Do you understand?"

I did. He had made this point before, and there was no reason to respond.

"Campbell might be killed, too. There's no guarantee both of you will be alive to take care of this. So I'm going to give you the same thing I gave him."

Both of our weapons had been pointed at the floor, producing a reflected twilight. The pipes, wires and machinery in the background were black-on-black, unseeable.

Out of the artificial night had come Larsen's hand, reaching toward me. In its palm had been a hand-sized gray slab with a black piece of plastic embedded in it.

"It's C-4. Three door-busting charges molded together. Enough to put a hole in the pressure hull, I think. But if you want to make sure the sub goes down, put it on the oil or fuel tanks in the engine room. Obviously, the torpedoes would make a pretty big bang, too."

The explosives had been lighter than I expected and had a greasy texture.

"The timer's simple. It's got a readout like a digital watch, you see there? All you have to do is use these arrows to set the minutes and seconds. Then push the red button. You can't disarm it after it's set, and if you pull the trigger out of the brick, it will fire."

"So once it starts, there's no going back."

"No going back, no backing out. I don't think you'll need to use this. But you know how important it is. I know you do."

"Yes. I can do it."

And he had nodded, letting go of my shoulder as Moretti and Reyes had arrived for their briefing, hustling down the stepladder.

Now, as I squatted there in the control room, waiting for the shooting to start, I could feel the explosives in the pouch he had given me, hanging from a loop on my jeans. I tried to banish the sensation and focus on the immediate future.

Tried to pretend that I still was just a forensic scientist, not a conscript in a fast-dwindling army. Tried to ignore the blood-sodden body on the floor beside me. Tried to follow my own advice and allow pleasant memories to keep my thoughts from descending into inescapable darkness. There was going to be a tomorrow, I kept telling myself.

But I had to survive today first.

We had all been listening. No sound of the hatch opening. No signal. The Serpent was still there. Was it aware of what we were planning? Did it even want to avoid our final assault? It had shown little desire to back away from conflict, but I agreed with Larsen and Grimm: If the SEALs did this the way it was supposed to be done, there was no way the Serpent would be able to fight off the two-pronged attack. It was too small a space, and there would be too many bullets in the air.

There was no sign—to us, anyway—that two SEALs were creeping through the corpses on the lower deck, either. If they were quiet, evading even the Serpent's enhanced hearing, surprise might be total.

The agony of waiting was exquisite. I thought of Campbell in the captain's room; he must feel even more helpless. The bleeding from his leg had stopped, for the most part, but his cognitive functions seemed impaired. No way of knowing for sure at this point, but I guessed that his concussion was worse than I had diagnosed it as being. Forget secrecy, I thought; if this attack goes as planned, our priority afterward should be getting Campbell to a hospital before he slipped beyond help. But I knew Larsen wouldn't see it that way.

After checking him one final time, I had left Campbell sitting on the edge of the bed—he'd refused to lie down—keeping the cone of light from his assault rifle pinned on the doorway. Other than that focused illumination, he sat in darkness and anticipation. I turned to look at him as Larsen led me out of the room, and he had smiled. A gentle, kind expression that I was becoming used to. More than Larsen's plan or the massed firepower of the rest of the SEALs, it reassured me.

"Hey," he had said. "Keep your finger on the trigger and the barrel pointed downrange. I've got your back covered. But you owe me a beer on dry land."

"Deal," I'd replied, and I'd meant it. That was the last time I can remember smiling.

Clang.

Reyes and Grimm hadn't moved, but somehow their shadowy shapes seemed more alert. Ready to pounce and kill.

But where were the second two knocks? I was bowled over by billowing panic and sudden realization. It might not be the second team signaling us. It might be Grimm's makeshift alarm sounding. I swallowed a scream. How could we tell whether the Serpent was escaping or the attack was on? How could . . .

Clang. Clang.

The world slowed down again.

I don't remember breathing. Grimm grabbed the dogging wheel and gave it a vicious spin, allowing the wheel's momentum to do most of the work of unlocking it. Behind him, Reyes's right hand came off his rifle and danced in front of his chest. He was making the sign of the cross.

The wheel stopped, and Grimm shoved the door ajar with his shoulder as he bulled through. Reyes followed, his head entering the opening as soon as Grimm's combat boots were clear. They were no more than moving outlines now, made sharp by the jerking lights at the other end of the electrical compartment.

So the SEALs were coming through the aft hatch, too. If the lights overhead had been functioning, the scene would have been more real. I might have seen their fluid, sure entrance, four rifles pivoting to strip away all the compartment's defenses.

But their actions were lost in the maelstrom of shadows. Boots slapped against the deck, metal struck metal as the doors swung against the adjacent bulkheads. No shouting or talking. The shifting patches of light and dark made shapes emerge where there were none and blurred perception of what was alive and what was not. The room's walls seemed to undulate.

I'm not sure when the shooting started. There was a short, stuttering burst that made the silence afterward sound absolute. Then, a voice.

"Reyes! Chacho, please, no!"

I couldn't tell who said it. The voice was strong and full of earnest emotion.

Then the room exploded with gunfire. Someone fell on the other side of the hatch, passing through the light from my rifle too fast for me to make out who it was. Sprays of red on the lip of the door were left behind.

The shooting continued, and I found myself standing, trying to sprint across the control room. My feet didn't react as fast as the rest of my body, however, and I fell face-first not out of panic, but clumsiness. I caught myself, the MP-5 smacking into the deck and skittering away as I let it go. The light on the barrel winked out.

I lay there, looking up. I was more shocked by the sudden darkness than by the violence blossoming in the next compartment.

Sparks now had joined the visual cacophony as bullets plowed into the instrumentation and controls. I heard a scream. It wailed and wailed, an alto counterpoint to the firing, then just disappeared, as if it had been severed from its source.

My world was illuminated by the pulses of light darting through the doorway. It no longer was possible to distinguish muzzle blasts from flashlights from electrical shorts, and the shadows whirled among them. There was an army in there, a thousand soldiers forming and reforming as they fought.

Was that a pair of legs that just moved in front of the door? The shape soon was gone, or replaced by another indistinct form. Now a pipe had been hit, a line carrying compressed water, which sprayed into the compartment. The mist hissed and popped as it settled on the equipment.

And then that sound was all that was left. The darkness and light untangled and stopped moving. The only illumination came from outside my field of view in the other compartment, and it seemed to be facing the wall, offering only an ineffectual reflection of light to the rest of the room.

Something moved by the aft doorway. Maybe. I picked myself up, but remained on my knees. Larsen's orders—all of them—were shouting at me to act. Drawing the pistol, I called out.

"Hey! Who's there?"

Stupid.

And there was no answer.

I crouched and moved forward. Yes, there was blood on the doorway, snaking down its edges. As I got closer, I could see that a hand rested on the lower lip. Its fingers were limp and pale.

If I stayed close to the wall, I'd have the best view into the next room. I squatted over Jakes's body, ignoring the knife sticking from his back like a lever. It was impossible to glean any details of the electrical control room's interior from this angle. I couldn't see the face of the corpse by the door.

What was in the corner with the compartment's lone light source? A huddled lump on the floor. A SEAL? The Serpent?

Fuck. Fuck, fuck, fuck.

"Hello?" I asked.

Still nothing but the water drizzling from above.

The SEALs had planned to return via the lower deck. But if they still were alive, why weren't they replying?

I would have to look. I would have to dive into this nightmare and see what had happened.

First, who was on the other side of the door? Keeping the pistol in front of me, I craned my neck enough to see over the hatch's rim. Even in the damp gloom, I could see Reyes's face staring back at me, eyes wide. His mouth was open, too, as if he'd been trying to yell when he died. The cause of death was the dozen still-oozing bullet holes in his chest.

The professional side of me, the side that had examined a thousand mutilated bodies, was fighting a losing battle. I was afraid. Yes. It was in-escapable, the fear. I knew that each corpse I encountered in the room would make me see how close I was to becoming one as well.

But I climbed through the hatch anyway, stepping over Reyes's splayed legs. I had been right about the light on the other side: it was emanating from an assault rifle lying in the corner.

A little water had collected on the deck, but no more sparks were jumping from the equipment. As I stopped next to the mass on the floor, I could see that the puddle around the body–and it was a body–was cloudy with blood.

I picked up the rifle. The space where the magazine fit into the under-side was empty, and the bolt was thrown back. Whoever had been firing this had run out of ammunition.

Using its light, I discovered the corpse's identity: Grimm. He was in worse shape than Reyes. I was surprised there wasn't more blood.

His throat was hacked apart, and several bullet wounds pocked his back. I couldn't see his face. I didn't care about what it would tell me. His hands were empty; I must be holding his rifle. There were two empty clips by his feet.

I swung the light aft and moaned. It was all I could manage.

Moretti sat with his back against the wall, knees to his chest, staring through me. One hand was pressed to his torso, where it had been strug-gling to stanch the flow of innumerable wounds. The other was wrapped around the MP-5 on the floor next to him.

I stepped closer through the crimson-tinged water. He looked alive, as if he were listening to an unseen speaker in front of him. I could see his rifle better now, and its bolt also was all the way back. Cartridge casings around him threw twinkling reflections across his body and the walls.

It would be impossible to reconstruct who had been shooting at whom and where everyone had been standing. But I had only found three bod-ies so far and was running out of places to look for them. Maybe Larsen had survived. Maybe the Serpent had not.

But the answer to that question lay in the doorway to the engine room. It was Larsen. His body sprawled in the electrical compartment, a clip-less rifle by his side and a combat knife in his hand.

Unlike the other three, no bullet wounds were visible. But I didn't need to check his corpse to see what killed him. His face was resting on the edge of the hatchway, deformed by the impact. Larsen had run out of bullets. He had tried to escape. And he had died.

The pistol in my hand now seemed too heavy to keep a grip on. Had

Larsen reached for its empty holster, ready to finish off the Serpent? Had he panicked when he discovered himself defenseless? Had the Serpent dragged him back through the door, then killed him with a quick thrust of its arms?

I found that it didn't matter. Nothing did. Nothing except the pouch on my belt. Forward torpedo room? Or engine room?

The engine room was closer. I would choose the manner of my death based on convenience. It seemed random and appropriate, and the thought made the water, the blood and the killing seem less real.

I pulled Larsen's body from the door, trying to ignore the moist thump as his head hit the floor. Holding the useless assault rifle in one hand and the pistol in the other, I entered the engine room. It was tranquil, the beam from my light showing dormant machinery waiting for someone to throw the switch.

Pausing at the ladder to the lower deck, I thought of Campbell. Maybe I should go back and get him, and we'd set our explosives together in the torpedo room. There was no reason to die alone. We'd each mold the C-4 around the torpedoes' warheads and stand there, surrounded by what was sure to be an instantaneous death, and wait next to the executive officer's corpse.

The executive officer. Lee.

Shit.

One of us could get off this boat. That yellow suit on Lee's body was for escaping a submerged submarine, and the Korean had been trying to do just that when he had expired. I didn't know how deep we were or how to operate the escape hatch, but I didn't care. A shaft of hope now pulsated in my mind.

Set the explosives, then run. What about Campbell? What would he do? I already was in motion down the ladder and across the lower deck to the oil-storage area Larsen had told me about.

I was sure I could set the timer. After all, I had been ready to do so when I thought I would perish as the ship's hull tore open. But I wasn't sure I could just leave Campbell. It was the rational thing to do, I suppose—after all, was it better for one of us to survive, or for both to die? What a disgusting thought. Drowning Campbell. Because one of us would surely have to suffer, if not die. Would he try to stop me? I couldn't picture him threatening me. It *hurt* to imagine that. Would he agree to stay behind and do the noble thing?

Shit, why shouldn't I be the noble one and allow him to escape? Maybe there was another pressure suit someplace. I didn't think we had time to look for it, though. The Serpent, even if it had been seriously wounded, wouldn't wait long to try to wipe out the remainder of the force trespassing on his ship.

The prospect of survival made me sick.

I packed the explosives into place and crouched there, back against the wall, certain an attack would come streaking from beyond my flashlight's beam.

Then I made my decision. I'd set the explosives. I'd go tell Campbell what was going on. And we'd both go through the hatch. He was trained for underwater work. Maybe he could make it to the surface. I kept repeating that to myself, mentally. It was the only way I could keep moving.

If it looked like he was going to kill me and take the suit, I'd fight back. But he could either stay here and die, or take a chance at survival. It was all either of us could do.

My plan was driven by what I had seen so far, I think. I realize it sounds ruthless and chilling. And it was. But there was only one acceptable outcome now: destroy the Serpent and escape. I knew that I would do whatever was necessary to make that happen, including murder my last link to human kindness.

The timer was simple to operate, as Larsen had told me. Five pushes of one arrow set the red LED display to seven minutes. Four hundred and twenty seconds. An arbitrary number, but it seemed like enough.

My finger hovered over the red button. Then jabbed down.

I hurried up the ladder, the bobbing light in my hand creating wild patterns on the bulkheads around me. Then through the electrical control room, my breathing seeming to echo off the dead walls, water trickling down my face as I ran under the leaking pipe.

Into the control room, where I stopped. Campbell stood at the other end of the compartment, his light in my face. He lowered his rifle and, as the blobs of color faded from my vision, spoke.

"Christine . . . what happened? Where are they?"

"They're all dead. I looked, but there's no sign of the Serpent's body. Nothing."

I still couldn't make out his features, but his voice told me what they must have looked like.

"We're going to die."

"We don't have to," I said, taking a step toward him but stopping short. I didn't want to be too close to him if he decided I wasn't going to be the one wearing the pressure suit. "There's a way out."

"I don't understand," he said. "We need to do what Larsen ordered. We've—"

His words ceased as a hand emerged from the darkness behind him and fastened around his throat. He dropped his rifle, the weapon dangling from its strap, and reached up to the fingers crushing the life out of him.

I could see a pair of feet and legs behind him, but the assailant's upper body was hidden by Campbell's. Another hand pulled at the MP-5, though, and yanked it out of sight.

Campbell's eyes screamed at me.

And then his face exploded as a burst of gunfire ripped through it, leaving behind a glistening pink crater. The hand around his neck pulled away, and Campbell collapsed in a pile of twitching limbs.

I'm not sure what I yelled. "No!" maybe. I just remember the anguish bursting out of me, raw in my throat, as I watched him die.

The Serpent stood behind him. It was naked; that much was apparent. Its skin was mottled gray and black, the camouflage turning its face into an indistinguishable surface with two eyes, a nose and a mouth. I could tell its mouth was there because it was smiling.

The pistol came up. I had begun squeezing the trigger before I even realized I was going to shoot. The Serpent was there in front of me when the first slug left the barrel, I swear.

Then it was moving, an impossible smear of darkness amid shadow. It ducked right, trying to put the periscopes between us, and I kept shooting. Sparks exploded from the walls and equipment. The steering control station vanished behind a puff of smoke, the diving switches shattered, spraying glass across the floor, and the sonar screens broke with the dull pop of a failed vacuum tube.

It kept moving aft, circling, its movements both fluid and jerky. The gun seemed to fire in silence, each flash capturing and preserving the action. I could hear only the beating of my heart. Slow, like the rest of the world.

My last shot ricocheted off the nav periscope, sending a billion tiny fragments of metal whirring back at me. I didn't blink.

And it was there. In front of me again. One hand on the barrel of my gun. I knew what was coming and tried to let go, but one finger caught in the trigger guard as it wrenched the weapon out of my grasp. I felt nothing as the digit broke with a faraway snap.

The Serpent did nothing further to attack me. It just stood there, looking down into my face, still smiling. Its features swam in front of me as its coloration rearranged itself, then faded to a uniform, olive flesh tone.

As its face coalesced, so did recognition.

Vazquez.

"Just you and me now, Doctor. I have to tell you, it took a great deal of work to get us to this point, but it was worth the effort. And I can't say it wasn't fun, as well. I find blood invigorating."

I couldn't move. My body was unrestrained, but my mind had settled into a circular track of disbelief, denial and terror.

"Oh, come on," he continued. "Not even a 'hello'? No 'Wow, Vazquez, you killed fifteen SEALs all by yourself, and that turns me on'?"

"Vazquez," I whispered. I had meant to speak in a normal voice.

"Yes and no. I think I'm still me. But better. You have no idea what it feels like to see the whole world become so . . . obvious. So slow. So weak."

The rifle in my left hand had begun to drift toward the floor, but Vazquez reached down and forced its light back up. His face was all I could comprehend. My environment was just a footnote to this moment, as were the past and future.

"You're dead." Again, a ragged whisper.

"Am I? I don't feel dead," he said, examining his body. "Although the boys did put a couple of holes in me back there. Maybe a weaker person would be dead now—look at this."

He brought his right arm into the light. The bulging bicep was smeared with blood, but no wound was evident. Then he pointed at his stomach, which also was bloody but undamaged.

"It's amazing, isn't it? I headed aft for a few minutes, and that's all it took to heal both of them."

"The torpedo room. We all heard it." But we hadn't. We had heard what Vazquez wanted us to hear and drawn the conclusion he wanted us to draw.

"That was great. I killed a whole flock of birds with one stone there. Plus Matthews, who kind of looked like a bird." He laughed, and I could taste the vomit in my mouth. "My skin had just started to change. There was no way I could hide that.

"Besides, my natural camouflage didn't do me much good with clothes, so I had to get rid of them. Do I have to spell this out?" He didn't allow me to answer. I don't think I could have, anyway. "Clothes in the tube, then whoosh—out into the ocean. Plus you all think I'm dead. After that, it was just a matter of jamming myself into a dark corner and blending in with it. At the time, I was angry—furious, really—that I hadn't been able to kill Campbell. But what he told you added a certain extra credence to my death."

Vazquez was using words that I was sure hadn't existed in his world when he woke up that morning. Obviously, his vocabulary was growing along with his intellect.

"And, of course, I got to kill Campbell in the end," he added.

Yes, he had. He had killed everyone in the end. My brain paused in its pointless scurrying long enough to fix on an image of Campbell's head disintegrating, the humanity and concern on his face erased in one bloody instant.

"But you're still here. So am I. Which is exactly the way it should be. Can you see that? Didn't you feel how much they wanted you? I did. But you're mine."

He had an erection. His member was just a dim shape, almost lost in the darkness between us, but it was there, aiming at my midsection like a gun barrel.

"You like that, bitch? I'm going to make sure you like it." Now his hand was on my shoulder, squeezing hard, the bones beneath his fingers grinding against one another. He took a step back, yanking me toward him. "The nav table looks like a good spot. Bend you over or lay you down? Now that's a tougher decision."

As he moved, I attacked his grip. But it was like struggling with a tree trunk.

"Miller and Martin, you know, I killed them because it felt right. Hell, it felt *good*," he said, sweeping papers off the tabletop with his free arm. "I knew they were trying to stab me in the back and keep me from something. I wasn't sure what that something was right away. But then I knew."

He whipped me around, shoving me backwards onto the table. Its edge jammed into the base of my spine, and I dropped the light. Vazquez's features dimmed, but the whites of his eyes still gleamed in the air above me.

"It was you. They were trying to keep me from you, just like everyone else. So they all had to die. Because you're MINE and not theirs! MINE!"

His voice had leaped from an even, reasonable tone into sudden hysteria. Eyes wide, he screamed down at me.

"MINE! MINE, MINE, MINE!" He was fumbling with the front of my jeans.

I tumbled out of my mental paralysis.

"You're going to die, Vazquez."

He froze in mid-shout and closed his mouth. His head vibrated with tension.

"Nobody can kill me."

"I already have."

The hand on my shoulder pushed down harder, flattening me against the glass surface.

"You're not going to do anything but lie there and watch me FUCK you! I don't think I'll kill *you*, not yet, but . . ."

"You don't understand. There's a block of C-4 in the engine room, and its timer is running."

I wasn't going to outsmart Vazquez. I had to offer him a scenario in which he didn't see any possibility of defeat. If Larsen had been telling the truth–if there were no way to stop or reset the timer on the explosives–he would rape me, and afterward we'd both die.

But I could see a million potential futures flashing behind his eyes. Here was the one I wanted him to settle on: Go see whether there is C-4 back there. If there is, defuse it, then finish with me. Because I couldn't get away, right? He had the only functioning firearm. He could force his way into anyplace I tried to hide, he could overwhelm me in a hand-to-hand fight and he had control of the entire sub.

Go on, I willed him. Let the bitch go, then come back and punish her. She'll get what's coming to her, no matter what. There's nothing left to stop you.

When his grip loosened, I think he mistook my sob of relief for pain.

"Oh, there's more of that in your future. I hope you weren't counting on a bang, a flash and a quick end. I'm enjoying this too much not to savor it. You and I . . . we're just getting started."

And he was pulling away, flashing through the aft hatch so fast it made me wonder whether he had been standing over me at all.

But I knew he had. A lance of white-hot pain was imbedded in my finger, and my shoulder made me gasp as I sat up. How much time had passed since I pushed the red button? Thinking about it wouldn't slow the countdown.

I picked up the rifle and ran through the control room, stepping on and around the two corpses by the door. Ridder was just an obstacle. But I found myself gripped by chest-constricting sadness as I moved past Campbell's crumpled form, and I tried not to look at what remained of his face. No time to grieve.

The hallway in the next compartment seemed unending, and I expected to feel Vazquez's fingers sink into my flesh again, pulling me away from a chance at life. But the circle of illumination thrown by my light led me onward, focusing my attention on the deck in front of me, the hatch beyond it and what must come next.

How long would it take him to defuse the C-4? I thought as I scrambled down the stepladder. He believed he could do it—otherwise he wouldn't have let me go. So far, it had been a losing proposition to bet against him, and the prospect of him appearing in the door to the torpedo room tore at my hopes.

I tripped over the chain piled on the floor and screamed. But it wasn't fright that moved me. It was elation.

Slamming both hatches, I spun the dogging wheels until they wouldn't turn any more, ignoring the rubber band as it snagged, broke and spurted away. I slipped the chain through the mechanism on the lower door, then stood and threaded the other end through the wheel on the hatch to the hallway. The chain had been wrapped multiple times around the lower door's latch when I first encountered it; now, uncoiled, it was long enough to loop through both wheels.

The lock. Where the fuck was the lock? I cast the light about, imagining heavy, purposeful footsteps in the next compartment. After a few seconds, I saw it: a scuffed hunk of metal, partway under a torpedo rack, perhaps kicked there when I stumbled over the chain.

I gathered the loose ends, pulled them taut and slipped the lock through a link on each side. Click. It was done. I imagined the chain jerking out of my hands, its links groaning as Vazquez arrived at the door. I imagined the dogging wheels distorting as the chain vibrated between them, humming with tension. I imagined a link popping, sending two steel whips ricocheting off the bulkhead in a splash of sparks.

But it didn't happen. And whether it was going to or not, I was never going near those hatches again.

The torpedo room's machinery seemed ancient and abandoned in the focused glare of the flashlight, offerings left for some god in a metallic tomb. The smells had become closer, more concentrated. The pervasive odor of oil dripped over my body, tangible enough that I wiped my uninjured hand on my shirt without thinking.

Lee's body hadn't yet added its own pungent aroma to the atmosphere. The pressure suit was already two-thirds removed, making it easier to strip the rest of the way off. My finger screamed at me, pleading for mercy as I pulled at the rubbery material. I relished the agony. The pain let me know that my rational side was back in charge.

Still no sign of Vazquez. Maybe he hadn't been able to disable the timer. It almost would have been comforting to hear him pounding on the hatch, screaming epithets through its steel. It would be less frightening than letting my imagination paint its own dark pictures.

I *did* know what real threats I faced, though, and focusing on anything else would be a waste of energy. If the timer still were functioning, I had to get off the boat before it reached 0:00, and that could be seconds from now. If Vazquez had foiled it, I had to get off the boat before he found a way to get past my makeshift barricade. Of course, I might use up all the oxygen in the torpedo room before then.

My hands never stopped working. I had that much presence of mind, at least. I got Lee's legs out of the suit, thanking a god I didn't have much faith in that the executive officer had removed his shoes. I wouldn't need to do that myself, I discovered as I thrust my own legs into the yellow folds.

No time to check for punctures, and what good would that do, anyway? Would I stay here in Vazquez's domain if I found a tear in the fabric?

There was a seal up the front. It didn't look durable, but I guess it didn't have to be. Just had to last long enough for the wearer to reach the surface.

A hood with a transparent face was supposed to pull over my head. But I hesitated. How the hell did this thing work, anyway? Was there an air supply? Was I going to suffocate after I sealed the hood?

OK, then, I'd do that last. I didn't have much choice.

The hatch was going to be difficult to get to, I thought, then realized there was a rudimentary ladder built onto the torpedo rack nearest to it.

I climbed up, using three fingers of my mangled hand to brace the light against my body, and shined the beam on the Korean instructions. Did they say "Open door, hold breath?" Wait. Larsen had explained this.

There was an inner door. You opened that, climbed in and shut it. Then you let the ocean in.

The red striping on the hatch was bright and inviting. I jammed the rifle between the top torpedo and the ceiling, hooked my right arm through the ladder, then gripped the dogging wheel with my left hand. I could see gnat-sized beads of condensation hanging from the door's surface.

The wheel wouldn't turn. The ladder dug into the crook of my bracing arm, the sinews of my left wrist rippled beneath the skin and my palm ground against the cold metal, but the hatch and I were frozen there in an isometric struggle.

I felt sweat trickle down my back beneath the suit. Disengaging my right hand, I added it to my efforts, trigger finger a jagged protrusion from the fist formed by its four companions. I squeezed the ladder with my knees and twisted. Pulled. Threw every cell of my upper body into the task. Shit, was I even turning it the right direction?

Then the wheel slipped into motion with a shriek. I let go of it with my left hand, scrabbling for a grip on the ladder as I pitched backward. My right hand got caught for an instant, jerking my arm and bashing my injured finger against a spoke of the wheel.

The pain this time was searing. It pulsed through my hand and arm into the pit of my stomach, and as I clung to the ladder, panting, I saw specks of light floating in my vision.

I'm not sure how long I clung there, tears and sweat winding their way down my face. And it's an even greater mystery how I managed to steady myself again with my right arm, reach out with the opposite limb and turn the wheel the rest of the way.

The hatch swung open and dangled there.

"No!" Not a denial, but a sharp, painful syllable filled with all my fears and frustrations. The space on the other side looked about the same size as the inside of a clothes dryer. A child could fit in there, maybe.

I was sobbing now, angry. There were handholds set on the inside of the escape tower—how could they call a space that small a "tower"?—and on the hatch. I'd have to climb off the ladder, up the hatch and jam myself into the area above. With one hand.

But first, I shined the rifle-mounted light through the opening. There were two softball-sized knobs set into a recess in the chamber wall. Both had bumpy red handles, and both were surrounded by instructions in Korean. Not that I would be able to read the characters, even if I'd known the language. There was no chance I'd be able to fit the light in there.

I reached up as far as I could and grabbed a handhold, then pulled one foot free and rested it on the lowest notch on the hatch's surface. My momentum and leg would have to propel me far enough up into the space that I could find a rung with my other foot. If I didn't, I could hang there, bent into an L shape, and keep trying. Or I could fall, my head bouncing off some piece of unforgiving metal, and lie there until I died.

There was no reason to count to three. If I couldn't do it now, I couldn't do it three seconds from now.

The suit's material squeaked, and I felt my fingers slip. But my leg straightened, pushing me up, the edge of the hatch scraping against my back. The other foot landed on something solid enough to brace on. And I was in.

Below me, the gun fell to the floor. Already, the clatter seemed part of a different plane of existence. The rifle a million miles away, casting a beam back aft across the floor. In its distant light, I could see that the tower was a little bigger than it had appeared. There was a lip around the bottom edge, a shelf a few inches wide on which a person could brace himself.

Or herself. I reached through my legs, my hand touching, then grabbing the hatch. It took all the remaining energy in my shoulders and back to haul it closed and turn the wheel until it stopped.

And now I was alone, more so than I had ever been. Lost in a blank, featureless reality that echoed with the frantic sound of my own breathing. Where were those knobs?

No, not yet! I stopped myself just as my searching fingers found the switch. I needed to close the suit's hood. I considered taking a deep breath before I did so, but it seemed like such a ridiculous, futile gesture that I laughed instead and spoke into the nothingness.

"Don't go off the deep end, Christine."

But I already was there. The trick was to get back to the surface.

With the hood in place, the slick odor of the submarine was replaced with a synthetic smell, like the inside of a newly made plastic bottle. It was getting difficult to breathe.

The first knob I tried didn't move. I gave up. But it was the other one I had been looking for, anyway, as I saw when water began to gush into the chamber from vents around my head. I sat there, knees to my chest, and watched the sea rise around me.

It didn't take long. Fifteen seconds, maybe, and then the entire space was filled. I felt my ears trying to pop, my body compressed by countless tons of water. But I realized the suit had inflated, perhaps triggered by the water.

There was a wheel—just like all the others—on the inside of the outer hatch, and I felt panic swirl in my chest as I placed my hand on it. What if it wouldn't open? What if it were damaged? What if . . .

But the wheel turned. And after a few revolutions, the door swung back and my darkness gave way to a different shade of night, just as thick but somehow perceptible as blue.

The suit now was puffy and stiff, protecting me from the depths. If I let go, I would float up.

A sudden urge gripped me. For the first time since setting foot on the submarine, I was in a position to escape. To win. But I wanted to ensure that victory was total.

I couldn't see the lower hatch, but I could feel it with my foot. I slid a toe into the dogging mechanism and began pushing it. It wasn't designed to be open in this circumstance and fought my efforts in a way that would have made its engineers proud. After a few moments, however, I noticed thin threads of bubbles streaming past me.

Almost there. The threads became ropes, and suction tugged at my leg. Maybe that would do it. Maybe Vazquez wouldn't be able to get into the torpedo room, and it would flood with the water already jetting around the edges of the escape hatch.

But that same impulse, that primal desire to destroy, seized me again, and I kicked out, bashing the wheel and pushing off at the same time.

For a second, the water rushing into the submarine seemed to grab me and try to yank me back into its maw. The hatch had swung open. Hovering there a few feet above the sub, on the razor edge of capture or escape, I saw the light dancing inside the compartment, distorted by a shimmering torrent of seawater. Then I was free, floating upward, I guess, although there was nothing by which to judge my progress.

Except the *Dragon*.

I saw it below me, a menacing shape against a lighter background, its life bubbling from a wound in its snout. It was visible for just an instant before being swallowed by the sea's murkiness.

And I rose, looking upward, seeking deliverance.

[Transcript continued]

MYERS: I can't say that I remember much after that. I just have a vague recollection of breaching the surface, pulling back the hood and bobbing there, staring at the stars. I have no idea why I didn't sink after I opened the suit.

TRENT: It has a flotation device built into it. It's triggered by contact with water, just like the rest of the suit.

OLSEN: Don't worry about what you remember. You've done a really remarkable job.

MYERS: Remembering is easy. I think my problem is going to be forgetting. That's what I want to do.

OLSEN: Well, regardless. You've been very helpful. Now, do you have any memory of being picked up? Of what happened then?

MYERS: I told you, it's all dim. I don't even know how long I was floating there. How did anyone know where to look for me?

OLSEN: The *Rickover* called for search and rescue after it heard the submarine begin sinking. We'd had vessels on standby since it reported hearing gunfire on passive sonar.

MYERS: So it sank? The C-4 detonated?

TRENT: We'll get to that in a second. Right now I have a few things I'd like you to elaborate on.

MYERS: God, I haven't been elaborate enough? What's your question?

TRENT: Several questions, actually. First of all, you said Vazquez was infected with this virus. But why were none of the other SEALs infected, and what happened to the infected Korean crewmember you said started this whole thing?

MYERS: Well, the two are connected. As I mentioned, the documents we saw said it was transmitted only through body fluids. And Vazquez was the only one of us to come in contact with the body fluids of the Korean sailor who had been infected.

TRENT: You lost me. Could you—

MYERS: Remember how Vazquez said he fell on a corpse in the battery bay? And how his description of blood spraying from the corpse's mouth helped me determine a cause of death? Well, that must have been the body of the first Serpent. Lee's last-ditch attempt to kill it was successful. But the virus stayed alive in the man's blood. It wouldn't have survived much longer as the body's temperature continued to drop. Unfortunately, it found a new host before that happened.

OLSEN: You're saying the new host was Vazquez. He was infected when the blood sprayed on him.

MYERS: Exactly. It got in his eyes, his nose—we'll never know for sure. All it needed was a mucous membrane, and it obviously found one. Soon after, it began working its magic on Vazquez. And then he became the Serpent.

TRENT: But how did the virus begin spreading to begin with?

OLSEN: Do you think it was released from the locker you described? The one in the battery bay?

MYERS: One at a time. First, yes, I think it was being stored in that locker. Everything we read about the transfer of the research to the sub seems to indicate that it was transported in a container like that. And hell, the locker had "biohazard" stamped all over it.

TRENT: And how did it spread?

MYERS: I heard you the first time. I have no idea. Make up a story—it's just as likely to be right as anything I can come up with. The question is totally irrelevant at this point. The virus got out, that much is clear.

TRENT: No speculation at all?

MYERS: You want me to guess? Fine, I'll guess. Um . . . there was an interruption of the locker's power supply, and the virus's temperature rose to the point where it became active. Then a crewman trying to fix the locker accidentally got some on himself without knowing it. Then he set out to kill his fellow sailors. Happy?

OLSEN: You're saying it could have been anything.

MYERS: I'll say it again if you want.

TRENT: That's not very helpful, Dr. Myers.

MYERS: Not very helpful? Fuck you! I've told you everything I know, every fucking nuance I can recall. What's more, I eliminated this living, breathing bioweapon after fifteen SEALs died trying to do the same thing. I'd call that helpful. I'd call that a big debt that you owe me, and I'd call that a reason you should take your "helpful" comments and cram them up your ass. Is that helpful?

OLSEN: Doctor, try to relax.

TRENT: That's not what I meant.

MYERS: Yeah? What did you mean, then?

TRENT: Well, our people are going over the sub, and we want to make sure—

MYERS: Hold on a second. You have people on the sub? I sank the sub. I saw it going down. You said that ship, the *Ricker*, heard it sink.

OLSEN: Well. The *Rickover* did hear what sounded like a hull breach, and that's when it called for surface ships.

MYERS: So the *Dragon* didn't survive, right? Then how did you have people onboard? Wait, why did you just look at him like that?

OLSEN: Go ahead, Captain.

TRENT: Dr. Myers, the *Dragon* went down in less than three hundred feet of water. Its hull survived the low-speed impact with the seafloor.

MYERS: No.

TRENT: A salvage team used pontoons to raise it.

MYERS: Raise it?

OLSEN: The sub and pontoons were covered and towed to shore.

MYERS: Oh, fucking Christ. You've given it a chance to get away! It's going to get off that boat and it's going to spread the virus and it's going to kill and kill—

OLSEN: Doctor, the sub was completely searched. There was no one alive onboard. We didn't find Vazquez, but we did discover that one of the torpedo tubes had been flooded and fired. His fingerprints were found on the inside of the tube.

MYERS: I told you already, he faked his death there!

OLSEN: None of the documents you described were found. No diaries, no references to a super-virus, no reports on its development. The biohazard locker was empty. Completely empty. There weren't even any racks inside.

MYERS: Check my bag. I took notes, recorded observations.

OLSEN: No. All the tapes we found were blank. There were no fingerprint records, none of the evidence you said you collected.

TRENT: And the recording device in your bag had been disabled. Why did you destroy it, Doctor?

MYERS: Recording device?

OLSEN: A digital recorder was sewn into your bag before you left shore.

MYERS: Why?

TRENT: This was too sensitive an operation for us not to keep track of exactly what you knew. But you already understood that, didn't you? That's why you smashed it.

MYERS: Smashed it? I didn't smash anything! I didn't know there was anything to smash! Why would I think there was a bug in my bag?

OLSEN: It doesn't really matter.

MYERS: Don't you people understand? You've set a bioweapon loose on your own country! Check the crime reports in—where did you tow the sub?

TRENT: We can't tell you that.

MYERS: Wherever the *Dragon* was taken, check the crime reports. There will be rapes, lots of rapes. And murders. Those numbers will grow exponentially as more people become infected. It's happening right now. Why can't you see that?

OLSEN: We have no idea what happened onboard the *Yong,* Dr. Myers. But we suffered 100 percent casualties in a mission that yielded nothing. The sole bright spot was that secrecy was maintained. This was a black operation to begin with, and it's going to be invisible now. Absolutely invisible.

MYERS: That's it? That's your answer? Charlie—the division supervisor, Charles Weber—he knows where I was. He and Gen. Patterson aren't going to stand back and write all this off. What you people are doing is insane and illegal.

TRENT: Gen. Patterson authorized every step of the salvage and recovery process.

OLSEN: Operations just don't go this badly. Sometimes, in cases like this, you have to simply tie off the loose ends and stop asking questions.

MYERS: But I told you what happened. I told you everything. I answered your questions.

TRENT: Yes. You've done all you can for us.

MYERS: But you're not listening! Dammit, Vazquez is smarter than the three of us combined now. He sneaked off the boat after it was raised—remember what I told you about his skin camouflage?—and he covered his tracks. What's so hard to grasp about that? He took or destroyed everything that could substantiate my account of what took place on the submarine, including the virus samples, which he could be dumping in a reservoir right fucking now!

TRENT: We've been over that, haven't we?

MYERS: You don't believe me. I'm telling the truth, but I can see it's not registering. Why would I lie?

OLSEN: It's not a question of lies or belief. There comes a point where our views of truth—yours and mine—cease to matter.

MYERS: You don't understand what you've set loose on—

TRENT: Here's what we understand, OK? A mission to secure a foreign submarine and the weapons research it carried failed completely. The research, if it was there to begin with, disappeared. The inside of the submarine is shot to hell and one compartment is flooded. We have sonar audiotapes of shooting and a torpedo tube firing. All other evidence of what may have occurred is missing, including a listening device in your bag that was deliberately destroyed. And none of the mission's personnel survived.

MYERS: Why do you keep saying that? I survived. I'm here to tell you exactly how it all . . . what? Where are you going?

OLSEN: This interview is over.

END TRANSCRIPT

060602:1732

File No. 487-29800(C6)